Maybe Love Likes Crazy

By G.R. Minner

Produced by

MECHLING
BOOKBINDERY & BOOKBINDERS WORKSHOP

124 Evans Road
Butler, PA 16001
www.mechlingbooks.com
1-800-941-3735

Printed in the United States of America

Prologue

When Katie rose to leave, Mark held her in his arms for the second time. She came around the table, never taking her eyes off his and boldly embraced him. This time, he knew it was coming and was ready. She stood on her toes and slid her cheek alongside his. She wrapped her arms around him and pulled him tightly to her, pressing their bodies together. Mark did the same, and each felt the full measure of the other's physical presence. It was a measure neither would soon forget.

Katie whispered into his ear, "Thank you," then she released him. Mark wanted to pull her back and ask her to stay forever in his arms, but he dared not, and let her go, remembering everything, including the scent of her.

Mark and Katie, Katie and Mark
All it took was just a spark
For our love to begin to grow
Out of control, a celestial glow.

Blessed by God yet unseen by man
We vowed to keep the upper hand
Should life together ever get hazy
We'll just hang on and love like crazy.

~by Mark Lane, 1966

April 1963
Powder Mills, Pennsylvania

Mark's alarm clock went off at five like it always did, except when his flailing hands knocked it off the nightstand while some nightmare raced through his sleep. As Mark's feet hit the floor, his stomach rolled. He reached for the waste basket beside the bed and lifted it under his mouth just before last night's supper emptied out of his stomach.

"I'm sick, Mom," he groaned as his mother entered his room, clearly having heard Mark's retching. "I think I have a stomach bug."

"You definitely don't look well, you poor thing," Ann Lane said, studying her fifteen-year-old son. "I'll hurry downstairs and catch your dad before he leaves the house. Eli will need to help him with your chores. Go back to bed, and I'll bring up some hot tea and toast. Did you have anything important at school today?"

"Nothing I can't make up tomorrow."

"All right, Sweetheart, back to bed with you."

"Thanks, Mom," Mark mumbled.

In mid-morning, the slam of the washer lid from downstairs roused Mark from his sleep. Laying there in his double bed, he realized he felt better. Mark sat up on the edge of the bed and spied the partially uneaten slice of toast. He finished it off and washed it down with the cold tea left in his cup. Soon his mother would begin to prepare lunch for the men. Things ran promptly by the clock at Lane Farms: breakfast at 7:00, lunch at noon and supper at 5:30.

Mark descended the steps of their two-story farmhouse and found his mother by the washing machine in the mudroom. She turned her head toward the doorway as he entered.

"You look better," she said. "But no one else in the house wants your germs, so don't be drinking out of the bathroom cup. Go to the kitchen and

1

get your own. And wash your hands with soap and hot water before you touch anything."

"Geez, I'm almost sorry I found you," Mark said, feigning indignation.

Ann glanced at him, but kept stuffing clothes in the washer. "What do you want, Mark?" she asked, with just a hint of humor in her eyes.

"I wanted to place my lunch order with the cook."

"Come here and let me check your temperature. Put your forehead on my cheek." Mark bent down to her eight-inch shorter frame.

"No fever," she said. "I don't know what could have disagreed with you about supper. You must have picked up a bug somewhere. That, or you ate too much of the candy you have stashed away in your room."

"Me? Eating candy?"

Ann chuckled. "Now go get dressed."

Mark gave his mother a cheesy grin. "Yes ma'am!" Laughter filled the mudroom when Ann snapped a dirty towel toward him as he escaped.

If Mark was anything, he was intuitive. He headed for the kitchen with the smug satisfaction that his mother thought he was special. He and his mom had always shared a closeness that was truly rare.

When everyone was seated around the table for lunch, Mark asked, "Where's Eli?"

Eli Yoder was their Amish worker who had just started at Lane Farms a few months earlier.

"He had to help at home for the rest of the day," Mark's father, Harold, replied. "He took off as soon as he got the chores done. His and yours, that is."

"Did he get Nasty's pen cleaned out?"

A grin spread across Harold's face. "Yes, he did, although for some reason Nasty makes Eli nervous. I asked him if he was afraid of a little 'ole five-month-old Angus bull. He assured me that he wasn't afraid and cleaned the pen, but Eli never took his eyes off that calf." Harold laughed. "I swear Nasty torments him on purpose."

"What was he doing today?" Mark asked.

2

"The usual. You know how he shakes his head, gives you the beady-eyed look with those black eyes, then tosses that head around while pawing with his hoof. Hey, you didn't name him Nasty for nothing!" Harold studied his son. "You seem to be feeling better now. Your mother said you looked awful this morning. How are you feeling?"

"It's almost like I wasn't sick."

"I have hay bales to load onto the wagon and deliver this afternoon to the Jankoski farm over on Red Oak Road. If you're feeling up to it, you could help, but it's your call."

"I can help. Why are the Jankoskis buying hay from us?"

"They took a big gamble last year with their first cutting. They cut half of it down with the intention of running two balers to get it all up in one day. Unfortunately, it rained for five straight days, and the hay was ruined."

"Huh," Mark said, as he shoveled another forkful of food into his mouth. "One person's loss is another's gain."

"Mark!" Ann chided. "Was that said in a Christian spirit?"

"Yes," he answered. "The Lord helps those who help themselves."

Mark's plate disappeared from under his nose and he soon heard his mother scraping the remainder into the garbage.

Mark lifted his face to the sun and leaned against the wooden-slat tailgate of the now empty wagon as he and his father were returning home. Mark stood on the wagon, enjoying the tug of the wind on his face and clothes. As the John Deere tractor sped along Moorefield Road, he relished the feeling of freedom and speed. It was like riding the roller coaster with no hands and no safety bar. He thought about the Blue Streak at Conneaut Park.

They were approaching the Amish school, and children in their plain-colored clothes walked along the side of the road, heading for home.

The Amish called anyone not belonging to their society "English." While there was talk in the Amish community about switching to Amish teachers, as of yet no action had been taken, so there was a car sitting beside the school.

3

Mrs. Walker, the teacher, was standing out front seeing the last students off when Harold and Mark passed by. Harold waved, and she returned the greeting. Mark's attention however, was on her blue and white Ford.

Mark was already looking forward to the following year when he hoped to get his first car. He was determined it would be a blue one.

His daydream was interrupted when he was thrown forward. He ran partway up the wagon to keep from landing on his face as Harold braked hard.

"Geez, Dad, how about a little warning before you stop?" he groused quietly. With Mark's mild manner, "quietly" was the only kind of complaining there was. And always to himself. He never forgot one of his grandmother's favorite maxims – "If there's anything I can't stand, it's a whiner."

His dad came to a stop beside the four Byler children who were walking along the side of the road.

"Hello Katie!" Harold called out. "What brings you to school today?"

"I was visiting a friend, so I thought I'd say hello to Mrs. Walker."

Harold nodded. "Did she give you any post-graduation assignments?"

Katie blushed as she returned Harold's smile. Mark couldn't help but notice the subtle line of freckles under her eyes and across her nose. And it was an attractive nose, at that. In fact, there wasn't anything about Katie that wasn't good-looking.

"No, Mr. Lane," Katie said, "but she did loan me one of her books to read." She held the book up for him to see.

"Wow, that's a big book!"

"It's a picture book on national parks and wildlife."

"When you're finished with it, you should come to our house and see Mrs. Lane. She has a whole stack of them you would probably enjoy."

"Oh, thank you! I will come with Mama to borrow one. I'd take very good care of it."

"I'm sure you would, Katie. Come on! We'll give all you kids a ride home if you want to climb on the wagon." He looked at the other children. "Wouldn't you like a ride?"

The three of them all looked to fifteen-year-old Katie for direction. Eleven-year-old Jacob asked, "May we ride on the wagon, Katie?"

4

When Katie hesitated, eight-year-old Sarah chirped, "Beats walking."

Little six-year-old Daniel added, "Yeah, Katie, can we?"

She finally relented. "Okay, but all of you must sit in the middle of the wagon."

"Help them up, Mark," his dad told him.

Harold instructed the children to come to the front of the wagon and give Mark their hand as they stepped up on the wagon tongue. Mark helped Daniel and Sarah climb aboard, but Jacob scampered onto the wagon without assistance which made Mark smile inside.

He held out his hand to Katie. Her hand was much smaller than his own, though the strength of her grip and warmth of her skin surprised him. She held on snugly to steady herself and easily stepped onto the wagon floor. "Thank you," she said, without meeting his eyes.

Katie sat down gracefully in the center of the wagon and wrapped her arms around Sarah and Daniel, one on each side of her.

"I can stand up with Mark," Jacob said.

Katie sternly addressed him. "No! You can't, Jacob. You will sit here with the rest of us or walk home."

Jacob trudged to the center of the wagon and plunked down near the other three, but behind Katie where he didn't have to look at her face.

Harold revved up the tractor and continued toward home. Along the way, they passed gently rolling farmland. The topography sloped downhill to the right, and the road traversed the rim of a gentle valley. At the bottom of the valley ran a medium-sized stream.

Eventually, the "lower farm" came into view. Everyone at Lane Farms referred to it as such because it was lower in elevation than their home farm. The Lanes rented the 110-acre, former dairy farm from Elsie Lane, a distant relative.

Mark watched the scenic farmland stretch along the valley to his right. The view was the most picturesque of all their farmed land. His dad had promised that they would own it one day soon.

They passed the long lane leading down the hill to the farm buildings, and Mark eyed their herd of Angus cattle grazing in the large, open meadow dissected by the stream.

Continuing on, they neared Old Mill Road, and Harold slowed and made the left turn. He throttled ahead as fast as the tractor would go, racing up a small grade and then downhill into a depression. Katie smiled when the younger children squealed their delight as the wagon bounced along the dirt road. She had a really nice smile. Even her eyes joined in.

The Byler house and farm buildings sat on both sides of Old Mill Road, less than two hundred yards from Morefield Road. Harold pulled off to the right, into the dirt parking area in front of the bake shop. The Bylers' large, two-story house sat seventy-five feet farther from the road and up a slight grade to the right of the small store. A freshly painted white barn sat beyond the courtyard on the left side of the road, with the tack shop and smokehouse situated closer to Old Mill Road.

Harold killed the motor and turned his attention to Katie. "When will you be opening the bake shop this year?"

"Another three or four weeks."

He called out, "Mark! Jump down and help the kids off the wagon."

When the children approached the edge of the wagon, Mark reached up and took Sarah by the waist and swung her around. Her dress billowed out as he lowered her gently to the ground. Mark obliged Daniel with an exaggerated swing as well. The two children laughed and ran toward the house. Suddenly, Sarah stopped, wheeled around and yelled, "Thank you, Mark and Mr. Lane!"

"Yeah, thank you!" Daniel echoed.

Jacob had already jumped down without assistance. After thanking Mr. Lane for the ride, he sauntered toward the house. Katie laid her book down at the edge of the wagon. "You're not going to try to swing me around, are you?"

Mark eyed her slim frame and grinned. "Nah. You're way too big for that."

He held out his left hand to steady her as she jumped down, but when she reached to grasp it, her heel caught on the raised board that ran the perimeter of the wagon. Leaning forward, she missed his hand altogether and pitched into empty air.

Mark shot his arm out to the left and side-stepped toward her. At the same moment, Katie reached out and encircled his neck with her left arm. Mark pulled her toward him as the two went down in a heap. He grunted hard when he became her landing pad. The wind rushed out of him, but Katie got the worst of it. She had a bruised left hand, scraped right palm, and a cut on her forehead near the hairline.

"Oh, my gosh!" Harold exclaimed. He jumped off the tractor and used his handkerchief to stem the flow of blood from her head. "I'm so sorry!" he said to Katie.

"It's my fault," Katie insisted. Still trembling, she looked over at Mark lying in the dirt.

"Are you all right?" she asked urgently.

Mark was panting for air in an attempt to inflate his lungs. "Fine. Can't talk now."

"Can you make it to the house?" Harold asked Katie.

She hung onto his arm as she stood up.

Mark rolled over and heaved himself to his feet.

"Bring her book, and I'll help Katie up to the house," Harold said.

When they reached the porch, Harold helped Katie onto a bench then glanced at Mark. "Stay with her and make sure she keeps the pressure on the cut, while I get her mother." Harold opened the door and called out for Mary.

"Harold, what are you yelling about?" Mary asked.

He told her about Katie's fall from the wagon. Mary swiftly took control and began nursing Katie's injury.

"Do you think the cut is bad enough to need stitches? I can have Ann come right down and drive you to the doctor," Harold said.

"Thank you, but I don't think that will be necessary. I'm sure if we keep the skin pulled together, we can avoid stitches."

"All right, if you're sure. Do you have plenty of the large Band Aids? If not, I'll send Mark with more from our house."

Mary smoothed a bandage on Katie's forehead. "This is the last one we have, but I wouldn't want to inconvenience you."

"Nonsense," he replied. "It's no inconvenience. And Mary, I just feel awful about this accident."

"Harold," Mary said gently, "it's all right. It was an accident, and accidents happen."

"Thank you, Mary." Harold placed his hand on Katie's shoulder and looked her in the eye. "You are going to be even lovelier after it heals," he told her with sincerity and a wink.

She smiled sheepishly. "You know just what to say, Mr. Lane. Do you have any Band Aids at your house for wounded pride?"

"Yes, I believe we do," he responded with a chuckle. "I'll send a couple of those along with the regular ones."

"Your pride is probably pretty banged up, Katie," Mark chimed in. "Mom always told us, 'Pride goeth before a fall.' If that's true, then your pride hit the dirt before we did."

Katie glared at Mark as Harold grabbed his arm and hurried him off the porch. "Now, why did you go and say a fool thing like that?" he hissed in Mark's ear.

"What? I was only trying to make her laugh."

"You sure have a lot to learn about women." Harold shook his head.

Harold drove the three quarters of a mile up Old Mill Road to the Lanes' home, while Mark sat at the back of the wagon and replayed the scene in his mind. He couldn't get Katie's fall out of his head. He had known her all of his life, but she was just the Amish girl who lived at the end of the road. She and her mother supplied the baked goods at their small shop to satisfy his sweet tooth. Nothing more. After all, she was Amish.

However, deep down inside, Mark was acutely aware that Katie was no longer "just an Amish girl." She was a very becoming young lady. To top it off, she had been vulnerable and he had succeeded in helping her. He just wished he had been able to do more. And what in the world did his father mean about him having a lot to learn about women?

Harold pulled in front of the machine shed and hopped off the tractor. "Your mom just bought a new tin of bandages the other day. Get them from the medicine cabinet and run them down to the Bylers. I trust you are okay to drive the pick-up?"

"Sure," Mark replied. He never turned down a chance to drive the truck. He still couldn't legally drive, but the truck had farm plates, so he was allowed to drive it between their properties.

Mark parked in front of the Bylers' bake shop. He approached the house on the flagstone walkway and spotted Katie sitting in a rocking chair on the porch looking at Mrs. Walker's book.

"Hi, Katie," Mark said. "Mind if I sit down?" She looked at him and nodded but didn't say anything. He held out the tin of bandages. "Here are the Band Aids Dad promised you."

She gave him a polite smile. "Thank you," she said as she accepted them then returned to her book. Mark sat down on the bench next to her rocker, careful to leave adequate space between them.

Back to polite but distant. Did Katie have something against him? Mark stared blankly out across the yard. Right after Katie fell from the wagon she asked him if he was all right. He could still hear the concern in her voice. She had been worried about him! In fact, that was the only time he could ever remember Katie talking to him in a friendship way.

Her voice interrupted Mark's thoughts. "Why aren't you in school today?"

"I played hooky."

"Does your father let you get away with that?"

"Not unless he thinks I'm sick," Mark said with a grin. She gave him a hard stare. He had no idea what she was thinking. Until today, he hadn't really cared either. But Katie's fall from the wagon had awakened something in his spirit.

Her expression softened. "Well, maybe God wanted you to play hooky today."

"Hey, I like the way you think. If you're going to be talking to Him later, maybe you could ask if I could play hooky tomorrow, too."

Katie cocked her head and studied him. "You don't like school?"

9

"It's okay, but if I had to choose between spending my days in the meadow or in a classroom, it's a no-brainer. So, do you really think God made me sick this morning?"

She raised an eyebrow. "You really were sick then?"

"Yep. First thing I did after I sat up on the edge of my bed was throw up into my wastebasket." Katie wrinkled her nose. Mark found himself staring at her subtle band of freckles again, as well as her striking set of hazel-blue eyes.

"Was there any reason for you to be sick this morning?"

"Nope," Mark said, shaking his head. "I was fine by lunchtime."

She gave him a wry smile. Did she know something he didn't?

"You don't think God would make me sick just so you could land on me, do you?"

"It says so in our Bible," she replied with a confident nod.

Mark couldn't validate her claim, so he leapt to his feet and changed the subject. "I have to get back home. Dad said to remind you about my mom having lots of those books you can borrow. Why did Mrs. Walker lend you a book about nature, anyway?"

"Because she knows I very much enjoy the subject."

Mark nodded. "Last year I made a book of wildflowers as a project for my science class. I collected them from the fields and woods and then preserved them."

"How many did you find?"

"More than sixty."

"Sixty," Katie remarked. "I didn't know we had that many. I'd like to see it, if you don't mind."

"Sure, I'll show it to you. Maybe when you come to borrow Mom's books. Well, see ya!" Mark said, as he started down the steps.

"Bye, Mark." Katie returned to her book.

Chapter Two

"Mark Lane!" Mrs. Bacco exclaimed. Mark's mind instinctively flipped to autopilot like it so often did when she went on one of her rampages. Uh oh, here comes "The Backhoe." Mark envisioned the big yellow machine with its giant arm swinging back and forth, wildly out of control, as the operator frantically worked the levers, to no avail. The machine had a mind of its own. "Run for your lives!" he imagined someone yelling. Mark looked up the row to see his oversized teacher powering down the aisle toward him.

"Is my class not interesting enough for you, Mr. Lane?" Mrs. Bacco barked in his face.

"No, Ma'am, your class is the Goldilocks of schooldom: not too boring, not too hard, it's just right." The room echoed with his classmates' snickers, but Mark's attention was on the menacing figure towering over him.

"Are you smart-mouthing me, Lane?"

"No Ma'am. Everyone in this class knows you only do that at your own peril. I'm sorry, I was just lost in thought."

"You are only here for forty-four minutes each day. I would appreciate your attention while you're here." Mrs. Bacco returned to the front of the class, and Mark's thoughts returned to where they had been before the interruption: Katie Byler.

Lately, Mark found himself thinking about her a lot. The scene that replayed most often was Katie's fall from the wagon. During the actual event, the high emotion and physical pain played the lead role. However, time allowed the secondary entities to come through loud and clear. The fear was raw on her face when she tripped and began to fall. She turned toward him and reached out for him to save her. He thought of his automatic response: arm out, step sideways, and encircle her.

Holding her as they fell became his favorite memory of all. It had become a sensual memory. He went back to it over and over again: she held him tightly, her whole body pressed firmly against him.

The memory simply would not go away or even subside. His emerging infatuation with Katie was beginning to consume him, so he embraced the memory and even enhanced it: the feel of her hand on the back of his neck, her soft cheek against his while falling, her breasts against his chest, her warm body against him. It was intoxicating, and he wanted more of it. But she was Amish, and he was English. He knew better than to hope for affection between them, though that knowledge did not quell his daydreams, and his nights were a whole other story.

Mark muddled through the rest of the semester until finally, school was out.

Summer was upon the inhabitants of Old Mill Road. Spring planting was over and hay season was in full swing.

Mark had just finished raking a field of freshly cut hay at the lower farm. It was only midmorning, but already the sun was like a demon in the cloudless sky. Two fields down and countless jobs to go. He pulled the tractor onto Morefield Road while surveying their new land holdings with an appreciative gaze. His parents had just purchased the farm last month.

Mark made the left turn off the blacktop onto Old Mill Road. He dropped down into the dip where the small stream crossed under the dirt road and began the long gradual climb to the knoll. He soon came upon the Byler farm buildings.

He eyed the springhouse attached to the front of the big white barn and considered stopping to get a drink. The springhouse had a large cement trough with cold water continuously flowing through it, fed by a pipe that led to a spring up on the hillside. The trough was a godsend for keeping things cool in the summer. When out on his bicycle over the years, Mark had often stopped for a cold drink and some water splashed on his face.

On the right, the bake shop was built under the canopy of a huge oak tree. Today, the front door and the venting sidewalls were open in an attempt to keep it cooler, turning the shop into an open-air stand. Inside, the shelves would be filled with baked goods, canned goods and seasonal produce.

12

As he approached, Mark glanced at the spot on the ground where Katie had knocked the wind out of him. The memory instantly brought a smile to his face.

In the shade under the oak tree, he could see one-year-old Ruthie in her wooden playpen and four-year-old Rebecca keeping her company. Through the open door, he caught a glimpse of their mother, Mary, behind the counter.

Mark puttered past the store and saw Katie, Sarah, Jacob, and Daniel working in the large garden to the left of the house. The garden supplied the produce for the small store as well as food for the Byler table all year round.

Jacob saw Mark and waved. Mark waved in return. If Katie saw him, she didn't acknowledge it. He took one long look at her form and turned his attention back to the dirt road. It was too hot for dreaming, and too much work waited to be done.

Mark continued past the Byler fields on each side of him and finally reached the knoll that marked the highest point on Old Mill Road. It was the dividing line between the Byler and Wagner farms. One could see clearly for more than a mile to the next rise of farmland. From the deep woods on the far left to deep woods on the far right, Mark's gaze swept across the checkerboard of hayfields, wheat, corn, soybeans and pastures, encompassing hundreds of acres of prime farmland.

Wagner's dairy farm and most of Lane Farms Angus beef and crop operation were visible from this promontory. Off to the far right, the drop of the landscape hid the Wagners' two ponds and the 15-acre meadow of Lane Farms. The forest behind them formed the skyline.

No matter how many times Mark drank in this view, his chest swelled with pride, and a lump rose in his throat as he surveyed its beauty.

Seven hayfields and three brutally hot work days later, Saturday evening arrived. Close to a thousand bales of new hay resided in the barn. The entire Lane family - minus the eldest son, Doug, who was away at college - relaxed in the cool evening air on the back porch. A half-empty pitcher of iced tea sat on the table while everyone enjoyed the cold drink and the camaraderie of the family. The setting sun cast everything in a warm glow.

Mark's mom and dad were sitting on the glider with his ten-year-old sister, Brenda, between them. His thirteen-year-old sister, Peggy, occupied a rocker that matched Mark's.

Mark looked at his older sister, Karen, who was twisting her empty iced-tea glass around in her hands. "Why aren't you and Todd doing something tonight?"

Karen let out a big sigh. "He went with his parents up to their cottage on Lake Erie for a whole week."

Mark looked at Peggy. She made her saddest face and dramatically mouthed the words, "for a whole week." It was all Mark could do to keep from laughing. He conjured up his most sympathetic look for Karen. "Wow, that's two whole weekends you won't be together. You should have gone with him."

"I know," Karen moaned. "Todd wanted me to go, but his parents didn't have enough room because friends were going, too."

"Todd was taking friends?" Mark asked. "Boys or girls?"

"Not Todd, his parents!" Every word was exasperation.

When Karen saw the devilish look on his face, she scowled. "You are such a twit!" She flipped her red hair behind her shoulder.

"What's a twit, Mark?" Peggy asked.

"How is he supposed to know, Peggy? He's only a ninth grader," Karen said smugly.

"Am not!" Mark countered.

"Oh, excuse me… three weeks past a ninth grader," Karen corrected herself.

That was enough to egg Mark on. "Do you think you'll be able to make it till Todd gets back? That's a long time to go without any kissing or hugging." Mark hugged himself and made kissing noises. Peggy began to imitate his actions.

"What do you know about it?" Karen snapped. "The closest you ever got to a girl was when one fell on you!"

Mark was caught off guard and didn't know what to say. Peggy looked at him in anticipation, waiting for his great comeback. His parents stayed quiet, looking on with raised eyebrows.

The silence hung in the evening air, and it was Karen's turn to gloat. She leaned toward him and softly said, "Gotcha!"

Harold spoke up before Mark could respond, "You see Katie every now and then at the bake shop, Mark. How is her forehead doing since that nasty fall?"

"Wrinkled," Mark answered.

Harold's look turned to one of genuine concern. "Why is that?"

"From scowling so much, but the cut has healed fine, Dad."

"Who is she scowling at?" his mother asked.

"That would be me, mostly. Maybe, only me, for all I know."

"Well, what are you doing to her? You don't treat her like your sisters do you?"

"What's that supposed to mean?" Mark asked.

Ann gave him a knowing look. "You are a little hard on them sometimes."

"I'll kid with her, but Katie holds some grudge against me, and I don't know why."

Ann shook her head. "That's odd. I can't imagine why you have that effect on her, because Katie is a sweetheart. She's pleasant-natured and friendly with everyone she comes in contact with. Have you ever seen her with the customers at the bake shop?"

"Yes. She's nice to them, but she's not nice to me. She warmed up to me a little after I saved her bacon, but that didn't last long."

Mark changed the subject. "Dad, I've been thinking about a project I'd like to undertake. In American history, we studied the Plains states. Sometimes the pioneers made their homes by digging back into a hillside. You know that dirt bank in the back-left corner of the meadow near the old oak tree? I'd like to construct a bankhouse with a sod roof. That way, I could camp out overnight once in a while."

A thoughtful look crossed Harold's face. "There's that old shed up at the Mitchell property I've talked about tearing down. You could use the materials in it to support the roof and form the walls that project out of the bank."

"I was thinking of using more of the materials close at hand," Mark said. "Is it okay to cut the framing that I need from the forest?"

"As long as you don't go hog wild.   How many will this house hold?"

"Three or four," Mark answered, while looking at Brenda and Karen.

"Don't look at me," Karen scoffed. "I'm not sleeping in some hole in the ground."

Brenda looked apprehensive. "Will there be bugs or snakes? You know I don't like snakes."

"Like that five-foot black snake I caught last summer?" Mark asked.

"You were just mean, Mark. I told you not to come near me, and you chased me all around the yard, swinging it at me."

"Yeah, and boy were you screaming!" Mark hooted.

"Self-defense," Brenda said, "'cause when Mom heard me you got in trouble. Nah, nah, nah, nah, nah!"

"That's enough for me," Ann said. "You can continue picking at one another the rest of the night if you wish. Your father and I are going to bed."

Chapter Three

Once the Lanes finished the first cutting of hay, everyone enjoyed a temporary lull in the usually hectic pace, and Mark was finally able to start digging his bankhouse. He was rummaging for tools in the shanty when his mother called his name.

The shanty was a combination former living quarters in the front end – now used for storage – and toolshed in the back. At the turn of the century, the shanty had been the first home of Mark's grandparents while his great-grandmother and her remaining children still lived in the big house.

Ann approached and gave him money. "I need you to go down to the bake shop and buy a loaf of bread for supper. I didn't have time to bake today. You'll have to take your bike, though. Your dad has the truck."

"Okay, so why are you carrying the pail?"

"It's for you. Get a dozen eggs while you're there. I put a towel in the bottom, so they won't break. If Mary is minding the store, tell her I said hello and I'm sorry I haven't had time to visit her for the last couple of weeks."

Mark was sure his mom and Mary Byler would have been best friends, if not for their different societies. They were enough alike in appearance and personality to be sisters. They even celebrated birthdays back and forth, sometimes with the two families getting together for the occasion.

When Mark came out of the shanty with his bicycle, Bella, his two-year-old Border Collie was sitting at the edge of the yard. Her eyes pleaded as she waited expectantly for permission to accompany him, her tail thumping against the ground. He smoothly mounted his bike and started out the driveway. Mark glanced back, made eye contact and said, "Come, Bella." She shot from the yard and caught up to him in just a few quick strides. "Good girl," he praised her.

The bake shop door gaped open, and Mark sauntered up the two steps into the small store. Sitting behind the counter, Katie gasped.

"I didn't mean to scare you, Katie."

"I didn't hear you come in, was all," she replied coolly.

"Lost in your book?" His eyes darted to the cover. "What's it about?"

Katie closed her book and set it upside-down beside the money box on the shelf behind her. "No, I didn't hear a motor pull up."

"I'll bet you didn't know I like to read." His eyes danced with good-natured humor, but she remained aloof. "Can I borrow the book when you finish reading it?" Again, Katie ignored his question, but he was persistent. "Maybe there's stuff in it I shouldn't read. That's it, huh?"

Katie raised an eyebrow and tapped her foot on the floor, so he decided to lighten up a bit. "I rode my bike down. Mom needed a loaf of bread for supper tonight, and Dad has the truck, so I'm slumming it. I complained to Mom about my mode of transportation, but she said it would be good for me. Make me feel like a kid again."

Katie's eyes brightened, and she quickly turned away from him, and refolded a couple cleaning rags on the shelf behind her. As she turned, Mark could see the beginning of a smile on her face. "You shouldn't hide your smiles from me, Katie Byler."

Her ghost of a smile vanished. "I'm not smiling."

"You were a moment ago. I'll banter with you all day long if it means I get to see you smile. By the way, I see your cut healed nicely. Just the other day, Dad asked me about it. I told him I'd check it out the next time I saw you." He stepped closer and looked a little more intently at her forehead. "It's still a little pink there, isn't it?" Katie's whole face turned pink, and Mark couldn't help noticing those freckles again, or thinking how incredibly attractive she was. Her demeanor softened, and he took full advantage. "How tall are you, Katie?"

"Five feet, five inches," she replied guardedly.

"Well, I'm five inches taller than you, and I told my mother that kids are five feet one or shorter."

She gave him a puzzled look. "Where did that number come from?"

Mark hesitated. He knew he was reaching. This lovely girl standing before him was growing larger in his mind, and he wanted to prolong his time in her presence. "Thin air," he offered at last. "I was standing on top of a mountain when I thought of it."

She rolled her eyes. "You've never been on top of a mountain. You've only seen them in pictures, just like me."

"Have too! I've climbed a lot of mountains in my mind. What's the tallest mountain in the world?"

"I don't have to tell you."

"You mean you can't tell me 'cause you don't know," he corrected her. Katie was silent. "I'll pay you double for the bread if you know the answer to my question."

With a smile on her face, she held out her hand. "It's Mount Everest, and that will be seventy cents."

The wind left Mark's sails, and he begrudgingly handed her the money.

"Thank you," she chirped. She put half of the money in the cash box and the other half in her apron pocket.

Mark was certain he would have stumped her with his question, and now he didn't have enough money for an extra sweet for himself.

"Is that your mom's egg bucket in the bike basket?"

"Oh, yeah. I was supposed to get a dozen eggs while I was here."

Mark followed Katie across the road to the springhouse. He set the pail on the edge of the trough, and she placed the eggs in the bottom, one at a time.

"Do you ever drink out of this trough?" he asked.

She nodded. "It's good, fresh spring water."

"I used to stop here when I was riding my bike on hot days and I was thirsty."

"I know you did. I've seen you come in here when I was over at the house. Mama told me she gave you permission to use it whenever you wanted."

"Yes, she did. That was very nice of her."

"One day, I watched you go in, but you didn't come out right away. You were in here a long time. I asked my mother why you took so long. She smiled, but all she would tell me was, 'You should ask Mark.'"

Mark grinned, then reached over and picked up an empty can from the nearby table. He dipped the can deep into the cold, dark water. He plunged his arm in almost to his shoulder and scraped the can along the bottom of the trough. Then he dragged it along the side and out again. He put his hand over the top and carefully poured some of the water back. He grabbed an old mason jar he saw sitting on the table and handed it to Katie. "Come on." He clasped her hand and led her out into the sunlight. "Let's see if we were lucky."

He hadn't planned to take Katie's hand. Nor did he dwell on it, until it occurred to him later that she didn't pull away. Mark became convinced that when Katie was distracted, she really didn't dislike him.

Standing in the courtyard outside the springhouse, Katie held the jar, and Mark poured slowly, dragging the event out as long as he could. He was inches from her and in no hurry to end it.

"What is it?" she asked, leaning toward him.

As Mark emptied the water into the Mason jar, out plopped two coal-black water bugs. They dived for the bottom of the jar. Katie squealed and jumped back, the jar slipping from her hands. Mark caught it just before it hit the ground.

Katie gawked while Mark held the jar up with the two black bugs frantically swimming around and around. "You aren't bothered by them, are you?" he asked.

"No, I was just startled. Nice catch, by the way."

"Thanks, and I can understand that."

"You can?" Katie narrowed her eyes.

He gave her a tentative smile. "Sure. It's a natural reflex."

She lowered her eyes and studied the bugs while Mark studied her face and secretly rejoiced. Katie broke up the parley. "I should return to the shop. Let's finish getting your eggs." While she filled the small bucket, she kept looking into the water. "How many of those creatures are swimming around in there?"

"Lots, I'd bet."

"And you still drank out of it knowing that?"

"It didn't bother me."

"Yuck!" was Katie's response.

Mark and Bella slowly reached the top of the knoll. Bella kept looking at him as if to say, "What's your problem? You never go this slowly."

Stopping on the hilltop, Mark checked the eggs to make sure they were surviving the trip. He glanced back down to the Byler farm and saw the children playing in the backyard. For several moments, he gazed at the bake shop nestled under the big oak tree then turned his attention in the opposite direction.

Mark looked toward home. He drank in the beauty of the panorama before him. Looking across the fields to the north, Mark squinted as if doing so might bring into view that which he could not see: the meadow. His meadow. The one where starting tomorrow, he would build the bankhouse. The meadow that had nurtured him through his early years. The one that had saved him - after his mother had saved him first - when darker days had scarred him and threatened to destroy him. Back when he had given in to the hate in his heart and leapt at the chance to avenge. He had made them pay - in blood. But things were different now. He had let go of his hate, and he was different now.

Mark gazed at the treeline meeting the sky in the far distance. He closed his eyes and he could see the lush green paradise even though it was out of view – his Shangri La, his escape from memories that shadowed him.

His mother would be waiting, so Mark pushed on toward home. He soon reached the Wagner dairy farm. The Wagners milked their cows twice a day, seven days a week, 365 days a year. And that is why Lane Farms raised beef.

He looked ahead at the sprawling acreage that the Lane family called home. Years ago, Harold began buying any land that came up for sale near the original 200-acre homestead, and last year changed the holdings to a legal entity titled Lane Farms. It was a heritage that had been nurtured by six generations. He would never take it for granted.

Three buildings sat on the left side of the road and two on the right. On the left, the original two-story farmhouse still had its wood clapboard siding and slate roof. It was painted white, along with the nearby shanty.

A driveway forty feet wide ran between the side yard and the large t-shaped red barn. Two silos for corn and grass stood next to the barn with a cemented feed lot attached. Across Old Mill Road were two large, red storage buildings.

Harold and Ann were fussy people. Everything had its place, both inside and outside the buildings. It was only natural that Mark followed in their footsteps.

Mark entered the house through the back door and placed the eggs and bread on the kitchen counter. He was looking in the fridge when Ann entered the room.

"Get your nose out of that fridge and close the door. You're wasting electricity. What are you looking for, anyway?"

"Just checking to see if anyone has been taking my stuff."

"If you didn't have so much stuff in there, you wouldn't have to worry about it."

"You know, Mom, if you would buy goodies for everyone, I wouldn't have to spend my own money on them."

She raised an eyebrow. "You know perfectly well that your dad wouldn't want me to waste money on frivolous items."

Mark rubbed his stomach and licked his lips. "Frivolous, perhaps, but definitely tasty! Anyway, I only broke four eggs on the way home."

"Mark!" his mother exclaimed, looking into the bucket, "I told you to be careful!" When she looked up, Mark had retreated a couple steps. He stood grinning at her.

Ann shook her head in exasperation. "What took you so long? I was beginning to think you got lost."

"Yeah, I told Katie you'd be worried. We were busy holding hands in the nice, cool springhouse. She had me so discombobulated I forgot to get myself anything at the bake shop."

"Then where's my thirty-five cents change?" she asked, ignoring his other comment.

"I bet Katie she didn't know the name of the tallest mountain in the world." He grimaced. "Unfortunately, she did."

"You know your dad and I don't agree with gambling," Ann scolded.

"I honestly didn't think I was going to lose, Mom."

"Well, so far, you haven't lost, I have. Go up to your room and get my thirty-five cents. If you are going to gamble, you can at least pay the piper."

"Katie doesn't even have a pipe."

Ann stomped her foot on the floor and pointed toward the doorway. Mark quickly vanished. When he returned with the money, she asked, "So, what did take you so long to get back?"

"Katie didn't know there were water bugs living in the springhouse trough. I was showing them to her."

A puzzled look crossed Ann's face. "Was she interested in bugs?"

"Amazingly, she was."

Later that night, Ann and Harold were talking when she mentioned what Mark had said about holding hands with Katie.

"Surely, you didn't take him seriously, did you, Sweetheart?"

"I'm not so sure it was all kidding. His voice sounded like it had a hint of truth in it. And another thing, if he wasn't at least thinking it, why would he mention it?"

"You've got a point there," Harold agreed. "You've got to admit, Katie's going to be quite a catch for someone. Mark with Katie Byler. Wouldn't that beat all? "

Chapter Four

January, 1964

One sunny day in late-January, Katie sat on the front porch floor with her feet on the steps. It had snowed five of the previous six days, but today the temperature approached forty degrees, giving a short respite in the middle of a harsh winter. The south-facing porch was the perfect spot to take in some sun.

Taking a short break from her afternoon work, she leaned back on her hands and let the sun warm her dark blue dress and black stockings. She tolerated the cold, but didn't like it much. And why couldn't the sun shine more often?

Even her own lifestyle was a wonder to her. Although she dared not voice it, Katie often wondered about a lot of things: who would it hurt if they farmed with a tractor instead of a horse? A propane or gas stove would make life so much easier for running the bake shop and heating the house. Wash day, making clothes, going to town… all of these activities would be less of a struggle if they could only adopt more modern ways.

Her best friend Lydia Zook reinforced her doubts about the necessity of some of the old ways. Lydia and her family had come from eastern Pennsylvania four years ago to lease a farm on Hogback Road, just past the Amish school.

Katie and Lydia were the same age and immediately became inseparable friends. They were true kindred spirits. As one thought and felt, so did the other. Lydia came from a more progressive society, and it was an adjustment for her family to leave behind their former practices.

From her good friend, Katie had learned about belt driven washing machines, a wider variety of clothing colors, and riding bicycles. She had even been told stories about teenage girls and young women working in stores and restaurants.

A honking horn snapped Katie back to the present. She knew that sound. It was probably that bothersome Lane boy. She looked up, ready to roll her eyes, but it was actually Mark's dad who waved as he drove slowly by. She happily waved in return. Katie liked Harold Lane because he was always kind to her and he had a nice smile.

She thought about going back inside then heard a horse and buggy coming off Morefield Road. It pulled into the courtyard by the barn. When the driver stepped out, she immediately recognized Uncle Amos, her father's eldest brother.

While he walked toward her, apprehension began to seep into her. She waved cheerfully when he looked in her direction, but something was wrong. His normally brisk gait was slow and methodical. She had always liked Uncle Amos the best of all her uncles. He was the happy, friendly one, more interested in talking about others than about himself. But today, he looked sad and old. His eyes were red and Katie knew he had been crying.

"Hello, Katie," he said huskily. "Is your father home?"

"No, Uncle Amos. He and Jacob took advantage of this beautiful day to work on the garage the crew is building over at the Jankoski Farm."

Amos expelled a heavy breath. "Mary is in the house, I suppose?"

Katie's heart sank as she nodded her head.

"Let's go on in and tell her the news," he said.

They found Mary in the kitchen. Amos collapsed onto a chair and sighed.

"What I've got to say is bad, Mary. It's about Mother and Father. You decide whether you want the children to hear it from me or you'd rather tell them after I leave."

Mary gathered all the children around her and sat down. Her eyes were already filling with tears. "I'd rather we all hear it together… from you, Amos."

"There has been an accident. Mother and Father were headed west in the buggy. The berm was snow-covered, so they were on the road. A large coal truck came over the hill behind them, going west, as well. He was blinded by the sun because of how low it is on the horizon at this time of year. He never saw them." Amos paused and ran a hand across his eyes. "They were both killed instantly. The horse, too."

The children hugged their mother. Sarah burst into tears. Katie heard what Amos had said, but she didn't want to believe. The color drained out of her face. "Grandpa and Grammy are dead?" she asked, her voice trembling.

"Yes, Katie."

On shaky legs and with tear-filled eyes, Katie stumbled up the stairs to her bedroom. She groped for the quilt draped over her footboard, and curled up on her bed, clutching the blanket her "Grammy" had made her. Her stunned disbelief turned to sorrow, and she was racked by great sobs of grief.

When she was little, Katie couldn't say "Grandma Esther," so she just called her "Grammy." As Katie grew older, "Grammy" became a term of endearment. Once, Katie asked her grandmother if she minded that she still called her by that name. Katie still remembered her grandmother's gentle touch to her cheek, the smile on her face, and the twinkle in her eyes as she replied, "Ah, my sweet Katie, I wouldn't want it any other way. I will be your Grammy, always and forever."

Now, anguish stabbed her like a knife, threatening her ability to function, but Katie knew that there were still the everyday responsibilities and chores riding on her shoulders. She was the oldest, after all.

She would get through it. She had to get through it.

The big trucks had passed her many times while she traveled in the family horse and buggy. She was all too familiar with the whoosh of wind and the whipping of the buggy canvas as they went by in either direction going much too fast. She cried out, "It's not right!" as she imagined the impact when Grammy and Grandpa Byler met their end.

Hundreds of people turned out for the funeral. Even the coal truck driver attended. With tears in his eyes, he offered the family his sincere condolences.

The Lanes attended the funeral, too. Katie's emotional devastation caused Mark's heart to ache. When he offered his condolences, all he could utter was, "I am so sorry, Katie."

Her face was ashen with grief when she responded, "Thank you for coming." He wanted to hold her, comfort her, and take away the pain.

Mark was moved to mail her a sympathy card, including a handwritten note:

Katie,

You probably remember that I lost my Grandad not long ago. I was only three years old when my grandma died, so I never got to know her. However, I was close to my Grandad, and I just called him "Gramps." I loved that old man. We used to pick wild blueberries in Thompson's Woods. He is the one who taught me to love blueberry pie.

Gramps taught me so many things about nature and life. My love for the meadow comes from all I learned from him and the time we spent together there. I still miss Gramps fiercely from time to time, but I carry the good memories of him with me always and they make me feel better.

Gramps bought Bella for me the year before he died. I believe, he knew he was going away and bought her to ease my pain. We trained Bella together. There is still a part of Grandpa in Bella, and I take comfort in that.

It is sad your grandparents didn't know they were going away and couldn't prepare anything to ease your pain.

Mom said you were very close to your grandma. Take possession of something that belonged to her and let it give you comfort, as Bella does for me.

With deepest regrets,
Mark Lane

On Katie's sixteenth birthday, her mother presented her with the rolling pin that Grandpa Byler had made for Grammy. It went unspoken, but she believed her mother had seen and read Mark's note.

When the tears would no longer come, Katie accepted the reality that Grammy was gone. Deborah Yoder reached out to her, but theirs was a casual friendship. Lydia carried her through the hard time.

It was not surprising that the two girls became close. Both were the eldest child in their families, and their life situations were similar. Katie had five younger siblings, while Lydia had six. Responsibilities were placed on them that younger sisters did not bear. This was especially true of Deborah, who was the youngest of seven children.

There were other ways in which the two friends were alike. They both loved nature, the outdoors in general, and working outside. Both disliked laundry day - probably, because they didn't have sisters old enough to help with the chore.

Lydia earned money for her household by helping to care for an eccentric, disabled widow, Greta Kimes, who lived next door with her son, Will. Sometimes Lydia stayed overnight with her when Will went out of town on business trips. Greta had an extensive library, and Lydia had open access to it. Lydia shared what she learned from Greta's books with Katie.

They talked about traveling out West, if only they had money.

They fantasized about going on an extended vacation together, before they joined the church. They never doubted they would join the church, it was only a question of when.

In all their discussions, boys only came up in regards to their distant future. Mark Lane's name was mentioned once in a while, but not in a good light. Katie had grumbled about her neighbor on many occasions. She felt sure Lydia understood that he was to be avoided.

The farming industry was changing. Harold and Mark knew they must change also, or be left behind. Harold had been progressive and had already added the acreage.

Mark looked forward to attending the agricultural state college to pursue a degree in Animal Science and Agronomy. After four years of schooling, he would come home and take the family farm into the twenty-first century.

The multi-year conversion of Lane Farms was already underway thanks in part to Katie's father, Moses Byler. Byler Construction spent weeks at the Lane's remodeling the farmhouse and building a large, double-sided corncrib.

Harold had purchased their first modern tractor in time for the spring plowing and planting. It was a John Deere 3020, and a more powerful 4020 was already ordered for the next planting season.

Mark's favorite upgrade, however, was the new baling machine with a bale thrower. No more ninety-degree days spent carrying and stacking heavy bales on a flatbed wagon. Baling became a one-man job, though unloading them into the barn remained a group effort.

Although the transformation was bittersweet. Katie could not have fallen into his arms from one of these new pipe-frame wagons.

Mark again frequented the Bylers' bake shop during its open season which ran from late May to the middle of October. Mondays were wash day for the Amish, so the bake shop was open Tuesday through Saturday. Whenever Mark got a craving for something sweet or his mom ran out of something that the Bylers sold, he stopped at the shop. His favorite was the deep-fried, maple-glazed donuts. They were so huge that one was practically a meal in itself. The Bylers sold them every other Friday, which guaranteed that Mark would stop by. He also bought fruit pies on a regular basis.

More often than not, Katie worked behind the counter, and those were the special days. Mark would browse around the small store looking at this and that, trying to stretch out the time he spent in her presence. Katie mostly ignored him while she read a book or worked on some sewing. Stolen glances were the order of the day for Mark. He tried to be discreet, but once in a while, she would glance up and catch his gaze for a fleeting moment.

In-depth conversation with Katie was a mere fantasy, but Mark talked with her about anything that came to mind. He tried to formulate his questions so Katie was forced into more than one-word answers. He loved the sound of her voice and watching her facial expressions as she spoke. Katie was always polite but distant, responding only to the questions he asked.

Mark had always excelled at drawing, and for months, he had been secretly working on two drawing projects using colored pencils.

One of his drawings showed Katie standing behind the counter in the bake shop. Her eyes shone brightly, and there was a welcoming smile on her face. It was his version of how she would look if she was in love with him and he had just walked through the door.

The other picture was of Katie on a sunny day. She wore a yellow sundress and sat on a small blanket beside a stream with wildflowers all around her. While she looked into the eyes of the viewer, her long, wavy, strawberry-blonde hair hung down her back on one side of her head. On the other, it cascaded around her ample breasts. Mark had drawn the look on her face to perfection. It was mesmerizing and tantalizing, all at once. He titled the picture, I Await My Prince.

Each time Mark saw her, he gleaned another detail to enhance the pictures. When the drawings were finally finished, they resembled photographs. He had them laminated at the stationery store in Granville and then hid them away in his room.

For years, Mark had anticipated his sixteenth birthday, getting a driver's license, and buying his first car. He had hoped to accomplish all of that in quick successive order this year, but his parents derailed those plans.

A brick wall did not even exist at Lane Farms, and yet Mark could have sworn he ran into one. "But Doug had a car," he argued.

Ann smiled. "Is that what you'd call that thing he drove?" She corrected him. "Doug had a clunker, and not until he was a senior. I can't see you driving a clunker."

"Me either," Mark admitted.

"College costs a lot of money," Harold reminded him. "How will you have money for college if you spend it on a fancy car?"

"Your father and I agree that you may get your license and operate our vehicles, but a car of your own should wait."

"Wait until when?" Mark asked.

A look passed between Harold and Ann.

"Wait until you've proven yourself," Harold answered.

Mark did the only thing he could do. He bargained. "I'll agree to wait until next March, but I want your promise that I can buy a car by then as long as I've proven I'm a responsible driver."

Another look passed between his parents, with Ann finally giving a nod of consent.

"You've got a deal, son," Harold agreed, extending his hand.

The day Mark passed his driving test he stopped at the bake shop and told Katie the news. She listened politely, but he knew she couldn't care less what he did. She never cared. Finally, after all this time, it angered him. He had continually extended the hand of friendship to her and received nothing in return.

As Mark headed for the door, he told himself, "Go back over there and ask her, 'What's your problem, girl? What the hell have I done to you?'"

Walking to the truck, he chastised himself for the fact that he cared. "She's Amish, bird brain. How could you ever expect to be the object of her affections?"

It was a setback. But as annoyed as he felt, Mark recovered and persisted.

One day, Lydia was visiting Katie at the bake shop when Mark and Bella stopped in. Soon Mark and Lydia were chatting away, and Lydia explained where she lived.

"You must be neighbors to Mrs. Kimes," Mark said.

"Why, yes. How do you know her?"

"She buys sweet corn from my mother. When I was younger, I'd go along with Mom sometimes, to her house. Mom would visit for a while, since Mrs. Kimes was disabled and didn't get much company."

"Do you know how she got injured?" Lydia asked.

"No, but knowing that feisty old gal, nothing would surprise me.

Lydia nodded with a smile. "She broke a couple vertebrae in her back by falling off a ladder."

"What was she doing, painting your barn?"

Lydia chuckled. "No, but she was outside cleaning out the gutters on her son's house."

Mark smiled. "That would be Mrs. Kimes."

"Sometimes I help care for her when her son is working."

"In that case, you probably know she immigrated to America from Germany, when she was in her twenties."

"Yes, she told me," Lydia said with interactive eyes and a nod.

"By the way, do you know why they call your road Hogback Road?"

"No. Why, Mark?" She stepped closer, only an arm's length away.

"You know that one stretch that is hilly, wooded, and wild? Everyone around these parts knew that if one of your pigs got out that was where you went... if you wanted to get your hog back."

Katie groaned, but Lydia laughed heartily. She laid a hand on his shoulder and asked if the story was true.

Surprised that her touch awakened his heart, Mark simply shrugged and said that he didn't know.

Lydia spied Bella with her nose poking in the door, sniffing the aromas. She laughed again and went out to pet the Border Collie. They quickly became friends. "She's so beautiful," Lydia sighed. "What do you do with her?"

Mark was enjoying this attention more than Bella. He spotted Jacob coming off the front porch of the house and called out to him. "Jacob! Stand still for a minute." Mark told Lydia, "Okay, now walk up by Jacob."

Bella was keenly eyeing Jacob and Lydia, then Mark, then Jacob and Lydia again. She loped out into the yard, and when Mark slightly raised his index finger, Bella circled up toward them. Mark whistled, and Bella went around behind them, nipping at Jacob's ankles, then Lydia's. She steadily ushered them down through the yard. Katie's mouth gaped while she watched the scene from the vented side wall of the bake shop.

Mark gestured toward the front door of the shop. Bella quickly and expertly herded Jacob and Lydia inside, with Lydia laughing all the while.

"Well, I'd best be going, but it was a real pleasure to meet you," Mark said with a smile from ear to ear and his eyes ablaze. He held out his hand and Lydia shook it warmly, turning a light shade of pink when they made eye contact.

"Oh, my!" Lydia said when Mark and Bella had left. "So, *that* is Mark Lane. I can see where he could be a handful."

Katie nodded in agreement as Lydia sighed. "Those blue eyes and his muscles. Did you see the size of his hands? They are hands made to protect and hold a girl close. But *oh, how I would love to have my hands full of him!* It's too bad he is not Amish. I would bundle with him, anytime."

Katie was speechless. Why would Lydia say such a thing? Before she could comment Lydia added, "You should ask your dad if that story about Hogback Road is true."

"You ask him, not me. He's going to want to know where I heard it."

"So?" Lydia replied.

"I'd have to admit I was chatting with Mark Lane."

"Go easy, Katie. He's just your neighbor. It's not like you want to bundle with him!"

A customer coming into the bake shop interrupted their conversation, and Katie was thankful for the distraction. They did not return to the subject of Mark again, but Katie couldn't forget the conviction with which Lydia had said, "Oh, how I would love to have my hands full of him."

Chapter Five

Katie bolted upright in her bed, suddenly wide awake. The clock on her nightstand glowed in the pitch black of her room – 3:30. She tried to grasp what woke her but sat there in the dark with no answers until the memory of Lydia flooded her mind. She sank back onto her pillow, pulling the covers tightly up against her chin. She was helpless to control her thoughts and relived the events of the past few weeks.

Lydia was gone. There would be no more visits, no more whispered secrets, and no more loving embraces. Katie's only true confidant, the only one she could spill her heart to, had left Powder Mills. She had left all of Wilson County and moved hundreds of miles away, returning to Lancaster where her family had come from five years earlier.

Katie burrowed farther into her bed and pulled the covers over her head, hoping to ward off any thoughts of Lydia's departure. Sure, she had many other friends, but they were just that – friends. Lydia was and always would be her kindred spirit no matter how far they lived from each other.

They had said their goodbyes last night at Katie's seventeenth birthday party. Their tears had intermingled, and Lydia had whispered "I will always love you. We will keep in touch."

Now Katie was confronted with the heaviness of her loss, remembering how Lydia had helped her through the tough times.

Lydia was there for her when Grandpa and Grammy died. And it was Lydia who Katie had leaned on, instead of her own mother, to weather the emotional storm when she discovered she once had a brother just two years younger. An older cousin told Katie his name was Matthew, and he had been killed in an accident on the farm. Katie had often wondered about the four-year gap between her and Jacob. It had never been spoken of in the Byler house, and she still had not asked her mother about him.

Katie remembered, too, the good times she and Lydia had shared. She thought about visits to the Zook farm and their times together: long talks, sled riding, and swimming in their pond. Lydia had taught her how to swim. They pushed snow off that same pond so they could ice skate. Katie relished the feel of the wind on her face and the exhilaration of flying across the ice. It was a feeling of freedom that had no equal in her entire existence.

All too often Katie suffered from sleeplessness. She would wake in the night and struggle to get back to sleep. These last three weeks, lack of sleep had been particularly prevalent, and it was beginning to wear her down. As she lay in bed thinking about her life without Lydia, the weariness finally overcame her.

It seemed that only a moment had passed when a sudden din shook her awake again. "What is that?" she muttered. The fog in her brain cleared, and she groaned while reaching for the noisy offender on her nightstand. Katie fought the urge to roll over and go back to sleep. She forced her eyes open, threw back the covers, and put her feet on the cold floor. There were chores to do and mouths to feed.

Later that morning, Mark waited by the smokehouse. When his mother stopped the previous day to drop off a few items for Mary, she had asked if he could come by the next morning for a smoked ham and two dozen eggs.

Even though Moses Byler's carpentry work and farming kept him busy, he also operated a part-time butcher shop, specializing in smoked meats. The Lane family often enjoyed one of these hams for their Sunday dinner.

Leaning against the old pick-up truck, Mark began to wonder if the Bylers had heard his three quick beeps on the horn. He wasn't in a particular hurry, but he had chores waiting at the lower farm. Waiting patiently was not high on Mark's list of things to do, so he headed for the house. He had just crossed the road when the door opened and Katie came onto the porch. That's better, he thought. Now I'll wait patiently. He returned to the truck and leaned against it while she walked toward him.

There was something different about the set of Katie's face and the way she carried herself. Mark sensed that something was bothering her.

He greeted her cheerfully, "Hi, Katie! I came for the ham and eggs. I'll take my eggs over-easy with white toast." His bright blue eyes twinkled as he smiled.

She looked at him steadily. "Not today, Mark." She disappeared into the smokehouse, retrieved the ham, and tossed it to him.

"I'll get the eggs," she muttered, walking by him. When she returned from the springhouse and handed him the bucket, Mark gave her the money. She turned to go without saying another word.

"Please, Katie, don't go." Something in his voice made a connection, and she turned back toward him. "I know you're hurting. Please, tell me about it."

She studied the seriousness on his face. "Why should you care?" she finally asked.

"I'd like to help, if I can."

He saw a flicker in her eyes as she thought, and he waited quietly.

"No one can help me with this," Katie murmured.

"Try me," he challenged.

Katie squared her shoulders, straightened her back and said, "If you must know, Mark Lane, my best friend in the whole world has moved to Lancaster. How can you possibly help with that?" She glared at him, and he could feel the pain emanating from her.

"Lydia Zook," escaped his lips, and a pensive expression registered on his face. "I had heard the Zooks were leaving, but I didn't connect the dots."

"I'll bet that never happened before," she said with a smirk.

He was quiet for a moment. "I'm sorry to hear about Lydia." His face brightened when he recalled the day at the bake shop. "Do you remember that day when Bella herded Lydia and Jacob through the yard?"

"Yes, I remember the day well, and Lydia enjoyed it, too."

Mark saw the clouds part just a wee bit on Katie's face. "I know it's not much consolation, but I know how you feel."

"How could you *possibly* know how I feel?" Katie demanded tersely.

Mark blinked and looked off into the distance. For a moment, he didn't answer while she still glowered at him. "Because when I was ten, my best friend also moved. We had spent a lot of time together playing in the meadow, catching frogs and tadpoles or climbing trees. For a time after he left, I avoided the meadow."

Katie's features softened. "I'm sorry for snapping at you. Lydia leaving truly has me upset. What did you eventually do about your feelings?"

"Well, it took some time, like I said, but I finally came to the realization that I should go back to enjoying myself in the meadow."

"Why?"

"Because it's fifteen acres of pure heaven, bordered on two sides by twenty-five more acres of woods."

Katie bit back a smile. "What's on the other two sides?"

"Our hay and corn fields are on the south side, and Wagner's pasture with the two ponds are to the east."

"What I meant was," Katie softly clarified, "why did you decide you should go back to the meadow?"

"Oh." A flash of disappointment crossed Mark's face. "I decided that staying away was dumb. I should go back to doing all those things my friend and I did together. That was how I could celebrate his memory and the fun we had."

"Did you find another friend to take his place?"

"No, I never found another best friend who could replace him." Mark shrugged. "You get used to it in time."

All the while Mark had been talking to Katie, he was aware there was something different about her. Finally, he realized that she was taller, somehow.

She followed his gaze down to her black leather work shoes. "What is it, Mark?"

"You. There's something different about you. I haven't seen you much since last fall, but are your shoes taller?"

Katie blushed. "I grew another inch and a half. I had to let down my hems."

"Oh, what I could do with this," ran through his mind, but he knew Katie would be in no mood for his shenanigans today. He simply replied, "Wow, Karen was done growing by the time she was fifteen. I guess we could call you a late bloomer, huh?"

38

Mark had seen Katie blush many times, but he didn't think he'd ever seen her get as red as she did at that moment. Without another word, she left him standing there dumbfounded as she walked away.

Katie's first letter to Lydia summarized the talk she'd had with Mark. While she wrote, she remembered the look of disappointment on Mark's face and smiled. She thought about his literal answer to her question about the meadow.

"Now that you are gone," she wrote, "how will I put up with him all by myself?" Lydia's response puzzled her. "The polar caps are melting," she wrote back. "Someday you are going to have to deal with that boy."

Maybe, if Lydia hadn't used the word "boy" it would have gotten more traction, but then again, maybe not. In Katie's mind, "The Grudge" was still alive and well.

"Mary, your birthday is fast approaching." Ann said, one afternoon over tea. "We need to make plans for our families to get together for the annual gathering. You're coming up to our house this year. I'll make a German chocolate cake, and Mark can make homemade ice cream. We'll have the usual strawberry sauce or chocolate syrup toppings."

"By the way," Ann warned, "Mark has a bargain for you and Katie."

"Oh dear. Should I be worried? What sort of idea has he dreamed up this time?"

"He wondered why your bake shop doesn't sell blueberry crumb pies. I told him if he wanted to buy them from you, it was his job to convince you to make them. But he thought since it was my recipe that I should convince you."

"Your recipe?" Mary raised an eyebrow.

"Actually, it's my mother's recipe, handed down to her by her mother and so on."

"You would consider sharing this recipe with Katie and me?"

"You know I would," Ann replied, patting Mary's hand. She leaned closer to Mary and confided, "Mark has a girlfriend."

"Tell me all!" Mary exclaimed.

For the next ten minutes they gossiped away. "Her name is Sandy and she lives in Granville... she's Mark's age... Mark met her at a church conference in the cafeteria line... he got her name and phone number before the day ended... took him four days to get up the courage to call... they met at the roller skating rink, once... Harold and I had to put our foot down and inform him that he's paying the long distance phone bill to her house... the other two people on our party-line are not happy with him hogging the line."

"Oh my, Ann! A city girl... is she pretty... is she nice... does she go to church... well, I guess she must if they met at a church conference... how is Harold taking all this?"

"Truth be told," Ann said, "Harold isn't too crazy about the city girl part."

"At least Moses and I don't have to worry about that."

Ann glanced at her watch. "I had better let you get on with your work. I believe we've both exercised our tongues enough for one day."

"See ya, Harry!" Mark said to the driver, as he bounded off the school bus. His day looked a whole lot brighter now that he was home.

He stopped at the mailbox to retrieve the mail and newspaper. Once inside, Mark flipped the *Granville Herald* open to the last couple pages in search of the classified section with autos for sale. He had been looking for months in hopes his dream car would magically appear. Even though Mark would be hesitant to admit it, there were two things he asked divine intervention on, and a blue convertible was one of them.

"Autos," he muttered as his finger trailed down the column. His index finger stopped, and his eyes raced across the lines – "1962 Chevy II Nova 400, convertible, straight 6, 194 cu. in., low mi, good condition, $1395 or best offer, must sell. Ph. 555-4865."

Mark exhaled heavily and read it again. He could scarcely believe it. His fingers shook as he dialed the number. When a young female voice answered, Mark told her who he was and why he was calling.

"I have a few questions, if you don't mind," he began. "What color is the car?"

"Bright blue," the woman pleasantly replied. "It's called Nassau Blue

Metallic." Mark's mind went blank. "The car has about 21,000 miles on it," the sweet voice offered. "It has never been in an accident, and we have two winter tires."

"When can my dad and I come to look at it?"

"I would want my husband to be here, so after 4:30 each day or on Saturday. We would like you to make an appointment, though."

He promised to call back as soon as he talked with his father.

"Mom! Mom! Where's Dad?" Mark hollered as he hung up the phone.

"He's out and won't be back until supper."

Mark groaned and headed for the kitchen. "I really want Dad and me to see a car that's advertised in the paper, but we have to go after 4:30 or on Saturday. Can we eat a little later tomorrow night, if I get Dad to take me?"

"That won't work. Did you forget that tomorrow is Mary's birthday party?"

His disappointment turned to apprehension. He started to leave but Ann asked, "Aren't you going to tell me about this car?" Mark explained all the details and left the kitchen.

He didn't want someone else to buy the car without him even having a crack at it. He dialed the number again, and the same voice answered. He asked their name and address and promised to be there on Saturday morning at 10:00 sharp. He also gave her his name and number. Mark added, "Mrs. Kelly, please don't sell your car before I can get there on Saturday."

"But it is for sale," she replied kindly.

Mark explained why he couldn't come until Saturday and added, "I'm really anxious to see it."

Mark and his fifteen-year-old sister, Peggy, had almost finished turning the homemade ice cream when the Byler family arrived promptly at six o'clock. "My ice cream is getting hard to turn," Peggy complained.

Mark gave her ice cream maker a few turns. "Still a ways to go, Piglet. Keep turning."

"You know I hate when you call me that."

"If you'd tell me you like it, I might quit doing it."

"Reverse psychology, huh?"

"That's the name of the game."

Peggy quipped, "You are *really* good looking, and all the girls adore you."

Mark grinned at Peggy then turned his attention to Katie. He watched as she stepped out of the buggy and continued with an occasional glance while the Bylers approached the house. He never tired of seeing her. He wished that Sandy could be Katie.

The evening passed quickly and everyone had a good time. Ann presented the birthday cake with lit candles, and they sang a rousing chorus of "Happy Birthday."

Mark's eyes moved to Katie, and she held his gaze for just a moment. Mark would have given anything to know what was going through her head. Now that he'd seen her with her coat off, he knew exactly what was going through his... up wasn't the only direction that Katie had grown.

They ate too much cake and especially too much ice cream. Jacob gladly accepted his third dish when Ann handed it to him.

When all were done eating, the four parents, along with Katie, Jacob, Mark, and Peggy, sat around the large dining room table and played card games.

As the last game of the evening came to a close, Mark was left holding the "Old Maid." Everyone but Mark agreed that was a good way to end the games.

"You should change the name of that card to 'Old Bachelor,'" Katie exclaimed. That gave everyone the opportunity to have a good laugh on Mark. Smiling good naturedly, he used the time to fully observe Katie's laughing face, that oh so lovely, orb of delight... perfection enriched by freckles subtly displayed beneath her dancing, blue-green eyes.

Mark placed a paper sack in her hands when the Bylers were leaving. "Maybe you'll enjoy these. You can return them when you're finished."

Alone in her room, Katie emptied the contents of the bag onto her bed revealing a stack of "Ideals" books. She smiled at the thought of the coming hours she would spend leafing through pages and pages of beautiful scenic pictures.

Ann was working in the kitchen late the next morning when she heard a car horn. She smiled as she watched Mark and Harold pull up near the shanty in a bright blue Chevy convertible.

She hurried outside. "Oh, Mark, this is a pretty car," she complimented him. "I guess your dad thought it was a good deal."

Harold sighed and put his arm around Ann's shoulders. "You know, Mark should be in sales instead of farming."

"Why is that?"

"He surely did a sales job on me!"

Things were looking up for Mark at Powder Mills High. He could drive to school rather than ride the bus, and the end of the school year was fast approaching.

One Friday night in early May, Sandy accompanied Mark to the junior/senior prom in the high school gym. They danced the night away and were thoroughly entertained at the After Prom – at the expense of a few of their classmates – when a hypnotist performed his act.

Mark and Sandy got along well enough, but he wondered if women were simply enigmas to the male gender. Katie continually acted like she was holding a grudge, and Sandy had become reserved around him. He couldn't help wondering why she was distancing herself lately.

One evening, the telephone rang when the Lanes were finishing supper.

"Hi! This is a surprise," Mark said when he recognized Sandy's voice. There was a pause on the other end. "Is everything all right?"

"I'm calling about our date Friday night. I don't think you should come."

"What do you mean?"

"I don't think we should see each other anymore."

"What happened? Is it something I did or said?"

"Not really," Sandy replied. "I can't see any future in our relationship, so I think it would be best if we end it now."

"Are you really breaking up with me on the telephone?"

There was another silence on the other end of the line.

"Seriously, Sandy. I believe I am owed some type of explanation. If breaking up is what you want, I have no choice but to comply. However, I would like to point out that I met you at a church conference."

"What's your point?"

"Christians are supposed to be honest."

There was a long pause at the other end of the line, and Mark waited. He did not irritate easily, but Sandy was testing his control.

Finally, she said, "You told me that it's your dream to be a lifetime farmer. I can't see living my life on a farm."

"You mean you can't see yourself as a hardworking farm wife?" Mark rephrased with a touch of bitterness.

"That's another way of putting it."

"I'm sorry you feel that way, but I'm not changing."

The phone line went dead.

Chapter Six

Harold finished tinkering with the tractor in the machine shed as dusk settled in. "I'm calling it a day," he muttered to himself and started toward the house. He spotted Ann on the double swing under the big maple tree enjoying a few precious moments of peace and quiet. To him, she was as beautiful as the day he met her. A smile spread across his face as she watched him draw near. "Mind a little company?" he asked.

Ann returned his smile. "You're always welcome to join me."

Harold sat down while Ann ran inside to get him a glass of sweet tea. "How was your day?" he asked when she returned.

"Mark gave me a good laugh."

"Well, that's not unusual," Harold chuckled.

"We were talking about Sandy ending their relationship and Mark said, 'I wish I could find a girl like Katie Byler.'"

Harold sputtered on his mouthful of tea.

Ann patted him on the back and continued, "I'll admit, I was a little taken aback by that statement, too. I asked him why. Mark said, 'Well you might not approve because she is good-looking.' He went on to say, 'I was admiring a pretty girl once, and you told me that beauty is only skin deep. You might be happier with a girl who isn't as pretty.'"

"What does this have to do with Katie?" Harold asked.

"He said that Katie's good-looking, a hard worker, and a farm girl. He doesn't know what she's like on the inside, but he needs a girl who's not like Sandy."

Harold nodded, "When he takes over the farm, he will need a wife who supports him." He squeezed Ann's leg. "Of course, he'll never find one as good as the one I found."

She rewarded him with a kiss. "You do say the sweetest things - sometimes."

"I try." Harold said proudly.

"That's right, you do try. Time for bed," she said with a suggestive look.

School let out, spring planting was finished, and hay season was in full swing. English and Amish alike were busy tending their plantings in fields or gardens and coaxing the crops to be plentiful.

Katie was working in the garden, glad she didn't have to be in the bake shop. Normally, she enjoyed the social interaction, but today she was glad to be working outside. Something had been bothering her lately and that something was Mark Lane. For several weeks now, he had been especially irritating. The other day she overheard Mrs. Lane tell her mother that Mark hadn't been himself since his girlfriend broke off their relationship.

"He's not much different than usual," Katie muttered to herself. "I swear he has been trying to get my goat."

Just yesterday, Mark asked if she was wearing a new dress. When she nodded, he said he liked the color. It was the same color she always wore! And the time before that, he made a wise crack about her flip- flops. Why did she let him irritate her and why did he bother to do it?

"Oh, Lydia, I really wish you were here," she sighed. Katie picked up the hoe and attacked the weeds with renewed vigor.

Most of the girls her age were already interested in boys. Even her own mother wished she was interested in boys. Deborah Yoder was what Katie called, 'borderline boy crazy.' All Deborah thought and talked about were boys. She couldn't wait to find her future husband. She was one year older than Katie, but there was plenty of time. What's the rush?

Lost in thought, Katie continued working, but soon the silence was broken by the sound of an approaching vehicle. The sight of the Lanes' pick-up coming down the road put a smile on her face.

"Here he comes, and I don't have to wait on him. Let's see him try and irritate my mother!"

Mark bounded up the steps of the bake shop. "Hi, Mrs. Byler. I'm glad to see you here today." She looked at him with raised eyebrows.

"Not that there's anything wrong with Katie minding the shop," he added. "What I mean is, I came to talk with you about making blueberry crumb pies.

Mom told me she discussed it with you a while back, and I wish you would consider it."

"Well, Mark, I would need to have the recipe to check the ingredients and the preparation instructions."

"I just happen to have the recipe right here." He grinned as he handed it to her. "This is an excellent pie, and I'll bet you could sell lots of them."

Mary studied the recipe. "It seems like the usual, except it requires walnuts. We rarely use them. I'll go over this with Katie and see what she thinks, since she bakes most of the pies these days."

Mark had expected Mary to be in charge, and he frowned as he wondered if Katie would take this opportunity to get even with him. He sensed that he was getting under her skin a little more than usual, lately. Now he was depending on her not to derail his pie hopes.

Early the next morning, Mary and Katie were cooking goodies for the bake shop, filling the kitchen with heavenly smells when a small voice from the doorway interrupted them.

"Mmmmm, it smells really good in here." Katie looked up to see Sarah with her teddy bear clutched under one arm.

"When will I get to help make all this stuff?"

"Soon enough," Katie replied, sizing her up.

Mary brushed off her response. "Why don't you go back to bed for a little while? Then I'll fix breakfast for everyone."

"All right, Mama." Sarah yawned, and her little bare feet padded back up the stairs.

Mary turned her attention to Katie. "Yesterday Mark asked me to bake a blueberry crumb pie and add it to our baking list. Ann has provided her secret family recipe. I said I'd have to discuss it with you."

"I think Mark Lane is more trouble than he's worth. Why should we bake special pies just for him?"

"Katie Byler!" Mary exclaimed, "I know you're strong-willed, but I have never heard you talk like this. What is vexing you so?"

"Mark Lane is vexing me so."

"Why does he vex you?"

"He says things to get under my skin. He's aggravating. He likes to smell the bread."

"Does he ever buy the bread?"

"Yes."

Mary smiled at Katie. "Do you like to smell the bread?"

"Yes, but it's my bread. And he ogles the jams."

"He tastes them with his eyes. As often as he comes here, Mark obviously likes the goods we sell, and he spends his own hard-earned money to buy them. I'm sure he means no harm by what he says."

"I just wish he'd stop doing it," Katie complained. "And why should we have to bake something special just for him? No one else tells us what to bake."

Mary contemplated her daughter's strong response. "Did something happen in the past between you and Mark that needs to be resolved?"

Katie thought for a moment. "Nothing I can put my finger on. We've always been around each other, yet I can't remember a time when I liked Mark as a friend."

"Think about it, and maybe it will come to you," Mary told her. "You've always had a competitive spirit, but I can't remember a time when it led to long-term hard feelings. I can see this thing with Mark has truly disturbed you, and it's not like you. Hopefully you can get to the bottom of why Mark makes you feel this way."

Katie nodded.

"What answer should we give Mark about the pie?" Mary asked.

"It's a little more time-consuming, and we have to buy walnuts. Tell him we'll make it, but they will be fifty cents extra. Hopefully he won't want to spend the money."

On Monday, Mark was on his way to the lower farm when he spotted Mary in the side yard, hanging out a load of wash. "Good Morning, Mrs. Byler!" he said, approaching her. "Did you get a chance to talk with Katie about the pie?"

"Yes, we discussed it." Mary explained about the extra charge.

"Could I order one for Wednesday?"

"That would be fine. We are planning a trip to town tomorrow, so we can get the walnuts then."

While Mark talked with Mary, he was acutely aware of the underpants and bras hanging on the line. Walking away, he couldn't help but wonder if they belonged to Katie, and he couldn't help the new vision of her that crept into his mind.

Katie was behind the counter of the bake shop when Mark arrived to pick up his pie. She looked up from her sewing. Here comes trouble, she thought. Katie could tell he was in a good mood today - better than in a long time. She was about to wipe that smile off his face, and there was a part of her that was looking forward to it.

"We don't have your pie today," she said nonchalantly, not bothering to look up from the shirt she was mending.

"You're kidding, right?"

"I made a regular blueberry pie if you'd like one." She gave him her best innocent look.

"Are you serious?"

"Very serious." She narrowed her eyes, daring him to challenge her.

Mark frowned. "When do you think you'll have one?"

Katie had the upper hand in this conversation, and though she normally would just want him to leave, she savored every moment. She looked into his blazing blue eyes and thought of a picture she had seen in one of Mrs. Lane's *Ideals* books of the glaciers in Alaska. Near the bottom, the ice was brilliant blue. The caption said it was from the intense pressure. Katie almost laughed aloud.

She informed him, "We didn't have time to go to town yesterday, so no walnuts. We'll probably go tomorrow, because we have other things we need to stock up on. Why don't you come by on Friday... if you *want* to," she said with a smirk.

"I'll stop Friday afternoon then," he returned grimly. He left the shop without saying goodbye. As he went out the door, he whispered under his breath, "Stupid girl."

49

Maybe it was the wind direction. Maybe Katie was listening for trouble. When the barely audible sounds reached her ears she glared at the empty doorway.

The next afternoon, Katie pushed her shopping cart through the grocery store when the condiments section caught her eye. She reached up and grabbed a bottle of hot sauce. In the blink of an eye, she knew how to put Mark in his place.

One time, Mrs. Lane had bought a quart of their chili. Afterwards, when Katie had asked how they liked it, she told her everybody was fine with it, except Mark, who was very sensitive to spicy food.

Katie stood in the kitchen on Friday morning humming a tune while she mixed up the ingredients for Mark's pie. She'd had another restless night, and her mood was on shaky ground. She reached to the back of the cupboard to retrieve the hot sauce she had hidden there. The sauce came out of the bottle faster than she had anticipated, and a lot ran into the mixture.

"Oh well," she shrugged, and kept on humming.

Mark was dirty and sweaty from baling and unloading hay when he entered the bake shop later that day and noticed that the shelves were bare. "Looks like it's been a good sales day for you, Katie."

"Hello, Mark," she said cheerfully. "I was beginning to think I might have to eat this pie myself." She pulled it out from under the counter.

Mark leaned down and inhaled its familiar aroma. "It looks just like Mom's," he said appreciatively. "I can already taste it."

Katie smiled and told him she hoped he would enjoy it. She's actually being nice to me, he thought. He wished it was that way all the time, but what did it matter? Yes, he had been secretly attracted to her for over two years, but he certainly couldn't tell anyone about it, especially Katie. Yet here he was in her bake shop, and she was being friendly.

Mark let his guard down. "Why, thank you. You didn't have to do that just for me, but I'm glad you did." He delayed an extra moment to observe the pink tinge of her sun-kissed skin on her oh-so-lovely face. Beauty in its purest form—devoid of make-up.

He paid for the pie and began to leave, then turned to see her watching him. "Katie, I know I tease you a lot, but I don't mean anything by it. I'm sure it must bug you sometimes because it does that to my sisters. Would you prefer I scale it back a bit?"

After a brief hesitation Katie asked, "Are you trying to apologize to me?"

"I guess I am."

Mark could see indecision in her eyes, and he knew that she was struggling. He turned to leave, while she stood behind the counter with her mouth open and no words coming out. He walked to the door and said, "I'll see you next time, Katie. Thanks for the pie." Then he was gone, and she heard the tractor start up.

Katie ran around the counter and burst through the door to catch him, but it was too late. Mark was too far up the road to hear her over the sound of the tractor's motor, and he never looked back as Katie stood in the middle of the road waving her arms. He crested the hill between their houses and was soon out of sight.

All the way home, Mark couldn't get two things out of his mind. Katie was nice to him, and why did she look at him like that when he left?

He was famished from working hard all day on the lower farm. Lunch had worn off hours ago. As soon as he shut the tractor off, he jumped down with pie in hand and strode quickly to the house.

In the kitchen, Mark poured himself a tall glass of cold milk, cut a big piece of pie and set it on a plate. His stomach rumbled with involuntary anticipation. He stuffed a large forkful into his mouth, and as he began to chew his brain went numb. Instinctively, he began to swallow when his body decided it had all that it could take.

Mark stood by the sink in front of the window and Ann's curio shelves when Mount Vesuvius released its second catastrophic eruption. And there he remained while rinsing, gagging, gargling, and spitting. Tears poured from his eyes, and he splashed cold water on his face and continued rinsing. After what seemed like an eternity, the burning began to subside. Thoroughly spent, Mark laid across the sink with his face under the running water, letting it wash over him. He splashed more water in his still-burning eyes, for they felt like they were on fire.

As he lay there, his brain worked out what just happened to him. Katie had filled his pie with hot sauce on purpose. Anger bubbled up in his chest. How could she be that vicious? He wanted to get even with her.

But even as his anger built, Mark felt the pain in his heart. Katie had been nice to him, yet it had all been a hoax.

Mark still had his face under the running water when his mom came in from the outside. "What happened?" she exclaimed.

"I'm sorry, Mom. The pie was spicy hot, so I spit it out. I'll help you clean it up."

Mother and son worked quickly with soap and water to put everything back in order. Finally, Ann asked, "Why was the pie spicy?"

"I really don't want to talk about it," Mark grumbled.

"Is everything okay between you and Katie?"

"Nothing I can't handle."

Chapter Seven

Mark spent the next three days trying to come up with a plan of retaliation: some were too harsh, some were too mild. All the while he couldn't shake the nagging thought of how Katie must be laughing about the joke she pulled on him. He could almost hear her cackling, "I got one over on you." He pictured the ear to ear grin on her face and the triumph in her eyes.

In a moment of inspiration, Mark recalled an incident that occurred in the bake shop a couple years earlier. While Katie had waited on him, a large wolf spider walked across the counter. She jumped back in panic and yelled, "Kill it, Mark!"

Quickly, he reached out and ended the spider's existence with one swift swat of his hand. He turned his hand over. "Ooo, look at that. Do you want to see it, Katie? It can't hurt you now."

"Go away!" she said.

Now Mark grinned – almost sneered - as he rehashed the event. The Lane barn was a treasure-trove of spiders. He headed out to the barn with a pint jar in hand and went from cobweb to cobweb until he had almost every type of spider known to man inside his jar: big ones, little ones, brown ones, black ones. With smug satisfaction, Mark eyed the twenty or twenty-five spiders.

He headed outside to find his father. "Dad, do you still want me to get that wagon at the lower farm?"

"Sure do," Harold shot back.

"Which tractor can I take?"

"The 4020 will do."

"Great," Mark thought. He loved to drive the new tractor.

Katie heard him long before he crested the top of the hill. She felt bad about what she had done to Mark and for four days had nervously expected his return visit. She hadn't had a good night's sleep in all that time. She even considered a visit to the Lane farm to apologize, but her pride got in the way.

Now she could see him. Katie worked the pleats in her dress as she waited for him to stop at the bake shop, but he didn't. Man and machine sped by without even a hesitation. Mark usually cut his speed when he passed between the buildings occupying both sides of the road. She always assumed it was because of the children who played here and sometimes darted across the road without thinking. And if anyone was outside, Mark waved and gave them a smile. Why had she never acknowledged this positive side of him before? All this time, had she allowed her attitude toward Mark to warp her image of him?

Not long after Mark went by, Katie heard him coming again. She scarcely took a breath, and her heart pounded as the tractor neared. She heard the dreaded sound of it slowing and then stopping in front of the shop. She knew it was coming, and she braced for whatever it might be.

Mark steeled his nerves as he hopped off the tractor and sauntered into the bake shop. "Hi Katie," he greeted her with a friendly wave and pleasant smile. "What kind of pies do you have today? I'm kinda hankering for a peach, if you have it."

"I do have a peach. Did you eat all the blueberry pie I gave you the other day?"

"Funny story about that pie. I had just got home and took it into the kitchen, all set to cut me a big slice, when Mom said she was going to come here and get a pie for the church bake sale. I told her she was going to be out of luck, since that was the last pie you had. I told her how you had hidden that one under the counter just for me. I also told her what you said. Do you remember?"

Mark gave Katie a chance to answer, but she just stood there looking a bit dazed.

"Well, as I recall, you said, 'If you hadn't come by, I was going to have to eat this myself.' Mom just stood there with her mouth open and looked at me. And trust me, it takes a lot for my mom to be speechless. Anyway, I was standing there with a big grin from ear to ear, and Mom finally said, 'I need a pie for tomorrow's bake sale.' Then she asked how set I was on eating your blueberry pie. Now it was my mouth that was open, but I knew exactly what I wanted to say: 'You have got to be kidding, Mom. You want me to give you

54

the pie that Katie made especially for me so you can take it to a church bake sale? See how good this pie looks, Mom. Just smell that aroma - blueberries, walnuts, and sugar? You'll never guess what Mom said next. Go ahead, I dare you to guess," Mark goaded her.

"I don't know."

"She said she'd pay me double what I paid you. Can you believe it? My own mother was trying to buy me off!" Mark shook his head in mock disbelief.

"What did you do?" Katie stammered.

"There was no way she was going to get that pie off me, but she cheated!"

"How?"

"She knows I have a soft spot for you, and she said to me, 'If Katie liked you enough to make this pie, you'll find out how much she really likes you by giving this one to me and asking her to make you another.' She had me. She can be tricky sometimes. I gave her the pie, and only made her pay the regular price. After all, it was for the church bake sale."

Mark bit back a tattletale grin at Katie's speechlessness. "So, will you *please* make me another blueberry crumb pie just like the last one? Do you like me that much?" He gazed at her with a look of sheer innocence and pleading.

She quickly responded, "I'll make you another one."

"How much do you like me?"

"When do you want the pie?" she asked, blushing brightly.

"That depends on whether you want to be my friend," Mark answered with his attention focused squarely on her.

Katie swallowed hard. "I guess that would be okay," she replied in a small voice.

"Good." Mark kept his steady gaze upon her. "Can you have it for this Saturday?"

"Yes, no problem."

"Here, let me pay you for today's pie." He handed her a ten-dollar bill, knowing she would have to turn to the shelf on the back wall and rummage in her money box for the right change. While her back was turned, he reached behind him and retrieved the jar full of spiders. He had hooked his belt on the very last hole leaving space to secure the jar. He unscrewed the lid and dumped all the spiders on the counter. He set the jar down and picked up the pie. When Katie turned around, he was waving the pie back and forth at shoulder height, and her gaze followed it. Mark smiled and reached out his hand for his change. Movement on her apron caught his eye. When Katie had moved forward to hand him the change, she leaned against the counter while the spiders scattered. Three spiders were in a race to the top of her apron.

Alarm must have shown on Mark's face because Katie instantly looked down. At that point, as Mark's grandpa would say, "All hell broke loose."

Katie screamed, and overcome by fright, she fainted. Mark let the pie and the money fall to the floor and leapt over the counter. He caught her as she collapsed and brushed the spiders off her apron. With his free hand, he reached up and grabbed the money box and used it to smash the spiders that were making a hasty get-away. The lid on the box popped open, and money flew everywhere. It was precisely at that moment Mary Byler burst through the door. She stared, wide-eyed, around the bake shop.

Mark quickly found his voice. "Katie had a spider on her apron and passed out. I caught her and was trying to kill the spider with the money box when the lid flew open."

Mary leaned against the wall and laid a hand over her heart. "Can you carry her outside for me?"

He scooped her up in his arms. Mary was waiting for him in the shade under the old oak tree. Mark gently laid Katie on the ground with her head cradled in Mary's lap. "I'll go back in the shop and clean things up while you help Katie."

Once inside, Mark killed spiders as fast as he could find them. He used his hands so as not to make too much noise. Sticky spider guts covered both hands when he was done, but he believed he had killed the majority of them. He cleaned his hands, collected the money, and placed it back in the box. He headed outside to Mary and Katie.

"Is she going to be okay?" he asked quietly.

"Yes," Mary replied, stroking Katie's forehead. "She's just sleeping now. Eventually, she'll wake up, and it will be fine. I want to thank you for helping her. Thank goodness you were here." Mark remained quiet and studied Katie as she slept.

Mary explained, "Katie is deathly afraid of spiders because she got bit by one when she was nine years old. We almost lost her, and the doctor warned we might not be so lucky the next time. That is why it worries us so that she likes the out-of-doors. We are very careful to keep the house spider-free, but we have no control over what's outside."

Mark did not want to be present when Katie woke up. "My dad is waiting on that wagon, so I'd better get going. When Katie wakes up, please tell her I'm sorry."

"All right, but what shall I say you're sorry for?"

"She'll know."

Mark did not return to the bake shop for two weeks. Katie saw him go by, but that was as close as he got. She welcomed the reprieve. She had learned a valuable lesson from this tit-for-tat exchange with Mark: it was time to grow up.

She wrote to Lydia, telling all. A sympathetic response soon arrived, but included in it were a few simple words of advice: "It's time to open your eyes to boys, Katie. Nothing serious, of course. Simply accept that they are a necessary part of our future. Dip your toe in the water, so to speak."

One night, when Katie was having trouble sleeping, she went for a walk behind the house. It was a beautiful moonlit night, such that she did not need a lantern. She enjoyed these nights almost as much as bright sunny days. She paused in the backyard beside the garden. She could see the worn spots in the grass that formed the ball diamond. Katie remembered the fun family and friends had had playing softball, Wiffleball, and kickball when she was growing up. She thought of how different things were now that she was of age.

The following day was Sunday, and in the afternoon the ball diamond was in full use. Katie sat on the backyard glider and enjoyed the chance to watch the game. Since there were two sets of cousins visiting, pitchers were aplenty and Katie got a break from her "designated pitcher" duties. As she watched the game, she was struck by both the competitiveness and the camaraderie of the group. Suddenly, one cousin said to another, "Come on, Sam, strike her out. She's only a girl."

Katie started to chuckle, then froze. It all came flooding back to her. About five years ago in this very yard, Mark was visiting, and they struck up a game of Wiffle ball. Katie was clearly the best player in her age group, even better than the boys, and they respected her for it. Mark and Jacob were on the same team, and they were winning. In the last inning, with two players on base, there was still a chance her team could win. Jacob was pitching, and after several bad pitches, Mark yelled to him to just throw her a good pitch. "She's only a girl!"

Katie remembered feeling so flustered that she swung at a couple of bad pitches and struck out. "I am a better player than that," she bemoaned to her mother at the time.

Sitting here now, all the hurt and humiliation of that day returned. She had always competed with boys, and she won most of the time. Katie had never been so casually dismissed or taken for granted as an "easy out." What made it worse was she struck out and proved Mark to be right.

Mark may have kept his distance, but that didn't mean Katie wasn't on his mind. He spent more time to make amends than he had to come up with his plan to get even with her. On three, twelve-inch squares of lightweight poster board he used colored pencils to draw a panorama of the meadow. The middle picture was a close-up of an Amish girl with her back toward the viewer. She sat on a small blanket beside the stream that ran the entire length of the meadow. The girl was surrounded by wild flowers in bloom. When the pictures were finished, he rolled them up and placed them inside a cardboard tube along with a letter of apology and a humorous poem he had written.

Exactly two weeks after the spider incident, Mark eased the tractor to a stop in front of the bake shop. Mary Byler greeted him when he stepped inside.

"Hello, neighbor," she said pleasantly, "You must have been very busy lately. We haven't seen hide nor hair of you except in passing. How have you been?"

"Fine, but busy." Mark handed the cardboard tube to Mary. "Would you please give this to Katie for me?"

"Certainly, Mark. No spiders inside, I hope."

"No spiders. Just some drawings I made of the meadow. I know how much Katie likes scenic pictures, and I've mentioned to her a couple of times how beautiful our meadow is down by the woods." He gestured in that direction.

"That was kind of you, Mark. I'm sure she will appreciate it."

"There is also a letter of apology in there for the prank I pulled on her with the spiders."

"Oh?" Mary studied his face.

"I also want to ask you and Mr. Byler to forgive me. I didn't know Katie was allergic to spiders. I was only trying to scare her, but the trick got out of control. It was a dumb thing to do, and I am sorry. I'm sure Katie told you all about it, and I don't blame you for being angry."

Mary shook her head. "No, Mark. She didn't mention anything about a prank."

Mark was surprised but continued. "I feel terrible about my actions, and I'll never do anything so idiotic again. You can tell Mr. Byler that, too."

"Do you mind telling me exactly what did happen?"

"I caught some spiders in a jar, and when Katie wasn't looking, I released them on the counter. You pretty much know the rest."

"What is the tiff between you and Katie about?" Mary asked in a concerned voice.

"You'll have to ask her. I try to get along with her, but she's holding a grudge about something, and I don't know what it is."

Mary reached out and patted Mark's hand. "I forgive you, and I will talk to Moses. I don't know if it will help you, but Katie and I just talked about this a few weeks ago. She admits to having a grudge, but she doesn't remember why."

Mark looked at her skeptically.

"I know it sounds odd, but Katie wouldn't lie."

Chapter Eight

A full day's work was done, and the sun was dropping below the knoll to the west when Mary sought out her oldest daughter. "Come, Katie. Let's sit on the glider and talk."

Katie noticed the cylinder in her mother's hand. "What's in the tube? Did you get me a present?" she asked lightheartedly.

"You'll find out after we have talked." Katie fell silent and looked down at her bare feet. "How have you been sleeping lately?" Mary asked.

"Not well. Especially since Sunday."

"Oh. What happened on Sunday?"

"I remembered why I have a problem with Mark."

"Tell me all, sweet daughter." Mary took Katie's hand in hers and squeezed it gently. Katie recounted the story of the ball game. "Why do you think you have carried this cross for so long?" Mary asked.

"He flustered me so that I played poorly and struck out, and then he and Jacob cheered and laughed together. Mama, you know I was better than most of the boys my age back then. I felt humiliated. My own brother laughed at me."

"Has Jacob ever laughed at you other than that time?"

"Yes, Mama."

"This event made you a better ball player. You were still beating boys when you were fifteen. Jacob would have laughed because he was happy to get you out. He knew how hard that was. Mark would have laughed because he was just being a twelve year-old boy. I'm sure he didn't do it to hurt you. I know from the stories Ann has told me that Mark has a kind, sensitive heart.

"Not too many years ago, he found a wounded young bunny that had been shot through the neck. Mr. Lane wanted to put it out of its misery, but Mark refused. For weeks, he fed it milk from an eye dropper. He named him Benny, which was kind of cute because he always called him Benny the Bunny. When Benny was healed and had grown large enough, Mark released him in the meadow. One Saturday last November, Mark came to Ann and asked if she would simply heat up a can of soup for his supper. When Ann questioned him on it, he said he knew that she would be cooking the three rabbits his brother and father had shot that day while hunting."

Katie's eyes grew moist.

"Mark said he knew for certain that one of the rabbits was Benny because the fur had never grown back on his neck where the wound had been. Ann reminded him that he had given Benny three good years, which is a lot for a rabbit."

Mary looked at Katie, catching her eye before continuing, "Mark does not believe in hunting for sport. Ann has also told me that there are squirrels in the meadow that will take nuts from his hand."

"Man has dominion over the animals," Katie said. "We hunt to put food on the table and utilize nature's bounty."

"This is true," Mary agreed. "It is also true that Mark exercises that dominion in other ways."

"What do you mean?"

"We don't have many groundhogs in these parts, thanks to Mark. We also don't have too many coons around here, either. You know how they love to raid our gardens and are especially fond of sweet corn. And every now and then, a family of muskrat will move into the Wagners' ponds. If they tunnel through the banks, they could drain the ponds."

"Don't tell me. Mark traps the muskrats," Katie said with a smile.

"He rids our neighborhood of vermin. Mark is being a good neighbor." She paused. "What do you think we should do about your anger at him?"

"As the Bishop always says, 'Utilize the power of the cleansing blood.'"

Mary patted Katie's hand and stood up. "You are wise beyond your years."

"Mama, wait! You forgot about the tube."

"Goodness, yes," Mary said. She retrieved the tube from under the glider and handed it to Katie. "Mark stopped at the bake shop today and asked me to give this to you."

"Oh."

"He also asked for forgiveness from your father and me for pulling the spider trick on you."

Katie's eyebrows shot up. "He admitted that to you?"

"He did, and he was genuinely remorseful."

"What did you tell him?"

"That he was forgiven. But now he knows why you are frightened of spiders."

"What else did he have to say?" Katie asked, ducking her head.

"Nothing, really. Knowing that Mark stayed out of our shop for more than two weeks was indication enough of how adversely this affected him." Mary stifled a yawn. "It has been a long day, and I'm going to turn in."

Katie didn't have far to walk, since her room attached to the back of the house. Inside, she lit her oil lamp, sat at her writing table, and emptied the tube's contents onto the hardwood surface in front of her.

The apology note was brief but to the point, and he seemed sincere. It concluded, "*I hope these drawings help you feel good and will at least replace the bad feelings I have caused you. I wrote you the poem to help you smile. Sincerely, Mark.*"

Katie unrolled the drawings. She never knew Mark could draw. In fact, she really didn't know much about him at all. She focused intently on the first picture displaying nature's beauty. A lump caught in her throat when her eyes gazed upon the second picture. The young Amish girl so perfectly drawn with her back to the viewer could be her. She realized it probably was her, and a tingle passed through her. Katie closed her eyes and imagined sitting there on the blanket. She felt a warming inside and let her mind drift, allowing the good feelings to wash over her.

After viewing the third drawing, she reached for Mark's poem.

Today in the Meadow

By Mark Lane

Today in the meadow I saw a bee.

I got too close, so it was chasing me.

I ran so fast across the grass

Until I thought I had lost him at last.

I was so glad I began to sing.
It was then I felt that mighty sting.
I jumped back and looked in his eye.
"Why'd you do that?" in pain I cried.

"I had let you off the hook," he replied.
"You began to sing and my ears were fried.
I had to act fast. I had no choice.
I had to silence that squawking voice."

So now the bee is a friend to me.
If I'm in the meadow and him I see,
I control my singing very well
'Cause I don't want my body to swell.

Katie's laughter could have been heard throughout the house.

She lay awake for a time and thought about how Mark had not tattled on her. She rehashed all her mama had said and looked at the drawings propped on the top shelf of her bookcase. She read the poem again and again, until she almost had it memorized. *What other talents did he possess?* Her last thought as she drifted off to sleep was that he had written a poem just for her. It was the best night's sleep she had in a very long time.

Katie awoke the next morning wanting to make her peace with Mark. She needed him to know that she, too, was sorry and that she wanted to thank him. She felt an urge to look into those beautiful blue eyes – yes, they were beautiful – and make him feel her regret. He made at least one trip past their house every day, and she wondered if he would stop today. But he didn't stop that day, or the next day, or the one after that, and her misery mounted.

By Saturday, Katie could stand it no longer. She made his favorite blueberry crumb pie in hopes she would hear his tractor today. Katie didn't have long to wait. She knew it was him before he topped the hill. He had the tractor revved at full speed, and he was flying.

She left the bake shop and planted herself in the middle of Old Mill Road. As he barreled down on her, she didn't even flinch. She simply raised her arm and pointed to the pull-off. Mark downshifted and turned into the parking area. He cut the motor and looked at her with wide eyes. She held his gaze and approached the tractor.

"Are you crazy, girl?" he asked with a grin, while the morning light danced in his eyes.

Katie walked over and stood beside the dismount step. "This is a big tractor," she marveled, "but would you, please, get down off this big, green machine?" She took a step back and watched the ease with which he swung to the ground.

"I love flying on this baby."

"I can tell. Maybe someday, you can take me for a ride."

Mark's eyes bulged, but all he said was "Yeah, right."

"I've wanted to settle this thing between us, and you've driven by three days in a row without stopping."

"I made the last move," he said.

"Until today!" Katie responded, not taking her eyes off him.

"I want my ten dollars that disappeared into your moneybox."

"Serves you right," she said with a thin smile. "That's less than fifty cents a spider."

"Well, if that isn't the pot calling the kettle black! I want my money back on the blueberry pie, too. I'm not paying for something that was defective."

She stood toe to toe with him. "It sounds fair to me. Your parents paid for you, and you're defective." She boldly held his gaze and scrunched her eyes together. "Your mother didn't take that pie to the bake sale, did she?"

He leaned down with their noses almost touching. "No, you little turd."

Katie let out a chortle. "You shouldn't talk like that. Your mother will need to wash your mouth out with soap."

"I meant what I said."

She looked up at him with devilish eyes, and a smile tugging at her lips. "I really got you, didn't I?"

65

"Yes, you did." Mark said grudgingly. "Big time, if it makes you feel any better."

"Why didn't you tattle on me?"

"I didn't want to get you in trouble. Why did you do it?"

"You called me stupid."

"Oh, you heard that."

"Yes. And just so you know, I tried to stop you that day. I stood right out here on the road, like I did today, and waved for you to stop. I was going to chicken out and stop the trick, but you didn't see me."

"Truth is, most days I would have looked back, but I was too engrossed in wondering why you were nice to me."

Katie reached out and wrapped her long, slender fingers around Mark's forearm. "I'm sorry I made you the spicy pie. Will you forgive me?"

"I guess, but what are you going to do for me?"

"I already did it. That's why I flagged you down. Come into my little bake shop."

He followed her through the door and watched as she went behind the counter and removed a pie box from the shelf. She motioned for him to come closer and opened the lid. "Blueberry crumb pie" escaped his lips. When he looked up, apprehension flashed across his face.

Katie gave out a bark of laughter, then brought a fork out from behind her back. "Care to try it?" she asked sweetly.

Mark scooped out a forkful and shoveled it into his mouth. "Mmmmm," he said, savoring the flavor as the ingredients blended together. He relished another bite, filled the fork again, and looked at Katie. "Have you ever had one of these pies?"

"No. We make them to sell." Mark held the treat out to her mouth, but she tried to refuse it. When he insisted, she accepted it, tentatively. He smiled as he watched her eat. She allowed him to give her another bite before she refused the third. "I see why you like them, but I made it for you to enjoy."

"How much do I owe you?" he asked. They burst out laughing together.

"I guess I'd better get back to work," Mark said. "Flag me down anytime."

"Not so fast. Here's your ten dollars, and I want to express my appreciation for the drawings you made for me. They're lovely, and I can tell you spent a lot of time on them. I can see why the meadow is dear to your heart. The poem was so funny, and I imagine the whole house heard me laughing. I hope you don't mind that I shared it with Mama the next day. She laughed, too. I'm going to have my uncle make frames for the pictures, so I can hang them on my wall."

Mark waved as he pulled away on the tractor.

Katie remembered the first words that came to her mind that morning while she lay in bed: "Go boldly to the throne." Boldly was good.

One evening, as the Lane family sat around the supper table, Ann mentioned blackberry season. "Mark, have you checked the bushes lately along the back edge of the meadow to see how ripe the berries are?"

Mark swallowed a mouthful of his mom's delicious country fried steak. "Not within the last week. They were still red then."

"Were they plentiful?"

"From what I could tell, it looks like it will be a bumper crop. They are big berries, and the bushes are loaded with them."

The next morning as Ann headed to town, she stopped to see if she could pick anything up for Mary.

"I'm glad you stopped. If you don't mind, I'm low on brown sugar. Also, a bag of walnuts would come in handy. Your blueberry crumb pie has been very popular. We thank you for the recipe."

"Last night at supper, Mark said there will be more blackberries in our meadow than we'll need this year. I'll let you know when they're ripe, and you can help yourselves. You've got lots of hands for picking."

"Only the customary two," Mary said as she held them up for Ann to see. They shared a laugh. "Thank you, Ann. We can always use extra blackberries for canning and pies. We would have no trouble selling them in the bake shop."

"You might have to tweak it a bit, but I have used blackberries in the blueberry crumb pie recipe. If the blackberries are a little tart, just add more sugar."

Mary nodded her head. "That's a good idea."

"What's new on the relationship side of our two children?" Ann asked guardedly. "I don't mean to pry, but Mark is pretty tight-lipped about it."

"I try not to involve myself in it," Mary replied. "Perhaps you know they kind of came to an understanding a couple weeks ago."

"No. I didn't know that. What happened?"

"Well, first I talked to Katie, and she had a talk with Mark. I think they're doing better now. Mark is back to stopping at the bake shop regularly."

"Back to stopping regularly?"

"That's right. A while back they got in a tiff, and he didn't come for over two weeks."

"I knew about the tiff, but I didn't realize it was that bad."

"Yes, but they're old enough to work it out themselves. So far, so good. Katie's best friend moving away was hard on her."

"And Mark's girlfriend breaking up with him had him in a foul mood for a while."

It was a testament to their friendship that neither mother told all they knew, and the information withheld was to protect the feelings of the other.

"I guess, I'm going to see your meadow firsthand," Katie said when Mark walked into the bake shop a few days later.

"Can I come, too?" he quipped.

"As long as the berries you pick go in my bucket and not your stomach."

"Did you just try to tease me?" Surprise etched his face.

She laughed and returned his gaze. "Is it all right that I do?"

"It's very much all right. It's just that you never did it before. Does this mean that teasing is on the table for a two-way exchange?" He looked at her hopefully.

"I'm game if you are, as long as it's not hurtful."

"Well, I hope I do better at this than I did at Old Maid, or should I say Old Bachelor?"

Katie snickered. "I think you're teasing me now."

"You catch on quick. Do you scrub up nice, also?"

"Now that was funny and harmless." She said with bright eyes.

"Let's talk about my meadow. What's the scoop?"

"Scoop?" she asked.

"Yes, scoop. Like you and me since I walked into this shop. There is a story begging to be told on both counts." Mark's piercing gaze held her captive, and they were stranded there for a few moments in time. She broke the spell by looking down shyly, then flushing under the intensity of it. Judging from her face, she probably blushed clear to her toes. He waited until she looked up and caught him fawning over her.

Katie felt her face warming again and he looked truly sorry for her. She gave him an impish smile while rubbing her hand along her arm. There was an element at play that she did not understand – something excited her.

"The story of today is forgiveness…"

"Forgiveness is good," Mark replied.

She continued, "The story of the meadow is your mother said we could pick blackberries because you don't need all of them."

"That's for sure, and that sounds just like Mom - thinking about someone else."

"I really like your mom."

"Yeah, she's sorta grown on me over the years," he said with a wayward shrug.

"You are terrible," Katie said, matter-of-factly.

"I know, and Mom knows, but she loves me anyway."

"Mama said for you to tell your mother when you have picked all you want, let us know, then we'll pick."

"If you would come picking with me, I could show you where all the berries are. You'd get to see the meadow, and by helping pick our berries, you could get your berries that much quicker."

Katie pondered his suggestion. "We're teasing again, aren't we?"

"You got me. But I would have preferred to show you the meadow myself." Mark folded down his lower lip in a pouty face. When she laughed aloud, he pretended he was wearing a dress and gave her his best curtsy. She laughed even harder. Katie told him about his mother's suggestion of the blackberry crumb pie, and that brought an abrupt end to Mark's clowning. "As soon as we begin picking, I'll bring you enough blackberries to make two pies."

"Why two pies?"

"One for the Lanes and one for the Bylers."

"By the way, I got the pictures of the meadow hung on my wall the other day, and they brighten it up considerably. Thank you again for your kindness." His eyes were on her, unwavering. Those expressive eyes that seemed to reach into her very soul were doing strange things to her – conjuring up feelings that were unknown. Her heart quickened, and a warmth spread through her.

Katie grasped the first thought that came to mind, "Numerous times, I have thought about the day I fainted, and I wondered about some things."

"Such as?"

"I'm lucky I didn't hit my head, but I'm not sure how I managed it."

"I leapt over the counter and caught you when you passed out."

"Oh. And what about the spiders that were crawling up my apron?"

"I killed them later. First, I brushed them off your apron as I caught you falling." Katie stared at him as heat crept up her neck and face.

"You are making me feel really uncomfortable," Mark confessed. "Would you have preferred I let them bite you? I brushed them off, scooped you up in my arms, carried you outside, and laid you on the ground with your head in your mother's lap."

"That's the second time you saved me, isn't it?"

He shrugged. "Who's counting? I'm just glad you weren't bitten."

Mark said goodbye and left the shop. A moment later he poked his head back in the door. "I'll gladly share my meadow with you, any time. And I'm always available for a personal tour."

With a wink of his eye, he was gone.

Chapter Nine

Katie couldn't get Mark's visit to the bake shop out of her head. Maybe if she had tried just a little harder...

He had teased her - in a good way - and she was sure he had intentionally flirted with her at least twice. A month ago she wouldn't have cared or given it a second thought. But she was different now, and she did care about Mark. However, she was acutely aware that she couldn't care. It was not permitted. But a little flirtation was surely harmless, wasn't it? Tonight, she gazed at the pictures hanging on her wall. She appreciated the beauty and what they represented: Mark cared about her and her feelings. It was a new and exhilarating thought. Another person had her solely in mind as he toiled long hours on something for her benefit and enjoyment.

Katie sat in her room while many thoughts and questions played in her mind. She was torn because these new feelings contradicted what had been a part of her for so long. This was the same person she had disliked for years.

She and Mark had forgiven each other their pranks and were trying to become friends, but what about his flaws? Should she simply overlook them and pretend they didn't exist? Were they even real or were they an illusion conjured up by her imagination? Deep in her heart she wasn't sure, and in spite of everything she found herself drawn to him.

When the revelation came, it hit like a thunderbolt. She was attracted to Mark. But how improbable was that? Not to mention unwise. Katie admonished herself, but it didn't stop the fluttering in her stomach or calm the beating of her heart. What bothered her the most was that her thoughts suddenly seemed to have a will of their own.

And speaking of botherations, she had tangible proof of Mark's caring: the pictures, the poem, and protection from criticism. However, she had given him nothing in return and it troubled her. After a few minutes of quiet thought, an idea came to her. She would embroider his initials on handkerchiefs for him. That way, he would have tangible proof that she also cared, and no one would need to know they came from her. The hypocrisy of this situation occurred to Katie. She rubbed the back of her neck and let out a heavy sigh.

As sleep gradually overtook her, Katie thought about the spider incident and imagined Mark catching her. She thought about being held in his arms when he picked her up and carried her outside. She tried to imagine the feeling of her head on his shoulder. She pictured Mark bending down and gently placing her on the ground, careful that his large hand supported her head while he placed it in her mother's lap. She envisioned him gazing down at her with sad eyes as he murmured, "When Katie wakes up, tell her I'm sorry."

When she woke the next morning a surprising thought raced through her head. What would it be like to have Mark pick her up in his arms and lift her out of bed? She immediately rebuked the thought and tried to put it out of her mind.

It was an exceptional crop of blackberries, big, juicy, and sweet. The Lanes had quickly picked and filled their needs, leaving a large volume for the Bylers. Mary and her children had tackled the challenge in full force. There would be canned blackberries to sell, and blackberry pie could become a regular item in the bake shop.

After the first day of picking, Mark delivered enough berries for two pies to the Bylers. When he stopped the next day to pick one up for the Lane household, Katie had the pie sitting on the back shelf beside the money box. LANE was clearly written on the pie box. "How can I help you today?" Katie asked pleasantly.

"Very funny. Did you enjoy your pie yet?"

"We're saving it for tonight's supper."

"Now that's what I call willpower."

Katie held his gaze, and pretended not to notice when Mark began to fidget.

"Well, um, I better pay you for that pie." He reached into his pocket.

"Whoa horsey," she said, holding her palms up. "You've got to leave it in there. The money leaves with you or the pie stays here - Mama's orders, not mine."

Mark's face lit up in a roguish grin. "If you'll recall, I jumped over this counter once before."

"And look how that turned out," Katie responded with a sassy grin of her own.

"Are you trying to imitate my grin? You've got it all wrong. That's more like a half smile. Your face doesn't have nearly enough of the look that irritates adults or make teachers want to give you an extra assignment."

She laughed. "I'll bet you know all that from experience, don't you?"

"Let's not go there," he conceded. "Okay, you win, *Miss* Katie. No money will be exchanged. Now may I pleeease have the pie?"

"It would be my pleasure to give you your pie, *Mr.* Mark."

"Tell your mom I said thank you, but please, no more free anything."

It was a warm Saturday morning in August, and by 9:00 the day was already hot and hazy. Mark had Wagner's big pond on his mind when he entered the bake shop. He greeted Mary cordially, grateful to be out of the sun. "Mr. Byler sure knew what he was doing when he picked the spot to build your store."

"Yes, he chose wisely. The huge oak tree provides the perfect shade. I'm glad you stopped early today. We'll be closing before lunch. After we grab a quick bite to eat, four of the children and I are going to the meadow to pick the last of the blackberries. Again, give your mother our thanks."

Mark passed that information along at lunchtime. "Well, let's hope they don't get wet," Ann said. "The weatherman is calling for a chance of rain. Mary's not taking Ruthie with her, is she?"

"No. She told me Daniel was staying home to watch her while Mr. Byler finishes painting the house."

Ann was working in the kitchen in mid-afternoon when a special bulletin came on the radio. "*This is an emergency weather alert. A narrow band of severe thunderstorms has formed in Eastern Ohio. This storm has already struck the Youngstown area, causing major damage. It is headed for Wilson County in Pennsylvania. This storm contains high winds, heavy rain, and dangerous lightning. All residents are advised to seek shelter immediately.*"

73

Mark was working in the barn when he heard his mother shouting. "Now what's her problem?" he wondered. He walked from the barn and spied her at the far side of the driveway. Even at this distance, he knew something was terribly wrong. "Mom!" he called out.

Ann ran to him and grabbed his arm. "Where's your dad?"

"He took the truck to get supplies in town." His mother's pallid face alarmed him.

"The radio just issued a warning of severe thunderstorms coming from the west. I can see the beginnings of them already. Mark, the..."

He knew what she was thinking: the Bylers are in the meadow. "Mom, take Bella with you to the cellar. I'll warn the Bylers." Mark sprinted toward the machine shed. He looked at the sky as he ran. Beiges were turning to ominous, swirling gray masses.

Mark leapt onto the 4020 and a second later, it roared to life. He slammed the tractor into gear and shot away. He quickly maneuvered through two sets of gates and into the lane that ran all the way to the meadow. He raced at breakneck speed down the lane between the fields. The uneven ground jostled the huge machine, but he never slowed.

Mark cut the throttle as he entered the meadow, scanning the entire length, searching the underbrush for any sign of a Byler. Finding none, he tore over to the spot where they always forded the stream. Reaching the other side, he opened the throttle and sped across the grass to the eastern end. Mark turned and began his search westward. If they were still in the meadow, he would find them.

At the Bylers' house, Moses was unaware of the storm rolling in. The last side of the house, the east side, was almost painted. He stood on a ladder at the top of the wall just under the overhang, and he couldn't see the approaching storm. He heard a loud noise, then the screen door banged. He thought that Mary and the children had returned, but the door kept banging. By the time he realized it was the wind slamming the door, the storm was upon him. He hurried down the ladder and into the house, where he found Daniel and Ruthie hiding behind the couch.

The wind howled and shook the large house. Moses quickly closed all the windows as the water poured inside. All the time he worked, his mind was on the edge of panic. My family? Where are they? A thunderclap shook the heavens, and the world outside disappeared. The wind and rain made it impossible to see another building. There was a pause in the torrent of water, but the winds came again, more fierce this time, followed by hail beating against the window. The big oak tree above the bake shop whipped mightily, then came a thunderous crack and a crash, as a large section of the tree fell on the shop.

Amid the deafening fury of the storm Moses dropped to his knees. While clutching his two children, he cried out, "Have mercy on my family, Father."

The heavens continued to roar, and lightning strikes, one after another, reached to the ground. The house shuddered and slate from the roof flew past the windows. He feared the roof would go at any moment.

The magnitude of the storm seemed to make time stand still, and all he could do was continue to pray. Then the storm was over as quickly as it had come. Moses descended the porch steps into the yard and looked to the west. The sky was already showing signs of clearing like it was just another day. He ran back into the house and sat Daniel and Ruthie on the couch. He looked into Daniel's face and said, "I need you to be a man and take care of your sister until I return, no matter how long it takes. Can you do this for me?"

Daniel nodded. "We will wait here together."

Moses left the house at a run and headed for the meadow.

Mary and the children were having a productive afternoon harvesting the remaining blackberries. They already had several containers full and considered calling it a day. "Why don't we pick for another half-hour?" Mary suggested.

While the others picked, Katie moved the containers under a tree and covered them with a vinyl tablecloth they had brought with them just in case it rained. It made no sense to have their hard work go for naught.

If they had been picking out in the open, the Bylers would have seen the storm approaching, but there were forests on two sides of them. Suddenly, the wind picked up and Katie looked at the sky. Her heart began to beat wildly, and her soul shivered.

Mary called out to Katie and Jacob, "Get Sarah. We must leave now!" Mary took Rebecca in her arms and headed toward the open meadow. Katie grabbed Sarah and followed her mother.

The wind had grown to a roar, but in a lull, Katie heard a tractor and a voice calling out. She could see the tractor through the brambles. She hoped it was Mr. Lane in search of them.

As the Bylers picked their way through the entanglement of berry bushes, Mark leapt to the ground and reached them as they broke free into the open. "We have to seek shelter!" he shouted to Mary above the wind as the rain began to fall.

She looked unsure. "We should try to make it home."

"There's no time," Mark yelled.

"We could all hide under the tractor," Mary yelled back. A lightning strike cracked just to the west.

"No! If the tractor gets hit by lightning, we all die. Follow me! I have a bankhouse not far from here."

Mary hesitated. Mark scooped Rebecca into his arms and ran toward the tractor. He hoisted her up and jumped up behind her.

Mark brought the tractor to life and called out to the others, "Follow me!" He sped across the gently sloping hillside, turning only once to assure himself that the rest of the Bylers were following.

It wasn't far to the bankhouse just outside the canopy of the big oak tree. Mark pulled the tractor to a stop along the west side of the hut dug into the hillside. He used the tractor as a shield against the fierce winds and to protect the bankhouse in the event that the tree might succumb to the storm.

Mark had already ushered Rebecca inside when the others reached him. "Watch your head," Mark shouted. "You can only stand near the center."

All of the Bylers hurried inside. Mark swung the door shut and fastened the slide bolts. They might be wet, but for the time being, they were safe.

For a minute, everyone peered out at the storm from inside their shelter. Most of the east wall was an old door Mark had found in the shanty. He had laid it on its side and attached a couple hinges at the back and two slide bolts at the front. The space above the door and the open foot above the west wall gave them a view of the meadow and the woods to the west. They watched in awe and then fear as the storm intensified.

Finally, Mary said, "I'm sorry, Mark. I'm sorry for not trusting you."

"We're not out of danger yet. Let's hope we make it through this storm. Why don't you take the girls to the back? Have them sit on the wood floor. The safest place is the back four feet. All of you may as well get comfortable."

"Can I stay up here with you?" Jacob asked.

"Sure Jacob. If things get too bad, I may need some help." Jacob's eyes grew wide, but he said nothing. Their attention was drawn back to the scene outside. They watched as the storm grew stronger. It was like a huge beast on a mad rampage. Trees swayed more than Mark thought possible. Lightning struck and the sky roared with thunder.

"That was close," Katie said.

"I'm not worried about lightning," Mark replied. "This place has lightning rods. We had a couple left over when we built the corn crib, so I used them."

The bankhouse shook, the roof swayed, and the west wall bowed. The space above the wall allowed wind into the cabin. Mark feared the sod roof would give way completely, falling on them or exposing them to the storm. The sod had already blown off in a couple places along the peak, allowing water to come in. The house was literally being shaken apart while outside the storm ravaged all that was on the land. Trees cracked, and limbs fell like rain.

Rebecca cried as the storm intensified. If not for the tractor, Mark felt sure all would have already been lost.

Mark turned to Sarah. "I need you to hold and comfort Rebecca while your mama gives me some help. Can you be strong for me, Sarah?"

She nodded, and Mark continued, "Stay at the back and hold your sister in your lap. Katie and Mrs. Byler, I need you to hold the roof down, or we may lose it. Each of you take a side. In each hand, grab a tree limb that supports the sod, and hang with your weight when you feel the upward pull. Jacob! We must hold back the west wall. If it caves in, the whole house will collapse or be blown apart." Mark ripped one of the narrow, short boards off the east wall behind the door. He jammed the board into the earth between the floor boards. "Put your foot against it, and use yourself to brace that wall."

The storm was upon them in all its fury. Whole trees crashed down, but the oak beside the bankhouse held strong. Lightning continuously turned the darkness outside brighter than daylight. A tree nearby was struck by lightning and then one at the far end of the meadow. Sparks flew, and half of the tree crashed to the ground. If not for the danger, the scene inside the bankhouse would have been surreal: Mary and Katie hung from the ceiling, Sarah and Rebecca cowered in the back, Jacob wedged against the west wall, and Mark held the front roof.

The battle raged between man and nature, while the outcome seesawed back and forth. Jacob cried out for help. Mark was just in time to hold back the wall, then Katie called for help as the roof lifted.

During a brief lull, Mark hoped the worst had passed, but the fury came again.

When the storm finally began to weaken, everyone was physically spent. The others collapsed to the floor while Mark peered outside and watched the storm diminish.

But once more lightning snaked its way toward the ground, and a thunderous boom shook the heavens and the earth. The bankhouse took a direct hit. The lightning rods, support pipes, and cables were instantly electrified. A flash of bright light filled the bankhouse as the sky drained its electricity into the ground. No one would ever forget the humming, buzzing and crackling of millions of volts of electricity as it overwhelmed the bankhouse. The very air was charged with electric current. As Mark looked at Katie, illuminated in the bright light, their eyes met and held. There was a connection between them that couldn't be ignored. They both felt it. More than simple affection – deeper than that.

Then it was over. A few minutes more, and the storm was gone. The sky was already clearing, and soon the sun would shine again. Six people emerged from the bankhouse into a different world than the one they had fled.

Mark's heart sank as he surveyed the damage to his beloved meadow. Large craters existed where trees had once stood. Whole trees and half trees lay where they fell. Limbs cluttered the ground, with some still partially attached to the tree trunks. A thin column of smoke rose from the base of a split tree at the far end of the meadow. Mark watched the five Bylers emerge from his cabin, and it struck him that what was truly important was that everyone survived.

Jacob came out last. He tentatively looked around and stood tall, breathing out a sigh of relief. Mark slapped him on the back and grinned. "We won, Jacob. We fought the battle with Mother Nature, and we won! Wasn't that exciting?"

"It really was," he agreed. "That lightning strike was incredible."

"Yes, but you did it, Jacob! Your holding back that wall was amazing. If you hadn't, we would have been goners for sure." Jacob beamed proudly, and Mark had made a friend for life.

"When the bright light came, my skin tingled," Rebecca piped up. Everyone laughed. It was a laugh of great relief.

"We must get home, children. Your father will be beside himself with worry," Mary said. She looked at Mark intently then hugged him in a powerful embrace. "Thank you, Mark Lane."

Mark watched them go, never taking his eyes off Katie, as she brought up the rear. After they all had crossed the stream, she turned back to him. Katie looked in his direction even as she walked. She finally gave him a wave before she turned her attention toward home. Mark waved in return and watched her go.

As Katie left the meadow, a part of her wanted to stay. It was another first for her… leaving a boy's presence had an element of regret. The fact that it was Mark's presence was not lost on her - once her adversary, and now her friend.

She wrote to Lydia who responded, "Be careful, Katie. I know him. You could fall in love with him."

When she read Lydia's words, Katie realized she would have to be careful what she told Lydia. If even a hint of her emerging feelings got out, things could become difficult for her.

Chapter Ten

Mark chose his way carefully while leaving the meadow on the tractor, zigzagging around fallen trees and limbs. Reaching home, he was relieved to see that Lane Farms had avoided serious damage.

Ann watched him come up the lane, and when he dismounted the large machine, she rushed to hold him.

"Tell me about it, Mark!"

"Can I tell you a little later, Mom? The Bylers hurried out of the meadow without taking their blackberries. I'll change into dry clothes then drive down to their house, and offer to get them."

Ann would not be put off. "First, tell me are the Bylers all right?"

She was staring at him, her eyes alive with concern. "Yes, Mom, they're fine. Somewhat wet and a little shook up, but they have good reason to be."

She let out a sigh of relief. "All right, you may go. But when you get back, I expect the complete story."

When he topped the knoll and looked down on the Byler homestead, Mark caught his breath. He scanned their property as he pulled off the road into the courtyard. Every building had been damaged in the storm. A large section of the oak tree had crushed the bake shop. Would Katie have been inside if not for the blackberries? He shivered at the thought.

Moses came out onto the porch and down the steps as Mark approached the house. Jacob trailed close behind. "Hello, Mark!" Moses greeted him. "My family has just been filling me in on all the details."

Moses strode up to him and shook his hand while clasping his arm. He looked into Mark's eyes and said, "Thank you, my son. We owe you a debt of gratitude."

"You owe me nothing. You would have done the same for us." Moses nodded and accepted his kind words.

"What brings you here on this calamitous day?"

"I was riding up from the meadow when I realized Mrs. Byler left without taking her berries. If she'll tell me where they are, I'll take the tractor and get them."

Moses called her name through the screen door, and Mary came out of the house. She explained where they were, but protested that he didn't need to bother himself with their berries. "We can do it," she said. "They might not even be worth much now."

"I don't mind," Mark assured her.

"I can help him," Jacob offered. "There are several pails."

Mark smiled inwardly at his eagerness.

"No, Jacob," Moses answered. "We've got work to do here."

Katie came out onto the porch, and Mark noticed she had changed into dry clothes.

"Katie," Moses addressed her, "fetch Mark a box that will hold all the blackberries."

She soon returned with two picnic baskets. "This should do it. Why don't I go with him and lend a hand? Plus, I know where the berries are."

"All right, but don't be gone long. We have quite a mess to clean up around here."

Mark led the way to the tractor with Katie close on his heels. She set the baskets down and asked him to help her. He gripped her waist with his hands and hoisted her up. He handed her the baskets as she stood by the tractor seat. She didn't know what to do, so she sat down.

He looked up at her and marveled at how remarkably his circumstances had improved in the last hour. "You know you're sitting on my seat, right?"

"Oh… well, where do I go?" she asked taking in her surroundings.

On his lap would have been fine, but Mark told her to sit on the fender.

Katie looked at the fender and then down to the ground. "That's a long way down. What if I fall off?"

He shrugged. "Then your worries will be over."

She stared at him blankly. "You saved me in your bankhouse so you could kill me on your tractor?"

Mark was grinning now, prompting Katie to smile.

"Show me how to do this. If you can save a whole family in a bankhouse, you can teach me how to ride a tractor."

"See the big hole at the front of the fender? That's where you hold on."

Katie stood up, placed her fingers in the hole, and leaned outward. "Now what? Do I lean against the fender like this?"

"Not unless you want your butt pointing at my face."

"That's embarrassing, Mark," she scolded.

She put her hand on her hip, pursed her lips, and looked down at him with narrowed eyes. "I should let you get the berries yourself."

He half smiled in return. "That would definitely not be a good idea."

"Why not?"

"Because it would be way less fun, and I want you to go along." A bashful smile lit up her face.

Mark mounted the tractor and leaned against the fender. "Hold on to the handgrip and scoot your backside up onto the fender like this," he said, demonstrating the proper procedure.

Mark dismounted again, and Katie followed his instructions. After the second try, she was sitting on the high fender. He walked to the other side of the tractor and mounted it easily, sliding onto the seat.

Mark assured her, "If you hold on, you're not going to fall. We'll just sit here till you feel comfortable." She took a deep breath and straightened her back. She turned and looked down on the outside of the huge tire.

"Starting and stopping," Mark informed her, "that's when you need to hold on. While we're moving, you can sit there and enjoy the ride - with your hand still in the hand hold, of course. Ready, Katie? I distinctly heard your old man say not to be gone long."

Her eyes became saucers. "Does your father allow you to call him your old man?"

"He never told me not to do it. After all, he is the oldest man of our house." Mark winked at her and started the engine. He smoothly ran through the gears as he picked up speed. He never opened the engine to full throttle but took a leisurely ride. With Katie at his side, he was in no hurry today. By the time they reached the meadow, he could tell that she was getting used to sitting atop the metal beast. The creases had left her forehead and she gently swayed to the movement of the tractor.

Mark crossed the stream and stopped at the far edge of the open grass. "We'll walk from here. When you dismount, turn around and look for the footstep."

"Just like getting out of a buggy," Katie said, giving him the eye.

"You got me there, but let me guide your foot to the footstep as you dismount."

With Katie in the lead, they started off toward one spot, but the berries weren't there. She went to another spot, but no berries. She looked around, trying to get her bearings as Mark watched with interest and amusement.

"You don't remember where you left the berries, do you, Katie?"

She frowned and in an uncertain tone replied, "I thought I did."

Mark's heart soared. She had come along on this adventure so she could be with him. "You just wanted to ride the tractor, didn't you?" he prodded her.

"What?" Katie glared at him.

"I remember the other day you said, 'Maybe someday you'll take me for a ride on the tractor.'"

For a second Mark thought she might agree with him. "No, that's not it," she said defensively.

He knew when to drop it.

"From what your mother told me, the berries should be over to the right." Mark headed in that direction. A turn here and a turn there, and they soon came upon them. In spite of the rocks Katie had used to hold the cover in place, the wind had blown it off. Three of the pails had upset, and their contents had spilled into the grass.

"We'll carefully pick these up," Mark said. "I think most of them should still be usable."

"I wonder how much water got in the pails?" she mused aloud.

"Let's see." Mark picked up the largest container, held his hand over the top and tipped the pail to pour out the water.

Katie watched his hands. They dwarfed her own. His little finger was almost the size of her thumb, and the fingers were long and perfectly shaped.

They were masculine hands – strong and well-tanned by countless hours in the sun. She remembered Lydia had remarked about them at the bake shop.

As Mark tipped the bucket, only a small amount of water came out. "The tablecloth must not have blown off until near the end of the storm. That's good, right?"

"Yes. The berries won't be waterlogged."

While they picked the berries from among the blades of grass, some invariably got ruined. "Oops, there's another one," Mark said. He tossed the damaged berry into the air, and caught it in his open mouth. "Betcha' can't do that, Strawberry Top."

"What is 'Strawberry Top'?"

"Your hair. We call the color strawberry-blond because of the red in it."

"Like 'Carrot Top.'" she stated.

"Yes, but Strawberry Top is way more attractive. How long is your hair?"

"We don't draw attention to such things."

"What kind of fool notion is that? Your hair is gorgeous. Why shouldn't it be celebrated?"

Katie gave a shy smile and resumed working. A moment later, she ruined a berry, and the berry-catching game began. "Betcha can't catch it!" She tossed the berry into the air toward Mark. It bounced off his nose, and she laughed. He threw one up for Katie, and it bounced off her chin. She managed to catch the next one, and the competition was on.

As they finished collecting the berries, Mark caught her gaze with his own. "We really ought to talk before long."

"What do you mean?"

"About our feelings and experiences."

Katie felt a tightness in her throat, and she looked down. Slowly she responded, "I don't know if that's a good idea."

"You know… about the storm," he explained. "I've had bad dreams, some of them full-blown nightmares, ever since I was a kid. Talking out a situation calms me down, and the dreams go away. My mother and I have done this many times, but you were there today. Maybe we could talk about our individual experiences?"

As Katie listened, her nerves began to settle down. "I know what you mean about the dreams. Sometimes I wake at night from a dream and can't get back to sleep."

"What do you do then?"

"Different things: read, go for a walk."

"In the dark?"

"Some nights have moonlight, and I have a lantern. I listen to the sounds of the night, which calms me and helps me sleep." Katie wished she could add, "Thoughts of you have helped me sleep soundly, lately."

"Maybe we could talk the next time I come to the bake shop, if you're not too busy."

Katie's hazel-blue eyes widened, and Mark could read the unhidden trepidation that was registered there. "The bake shop?" she questioned. "There is no bake shop."

"Damn," he said softly. She looked away, ignoring his transgression.

They finished their task and headed back across the meadow. Katie asked him to help her onto the tractor, again. She liked the feel of his strong hands on her waist and the power of his arms as he hoisted her up.

They were lost in thought on the way back to the Byler farm, occasionally making eye contact with each other. Once, Mark didn't turn away for several seconds and Katie tried to read the unspoken message in his eyes. She was unfamiliar with such things, though her pulse quickened and she tingled all over.

The story of Mark Lane and the Bylers' experience in the meadow spread like wildfire throughout the area. Jacob's enthusiasm was largely responsible for the entire Amish community knowing the intimate details. Meanwhile, Peggy had learned the facts and wanted to make sure all her friends were aware that she was living with an honest-to-goodness hero.

Mark tore down the old shed at the Mitchell property and rebuilt the bankhouse. He made upgrades to the design, and the recycled lumber came in handy. Lane Farms hired Byler Construction to repair the light damage that occurred to the buildings. Mark, Harold, and Eli cleaned up the meadow, as well as the rest of the property.

Soon after the storm, the Byler farm hosted a work day that would have made a barn- raising proud. Amish came from all around Powder Mills to put the house and buildings back together. The house suffered heavy slate loss, while the barn had lost a large section of its roof entirely. Of course, the bake shop had to be rebuilt. By the end of the day, all the repairs had been completed before the last buggy left for home. Along with the hearty meal served at lunchtime, everyone enjoyed a piece of blackberry pie.

The Byler bake shop was closed for only one week. The following Tuesday, Mark was one of its first customers. As he walked through the new and larger door, he looked around and smiled at Katie. "Bigger and better," he said admiring the new shop. "Love those wide steps. Good for people who don't watch where they're going."

She laughed and asked, "Are we speaking of anyone present?"

"Well, I remember someone who didn't know where she was going just a little over a week ago."

She blushed and chided him, "Stop it, Mark!"

"That's okay, Katie. Your red face goes nicely with your strawberry-blond hair." Her blush deepened.

"Have any of the young ones had bad dreams since the storm?" he asked.

"I don't know. Have you?" she inquired sweetly.

"Ouch," Mark said. "I'm beginning to regret that I struck a teasing bargain with you."

"What would you prefer? I throw more blackberries at you?"

Mark raised an eyebrow. "Hmmm, tempting, very tempting."

"To answer your question, there have only been a few bad dreams. That's pretty good for the severity of the storm," Katie opined with a shrug.

She didn't divulge that she had had a couple nights of restless sleep. She had mentally chastised herself about the event. She knew that Mark had only been there to save them because her mama had watched the bake shop that Saturday morning and told him about their plans. Katie realized she wouldn't have told Mark they were going to the meadow that day, because she still didn't create much conversation with him. She had promised herself that she would change.

"How have you slept?" she asked.

"Good. I guess we didn't need that talk after all."

"Jacob is still talking about that day. I think Father is growing weary of hearing it."

"Yeah, thirteen-year-olds are impressionable."

Katie had thought a lot about the impression Mark had made on her the day of the storm. She came out from behind the counter and approached him. "I never said 'thank you' for saving us all from what could have been serious harm. Please, don't make this any harder for me than it already is. I don't show my feelings easily, but I promised myself I would properly show my gratitude." Having said her piece, she walked up to Mark and wrapped her arms around him. She laid her head against his shoulder and gave him a hug. His brain went numb. She slowly backed away and turned to go.

Mark reached out and grabbed her arm. "That's not fair. You can't just walk up to a guy and grab him with no warning. He has to have time to think."

She smiled as he straightened up to his full height. "Please, thank me again."

Katie slid into his enveloping arms. Firmly embracing him, she laid her head on his shoulder once more. While he squeezed her tightly, she said, "Thank you, Mark."

Chapter Eleven

Mark stepped outside the school doors and breathed deeply. He inhaled the fresh, cooler air of this late September day and was happy to be free until Monday morning. It was going to be a glorious weekend.

The next morning, he took a walk with their two-year-old Angus bull, Nasty. The bull was anything but docile with every living thing on the farm, except Mark. The Lanes had raised the temperamental bull from a newborn calf. He was almost a pet to Mark, who would brush him, feed him, and clean out his pen.

Countless times, Mark had clipped a twenty-five-foot rope to the ring in Nasty's nose and then led him out to a pasture field like he was a pony. Only problem was, Nasty wasn't a pony. He weighed more than fourteen hundred pounds and was still growing. Harold had warned Mark to be careful with the bull and never take his eyes off him.

Mark knew well the story of a bull attack on Grandpap Lane in an open field. The bull knocked him down and trampled his legs while it drove its massive head into Pap's torso. Without quick action, Pap would have been killed. But Pap managed to get his fingers through the ring in the bull's nose. One powerful twist from his arm sent the bull to the ground on its side. His legs were injured, so he couldn't let go of the bull and run. He and the bull lay in the field for two hours before Harold found him. Pap recovered, but his legs were never the same.

Despite Pap's experience, Mark trusted Nasty. The bull had never given him any reason not to. Today, Mark took him across the road to the pasture field behind the machine sheds. He tied the end of the rope to a fence post so that Nasty could graze. That post held three rows of barbed wire. The top and bottom strands were dead, but the middle strand was electrified. As Mark turned to leave the field, Nasty's head caught him square in the sternum, driving him backwards against the fence wire. Pinning Mark with brute strength, Nasty's powerful neck muscles raised him off the ground, as if he were a rag doll.

The wind rushed out of Mark, and he felt the fence post snap as Nasty surged ahead. The barbs on the fence raked along and buried into his back, tearing the flesh. He reached for the nose ring but couldn't grasp it. The electricity from the fence flowed through him and into the bull. Mark was the conduit, and Nasty was the end of the line. Enhanced by the wet grass from the early morning dew, the electric jolt rattled the bull right down to his massive privates. He bellowed and jumped back, and Mark fell to the ground. The bull charged again as Mark gulped for air and struggled to get up. Nasty's huge head caught him on the side of his rib cage, but fate was on Mark's side. The blow knocked him out into the adjoining hay field. So close was his escape that the barbs on the bottom strand of wire tore the back of his shirt.

Mark was battered and cut, but he had escaped serious injury. As he heaved himself to his feet, blood ran down his back, soaking into his shirt, which stuck to him when he moved. He began to inhale, but stopped short as sharp pain overwhelmed his senses. Mark clutched his ribs on his right side and took slow, shallow breaths: better, but a long way from all right.

He was holding his rib cage and slowly making his way toward the house when Ann spotted him through the window in the kitchen door. She knew immediately that something was terribly wrong and began searching for her car keys. She had just located them, when Mark labored into the house.

"I think I need a trip to the hospital."

"Oh, Mark, not again. What happened this time?"

"Nasty attacked me."

"Who won that battle? Does Nasty look as bad as you?"

"Please, Mom, don't make me laugh. It hurts even when I smile. He caught my ribs, and my back is bleeding."

"Let's get your shirt off and have a look." She undid the buttons and carefully peeled off his blood-soaked shirt. She studied the cuts, rips, and puncture marks. "How did all this happen?"

"Barbed wire," he groaned.

"Lean on the counter, and let me clean this a little." Ann dampened a clean dish towel and mopped him up. "That's all I can do. Stay where you are, while I get clothes from your room for you to wear home from the hospital." She laid a towel over his back to absorb the blood while she was gone.

Before long Ann returned and helped him into a shirt then wrapped a towel around him for the drive to the hospital.

"What about Dad?" Mark asked on the way to Granville.

"I left him a note that he may be on his own for lunch… and to stay away from Nasty."

A few hours later on their way home from the hospital, Ann asked Mark if he would mind if she stopped at the bake shop for a loaf of bread and some pickled beets.

Mark gave her a weak smile. "Please don't be too long, I need to lie down. And I'm hungry. See if they have a blueberry pie."

Katie greeted Ann pleasantly when she entered the shop, "Hello, Mrs. Lane. What brings you here today?"

"Katie, you're almost eighteen, are you not?"

"Next March, I will be."

"Then, please call me Ann from now on… as one adult to another."

"All right, Ann," she said with a smile.

"Now what brings me here is a son, who I swear will be the death of me. Just a few hours ago, he came dragging himself into the house and almost gave me a heart attack!"

"What happened?" Katie asked, concern seeping into her voice.

"The bull attacked him. Mark's shirt was saturated with blood and ripped to pieces by the barbed wire fence. His rib cage was a big, red blob where the bull's head clobbered him. He's lucky to have escaped with his life."

"How is he now?" Katie asked with a quaver in her voice.

"The hospital gave him some powerful pain killers, so he's a little out of it. He's got two cracked ribs and a whole bunch of badly bruised ones. They had to stitch three places on his back where the barbed wire tore him up. He's all wrapped up like a mummy, and yet, he just now said he was hungry."

"Just now?"

"He's sitting out in the car. He's not able to come in himself. Do you have any pies? It's a special request, from *you-know-who*."

"I only have a small apple pie left," Katie said apologetically.

"It will have to do. Why don't you make him a blueberry crumb pie for Tuesday? That always makes him feel good. He says your blueberry pie is even better than mine. I just kidded him the other day by saying, 'I've been replaced by Katie Byler.'"

Katie looked down and smiled inwardly while Ann continued. "The doctor warned us about Mark's cracked ribs. If he exerts himself too much in the next few weeks before they have a chance to heal properly, a rib could break completely and puncture his lung."

"What would happen then?"

"If it wasn't a short trip to the hospital, he'd most likely bleed to death. The doctor was quite stern about what Mark shouldn't do. But you know Mark," Ann said with a sigh. "I will say that this has slowed him up for the time being. Why don't you go out and say hello, and tell him you'll make his favorite pie on Tuesday."

Katie's head spun as she approached the car. Mark looked drained and his eyes were closed. So strong and yet so vulnerable, she thought. She reached through the open window and touched his forehead with the back of her hand.

"Mom?" escaped his lips, and he opened his eyes.

Katie smiled sympathetically. He blinked a couple times, and she could tell his brain was in a fog.

"Hi," he said with effort.

"Your mom told me all about your mishap. You were fortunate that God was looking out for you."

"I guess He was. Good thing, too."

"You shouldn't worry me so, Mark. I was saddened to hear what you endured. I hope you sleep well tonight. Will you and Ann need to talk this out?"

"Ann?" he said lifting an eyebrow.

Katie smiled. "We can talk about it another time, when you feel better."

"Okay. Yes, I suppose, Mom and I will talk it out."

"I'd like to hear about it, too. Take care of yourself and get better. Ann told me about the ribs."

"This is probably a rib that God took from Adam to make Eve."

"What do you mean, Mark? You're not making any sense."

"It's defective."

A tightlipped Katie straightened up. "You are going to be just fine. And you are so exasperating!" She walked toward the bake shop but wheeled around and came back to the car.

"Back again?" he asked. "Are you a glutton for punishment?"

"I know you didn't say that to hurt me, because you promised you would never do that again."

"And I meant every word of it... Katie?"

"Yes, Mark?"

"You're so *damn* good-looking when you're angry."

She turned away, but not quick enough. He clamped his jaw so tight he couldn't even smile and held his ribs. He had clearly seen the amusement in her eyes.

Mark had a couple rough days but was feeling somewhat better by Monday. In the mid-afternoon he suddenly felt a whole lot better. "Mark," his mom called. "You have a visitor. Can I send her in?"

"Depends on who it is," Mark called back from the couch in Grandad's room.

"Just go on in there, Katie," he heard his mom say.

Katie peeked around the door jamb. "You must be feeling better," she said with a smile.

Mark smiled back and asked her to pull up a chair.

"How *are* you feeling?" Katie asked as she sat down.

"Another couple of days, and I might return to school. I'm getting behind. In fact, Peggy is bringing my books and assignments home today."

"She is a good sister, Peggy is."

"Yes, she is, most of the time. It's her and me against the rest of the world."

"Really?"

"Nah, I've got my mother on my side, too."

"You mean, Ann?"

"Yeah, what about that? Spill the beans. Clear the air."

"Spilling the beans would be better than eating them for keeping the air clear," Katie said with a twinkle in her eyes.

Mark began to laugh but grimaced in pain. He held his side and looked at Katie in amazement. "Oh, Katie! You made a joke. And a good one at that! I'm so proud of you."

Katie said nothing, but her eyes were doing the talking. "Your mom asked me to call her, Ann. That's all."

There was a lull in the conversation, then Katie said, "You used a bad word to me the other day."

"Yeah, and you enjoyed it. I saw you try to hold back your smile."

"Maybe, but it is ungodly to swear."

"Hey, I'm not perfect. Sometimes my spontaneity gets the better of me. I made my statement in the spirit of honesty."

"It is true that I was amused by it. It was the way you said it and the look on your face, combined with the complimentary statement. I asked God for forgiveness."

"Did you ask him to forgive me?"

"I did, but why is that important to you?"

"Because it means you care about me."

"I do care about you," Katie assured him. "We are friends."

"About that," Mark said. "If we're going to be friends, I want to make a pact that we will be completely open and honest with each other to minimize misunderstandings and heighten trust, thereby giving the friendship a chance to flourish."

An amused smile played across her lips. "So…" she began slowly, "you want us to be truthful because it will make us better friends?"

He tried not to stare at her, but that was hard. "Isn't that what I said?"

Katie smiled and gazed at the picture above the couch. "Not exactly," she replied.

Now Mark *was* staring at her, and he was in no hurry to have their verbal jousting end. He wished he could chase her around the room.

A slow blush crept into her cheeks and she closed her eyes.

"Did your dad ever turn you over his knee when you were young?" Mark asked.

Katie opened her eyes, and her look of amusement changed to one of mock indignation. "I was a *good* girl. Such actions were unnecessary."

"I'm sure you were, but did he ever turn you over his knee now that you're older?"

"No, because I'm still good."

"Some of the time," Mark added with a smile while he relished the looks she gave him. God knew, he wanted to touch her. His hand trembled just from the thought of it. "What do you think of my request?"

"It sounds reasonable to me, and I am willing to accept it."

"Can we shake on it then?" Mark asked, holding out his hand.

Katie offered hers in return and he took full advantage. He surrounded it with both of his and pressed gently as her warmth reached all the way to his heart. As comforting as gentle rain, he thought. Those hazel-blue eyes seemed to look into his very soul, and she didn't blush. *Surely that was a good sign.* "Total honesty," Mark said, as emotions flowed like a lazy river. "This is a good foundation for us to build on." He gently rubbed the back of her hand.

Katie was the first to break away. "Tell me about the bull."

"He's big—over fourteen hundred pounds, black as midnight, has four legs..."

She pinched him on the arm, and Mark yelped.

"Serves you right," Katie said.

"Okay, okay." Mark recounted the event from start to finish while she listened attentively.

"I am thankful you didn't get hurt worse, because friends care about each other. And as a friend, I have brought you a gift today." She held out a thin box with a single ribbon wrapped around it. Mark slid the ribbon off and lifted the lid. Inside were three white handkerchiefs. As he unfolded one, he noticed 'MBL' embroidered on one corner.

"These are very nice." Mark reached out and squeezed Katie's knee. "Where did you come up with the idea to use the blue for the embroidery?"

"I think it's a good match," she said.

"I agree. I'll look really cool blowing my nose beside my car." They both chuckled. "But seriously, what's the occasion?"

"I wanted to give you something in return for the three beautiful drawings that hang on my wall and for the very funny poem you wrote. I was making these for you when the storm hit the meadow, even though it would not be proper for me to give you a gift."

"So you recommended to your mother that your family should thank me for letting you stay in my bankhouse," Mark finished.

"Basically, that's it."

"Thank you, Katie. I'll put them to good use and I will always think of the Bylers when I use one." She smiled bashfully. "Did you bring me anything else today, or do I have to wait until tomorrow?"

"I think you already know the answer to that."

"How can you be so sure?"

"Because I know what the B stands for in your middle name," Katie said. Mark simply raised his eyebrows. "Bloodhound," she stated.

"Symbolically, you're correct, but actually it stands for Brandon. Thank you for coming today. I could play my guitar and sing a song before you go."

"Your mother cannot know I allowed you to sing to me—another time, perhaps." She laid her hand on his shoulder before she left and said, "Oh, and try to behave yourself... for your *mother's* sake."

Mark chuckled as Katie stepped out into the mudroom.

She realized they'd formed a friendship. There was a connection between them that couldn't be denied. She could feel it, and she wondered if Mark's feelings mirrored her own.

Chapter Twelve

A week and a half later on Saturday afternoon, Mark pounded on the Bylers' door. Mary and Katie hurried to see who it was.

"Is Mr. Byler or Jacob home?" Mark asked when the door flew open.

"No, they're gone on a carpentry job. What is it?" Mary asked.

"I have a young cow trying to calve on the lower farm. Dad's off to an auction two counties away, and Mom and the girls went shopping. This calf will have to be pulled out. I called the vet, but Doc Gruber's wife said he left on an emergency call and isn't expected back anytime soon. The cow has been in labor for hours, but only the calf's nose is visible, and it's turned blue. The calf may be dead already, for all I know, and I could even lose the cow. This is an extremely valuable cow and calf. I need help to pull the calf out."

Katie stepped forward. "Your mother told me the doctor gave you strict orders not to engage in any strenuous activity, or it might be you that needs burying."

"True, but the hole would be a lot smaller," he quipped.

"Hmph!" Katie reached for her cape. "You stay here, Mama. I'll go help Mark deliver that calf and make sure we don't have three corpses."

"Her name is Molly," Mark said in a calm voice as they entered the stall. "Dad bought her when she was just a young calf, and this is her first try at motherhood."

Molly was lying on her side, and she looked worn out when she raised her head to eye Katie suspiciously. He gently stroked her neck and spoke in a soothing voice. "This is Katie, and she has come to help you." Mark motioned toward Molly's shoulder with his head, and Katie knelt down and caressed the young cow.

Gliding her hand across Molly's neck, Katie assured her, "We'll make it all better."

Mark felt around the calf's protruding nose as far as his fingers could reach, but his hands were too big to explore much further. "I'm going to need the assistance of your smaller hands, Katie. Slide your hand into the cow under the calf's nose. You should be able to feel the two hooves."

She looked at him doubtfully. "I thought I was only going to help pull it out."

"It's okay. I'm right here to guide you. You'll simply do what I'm telling you." Mark squeezed her arm in encouragement.

"Have you done this before?" Katie asked, her voice dripping trepidation.

"Yes. You need to roll your sleeves up as far as possible."

"Now work your hand slowly into the cow," Mark instructed.

"I think I feel a hoof!" she exclaimed.

"Great! Now find the other one. The two hooves come out before the head. We may need to push the calf back in some to get the feet coming first."

Her brows furrowed as she maneuvered her hand inside the cow. "I can't feel another one. Wait... I think it's a leg. No, it's more like a knee."

"Damn... sorry Katie."

She waved it off. "What do I have to do?"

"The second leg is turned under. That's why she can't calve. We have to push the calf back inside far enough for you to bring the hoof forward."

"How far in will the calf need to go?"

"A ways. Put one hand on each side of the head, and push with all your strength."

"It won't budge!" she cried.

"Lock your arms. I'll push on your back and shoulders to add my weight to the task."

"Be careful, Mark, your ribs," she warned.

"I'm going to have to get up close and personal with you. Are you all right with that?"

"Do what you must. Let's save this calf."

Kneeling together on the straw behind Molly, they were able to get the calf to move. Mark could see Molly relax. "We need to push more, now!" The nose and Katie's forearms disappeared as the calf slid back into the mother. "You'll need to turn the leg with one hand. Find the knee and follow down the leg to the hoof."

"I feel it!" Katie said.

"Good, now wrap your fingers around the leg just above the hoof. Pull toward you and push up on the knee."

"It's hard. I don't think I have the strength. I need more room."

"Okay, then we have to push the calf further. Put your palm on the calf's nose, lock your arm, and push in. I'm going to help you." Together, they felt the calf move.

"I can no longer reach the hoof," she cried in anguish. She tried again even as Mark instructed her to remove her arm. "It's too far."

"Move away!" Mark barked. "I have to do this."

"No!" she said, gritting her teeth and driving her arm deeper, barely reaching the hoof. "I've got it!"

"Pull!" Mark urged. "Pull with all your might!"

Molly began to stir, and Mark knew a contraction was coming. Katie pulled with all she had and felt the hoof slide forward as Molly's muscles clamped down to expel the calf.

"The hoof is now forward," Katie said excitedly.

Mark patted her shoulder. "Thank God!" He rubbed her back appreciatively.

Katie added, "Both hooves are coming!"

Her arm was trapped inside the birth canal as the contraction intensified. Mark's hands were still on Katie's shoulders to steady her, and he squeezed them firmly in encouragement.

"When the next contraction begins, slide your hand out, and try to pull the hooves with it."

Katie could feel their position. "They are both coming now, and the nose is right behind."

Mark turned his attention to Molly. "Come on, girl, push."

Soon the hooves appeared, followed by the blue nose. However, try as she might, Molly could not expel the calf. Mark quickly looped baler twine around each leg above the hoof. He handed one twine to Katie. "Next time she pushes, we pull. The head is the hardest to come out. Once that's out, the rest is easy."

"What's this 'we' stuff? Give me both of those twines. You can wrap your arms around my waist and lend me your weight, if you must."

"Your hands can't take the pull on the thin twine of both our weights." Mark disappeared and soon returned with a short, round bar. He slid it through the end loops of both twines and handed it to Katie.

Molly's next push was unsuccessful, but Mark wasn't complaining. He had his arms tightly wrapped around Katie, and the two were one as they leaned back while she pulled.

"I think it will come the next time," Katie said, as they relaxed. A moment later they could see Molly begin to strain. "Hold me tight, Mark, it's coming again. Lean back as much as you can." With Katie's strength and the weight of the two together, the head slipped free. After another contraction for the shoulders, the rest of the calf easily followed, and the newborn slid out onto the straw.

"Now we get to see if it was all for nothing," Mark said. As the calf lay motionless, he handed Katie an old towel. "Clean yourself with this," he told her, then turned his attention to the calf.

Molly raised her head and tried to get up, but could not. She looked longingly at her motionless calf then dropped her head onto the straw. Mark picked up a couple stubbles of straw and cleaned the mucus out of the calf's nostrils. He leaned down and blew air into its nose. The calf's eyes popped open, and it raised then shook its head. Mark eased back onto the straw. He felt the pain in his midsection the adrenalin had previously covered. "You did it," he said to Katie, studying her as she stood before him.

"We did it," she corrected him. "You're a good instructor, but how did you know what to do?"

"Dad and I had a similar situation once, although that calf wasn't so lucky. Use the towel to dry her off. I'll see if I can help Molly get to her feet."

While Katie gently toweled the newborn, she asked, "How do you know it's a 'her'? You didn't check."

"It's just a figure of speech. I don't know yet. I'm afraid to look."

"Why is that?"

"Because whether it's a 'her' or a 'him' may greatly affect the welfare of Lane Farms. A couple years ago, Dad drove all the way to Oklahoma and brought Molly home when she was only a few months old. She comes from a great line of Angus cattle known for quality meat. Dad paid a lofty sum of money to have her artificially inseminated to a deceased Angus bull from the Midwest. He was huge and known for producing large offspring. This calf represents an opportunity to combine the best traits of both lines. If this is a bull, he could start a whole new line that would improve beef production throughout our nation."

"What does this mean to Lane Farms?"

"We raise beef to go to market. The profit margin is not as good as it should be. Dad believes if we would move toward raising breeder stock, we would do better financially."

"What is breeder stock?"

"Molly is breeder stock. She's not here to be put on our table."

He raised an eyebrow. "Does this really interest you?"

"I am a farmer's daughter. I am always glad to become more knowledgeable about such matters. I do have a question, though. What is artificial insemination?"

Mark looked at her, not sure what he should say next. "You can't tell anyone we were discussing this, okay?"

"Okay, not a word."

"Instead of impregnating a cow with a live bull, the bull lives at a special farm where they collect his semen, or sperm. They freeze it then bring it to your farm. After warming it up, they inject it into the cow's cervix, and she gets pregnant."

Katie nodded in understanding. "If this calf is a bull, will he go to live at that special farm?"

"If he proves to be the quality sire Dad believes he will be, the answer is yes, and we would make a lot of money."

"I see. Are you going to look, or should I?"

"Let's name it first. What do you think we should call it?"

"Midnight," Katie answered. "It's dark as midnight on a new moon night."

"Then, Midnight it is. I'll see that it's part of the registered name." He nudged Molly, and she struggled to her feet.

Meanwhile, Katie could wait no longer. "It's a boy!" she exclaimed.

"Yes! My dad will be so pleased. I can't wait to tell him. Help Midnight to his feet. Now that you've dried him off, the poor guy will be confused about which one of you is his mother."

Molly quickly brushed past them and began to finish the job of cleaning Midnight. She prodded the newborn with her nose, and he wobbled to a standing position. They left the mother and calf alone to bond.

Outside the stall, Mark dropped onto a bale of straw. "Let me rest. You did all the work, but that took a lot out of me."

"Is there anything I can do to help you?" she asked.

Mark patted the straw bale beside him. "Sit here with me. I just need to let the pain subside. I can't thank you enough for what you've done. Tell me how you feel." He looked into her eyes and in spite of his pain, a smile lurked in his gaze.

Katie's mind raced as she wondered what he meant. Did he know how he affected her? Could she be so bold when she wasn't even sure?

A squeeze on her arm brought her back to the moment. "I'm sorry," she said. "Did you ask me something?"

Mark's eyes exuded a tender intensity that was enough to take her breath away, and his mouth gave way to his teasingly boyish grin. "You were lost, but now you're found."

She banished her thoughts. "Are you teasing me, Mark?"

"Uh huh."

"Do you tease your sisters like this?"

"Of course! Why do you think God put them on earth?" Her jaw dropped and he laughed. "They don't call me *The Agitator* for nothing."

"What other names do they have for you?"

"Well, Instigator comes to mind, and Analyzer goes in the list somewhere."

"The list?"

"Sure. You didn't expect me to be one dimensional, did you? When I asked you, 'How do you feel?' I was referring to Midnight. You saved the life of a very precious calf. Wasn't it great?" Mark asked. "It was lost, and now, it's saved."

Katie broke into a big smile and her eyes sparkled even in the dim light of the barn. "It is a really good thing, no?"

Spontaneously, Mark threw his arms in the air as he shouted in celebration, "YAY!!!"

She saw the pain flash across his face, and he dropped his arms. He would have pitched forward onto the cement floor, if not for Katie's swift action. She reached out and pulled him to her. He sagged, lifeless, into her embrace. She scooted sideways to the end of the bale to allow his head to lie in her lap.

Katie was a willing participant as she sat on the bale, cradling his head. She admired the tan skin, so close she could reach down and kiss it. His skin was not like her own - with its fair complexion and freckles - but darker and a pleasing shade of tan. She studied his features as he lay there and resisted the urge to run her fingers through his light brown hair. The tousled waves were badly in need of a comb but complemented his boyishly handsome face.

Katie was content to let Mark rest while her arm held him firmly, and her lap was his pillow. She restrained her desire to bend down and kiss the top of his head. However, she touched her nose to his hair, and inhaled deeply, recording the aroma in her memory.

Finally, Katie ran her hands along Mark's arm to wake him. She squeezed his shoulder, and he stirred with a groan. He opened his eyes and looked up into her face. "I guess, I shouldn't have done that."

She said in a soothing tone, "You had me very worried. Are you going to be all right?"

Mark rotated onto his back and continued to use her lap for a pillow – if you have the advantage, use it. He studied her creased forehead, the sad eyes, and the drooping mouth. He wanted to cup her face with his hands then bring those delicious lips slowly and gently down to his. He wanted to tell her, but he was afraid – afraid that she might laugh at him for carrying "total honesty" a bit too far.

But Katie was waiting patiently. She didn't seem to mind that his head was resting comfortably on her person. And she was still looking at him with those beautiful eyes. "I think I just need to lie here for a few more hours."

She was fighting back a smile when Mark said, "Your lap makes a great pillow, by the way. Being the recipient of amazingly good fortune, I hate to ask, but why am I lying on it?"

Now her eyes were smiling. "You passed out, and I had to choose between catching you or letting you fall on the floor."

"Was it a hard decision?"

"You didn't give me much time to ponder," she said with a light voice.

"I appreciate your *instincts* then. If you'll help me up, I'll just sit here for a bit. I'm glad I have my car to get me home. Speaking of home, I need to take you home. Your mother will be worried."

"Yes, I should get back."

"Let me check on the calf, before we go." When he looked into the stall, mother and son seemed fine, and the calf was nursing. He asked Katie to throw in a couple slices of hay and dump a tin can of grain into the feed bucket. Molly's water tub was low, so Katie used the nearby hose to fill it.

Mark was leaning on the gate looking into the pen when Katie came and stood beside him. "What are you thinking?" she asked.

"I'm thinking about what those two have been through. Yet for them, all is forgotten. It is only people who seem to dwell on things. We would be better off if we could be more like Molly and Midnight." They stood side by side, watching the scene before them, contented to be in the moment.

Mark stole a sideways glance at Katie. He hated to, but he broke the silence. "You look satisfied." When she turned to him, he added, "You've done well today."

As they walked from the barn into the October sunlight, Mark took Katie's arm and guided her toward the old milk house left from the days when this was a dairy farm. "Let's get you cleaned up before I take you home."

She didn't resist the pressure on her arm, though she couldn't ignore the feelings it aroused in her. "I'm fine," she insisted.

"I've got hot water, soap, and clean towels. Roll up your sleeves, and we'll get the dried slime off your arms."

"I can do it," Katie said fidgeting.

"I know you can, but I want to do this for you." She sheepishly relented. "First, let's get that crusty spot off your cheek." He pressed a wet rag to the spot and then gently wiped it away.

"Now your arms," his voice guided her. She lifted an arm – fit and toned with a light dusting of freckles. He caressed it with the soapy rag. Her skin was soft and beautiful.

While Mark rinsed the soap off, Katie implored, "Please don't tell anyone how we pulled Midnight out of Molly. My parents would not approve. They would say it was not proper."

"But it was necessary," Mark stressed.

Katie struggled to maintain her composure while he was so close, while his eyes were on her, while she was feeling things she had never felt before – things that beckoned her. "I know it was, but please... do this for me."

"Your honor is safe with me, Katie."

A shiver went through her, and goosebumps sprang to life all along her arm while light blond hairs stood in salute. She gave him a look that caused his heart to miss a beat... a combination of "I'm sorry," "this is so embarrassing," and "I just can't help myself." She quickly looked down.

Mark dried her arm slowly, gently massaging her sore muscles. He wanted to reach out and envelop her in his arms like he had that day in the bake shop, but he didn't have the courage and the moment passed.

When both arms were clean, Mark said, "My chariot awaits you. You'll ride home in the manner befitting the heroine that you are, the saver of bovine!"

Katie laughed. "Onward, my charioteer."

Mark pulled his car over in front of the bake shop.

Katie let herself out, gave Mark a smile, and said, "Thank you for a delightful time."

Chapter Thirteen

The bake shop was closed for the season, and fall harvest was in full swing. Mark had to come up with excuses to stop by the Bylers, such as wanting "super-fresh eggs" or the occasional smoked ham.

Each time he stopped, he never knew who would fill his order. Sometimes it was Mary, but if he was real lucky, it would be Katie.

Today was his lucky day. "Your dad stopped by the other day," she told him.

"Really? What did he want?"

"To let me know he gave me a high recommendation to Doc Gruber in case he ever needs an assistant."

"Well, if you were to work for Doc Gruber, he ought to pay you double."

Katie wrinkled her brow. "Why?"

"Because, he'd get to work with you and look at you all at the same time," he said with a grin.

"Flattery will get you nowhere, Mr. Lane."

"Oh, now it's 'Mr. Lane.' So tell me, what did my dad really want?"

She returned his grin. "He wanted to thank me for saving his prize calf. He also brought me a really nice flashlight and a bag full of batteries. He said a little birdie told him that I go for walks sometimes when I can't sleep." Katie eyed Mark suspiciously.

"Don't look at me. Who else have you told that story to?"

"That's just it. You're the only one who knows, except my parents. Now what do you have to say for yourself?"

"Tweet, tweet."

Katie chuckled and added, "Your dad couldn't stop telling me how grateful he was."

"Trust me, he was being sincere. My dad doesn't pass compliments around freely. But you are real close to walking on water in his eyes."

"Hush, Mark."

"Speaking of Dad, he looked at me skeptically when I told him that you pulled Midnight out of Molly all by yourself."

Katie recalled the closeness she and Mark had shared. Many times since that day, she had dwelled on the sensations of his arms around her, locked in a bear hug. She remembered the pressure of his body against hers. And his hands, those big hands that had gripped her shoulders and tenderly massaged her sore muscles. The same hands that had gently cleaned her arms and cheek. It was exciting, yet soothing. Katie simply laid her head on the pillow at night, and the memory came alive. Lying on her back, she imagined that the mattress was Mark. She only needed to overlap her arms below her breasts and exert pressure to vividly evoke the entire experience. She could even imagine that the pillow was Mark's head beside hers. When she drifted off to sleep in his arms, she always slept soundly.

"Hello, Katie? Anybody home?"

She shook her head. "Sorry, I was just thinking. How is Midnight?"

"Growing like a bad weed, and he has a lot of spirit. But that reminds me, Dad wondered if we could get a picture of you to hang in his pen."

"You know that's not allowed. But why would he want it?"

"To make Midnight feel better when he misses his other mama."

Katie smiled, and Mark couldn't take his eyes from her. "Dad asked me who named him Midnight. I thought about telling him that I had, but fessed up. I wasn't sure how he'd take the news that our future prize bull was named by a girl."

"What did he say?"

"Well, he thought for a moment then a smile crossed his face. He said, 'That's very symbolic because Midnight is going to grow up to be a real ladies' man, so it's only fittin' that he be named by one.'" Katie blushed as the meaning of his statement sunk in.

As he walked toward his car, Mark fought off the desire to go back inside and tell her how he felt. Tell her she drove him absolutely nuts. Tell her she was never far from his thoughts. Tell her he lay awake at night wishing she was his.

Katie came out of the springhouse and Mark gave her a wave that she returned as he got into his car.

On a windy and rainy Thursday afternoon in November, Mark was driving on Morefield Road heading home from school when he saw a lone figure walking up ahead. As he approached, he could tell it was an Amish woman briskly walking with her head down, trying to shield herself from the wind and cold rain. Soon, Mark recognized that it was Katie. He slowed, beeped the horn, and stopped beside her. He reached across the front seat, threw the door open, and yelled, "Get in, Katie."

She replied, "I'll get your seat wet."

"I don't care about my seat." He reached for the knobs on the dashboard and turned the heater on high.

She got into the car and closed the door. "I'm sorry, Mark. I didn't know it was going to rain, or I would have taken the buggy."

"I'm glad I came along when I did. You need to get home and dried out before you get sick. This is not the time of year to come down with something."

Katie pursed her lips. "So tell me, what is the correct time of year to come down with something?"

Mark flashed her a grin. "If I didn't know better, I'd say I've been given a dose of my own medicine."

"I believe you have," she said matter-of-factly.

"What were you doing at Deborah's?"

"I didn't say I was at Deborah's."

"Do I look stupid?"

"Do you really want me to answer that?" she replied tersely.

"We're in a lovely mood today, aren't we?"

"I'm sorry, Mark. The cold and the rain really set me off. Deborah invited me to visit so she could show me the present that Chris bought her."

"Who's Chris?"

"Her betrothed. They got engaged last week."

Mark was quiet for a moment. "When will they marry?"

"Chris wants to wait till next October so he can save up more money. Deborah would marry him next week if he wanted to."

"Why do you say that?"

"Because she's always been boy crazy. She's more in love with the idea of being married than who she's marrying."

"What's wrong with Chris?"

"Nothing, really. She's just not madly in love with him."

"Interesting. Would you marry someone you weren't madly in love with?"

"I don't know about the *'madly'* part, but I'd certainly have to be in love with him."

"Do boys interest you?" Mark asked.

Katie's steady look gave nothing away. "One friend to another, boys haven't interested me in the past. As the oldest of six, I haven't had much time to think about boys."

She had avoided his question concerning the present. Did that mean she was interested now? Mark believed he had pushed the issue as far as he dared.

When they pulled up in front of the bake shop, Katie started to get out. Mark reached out and touched her arm, "Wait," he said. She looked over at him, and waited.

Mark fought off a case of the nerves. "I really like the color of your hair. Each time I see you, it reminds me of the harvest moon… bright and beautiful in the October sky. Your hair is beautiful. In fact, all of you is beautiful."

Katie was drawn to his simple, honest sincerity. "Thank you for the ride, and thank you for the kind words."

"I didn't mean to make you feel uncomfortable," he replied softly. "Now that I've come to know the real you, the *last* thing I would want to do is make you feel uncomfortable. Please don't be mad at me."

"I must go inside," she said. Exiting the car, Katie turned back quickly, smiling openly. "I'm not mad."

She sensed Mark watching her walk to the house and tingled all over as she repeated his words. She no longer questioned whether he liked her.

That night in the privacy of her room, Katie, too, thought about what had transpired over the last several months. It was so easy and natural to picture him there with her… and holding her.

"Why does he have to be English? Are you testing me, Father? Do you want me to love Mark Lane? Give me a sign."

The sun was out on Saturday when Mark stopped by for eggs. Katie came to open the door but before he could say anything to her, she fled to her bedroom at the back of the first floor.

As Mary came from the kitchen, Mark heard Katie coughing. She had not looked good. She was unusually pale with dark circles under her eyes, her hand had been pressed against her chest, and he could tell she was not breathing properly. Then he remembered the rain. "What's wrong with Katie?" he asked.

"She's come down with the flu, I'm afraid," Mary replied. "She was up most of the night coughing. She's having a hard time breathing."

"Is she running a fever?"

"She's hot to the touch. Hopefully, she'll be better in a couple of days. I'll get those eggs for you."

As they were leaving the springhouse, Mark asked, "Is she coughing up any phlegm?"

"She does have some."

"Katie probably has an infection in her lungs," he said. "If she doesn't get better real soon, will you take her to the doctor?"

"Our doctor retired last year, and we haven't needed another one yet."

"You used Dr. Bailey, too? So did we. Mom searched for a new one and found a young lady doctor who had just started a family practice in town. Her name is Dr. Janice Ford. She took the stitches out of my back, and she's really nice. If you decide to see her, any one of us who drive will be happy to take you."

"That's very kind of you, but we wouldn't want to put you out."

"It's not a bother," he assured her. "If Katie needs to make the trip, it would be better if she did it in a warm car. Tomorrow evening I have to go to the lower farm to feed the cattle. I can stop on the way home to see if she needs a doctor. Hopefully, she'll be improving by then."

"God willing," Mary nodded.

Mark drove home and called Dr. Ford's office. A pleasant female voice answered.

"Hello Dr. Ford, this is Mark Lane, Harold and Ann Lane's son."

"Yes, I remember you, Mark. How is your back healing?"

"Just fine. I have a question." He described Katie's condition. "Do you think she should see you?"

"I can't be sure from what you've described on the phone, but my first-time office visit is only five dollars. I'm trying to build up my practice, and this enticement seems to be helping. If she doesn't improve by Monday, why don't you bring her in? It's always better to be safe than sorry."

"God willing," Mark said. "Thank you, Dr. Ford."

Ann came out of the kitchen as he was hanging up the phone. "I couldn't help overhearing that conversation. Is Katie going to be okay?"

"Maybe as okay as your father, for all I know," he said sharply. He saw the sadness in his mother's eyes and went to her. "I'm sorry, Mom." He gave her a hug.

Ann gladly accepted the embrace. "You are forgiven, now tell me about Katie."

"She's got the same symptoms as Grandpa Samuel, and she looks terrible. I told Mrs. Byler I'd stop in tomorrow evening to see if she might need a doctor. I said I'd be passing by after feeding the cattle at the lower farm."

"You don't feed the cattle in the evening."

"I know that, and you know that, but please don't ever tell Mrs. Byler."

"Be careful, Mark. You don't want to stick your nose in where it doesn't belong."

"If Katie is seriously sick, shouldn't she see Dr. Ford?"

"I think so. However, it's the Bylers' responsibility to decide that."

"I hear you, Mom, but sometimes people don't make the right choice. We know Grandpa didn't."

"Katie is a minor, therefore, her parents decide for her."

"For three more months, she's a minor. I guess, as long as she gets pneumonia after her next birthday, she can decide for herself."

"Don't you think you're being a little melodramatic?"

"Maybe, but you didn't see her. *I did.* I know she has parents who love her, but not even your dad knew to get to the doctor. I'm concerned. I told you, I gave her a ride two days ago. She was soaking wet from walking in the freezing rain."

Ann paused to consider what Mark had said. "All right. Stop by tomorrow evening, and let me know how she is. I can always run her into town on Monday morning."

"Thanks Mom," he said as he kissed her cheek. What Ann didn't hear Mark say as he ascended the stairs to his room was, "Big deal, your dad was dead on Monday morning."

The following evening, as promised, Mark knocked on the Byler door. Sarah answered. As Mark stepped into the dimly lit room, Mary came through the doorway that led to Katie's bedroom. He could see the creases on her forehead, and he knew them well. Katie had those same creases whenever she was anxious or worried.

"Hello, Mrs. Byler. I was on my way home. How is Katie doing?"

"About the same, I'm afraid. She didn't go to church today, and when we got home, she seemed delirious in her sleep. She kept mumbling something about a rope and saying over and over, 'Hold me, hold me. Make it better.' I've been cooling her down with damp cloths, but her fever flares up again. It'll be a long night, I'm afraid. If only I could get her to eat something."

"How long has it been since she ate?"

"She's only had a small bowl of chicken broth since yesterday morning."

"I explained to my mother that Katie wasn't doing well. Mom is very concerned and she asked me to report back to her. She's offered to run you and Katie in to see Dr. Ford first thing in the morning. Do you think that would be okay?"

"If Katie worsens during the night, she will need to go."

Mark did not panic easily. He didn't panic in the storm at the bankhouse. He didn't panic when Katie was fainting and the spiders were scattering. And he didn't panic when Nasty was trying to end his existence. As Mark left the Byler household and drove home, he was teetering on the edge of panic. Katie was in danger, and there was nothing he could do.

"How is she?" Ann asked as he came through the door.

"Delirious and running a high fever. She hasn't eaten since Saturday morning. I could hear her coughing in her room." With a wild look in his eyes, he paced around the house shaking and shuddering like a machine about to explode. "I'm going to go crazy, Mother. Where does Dr. Ford live?"

"She and her husband have a house in town, but what does it matter?"

"It matters to me." He grabbed the phone book and thumbed to the 'F's.' "What's his first name?"

"Martin, I think."

Mark was shaking so bad that he couldn't read the print. He slammed the phone book on the dining room table and pressed his index finger into the pages to steady it. "They live on Cliff Street, number 105. It's only 6:00 pm, Mom. Dr. Ford's office hours don't start for sixteen more hours."

"Calm down, Mark. What do you propose that we do? Drag Dr. Ford out to the Bylers' house without their permission?"

"If we don't, Katie is going to be dead by morning."

"You don't know that."

"I do know that, and I'm telling you I have a bad feeling about this. I would do more for a cow than what's being done for Katie right now. What would you rather I do, Mother? Go to the Bylers', kidnap Katie, and take her to the emergency room? She's underage, and I might go to jail, but I swear I'll do it."

Mark paced some more. He stopped in front of Ann, his eyes wide and pleaded, "Come with me to Dr. Ford's house and ask her to follow us to the Bylers'. Once we're there and a doctor is standing on their front porch, what are they going to do... turn her away? All I want is to make sure Katie doesn't have pneumonia. If I'm wrong, I promise not to bother the Bylers

114

ever again. You can blame it all on me, and I won't set foot on their property for as long as I live."

"What if Dr. Ford isn't home? I really think it might be better if we wait till tomorrow morning."

Mark flinched and backed away. "No!" he yelled. "I love you, Mother, but you are putting more importance on your friendship with Mary Byler than you are placing on the life of her daughter." He snatched up his car keys. "I will be waiting in my car. Five minutes is all... just a reminder: your dad was dead by Monday morning."

Mark started the car and waited. He could not stop the tears that ran from his eyes. When the five minutes were up, he put the car in reverse. The passenger door opened and his mother slid onto the seat beside him.

"Do I need to drive?" she asked.

"No, I can manage it."

"Let's go then. Time's a'wastin."

Dr. Ford answered the door herself. "Hi, Ann! What brings you out on this cold, dark night?"

"May we step in to explain? You know my son, Mark."

"Yes, of course, come in. We just spoke on the phone yesterday morning. How is the Amish girl?"

Mark spoke up. "Worse than yesterday morning. She's not eating. She's coughing and struggling to breathe, spitting up infection, running a high fever, and is delirious."

"When was the last time you saw her?" she asked earnestly.

"Yesterday morning, but I spoke with her mother not an hour ago."

The doctor studied him for a moment. "I usually don't do house calls."

"If it's the money Dr. Ford, I'll pay you one hundred dollars whether the Bylers let you in their house or not. You won't make the trip for nothing."

"You feel that strongly about this?"

"I know when a cow is sick. I don't see how people are that much different. I know Katie Byler. I fear for her, and I'll pay you two hundred dollars."

"Keep your money," Dr. Ford said. "I'll get my bag."

115

Chapter Fourteen

Mark stayed in the car while Ann led Dr. Ford to the front door. Moses answered. They talked briefly then went inside. Mark's heart pounded as the seconds ticked by. How long had they been in there? It seemed like forever. Finally, the door flew open. Dr. Ford came first, followed by Ann. Moses emerged carrying a large bundle wrapped in a quilt. Mark's heart leapt into his throat. It had to be Katie.

He started the car, sprang out, and opened his passenger-side door. When Dr. Ford reached him, she said, "We've got a very sick girl here. Follow me to the Granville Memorial emergency room. Ann will ride with me. Help Mr. Byler slide Katie into your back seat and lay her down. I'll grab a pillow from my car for under her head."

They slid Katie into the car and took off.

Katie opened her eyes to strange surroundings. How odd… Mark was sleeping in a chair in the corner of her room. He had a pillow under his head and a blanket draped over him. She studied the hanging bottle and plastic hose beside her bed and followed it down to her arm.

She continued to look around her room. So, this is what it was like to be in a hospital. But how did she get there, and why was Mark there?

Bits and pieces came back to her, though some parts were missing. She wasn't sure what was real and what had been a dream. She recalled the kind lady who had taken care of her. She would have to thank her, if she ever saw her again. It was strange that Mark was here.

As Katie studied him, she remembered calling out his name, over and over. When the kind lady had come to her side, Katie told her, "Mark! I need him to stay." She remembered that the woman squeezed her hand and said, "Okay, Katie. I'll let him stay."

She hoped to remember the rest later, and if not, she would get Mark to fill her in. She wasn't even certain what day it was. She could tell it was still dark outside because only the light from a street lamp filtered through the curtains on the window.

She sat up and did a physical check of herself. Her feet and lower legs were bare. She wore a loose gown, but cold air chilled her back. Katie felt behind her and realized she wasn't fastened. In fact she was almost naked. She felt up to her hair. And where was her cap? She followed the long braid with her hand and brought it around in front of her. Mark had seen her like this. What else had he seen? She lay back and pulled the covers tightly around her.

"You're not going to get modest on me now, are you Katie darlin?" Mark asked. He smiled from ear to ear. He obviously had been watching her. She wasn't sure for how long. "Long enough," Mark said.

Katie's mouth fell open, and her eyes grew large.

"I know what you're thinking," he replied. "On the night you got deathly sick, I went a little crazy. I didn't know it at the time, but you were calling out to me. You were speaking to my spirit, my subconscious, or whatever you want to call it. I'd heard about such things, but didn't believe in them."

Katie motioned for him to come closer. When Mark was standing by her bed, she reached out and touched him. "No, this is not a dream, Katie."

She instinctively held out her hand and their fingers entwined. "You have been with me the whole time," she said.

"I have. You wanted me to stay."

"Tell me more about going crazy."

"You should have my mom tell you. She probably remembers it better than I do. It was the night we brought you to the hospital. I was flipping out at my house."

"Flipping out?"

"Yeah, acting goofy. Saying and doing things I wouldn't normally do. You were doing it to me."

"Doing what?"

"You were crying out: reaching across space mentally. You somehow knew that I could save you."

"And did you?"

"Not really. I was only the messenger. It was God and Dr. Ford who saved you."

"The nice lady with dark hair?" Katie asked.

"That would be her. You worked through me to reach her."

Katie nodded. "What day is this?"

"Wednesday, and your mother will be in at the same time as every day."

"I didn't ask."

"But you were thinking it. She comes about lunchtime. My mom brings her."

"Stop it, Mark."

"Geez, you've been awake fifteen minutes, and you're already bossing me."

"Am I allowed to boss you?"

"In a good way, only."

Katie squeezed his hand again while gazing up at him. "Sit beside me on my bed," she commanded with a steady look. "Now that you are close, tell me what we've done for the past three days." The room suddenly seemed to get a lot warmer.

Mark's eyes shone with an intensity that Katie had never seen before. "We held on to each other's hands and fought the enemy that was trying to destroy you."

"Did you see this enemy?"

"I never did, but you could. One time you cried out, 'He's coming for me, Mark!' I supplied the power to let you win."

"You did this all by yourself?"

Mark shook his head. "I had help."

"Who helped you?"

"My guardian angel."

Katie had heard about the angels in the Bible and the roles they played, though she was uncertain about Mark having his own, personal angel. "Did you actually see her?"

"I did. Her aura was warm gold, and she looked like a person in a white robe. She was right here beside me, kneeling and praying."

"Did you see *my* guardian angel?"

119

"Perhaps only you can see her. Have you ever?"

"No. At least I don't think so. I'm not sure," she stammered.

"You'd probably know if you had. Or maybe, you're like me. I saw mine when I was young. She was kneeling and praying beside my bed. I had forgotten about her until she came to this very room."

"Did she stay the entire time?"

Mark's voice cracked with emotion. "She only came once, but it was when we needed her most. You had just cried out, and I knew the battle was about to be won or lost." He took a deep breath and pinched the bridge of his nose to hold back the tears.

Katie squeezed his hand again. "What did I say?" she asked softly.

Mark looked deep into her eyes. "You said, 'I need you, Mark, now more than ever.'"

Katie was caught up in his gaze, feeling the emotional power surging through her. "Is that when the angel came?"

"Yes. My strength was not enough. I felt her power, though."

"What was it like?"

"Power without measure… timeless – I could sense forever. And then a great peace filled our being."

"What happened then?"

"We slept. And while we slept, she left."

"Where did you sleep, Mark?"

"Here, beside you."

"Were we touching? I don't remember touching."

Mark gave her a crooked grin. "Only our hands. That's why you slid your hand into mine just now. Our hands are intimate. They belong together."

Katie looked at their hands, still connected. She shook her head and sighed. "It's so hard to believe. Such a story, I've never heard."

"Tell me about it," Mark agreed. "While you've been waging your battle, I've had a lot of time to think. Why the hands? Hands will hold on to one another. I believe that's what it's all about: two people being together. It's all about connecting, like receiving your mental thoughts when you cried out from your bedroom. Now you are awake, and the whole world will start impacting us again. The connection between us will diminish, maybe disconnect all together. Perhaps tomorrow neither of us will remember what happened here."

"What do we do now, Mark?"

"Stay connected and let hands touch. Never forget, you cried out to me and I heard you." Mark reached out and stroked Katie's golden locks. "Your hair, your beautiful hair. Why am I drawn to it?"

"You complimented it right before our battle began. You're not even supposed to see it… but stroke it again, please." She smiled and looked into his eyes.

"Do you mind that I see it?" He scarcely dared to breathe as he awaited the reply, but Katie put him off.

Her heart raced at his nearness as she raised an eyebrow. "I thought you could read my mind?"

Mark placed the back of his hand on his forehead and exclaimed, "Alas, my powers are diminishing already!" Katie laughed, and he pressed the point. "Seriously, promise me some day you will show me your hair in all its flowing glory."

She held out her other hand and said, "Let hands touch."

Mark held both her hands and did not remove his eyes from the face he thought was beautiful. The answer was written on that face, and with it came the first thrill of love.

He glanced at his watch, making a mental note of the time. He did the math and recorded it to memory – two years, six months, twenty-two days, fourteen hours and thirty minutes. That was how long he had waited. He had just wanted to see the emotions he always felt in his heart radiating from Katie's face.

He didn't know where to go from here. "This is just crazy," he said.

Katie smiled bashfully. "Maybe love likes crazy."

Chapter Fifteen

While Mark and Katie struggled to comprehend the entire event, their parents understood it even less. Both sets of parents concluded it had to be the work of God and simply beyond man's understanding.

Ann claimed that it was a spirit that had possessed Mark, and she questioned whether it was her son at all the night of his rampage. The Bylers believed it was God working through Mark who had saved their Katie.

Even though Mark and Katie feigned virtual ignorance, reality was quite another matter. The exploration had begun and hands would touch. Katie began a quest to see her guardian angel. If Mark could see his twice, she could surely come face to face with her own at least once.

Dr. Ford provided the medical diagnosis, double pneumonia and acute respiratory failure. She claimed that less than ten percent of Katie's lung capacity was still functioning when she first examined her. Dr. Ford also believed Katie should have been dead from organ failure.

On that first night, as Katie lay near death on the hospital gurney, Dr. Ford told Moses that Katie had called out for Mark to stay and frantically reached for his hand. The doctor said, "When their hands touched, she improved almost instantly. I can't argue that Mark is her lifeline. I have no medical grounds on which to base such a conclusion, but if holding his hand helps her live, I can't argue against it, and neither should you." Moses gave his consent for Mark to stay.

The two families kept most of this to themselves because no one outside of their immediate circle would have believed or understood it. Not even the other Lane and Byler children were told.

Katie's illness was a life-changing event for Dr. Ford. "Mark is quite a character, isn't he Ann?" the doctor asked on the way to the hospital.

"He can be a handful. But tonight, he knew something. Somehow, he knew that Katie needed him. He was acting crazy at home before we came to your house. It was as if someone or something had taken over him. I didn't think we should come for you, but Mark wouldn't hear of it. He was going to come alone, when at the last minute I accompanied him."

"I'm glad you did, Ann. I don't know if Mark could have convinced me by himself."

Dr. Ford questioned Mark as she worked on Katie. "Did you touch her during the ride to the hospital?"

"Yes, I did."

"When?"

"Soon after we left the Bylers' - when we almost hit the three deer."

Dr. Ford looked up. "What deer?"

"You braked hard for the first one, the little one. Your brake lights put me on alert. You barely missed it. The next two came between us: a doe, and then a buck. I had to brake for the last one, the big buck. He sailed over my hood. I was afraid Katie would slide off the seat onto the floor, so I reached back with my right hand to brace her. As I braked, she slid into my hand. She grabbed onto it and said, 'Don't let go, Mark.' I'm sure Mr. Byler heard it. We looked at each other for a split second..." Mark hesitated.

"Go on," Dr. Ford encouraged him.

"I drove the rest of the way to the hospital with Katie clutching my hand. She wouldn't let go."

"You have a three-speed, right? How did you drive?"

Mark shrugged. "I never shifted again."

Dr. Ford looked steadily at Mark. "Three stop signs and two red lights. It is true, I drifted through all of them, but at speeds way below your third gear. What did you do?"

"I prayed."

Dr. Ford was silent as she thought. "You know, Mark, I didn't think Katie would make it to the hospital. It was nothing short of a miracle. I honestly don't know what's going on, and I don't know why, but you must stay. Hold Katie's hand until she awakes, and give her your strength." Before Dr. Ford left to talk to Moses and Ann, she said to him, "I saw no deer. I never hit my brakes. You can confirm this with your mother."

Katie was awake early Wednesday morning, and she and Mark were holding hands when the nurse walked in. "Oh, my goodness!" she exclaimed. "They held hands when she slept, and now they are doing it when she's awake." The nurse walked over and felt Katie's forehead. "Welcome back to the land of the living, child. As for you, Mr. Lane, vacate this room. It's time for Katie's bath."

Mark grinned and headed for the chair. "I'll just sit here and cover my eyes."

"Not on my floor, you won't. I don't care how much Dr. Ford likes you." With that said, she ceremoniously ushered him out of the room. Mark heard Katie laughing, as the door was forcefully closed.

"Feel better?" Mark asked when he returned to Katie's room.

"Much, but I'm glad my nurse is older."

"Why is that?"

"Because I can pretend it's my mother washing me."

Mark looked down. "I guess it would be a little embarrassing. You look better."

"I wish I could wash my hair," she sighed.

"Dr. Ford comes in early every morning. You can ask her when you'll be allowed to take a shower. There's one in your bathroom."

"I've never taken a shower."

"Well..."

"But I don't need you to teach me how," she quickly added.

Mark smiled. "Who's being the mind-reader now?" He continued to smile as he gazed upon her.

"What are you smiling about?" Katie asked.

"I'm happy that you're going to be all right. That first night was very stressful, and I was afraid I might lose you."

Katie held out her hand. "I need some more healing."

125

Mark sat on the edge of her bed and held her hand as they talked.

A knock on the open door interrupted their conversation. "Good morning, Katie!" Dr. Ford said as she entered the room. After a proper introduction, the doctor continued, "I'm so glad to see you're awake. How do you feel?"

"Weak. Does the hospital have any horses?"

Dr. Ford's eyes blinked, and she turned to Mark. He shrugged and shook his head, clearly as perplexed as she. "Umm, no Katie. Why do you ask?"

"Because right now, I could eat one."

A relieved laugh escaped from Dr. Ford. "Oh Katie, you had me worried there for a moment. I thought you were still delirious or the high fever had affected your mind in some way. Clearly, you must be feeling better today. You've got your hunger and your sense of humor back. You didn't tell me she was funny, too, Mark." She gave him a wink.

"Today, we're going to start you out slowly on a liquid and soft food diet. Tomorrow we'll move you onto regular food. Mark can tell you all about the hospital food."

He grimaced. "Lived on nothing else for three days."

"Don't believe everything he says. I've personally seen him at the hospital soda fountain multiple times. Isn't it cherry that's your favorite milkshake?"

"Yes, but trust me, they don't make pies that taste anywhere near as good as the ones Katie bakes." He grinned, and Katie smiled bashfully.

Dr. Ford watched their exchange with great interest. "I'll have the dietician come by with a list of your choices for the next three or four days."

"How long am I going to be in here?" Katie asked.

"That depends on how fast your lungs heal… and perhaps Mark."

Dr. Ford made sure she had their complete attention. "I think it would be best if we kept Mark's involvement in all this a secret."

"Suits me fine, but why?" Mark asked.

"I'm walking on thin ice," Dr. Ford said. "The hospital and the medical profession would frown on hand-holding and the power of God being part of my treatment plan."

They nodded. "It never happened," Mark replied.

"Thank you both. Now Mark, if you want to stretch your long legs in the hallway, I'll examine my patient."

Dr. Ford listened to Katie's breathing. "One lung seems to be coming along fine. However, the other one is not doing as well. We'll need to keep the antibiotic going a little longer. The steam from taking a long, hot shower would help clear out your lungs."

"When may I take one?" Katie asked, hopefully.

"Let's wait until tomorrow morning, okay? That way, we'll have the I.V. out, and you'll be free to move about. Plus, that will give you twenty-four hours to get some food in you and build up a little more strength."

"Dr. Ford, I want to thank you for all you've done for me. Mark told me I wouldn't be here if it weren't for you."

"I appreciate your gratitude." She gave Katie a long look and added, "However, I am only part of the equation. You are a very fortunate young lady. You have been given a second chance. I hope you make the most of it."

When Katie was alone in her room, she wondered if Dr. Ford had said that as her doctor or as a friend.

"I saved the cafeteria the trouble," Mark announced, entering the room and waving the meal schedule in his hand. "They said they would send someone to get it later."

"I would like to know more about the time I was asleep," Katie said.

"As you wish, Katie."

"If you are going to grant my wishes, then I *wish* you would sit beside me, so we can join hands. Please crank my bed higher first, though."

"Yes, your Highness."

She smiled and moved over some more. Mark filled her in on the minute details of the last three days.

During a lull, Katie said, "You never showed me the injuries to your back. Do you mind if I see them?"

"It didn't make my back look prettier." He unbuttoned his shirt, slipped it off, and turned his back to Katie. She studied the multiple light lines and their random pattern.

"Oh, Mark, I'm so sorry. I assume these three bold marks are where they had to stitch you up?"

"That's right."

Katie reached out and ran her fingertip along a line, stopping to touch the stitched area tenderly. Mark's full-body shiver startled her. "Do they hurt?"

He shook his head. Katie leaned over and laid her cheek against his bare skin, then kissed each of the stitched areas. "There," she said, "I've made them all better."

Mark had just finished buttoning and tucking his shirt in when his mother and Mary Byler entered the room.

After their mothers had left for home, Mark and Katie went for a walk. The nursing staff had encouraged Katie to exercise and had given her a robe and slippers. Holding firm to Mark's hand, she made the rounds of her floor – stopping at the nurses' station to thank them for their kindness.

At the end of the hallway, they stopped and peered through the window into the darkness. Barren trees and house lights in the distance made up the world outside as they lingered and talked.

"How are you feeling?" Mark asked.

"A little weak, but spiritually content," Katie replied. She studied his face and squeezed his hand as their fingers interlaced.

"I'm surprised how at ease you are while you're a fish out of water," Mark said. He ran his thumb and fingers down her braided hair like he would a guitar string.

"I feel safe and protected. You will protect me while I'm a little fish in this big pond, won't you?" she asked with a coy smile.

"Why, Katie, you surprise me. I didn't think your kind knew how to flirt."

"*My kind*?" Katie pretended offense. "That's going to take a chocolate shake from – what did Dr. Ford call it – the soda fountain to make it up to me."

Mark looked into her bright eyes and saw a glimpse of heaven. The only thing missing was a garden.

The next morning after taking a shower, Katie emerged from the bathroom. Her damp hair fell around her shoulders and cascaded below the middle of her back. "I must rest now. That took a lot out of me." Katie looked at Mark. "You know, if you don't close the barn door, the flies will come in."

He clapped his mouth shut. "Oh, how my God has not forsaken me," he uttered huskily.

Katie smiled, and her eyes were more full of life than he'd ever seen them. "You do say the nicest things."

"I'm going to call you Bright Eyes." The emotions coursing through him radiated from his voice.

"That's fine, but don't let anyone else hear you say it," Katie warned. "Time for healing hands." She stretched her hands toward him.

Mark complied, and as he sat on the edge of her bed, he couldn't take his eyes from her. He had desired her so much and now she was right there in front of him. He let his eyes caress her while the light shining in the window played off her features. God, she was beautiful. And his heart was doing cartwheels as she returned his gaze. He could get lost in those eyes. He wanted to get lost in those eyes. Did she feel it too? If only he could ask.

He reached out and touched the golden waves of hair. As she sought his free hand, Mark whispered, "It's so beautiful. Do you mind if I smell it?"

With big eyes Katie looked up at him… so close. "I don't mind." She leaned toward him, and his nose bumped the side of her head.

"Sorry, my fault," she said. "Let's try it again."

This time she let Mark make the approach, and he hovered over her, just inches away. His breath was warm against her cheek before he inhaled deeply with his nose gently touching her hair.

She lay quietly with every nerve on high alert, while her heart pounded with anticipation.

Mark brushed her temple with his forehead as he pulled away, sending a shiver all through her. She squeezed his hand more tightly and reached for his other hand to hold. "Please hold both hands. After my hair dries some, I'll put it into the braid."

"Do you have to?" he whispered.

"Mama is coming, remember? Just yesterday, she scolded me for not wearing my cap."

"What did you say?"

"I told her the hospital preferred I not wear it."

Mark let out a bark of laughter. "Katie Byler! You told a white lie. Is that your first?"

She studied his face. "Not quite my first," she said with a mischievous grin.

"I want to hear all about the rest."

"I'll tell you about *some* of them."

She exhaled a long breath. Her eyes were heavy now. "I'm going to close my eyes and rest for a while. I'll be all right if you want to get some exercise. Just because I have to be in here doesn't mean you need to stay cooped up. Please lower my bed some."

"I guess a walk in the outside air might do me some good."

As Katie lay with her eyes closed, he leaned over and touched her hair with his nose. He inhaled and moved his cheek against the silky strands. Katie's eyes remained closed, but the corners of her mouth curled.

"Before you go, I want to thank you for the milkshake you brought me last night. Will you bring me another tonight?"

Mark leaned down and softly kissed the top of her forehead. "It's a promise."

"There is something I need to do," Mark said later that evening when they were holding hands and talking. "I've missed four straight days of school, and the work is piling up. I need to go to school tomorrow."

"When will you leave?" Katie asked apprehensively.

"I could go home tonight; then I'd be there to do my morning chores. Dad and Eli have been filling in for me, but I know they've been grumbling about that."

"Oh," she sighed. After a long silence, she asked, "Is our time together over?"

"Do you want it to be?"

"No!" she answered, quickly and boldly. Katie settled back on her pillow, her eyes fastened on Mark, while she picked at her blanket. He fought off the urge to take her in his arms and surround her with his loving care.

"I'll be back after chores are done tomorrow evening," Mark assured her. He gave her hand a gentle squeeze as he looked into the eyes that he adored. Her roiling emotions were so clearly displayed. He wished he could put her mind at ease – tell her that he didn't ever want to leave her. He knew he must leave now, or he wouldn't be able to go at all.

"Please stay five more minutes, and then you can go," she said, her voice catching.

When ten minutes had passed, Mark leaned in close to Katie's ear. "I'll see you tomorrow evening, Bright Eyes. " He squeezed her hand one more time before leaving the room.

The Granville Herald ran a story on page two in the Thursday afternoon edition. The headline read, "Amish Woman Survives Near-Death Experience." An anonymous source had called the paper. Mark was left out of the article, but it identified Katie Byler and Dr. Janice Ford. It hailed the good doctor and Granville Memorial as heroes who saved the day. The new wing of the hospital with its modern equipment and medical procedures were given the credit. The article described in detail the dangers of double pneumonia and acute respiratory failure.

Friday morning, after making the rounds of her patients, Dr. Ford was summoned to the office of the hospital's chief administrator, Willard McDowell. "Welcome, Dr. Ford. Have a seat," he motioned toward the chairs in front of his desk. "Did you see your name in yesterday's paper?"

"Only after someone called to tell me about it."

"I have no idea how they got the story, but the hospital is getting great publicity out of it. It was picked up by the Youngstown and Pittsburgh papers today. The Press wants to do a follow-up story and would like an interview."

"With who?"

"With you, of course. You're the treating physician."

"We had very little to do with that girl's survival, Mr. McDowell. She should have died. Truthfully, I didn't think she'd live long enough to get to the hospital.

Mr. McDowell's expression hardened. "You are entitled to your beliefs and opinions, Dr. Ford. See to it that you keep them out of this hospital. It has been brought to my attention you gave credit to a boy who brought her in, and to God. Today's interview was granted to back-pedal from that position. We have a wonderful hospital here at Granville Memorial, and it is my job to look out for its benefit. Have I made myself perfectly clear?"

"So you want me to be a team player."

"One hand washes the other," he smirked. "I understand this story is benefitting your practice, as well. Keep that in mind."

Dr. Ford nodded and left the room. Later that afternoon, while talking with the reporter, she smoothed things over like a pro.

Immediately after the interview, she headed to Katie's room. She was concerned because early that morning Katie's condition had shown deterioration. The bad lung was definitely worse, and her good lung was no longer clear. She had changed the medication, hoping it would help.

Upon entering her room, Dr. Ford was startled to see Katie's condition was considerably worse. She struggled to keep the concern out of her voice when Katie asked, "How am I doing?"

"I'm a little concerned. Nothing to worry about." In truth, Dr. Ford was alarmed. The first medication had failed, and now the new one was failing. She made a slight adjustment to the dosage and hoped for the best. She stopped at the nurses' station and instructed them to check on Katie every hour. "Report to me immediately after each exam."

The word psychosomatic popped into her head. Could Katie's subconscious be willing her to be sick? While she didn't believe her illness started that way, it could be what was happening now. At the very least, she believed Katie's mind had to be weaned off Mark.

Dr. Ford contemplated her predicament as she returned to Powder Mills. Katie had told her this morning that Mark had gone home last night and was attending school today. She thought nothing of it at the time, but she did now. As soon as she reached her office, Dr. Ford called Ann Lane. "Do you know if Mark will be visiting Katie at the hospital this evening?"

"Yes, he plans to go in after he finishes his chores."

"You're positive?" Dr. Ford pressed.

"Yes I'm sure. He told me so."

"Please tell him to get there as quickly as possible."

"Why? What's the matter?" Ann asked.

"I can say no more," the doctor responded and then hung up.

Dr. Ford was standing at Katie's bedside three hours later when Mark rushed into the room. "I got here as soon as I could."

At the sound of his voice, Katie awoke from her sleep. She smiled at him, but Mark could see she wasn't the "Bright Eyes" he had left twenty-four hours earlier. He approached the edge of her bed, and Katie held out her hands. Mark slipped his into them and asked, "How are you feeling?"

"A little worse. I missed you. I tried to hold on without you."

"I know you did, but I'm here now, and I won't leave you. Rest and get better."

Katie closed her eyes. "Lay down beside me, Mark. Let the healing hands touch."

Dr. Ford quietly closed the door as she left the room and slumped against the wall in the hallway. Exhausted, she slipped into the empty room next to Katie's and lay down on the bed.

Several hours later Dr. Ford was awakened by a tapping sound coming from the room next door. It was followed by a voice, "Beat you again, Mark."

Dr. Ford could not believe her eyes as she opened Katie's door. Two surprised heads turned her way. Katie had a big smile on her face, but Mark wasn't so happy. On Katie's lap lay a checker board with checkers strewn everywhere.

"What in the name of heaven?"

Mark spoke first. "Katie woke up and wanted to play checkers."

"Yes, and Mark's not very good at them. I beat him four games in a row," she exclaimed happily, holding up four fingers.

"This is quiet time," Dr. Ford scolded them.

"Sorry," they whispered together, but a glance at each other started them giggling.

"We were just having fun," Mark explained.

"Yeah, don't be a poop-head," Katie added, and each put a hand over their mouth to muffle the laughter.

Dr. Ford made certain she was present when the hospital released Katie on Sunday. Taking Mary and Moses aside, she told them about Friday's events and explained that there was no medical reason for what happened.

"What Katie is doing by leaving this hospital today is a miracle. Her recovery time should have been three to four weeks, at best. We know Mark was a part of that, and no one knows it better than Katie. She believes that Mark is her lifeline. When the mind is convinced of something, it can control our physical bodies, even unto death. Katie needs to be slowly weaned off her mental dependence on Mark. I'm advising you to let Katie and Mark hold hands for up to an hour a day. Cut back as time goes on and see how she does… and make sure she finishes her antibiotic."

Dr. Ford observed the uncertain looks on the faces of Katie's parents. Her parting words were, "I want to make this very clear. Katie was away from Mark for twenty-four hours, and I was close to losing her a second time."

What a strange sight they must have been going down the road. Three Amish and one English in a blue-and-white convertible. Mark and Katie sat in the front and her parents in the back. There was a bump in the ceiling where Moses's hat was pushing it up.

As Katie prepared for bed that evening, she thought back to all that had happened since Friday night. After the checkers, they had slept until morning. Katie took a shower, and since her mother and Ann didn't come to visit, they had the whole day to themselves. They talked about Katie's love of nature and baking. They talked about Mark's love for Lane Farms and the meadow.

"You should see the wildflowers in spring," Mark told her, "and listen to the peepers at night. They're like a lullaby as you drift off to sleep."

"You sleep there?"

"Sure, in the bankhouse. That's why I built it."

"Do you ever sleep outside under the stars?"

134

"In the summer, I do. Then I get to enjoy the fireflies, thousands of them, like far away blinking stars." Katie imagined what it must be like in the meadow, but she especially imagined being there with Mark.

They talked about Mark's love of music and his ability to play the guitar. Katie asked him to sing her a song, and he sang two verses of Amazing Grace. She asked him to sing her another, so Mark gave her a fast-paced rendition of Oh Susannah. When he finished, she questioned, "I wonder what it's like in Alabama. Do you know, Mark?"

"No, but I intend to find out some day. Some good music has come out of Alabama. It was the home of country music's greatest star, Hank Williams."

Mark had brought the article out of the newspaper, and they read it together...'After making a house call, Dr. Janice Ford...'"

Mark made up limericks that made Katie laugh. He even wrote one down on a scrap of paper. "I'm not sure I should give this to you," he said.

There once was a girl named Katie,
Who was a horse manure shovelin' lady.
She'd muck out the stalls,
In winter, spring, summer or fall,
For she loved to do the chore daily.

Katie read it and laughed good-naturedly. "That's funny, Mark. Not true, but funny."

Later in a more serious moment, Katie squeezed Mark's hand. "You took a chance you know – with your limerick."

"What do you mean?" Mark asked.

"What if I didn't think it was funny and had been offended?"

"I needed to know the depth and quality of your sense of humor. I would have apologized, but then I would have known."

Katie playfully walked her fingers up his arm and smiled. "Did I pass?"

A smile played at Mark's lips, and she could feel the admiration darts he flung from his eyes. They were gentle pricks making her tingle all over. He drew near and kissed her on the forehead near the hairline. He filled the air around them with masculinity as Katie's own sexuality caught fire. "I'm pleased to say you got an A+."

She wished he would hold her in his arms but dared not ask. She settled for the warm feeling that stole over her and then fanned herself with the blanket as the heat threatened to burn her.

Mark ambled to the window and watched the world below till she called him back to her side. The sympathy in his eyes said he understood and she yearned to shed her cover for other reasons. But she was nearly naked already, so she patted the bed beside her and let her face do the talking. Nothing was said, yet everything was understood.

He offered to sing her a couple more songs, and how could she refuse him?

Katie divulged her dream of taking pictures of nature like the ones in Ideals. "Can you imagine traveling around the country getting paid to see those places?" she gushed.

"Ain't nothing stopping you."

"Owning a camera is not permitted," Katie said sadly.

"I'll loan you one."

"You'd do that for me?"

"Of course!"

"Mama brought me a letter from Lydia."

"What did she have to say?"

"She's got a suitor. Just met him a month ago. Says he's real nice, but she isn't in any hurry to get committed. I'd like to go out to Lancaster and visit her next summer."

"I could drive you."

"It would not be permitted."

Katie didn't mention that Lydia asked if she had made friends with "that Lane boy" yet. "If you haven't, I suggest you get on with it," Lydia had written. There were things Katie wasn't even telling Lydia.

Katie handed Mark a homemade card from her brothers and sisters. Each had drawn a picture and written their name. Jacob had written, "Rebecca says to come home."

"It will be good to go home." She looked at him and asked, "How will we continue to hold hands?"

"Why don't you ask God for help? It's obvious that He knows what He's doing," Mark suggested.

Now as Katie lay in her own bed, she thought about the ride home from the hospital. She had held Mark's hand most of the way, only releasing it when he needed to shift gears. It didn't matter that her parents were present. Katie truly believed that she needed him.

They were approaching the lane to the barn where Midnight was born when Katie asked if they could go down to see the calf.

Moses started to say no but then replied, "Well, I guess those waiting at the house will wait ten more minutes."

When they approached Midnight's pen, the young bull came right over to greet Katie as if they were old friends. Katie held out her finger, and he began to suck it. "You don't suppose he remembers me, do you, Mark?"

"Hard to say," Mark shrugged.

"That's a fine-looking calf," Moses said. "It was born the first part of October, no?"

"That's right."

"No wonder his mother had to have help with the birth. Already so big, and you can tell to look at him that he has character. You two did a good thing in saving him."

Katie shivered. "I'm cold. Let's get back in the car."

Moses spoke up as Mark started the car. "We've been advised by Dr. Ford to allow a very unconventional treatment for Katie's healing. She stated that twice she witnessed a miraculous transformation in Katie's condition after holding Mark's hand. I witnessed it once myself, so I am going to allow it. The rest of our children cannot know of this. It must be done away from our property. If you agree, every evening for two weeks, either Mary or I will come to your house and sit with you while you hold hands. We assume nothing improper will take place."

"You know I wouldn't do anything improper, Father," Katie stated matter-of-factly.

Mark spoke up. "I'll clear this with Mom and Dad, but I'm sure we can use Grandad's room. I have no idea what to tell my sisters. They're going to be curious. Let's see what Mom can suggest."

"It is agreed, then?" Moses asked.

Katie and Mark looked at each other and nodded. "Yes," they replied in unison.

Moses continued, "I know we almost lost Katie. I would not be doing this except for that. As I said, this is unconventional; none of us can tell anyone. Is the confidence of this assured?" Again, Katie and Mark affirmed it.

Moses concluded, "God works in mysterious ways, His wonder to perform."

Katie took Mark's hand for the short ride to the Byler farm. She felt a paper in his palm, took it from him, and slipped it into her pocket. Later, in the privacy of her room, she opened it and read…

Snow Angel

I met with her on a full-moon night.
We frolicked in the snow, just out of sight.
As angels were made upon the snow,
We asked our guardian angels to show.

To our dismay they never came.
We had a good time just the same.
Some night we'll have to go again
To play and frolic just as friends.

As we part and say goodbye
Fresh snow is falling from the sky.
Creations we made soon will be gone
But my Earth angel still lives on.

Katie already knew the poem by heart, and she said it quietly one more time. She promised herself that she would ask Mark to act out the poem one night this winter.

Lying snug in her bed, she was still processing the events of the last week. The memory of holding Mark's hands was giving her comfort when she called to mind her angst from ten days earlier on this very spot. "Do you want me to love Mark Lane?" she had asked God. "Give me a sign."

Katie knew that she had her sign.

Chapter Sixteen

After the main meal on Sunday afternoon, Mark approached his parents. "I need to talk to you. Could we go into Grandad's room where we can have some privacy?"

"That bad, huh? Come on, Ann, sounds like this is important stuff," Harold said.

Mark pulled the door shut behind them and launched into the story about Katie. He ended the explanation with Dr. Ford's advice.

"What a strange situation," Harold remarked. "If it weren't our own son telling it, how could we believe it? We can hardly refuse the Bylers' request to use our home as a meeting place, but we definitely need to have a reason to give Peggy and Brenda."

"I agree," Ann replied. "Let your dad and I think about it. Give us until tomorrow morning to come up with an explanation."

Mark headed to his bedroom to enjoy some quiet time alone. As he relaxed on his bed, he thought of Katie and how ironic things were. All this time he'd wanted her to like him and feel as close to him as he felt toward her. Now the connection was stronger than he could even have imagined, and they needed to disconnect her from him.

Voices in the hall outside his open door interrupted his thoughts.

"Go on in," a voice whispered. "No, you do it," was hissed back. Peggy poked her head around the doorjamb, and Brenda pushed her into Mark's room, following close behind. "Peggy wants to ask you something," Brenda blurted. Peggy gave her a dirty look and then a shove.

"Come on in, girls. No reason to be bashful since you're already here."

"We want to know about Katie. Is she going to be all right?" Peggy asked.

"I believe so, but she still has healing to do."

"The article in the paper said it was a miracle," Brenda stated. "Did you see a miracle?"

"Better than that. I participated. That reminds me, I want to explain a delicate situation to the two of you. The Bylers believe that God saved Katie by using me. They wish to keep the three of us together for just a little while longer until Katie is completely over her pneumonia. Every night for the next couple weeks, one of the Bylers and Katie will stop by. We'll fellowship in Grandad's room."

"You mean like Youth Group?" Brenda asked.

"Exactly. We may do some Bible study, have a snack, play some games, or put a puzzle together. Stuff like that."

His sisters nodded. "Did God get involved?" Peggy wanted to know.

"Yes, in a powerful way."

Peggy looked at Mark with newfound admiration. "Who would have thought… you and God. That is so neat. If I get sick, could you heal me?" she asked

"I didn't heal anyone, and it was probably a onetime event."

When Mark entered the kitchen, Ann had her nose buried in one of her cookbooks. "You saved your dad and me a lot of thinking."

Mark considered the statement. "It just came naturally, kinda like eavesdropping."

"I'm a parent, Mark. It's not called eavesdropping. Anyway, I wasn't eavesdropping. I heard it all from the bottom of the stairs. You have no idea how well your voice carries. I baked Katie her favorite cake. I'll take it to her in the morning and tell Mary it has all been arranged for tomorrow evening."

"What's her favorite cake, Mom?"

"German Chocolate."

"Figures," Mark muttered, as he left the kitchen.

Ann sought out her daughters to instruct them that what Mark had revealed was to be kept in strict confidence.

"Hello, Mrs. Barnes," Mark greeted the cashier of the five and dime store.

He headed down one of the aisles and stopped in front of the puzzle display. His eyes locked onto a puzzle of a farm with its various buildings and homey-looking white house. Katie would like it. He could easily picture her presiding over the entire scene.

Mark shuffled the boxes as he searched for a second puzzle. He was drawn to one that contained a picture of a country cabin nestled in a large clearing in the woods. There was a slight hillside just behind it and a fair-sized stream in front of it... good for trout. The scene reminded him of the meadow in late fall. It was done in shades of gray, brown, beige, and silver. The whole scene had a somewhat barren tone to it which drew the viewer's eye to the cabin: warm and inviting, a place of refuge and safety. He could easily imagine living in this cabin with Katie. Just the two of them with food and water right outside. And inside, the fire and blankets to keep them warm… and each other, of course.

Mark made his plans for that evening's meeting. Moses would probably accompany Katie this first time to assure himself he was satisfied with the whole situation. He remembered the poems he had written since summer and decided to pick out a good one to slip into Katie's pocket.

Moses and Katie arrived right on time. Mark led them into the room he had prepared for their gathering. He had set up the card table with two chairs on adjacent sides.

Mark explained to Katie, "You can sit on that side, and I'll sit here." He held her chair for her as she sat down.

"Thank you," she acknowledged.

"I see you brought some reading materials with you, Mr. Byler. Very wise indeed. I set up the floor lamp by the easy chair there in the corner so you'd have plenty of light."

Moses sat down with an appreciative nod.

Mark showed Katie the two puzzles lying on the table. "Did Mama tell you I like puzzles?"

"No," he replied. He could see that she was drawn to the one of the farm scene. He smiled inwardly. How well he knew her.

Mark surveyed their situation. From his chair, he had a direct line of sight to Moses facing them. Moses could not see their hands since Katie's body blocked his view. When she would turn to look at Mark, the back of her head would be Moses's viewpoint.

And so it began - a challenging game of two participants on an open stage with an observer not twelve feet away. Katie held out her hand to Mark.

"How did you know I like puzzles?" she asked.

"Mom used to go to your house at Christmastime to take presents, and she'd take me with her. One of the things she'd give you was puzzles. Also, I remember a small table where there might be a puzzle partially assembled."

"I'm surprised you can remember back that far," Katie teased.

Two could play this game. He started to pull his hand out of hers.

She grabbed onto it and hissed, "Don't, Mark! I'm only playing with you."

They worked together on the farm scene while they talked. "I can remember you coming to our house. I thought that your hair looked like a girl's."

"Gee, thanks," Mark said.

"No, that's a good thing. Now your hair is light brown and somewhat wavy. Back then, it was blond with a mass of curls. I remember wishing my hair looked like that."

"We have a picture of me hanging on the wall just as you've described. I did look pretty cute."

Katie squeezed Mark's hand. "Pride filled."

"No. Honest. Don't you wish you had a picture of when you were young?" Mark asked, keeping his head down to let the table muffle the sound. When he looked up, Katie was studying him. They were still maneuvering to figure each other out, and her response was going to tell him a lot. There was a kindness in her eyes now and a faraway look, almost wistful.

"Yes, I suppose I should. Sometimes I wish I did." Mark gave her a sympathetic look, ran his fingers up her arm and squeezed gently.

"Your mom gave me two dolls once," she said.

"Two at the same time?"

"Yes, a boy and a girl, with bright red hair."

"Oh, Raggedy Ann and Andy dolls. Do you still have them?"

144

"Of course! They sit on my top bookshelf. I talk to them sometimes, but they never talk back," she said coyly.

"Did you try kissing Andy? That usually works with boys."

Katie looked up from the puzzle to see his mischievous grin. She wondered what it would be like to kiss him. She glanced at his mouth and perfectly shaped lips and felt herself warming again. She quickly looked down. It was a good thing Mark couldn't really read her mind. But did he ever think about kissing her?

The time flew by as they worked on the puzzle. Every once in a while one or the other would steal a glance at their workmate.

"Did you bring me a piece of the cake Mom gave you?" Mark asked aloud.

"Of course not," Katie said.

"Oh, I see. Next time, I'll make sure I get my piece before Mom gives it to you."

Mark heard Moses chuckle and looked up to see him smiling. "Yup, when it comes to German Chocolate cake around our house, that's the only way you're going to get any. Well, it's almost time, Katie. I'll go out and get the blanket off Nellie."

Moses left the room and they heard him speaking with Harold in the dining room.

"Our fathers are talking, so we have a little time. You were acting cool to me most of the night. It's not like we were before," she sighed. "I miss that."

"So do I. If you want us to be like we were in the hospital, I'll come to your room after lights-out tonight. Then we'll be free to be just like we were."

Katie played along, "Would you sit on the edge of my bed and hold my hand?"

"Both hands," Mark replied.

Katie looked at him for a moment. "I'd like that. But you'd better not," she quickly added.

"Why not?"

"It's cold out tonight. You could catch pneumonia!"

Harold and Moses heard the laughter, looked at each other, and shook their heads.

"C'mon, Katie! Time to go!" Moses called, as he went out the door.

Mark remembered the poem in his pocket. "Katie, wait! Read it when you get home." She slipped it into her coat, and thanked him.

"Is it a love letter?" Katie wondered on the slow ride home. She couldn't wait to be alone in her room to see what he had given her. She unfolded the paper to reveal another poem. This one was titled, 'The Girl and the Spider.'

Mark had included a short note at the bottom:

I wrote this soon after the incident with the spiders but held on to it for a while in hopes you could enjoy it when I finally gave it to you. Sleep tight, don't let the bed bugs bite, and keep getting better with all your might.

Sweet dreams,

Mark

Sweet dreams were exactly what Katie had that night. She slept soundly with the poem under her pillow. The next morning she added it to the ones already in her journal. She had been afraid to write her new-found feelings into that journal, because she knew the consequences if anyone read it. She promised herself that someday she would write her feelings down.

Moses came with Katie again the next night, but this time he and Harold spent twenty minutes talking before he entered the room to sit and read. Mark and Katie could be themselves, and the freedom was inspiring. Their giggling finally drew Moses into their room. "What's so funny?"

"We were just remembering when Jacob came out of my bankhouse after the storm," Mark answered. "He looked like he was waiting for an errant lightning strike to get him any second."

"I guess you had to be there," Moses responded.

Once again, their time together flew by. "Why, you're almost finished with that puzzle," Moses remarked as he got up to leave. "How many pieces are in it?"

"One thousand," Mark answered. "It goes quickly because it's a labor of love." Katie's eyes grew large and Mark saw her look of alarm. He quickly held up the lid with its picture and said, "See, it's Lane Farms or the Byler spread. Take your pick."

"Before you go, Mr. Byler, there's something Katie and I have discussed that I wish to speak to you about."

"Oh?" Moses said.

"When Katie was in the hospital, she told me it's her dream to take pictures of nature." Mark retrieved an Ideals from the end table beside Moses's chair. He thumbed through it, showing Moses several of the beautiful photographs. "This is God's handiwork, but a person took the pictures so all of us could enjoy them."

"I see that," Moses replied.

"Katie would like to take beautiful pictures, so she'll be able to look at them when the seasons aren't just right."

"I understand," Moses said. He looked into Katie's anxious eyes, and his heart softened.

Mark continued. "She's been through a lot, Mr. Byler. I believe taking pictures would give her something to look forward to and help her heal in both body and spirit. It would help her become an independent person again. Mom and Dad are buying me a new camera for Christmas. We could learn to use it together, and I would be happy to loan it to her."

"I'm sure Katie told you that owning a camera is not allowed."

"She did. But I also know that owning a car is not allowed, yet riding in one is permitted. I wondered if such an exception might apply to Katie's situation since it's so unusual. I mean, look at what she's been through. What about the good it might accomplish? Her healing makes it worth considering."

Moses looked down and thought. He glanced from Mark to his daughter's hopeful face. "I will speak with the bishop to see if an exception may be granted. I can make no promises. This is highly unusual. I'll get the blanket off Nellie." He ambled out of the room.

When Katie rose to leave, Mark held her in his arms for the second time. She came around the table, never taking her eyes off his and boldly embraced him. This time, he knew it was coming and was ready. She stood on her toes and slid her cheek alongside his. She wrapped her arms around him and pulled him tightly to her, pressing their bodies together. Mark did the same, and each felt the full measure of the other's physical presence. It was a measure neither would soon forget.

Katie whispered into his ear, "Thank you," then she released him. Mark wanted to pull her back and ask her to stay forever in his arms, but he let her go, remembering everything, including the scent of her.

Moses was busy the next evening, so Mary accompanied Katie. The atmosphere lightened considerably. Mary liked Mark, and he could dazzle her with his boyish charm. He gave her a casual hug and a peck on the cheek when she entered the room. Katie just shook her head as she walked by him, and Mark knew she couldn't believe he got away with that.

As soon as they sat down, she squeezed his hand and said, "Mama has something to tell you."

Mary exhaled heavily. "Moses has spoken with the bishop about the camera. At first he said no, but then Moses took him into our confidence on all that has happened during Katie's illness, and the bishop was moved to grant an exception as long as certain conditions are met."

"What are the conditions?" Mark asked.

Mary unfolded a paper and began to read. "Katie can take no pictures of people. She can take pictures of nature and things. These pictures will be purely for enjoyment. It is against our rules to sell the pictures or receive compensation for them in any form. If these conditions are accepted, the bishop has given his permission for you to loan Katie a camera. However, Moses has a condition of his own. We will provide to your family six free pies of your choosing when the bake shop opens in May."

Mark looked to Katie. She nodded with hope-filled eyes. "You drive a hard bargain, Mrs. Byler, but I'll accept it," he said with a wide grin.

"It is agreed then," Mary replied.

Mark knew she wasn't on board with this idea, so he pressed the issue. "I would've received this at Christmas but Katie can use it now, so I'll get it right away. I can teach her how to operate it while she's coming here."

Mary nodded.

That evening they finished the farm-scene puzzle. Mark promised to mount it on poster board and frame it for Katie's room. "That will look nice above the head of your bed," Mary remarked.

"I'll have the camera when you come tomorrow evening, and we'll start your lessons on how to use it," Mark assured her.

"Mrs. Byler, there's an Ideals laying on the stand beside your chair if you want to look through it. That's the book I was showing Mr. Byler last night."

Mary put aside her knitting and browsed through the book. "So Katie could take pictures like these?"

"I don't see why not. She certainly has a good eye for nature."

Katie and Mark held hands while they played checkers. Mark won one out of three games, and he suspected she let him win that one to save his pride.

"I should teach you to play Chinese Checkers. We'll see if your luck holds out in that game too," Mark said defensively.

Katie said nothing, but her mother couldn't help laughing. "Don't take it personally. No one beats Katie at checkers."

Mark just shook his head.

Mary stood up and stretched. "I'm going to say hello to your mother." She patted him on the shoulder as she passed, "Be a good loser, Mark." Her chuckles could be heard as she went in search of Ann.

When Mary left the room, Katie smiled and reached for Mark's hand. "Now we can be ourselves—the way I want us to be. Can we just sit and talk like we did in the hospital?"

"Sure." Mark raised her hand to his lips and kissed it tenderly. He gave her a smile that was lazy, like a Sunday afternoon, and she relaxed into a state of warm bliss.

It was well past the allotted hour when Mary and Katie finally headed home. Mary had enjoyed the visit with Ann, and Katie was in no hurry to leave Mark.

Once in her room, Katie hung her coat on a peg by the back door. Hope caused her to search the pockets, and hope was soon rewarded in the form of another poem folded neatly and hidden away for her to find. She carefully unfolded it and read the title, *The Spider and The Bee.*

After Mary and Katie departed, Mark turned his attention to his mother. "Did you decide what you might get me for Christmas?" he asked.

"Isn't it a little early for that?"

Mark could have made a game of it but he cut right to the point. "How would you like to buy me a camera, so I can loan it to Katie?"

Ann's eyes bugged out and her mouth hung open. He truly enjoyed each time he invoked these reactions in her: the sputtering, the look of incredulity. It was so much better than beating around the bush.

"Do you want to explain that?" Ann asked when she'd recovered.

Mark started at the beginning and ran through the entire story. "Mr. Byler and I will be a lot happier when Katie doesn't occupy a fair amount of an evening's free time."

"But you're the one who saved her," Ann said, genuinely surprised.

"And you're the one who said I didn't." Then he made a scary ghost noise. "It wasn't me. It was a spirit, remember?"

"You think the camera will give her back her independence?"

"It's worth a shot, and I could use a more sophisticated camera, anyway."

"What if I wasn't going to spend that much?"

"Tell you what, Mom. I'll buy the camera, give you the receipt, and you can put whatever amount you wish in my Christmas stocking with nothing for me under the tree. Except for the usual box of socks, underwear, and undershirts, please."

"What was all that laughing about in Grandad's room?" Ann wanted to know. "Katie seems to be warming up to you."

"Yeah, how long do you suppose that's going to last? I keep telling you that girl doesn't like me. The sooner she gets distracted with something else, the sooner she stops coming here, and the better for everyone."

Ann threw her hands up. "Do as you wish, Mark. You're going to anyway. I guess you aren't breaking any laws."

No, just a few rules, he thought as he walked away.

The next day after school, Mark made a trip to the camera store in Granville. He bought a camera perfect for a beginner. It wasn't cheap, but he didn't care. He wanted Katie to have one that would help her take beautiful pictures. He also hoped to use it one day to take beautiful pictures of Katie.

That evening, Mark and Katie read through the instruction booklet together.

"Why aren't you allowed to sell pictures?" Mark asked.

"Father said it's because nature was given to us by God, so we can't profit from His gift."

"What do you think about that?"

"I can see both sides of it. On the one hand, nature is everyone's gift, but if the photographer didn't get paid there would be no books like Ideals for people to enjoy."

"How did you like the poem I gave you last night?"

Katie was slow to answer. "It was thought-provoking. Much deeper than your other poems. I guess a poem about a spider and a bee isn't going to end happily." She gave him a weak smile. "Are we the spider and the bee?"

Mark was stunned. He wrote the thing, and he hadn't seen it from the angle Katie did. "No, Katie, it was just a poem about survival in nature. We don't have to live like the creatures in the poem. We can overcome our differences while the spider and the bee cannot."

They began working on the second puzzle. "Why do you like this picture so much?" Katie asked.

"Because with very little imagination, I can pretend I'm living there."

She studied the picture and then directed her gaze to Mark. "A house in the meadow by a stream. You're a dreamer."

"Is that bad?"

"No, because I know at the same time you're well-grounded here at Lane Farms. I am just a farm girl, so the other picture was perfect for me."

"You're not just a farm girl. You're also a dreamer. You have a love of nature and a dream to capture it in pictures. We are more alike than we are different."

"Is there anything else you can tell me about your dream-life in this house in the meadow?"

"It's peaceful and quiet. I'm contented there because life is pure – a world without evil."

Katie sensed he was holding back. If it was too private to share, it most likely concerned her, and she was glad. She realized that she was falling in love with him, and that alone was a weight off her shoulders. Now that she knew, Katie was determined just to enjoy the journey.

"So good to see you, Katie," Dr. Ford greeted her warmly. "Has it been two weeks already?"

"Yes, and a couple of days on top of that."

"You look really well. I can't put my finger on it, but something is different about you. How do you feel?"

"Good most of the time, but sometimes I get weak spells and my cough comes back."

"Let's examine you and see what we find." After a thorough exam, the doctor said, "Go ahead and get back into your clothes. I'll be in my office when you're dressed."

Dr. Ford was looking out the window when Katie entered. "Have a seat," she said, motioning to the chair beside her desk. "How did the sessions go with Mark?"

"Very well. We held hands most of the hour at first. In the second week we cut back, but we often ran over."

"Why is that?"

"We were having too much fun."

Dr. Ford smiled. "You mean, you and Mark?"

"Well, me and Mark, my mother, Mark's mother, even Peggy and Brenda a couple times."

"And what would you do?"

"Played games: Stix, Old Maid, Cootie, lots of stuff."

"Are you ready to go it alone, Katie?"

Katie was tapping a heel on the floor when she started to speak but stumbled over her words. Starting again, she looked down at Dr. Ford's desktop. "I was thinking maybe Mark and I should still get together once in a while on account of my weak spells and cough."

Dr. Ford spoke in a soothing voice. "Let me tell you the findings of my exam. You're in better health than I am, and I found no reason for you to be weak or to have a cough."

Katie looked down again. "Oh," she said.

Dr. Ford reached out and raised Katie's chin until she was looking into her eyes. "I know I'm your doctor, but can I give you some personal advice?"

Katie nodded.

"Do you love him?"

"I won't swear to it, but I think I do."

Dr. Ford waited. Katie gave her an anguished look. "He's English. I can only join his world by leaving mine. Why can't he be Amish?"

"If he were Amish, he wouldn't be Mark."

"I know. That's what I keep telling myself."

"I understand that a choice must be made, but surely the choice can wait. I can no longer be your alibi to see him. I have to tell your mother there's no need to see you again unless something new develops. Promise me that you will listen to your heart as well as your head. Make the right choice for you. Sixty or seventy years is a long time to live with the wrong person. Do not let others make the choice for you."

153

Chapter Seventeen

"Hi, Sarah. Is your mom or Katie home?"

"Come in out of the cold, Peggy," Mary called from the kitchen.

Katie came down the stairs with her usual shadow, Rebecca. "Come in, come in, it's cold out there today," Katie said. Peggy and Katie greeted each other warmly.

"You surely didn't walk here, did you?" Mrs. Byler asked.

"No, Mark dropped me off on his way to the lower farm. We came in the new truck Dad just bought this week."

At the sound of Mark's name, Katie glanced out the front window.

"How will you get home?" Katie asked.

"He's going to stop on his way back past. I figured by then you'd have a good idea what time he should come to get me."

"So that has been your red truck we've seen go by a couple times this week?" Mary said.

"Yes. Dad bought it used, but it's only a year old and looks like new. Mark said he'd teach me to drive it."

"It sits high above the ground," Mary remarked.

"That's because it's a four-wheel drive. It goes a lot better in the snow. Mark can't wait for the first big snow to use the plow that came with it. You know boys and their toys."

Mary and Katie chuckled.

"Let's go to my room," Katie suggested. "We'll spread your squares out on the bed to see how they look."

"I'm so glad I thought to ask your mom for advice on the quilt when you were at our house a couple weeks ago. I suppose I could have picked an easier 4-H project," Peggy said as she followed Katie into her room.

"Yes," Katie agreed. "But it is winter, and we aren't that busy. I am happy to help."

Peggy spread out the squares in the pattern she had chosen. "What do you think?"

Katie observed the color scheme and overall appearance. "This is going to be a beauty, but quilting takes a lot of patience and strong back muscles."

Peggy glanced around her. "Wow, I'll trade you rooms. This is more like a private suite. Why is it so big?"

"It was built for my mother's parents when I was a young girl, but about six years ago they moved back to Ohio, where they grew up."

Peggy's gaze fell upon the picture above the bed. "Say, isn't that the puzzle you and Mark put together when you were recovering?"

"Yes. He mounted and framed it for me."

"A Raggedy Ann and Andy set!"

Peggy was holding the Ann doll when she noticed the three pictures on the wall.

"These pictures are colored-pencil drawings. I didn't know the Amish studied art in school."

"We don't. They were given to me this past summer."

"They're very good. Someone spent hours and hours on them. They seem familiar somehow."

"Maybe because your brother drew them," Katie offered.

Peggy gawked at her in surprise. "Yes, that's it! He has a smaller one, of the whole meadow, sitting on his desk in his bedroom. There are his initials in the lower corner of this one." She looked at Katie, "What did he do to you that he needed to apologize for?"

"What do you mean?" Katie replied hesitantly, delaying the inevitable.

"Mark doesn't know how to keep himself out of trouble. First, he does something dumb, then does something really nice to make up for it. What did he do to you?"

"I shouldn't tattle on Mark, but it was pretty funny, now that I look back on it."

Peggy pulled her down onto the bed beside her. "You sit right here and tell me all about it, Katie. I'll just die of longing if you don't. I'll be your best friend for life."

Katie chuckled. "How well can you keep a secret?"

"If it's about Mark, as long as I live, cross my heart and hope to die!"

She told Peggy the whole story. "I'm so excited I could just pee myself!" Peggy exclaimed when Katie had finished. She noticed Katie was looking apprehensively at her bed, and Peggy laughed. "Don't worry, that's only a figure of speech."

"Well, that's a relief."

"It's the ultimate payback. You got him with the pie, then he pulled the spider trick. It must have been traumatic for him to have his perfect plan go awry. You say he caught you as you fainted?"

"Yes, and carried me outside under the oak tree."

"Mighty Mark to save the day!" Peggy sang. "Oh, thank you, Katie. You have no idea how much you made my day, my week even."

"You won't tell anyone?"

"Not a soul." Peggy gave her a big hug. "Friends for life." She looked out Katie's hallway entrance then came back to sit beside her. "Mark likes you," she whispered.

Katie gulped. "What do you mean?" she asked.

"He has never given this kind of attention to any girl. There are some girls at school who would like him to, but he just treats them nice and lets it go at that. I don't get it because they clearly want his attention. Beneath his outgoing exterior, my brother is shy around girls, even backward sometimes. I'd say he's almost tongue-tied."

Katie cocked her head. Who was Peggy describing? Maybe she had two brothers named Mark.

The following day, Peggy feigned illness and stayed home from church… alone. Nothing was safe in Mark's room. She found the poems and after an exhaustive search, the two laminated pictures of Katie. She whistled. She knew it; he did like girls. No, she corrected herself, Mark liked *one* girl.

As Peggy studied the pictures, she shook her head in amazement. Katie looked so beautiful in the yellow sundress. Surely, he had never seen Katie in the dress, had he? Peggy's mind churned while she put Mark's room back in order.

Mark stopped at the Byler farm on his way home from school on Monday to get eggs and the ham his mom had ordered for New Year's. Due to unusually sunny skies, the weather had warmed some since the week before, and most of the snow had melted. Before he had a chance to walk up to the house, Katie came out onto the porch, still wrapping her cape around her shoulders.

"Now that's what I call service," Mark declared as Katie approached him.

"Only the best for you, Mr. Lane. What will it be today?"

"Another hug would be nice."

Katie stopped and studied him. "What's your second choice?"

"Hmmmm, I'd better not say, so I'll tell you what my mother's choice is: two dozen eggs and a ham for New Year's Day."

"Well, let's go get them," she said, tightlipped.

Katie carried the ham out of the smokehouse and tossed it to him.

"Nice catch," she said.

"Yeah, it's a good thing I was looking."

"Your mind-reading skills slipping, Mark?"

"Am I ever going to live that down?"

"That depends."

"Depends on what?" Mark asked as he followed her into the springhouse.

Once inside, Katie took the ham from him and set it on the table. "It depends on whether you get better at it. Go ahead, read my mind."

Mark had no answer.

She gazed up at him. "If you came to my room tonight, would you sit on my bed and hold my hand?"

"Both hands," he replied.

Katie held her hands out to him, and their fingers entwined. He leaned down and touched his forehead to where Katie's hairline began. She tilted her face up to him, and for a minute they stood with their foreheads pressed together.

"I've missed you," Katie said softly. He remained silent. "This is where you tell me you missed me too," she prompted.

"I have missed you," he assured her. "I think about you all the time. I wish it was summer and I could see you more often."

"It *will* be summer, and we'll still be here with intimate hands."

Mark straightened and looked down at her. He studied her face and saw it was different. Somehow, the last few weeks had changed her. Her look. That steady look. And the way she squared her shoulders - presenting herself to him without reservation. It took his breath away.

"Would you lie beside me while you held my hands?"

"I would," he answered.

"You'd better not. I'm sure I could feel you this time."

Mark enveloped her with his embrace. Her heartbeat against his chest emboldened him. "Oh, Katie, stay with me."

She pressed her cheek against his. "I will," she whispered.

Mark lifted her off the ground, and stood with their bodies pressed together - their faces cheek to cheek. He set her down and started to take a step back.

"Not yet," she urged, "I'm not ready to let you go." She grabbed him and buried her head against his shoulder, hugging him like her life depended on it. He could only try to match her embrace.

Katie finally released him and looked up at him once more. "Will you hug me the next time you see me?"

"There will be no stopping me. But only if we are alone."

"Yes, that would be wise," she replied, her eyes crinkling at the corners.

"I have a Christmas present for you, but I don't know when I'll see you again."

"Oh Mark, I didn't get you anything. I didn't know you would."

"You just gave me the best Christmas present ever."

"But if I had known, I would have bought or made you something. Can you come the day after Christmas? I'll tell Mama that you are stopping by to pick up my first roll of film to have it developed. I'll make sure I've finished the roll by then. When you come, you can show me how to put a roll of film in the camera again."

The day after Christmas, Mark headed to the Byler farm, as promised. "Ann shouldn't have," Mary said as he handed her a bag filled with presents. "I know we used to exchange gifts way back when, but we've gotten away from it."

Mark gave her a sympathetic look. "I told her you'd probably feel uncomfortable, but she wanted to do something."

"Tell her they are much appreciated. Come children, Mrs. Lane has sent you a present." Happy faces abounded as the Byler children gathered around their mother.

"Mama, Mark is going to show me how to put the next roll of film in the camera. Come on, Mark, it's back in my room." Katie grabbed his coat sleeve and led him in that direction.

"Merry Christmas," Katie said when they entered her room from the narrow hallway. She took both his hands in hers and stood facing him.

"Merry Christmas," he whispered.

"Why are we whispering?" she whispered back.

"Am I supposed to be in here?" Mark asked warily.

"Yes, if I want you to be. And I do. Now give me that hug you promised if we were alone, but first take off your coat." He did as she instructed, though swiveled her around, so he could keep his eye on the hallway that led to the main house.

"You give the best hugs," Katie said as he released her. "Do you hug all the girls like that?"

"Not my sisters."

She laughed. "I'll bet you don't, however, that's not the answer I wanted to hear."

"I don't hug girls, only you."

Katie looked into his eyes and knew he meant it. Giddiness burbled up inside her.

He removed her gift from the bag, "Merry Christmas."

"Thank you," she said sweetly, sitting down on her bed to open it.

"I wrapped it myself. It isn't my best work."

Katie smiled up at him and patted the bed beside her. "Sit."

Mark looked toward the hall again.

"No one is going to come here."

He took a step forward, but asked, "Are you sure?"

"This is where we Amish ladies entertain, and everyone knows not to enter without announcing themselves."

Mark sat down tentatively. "Have you entertained here?"

"Thank you for asking, but the answer is *no*, and I never wanted to, until now." Katie looked at him boldly, and Mark believed she wanted him to kiss her. But he couldn't do it. Not here, not like this.

"Open it," he prodded.

Katie slowly removed the paper and set it aside. She held up the gift in the bright light coming in her west window. "It's beautiful! But what is it?"

"A camera case."

She undid the clasp and looked inside. Katie inhaled sharply as she reached into the case and brought out a telephoto lens. "I read in the camera book about this and what it can do. I only hoped to someday get one. I've got to show Mama!" Katie took his hand and led the way into the big living room. "Mama, look what Mark got me for Christmas, a telephoto lens. I can take close up pictures from far away."

"That's very nice, Katie. Tell me about the bag."

Mark explained. "It's an insulated camera case. There are compartments for the camera and all its attachments. It has a strap to hang over your shoulder."

"I like the colors," Katie said. "How did you manage it?"

"They had a book in the camera store, and you could choose from a whole bunch of different colors, even two-toned like this one."

Katie held it next to her dress. "Look Mama, almost a perfect match. And I have a darker dress that will match the bottom part. Come on, Mark. Let's go see how close it matches." As Katie led the way, Mark turned to Mrs. Byler and shrugged his shoulders.

"Go on," she said as she motioned with her hand for him to follow.

While Katie searched her closet for the right dress, Mark observed his surroundings.

She laid her dress on the bed next to the camera case. "Look, Mark, a perfect match!"

She turned to the bookshelves and reached for her Raggedy Ann and Andy dolls. "Your mother gave them to me for Christmas when I was seven. They are one of my most prized possessions," she said, hugging them both. "I didn't buy you anything, but I want you to have Andy, and I'll keep Ann."

"Thank you, Katie, but how will I explain this to my mother?"

"The truth is a good place to start." She looked at him and laughed. "Did I sprout a second head, Mark?" He continued to stare at her in silence.

"You know what I mean. You got me a gift. I didn't buy you anything, and so on." Katie said while rotating her hand.

Mark devoured her with his eyes. To control his longings he said, "Let's load your film before we forget."

"When will I see you again?" Katie asked.

"I can run your film down to Sampson's Drug tomorrow morning, and I should have the pictures back by Thursday."

"Here's some money. Buy me a roll of film while you're there?"

"Why don't you ride along and get it yourself?"

"Don't make this harder for me than it already is. I'd love to go with you, but I can't."

"I know that, Katie, and I'm sorry for saying it. I won't do it again."

Mark put his coat on and Katie suggested that it would be easier for him to use the back door.

"Easier, but not wiser," he replied.

She agreed. As they were leaving her room, Katie turned quickly, bumping into him. She led him back to her bookcase and took down the Raggedy Ann doll. "Let's exchange."

"I'm going to have a *girl* doll in my room?"

"Yes, silly boy."

"Why the switch?"

"So you can hold her hand and pretend it's me. *Intimate hands*" she said, holding her hands up and waving her fingers. "I'll do the same."

That night, Katie retired to her room early. She wrote in her journal until bedtime, finally putting her feelings for Mark on paper. She fell asleep hugging Andy and thinking about Mark.

Chapter Eighteen

Mary spied Mark coming up the walk and hollered for Katie, who was in the sewing room working on a new dress.

"He's got my first pictures, Mama. I'm so excited to see them."

Mary smiled as she continued to work on supper.

Mark didn't have to knock. The door opened when he approached, and he quickly stepped inside and closed it. Katie looked at his empty hands, and her expression drooped. "Weren't you supposed to bring me something?"

Mark grinned and unzipped his coat, pulling out a large envelope. "Oh good," she exclaimed, "Let's spread them out on the kitchen table. Do I have any good ones?"

"How would I know? They're your pictures."

"But I want you to see them and tell me how I did."

"That's fine. I'm happy to help."

Katie laid the pictures on the table one by one, one row after another. "Let's study them," Mark suggested. After a few minutes, he set five pictures aside.

Katie looked disappointed. "Only five good ones?"

"Five great ones, and another ten good ones on top of that. I knew you'd have an eye for this."

"Mama, come look at my pictures."

Mary dried her hands and studied the pictures. "They *are* beautiful, Katie."

"What do we do now?" Katie asked.

"I'm sure Lydia would be amazed to receive some, and my dad would be especially impressed with these ones of the cows. You've captured the mood of winter in many of them. I know my mom would be interested to see them. If you don't mind, I could take the fifteen good pictures up to the house to show my parents, then bring them right back. Dad's ears perked up the other day when I told him you were taking pictures of the cows."

"Can I go with him, Mama? We wouldn't be gone long, and I'd get to see Mrs. Lane's tree. You know she always has a beautiful Christmas tree."

Mary debated her answer. "I suppose it is only up to the Lanes. Tell Ann I send holiday greetings, and we should get together soon."

"Thank you, Mama. I'll be sure to tell her." Katie headed for the doorway. "I'll be right back," she said over her shoulder.

"These pictures are very good, Mrs. Byler. She has a better eye than I do, and I have some experience at picture-taking."

"This seems to be helping Katie enjoy life again," Mary said. "That pneumonia took a lot out of her."

Katie came back into the kitchen wearing a new dress, cap, and fresh apron. "You didn't need to get all gussied up for my parents," Mark responded.

"Sure I did. We Amish ladies have pride, too, you know," Katie countered. Mary chuckled while they went out the door, pictures in hand.

"Thank you for inviting me," Katie said.

"I don't remember inviting you," Mark replied with a grin.

"But I played off your lead rather well, don't you think?"

"Oh, Katie! I thought of something painful, or I couldn't have kept a straight face."

"What did you think about?"

"I pretended you didn't like me."

"By the way, I didn't get cleaned up for your mom and dad."

They held hands all the way to Mark's house, down on the seat where no one could see them.

Ann heard the car door slam. "That's gotta be Mark."

"Uh huh," Harold said, not looking up from the stack of receipts he was sorting.

Ann watched out the dining room window, waiting for Mark to come into view. "I wonder why he's parking in the driveway, instead of across the road like—"

Harold looked up when she quit talking mid-sentence. Her mouth hung open as she stared out the window. He joined her, leaning sideways to get a glimpse out the window, too. He let out a soft whistle.

"Get back to the table," Ann hissed. "Let's pretend we didn't see them."

As Katie stepped onto the porch they heard her say, "That would be a great shot of the cats in their ragged winter coats sitting on the step of the old shanty."

Harold and Ann glanced at each other with a look that would have been truly a great shot. Katie came through the kitchen door first, while Mark held the door for her. She was beaming like a lantern on a new moon night. Ann rose and greeted her with a big hug and a warm, "Merry Christmas."

Harold rose, too. "Likewise."

Katie returned their warm greeting and passed her mother's message on to Ann.

"I brought Katie because I wanted you to see the pictures she's taken with the new camera," Mark said.

"Let's spread them out on the table," Harold suggested. "Mark has told us how enthusiastic you are to photograph nature. Did those books you always enjoyed help?"

"Very much, Mr. Lane. If I could have one of my pictures displayed in such a way it would be an honor."

"Let's see what you've taken so far."

"We didn't bring all of them. These are the fifteen pictures Mark liked the best."

Katie handed them to Harold, and he laid them out on the table, ignoring the receipts strewn everywhere. Mark pointed out the five best, including one of the Byler cows.

"These are *really* good," Ann exclaimed.

"This is only her first experience," Mark said. "She'll get much better as time goes on. I think two or three of them could win prizes at the Wilson County Fair."

Ann squeezed his arm. "That probably wouldn't be allowed."

He turned to Katie. "I'm sorry. I didn't know that."

"It's okay. But it is nice to know you think they are that good."

"I like this one of the cows," Harold opined. "It's almost like they're ready to speak."

"Yeah," Katie replied. "Feed me. Milk me. I'm thirsty. Clean my stall."

Everyone laughed.

"If Katie can bring her own cows to life, imagine what she could do with Molly and Midnight," Mark said.

Harold gave a nod then remarked to Katie, "I was just telling Mark the other day that we should document Midnight's growth with pictures at frequent intervals. If he becomes a famous stud bull, they might come in handy. Do you think you're up to the job, Katie? If you do, it's yours."

"I can't accept money, Mr. Lane, but I am happy to do it."

"I don't want you to spend your own money on this, so I'll buy the film and pay for the developing. I also heard what you said about the shot of the cats. I'd like you to create a photo album titled Lane Farms. It might contain two hundred pictures or more taken of the fields and meadows, woods, cattle, and buildings from a professional photographer's viewpoint. To the right eye, the lower farm is a treasure trove of old, outdated American farming with more dilapidated buildings, a varied landscape, and a fair-sized stream. Do you see what I mean?" Harold asked.

"I do, and I would love to do it," Katie answered.

"Then we've got a deal."

"I hate to break up this business meeting, but if I don't get Katie back soon, we're going to catch it from Mrs. Byler."

"But I want to see the Christmas tree," Katie objected.

Mark accompanied her into the living room and turned the tree lights on at Katie's request.

"It's so beautiful," she gushed. "Thank you for showing it to me."

Once they were alone, Harold and Ann sat at the table looking at each other. "I see storm clouds on the horizon," Harold said.

Ann nodded. "We may have to find new friends."

"Did you see? He was holding the door for her."

"She was beaming," Ann added.

"*We* didn't bring them all" Harold repeated.

"These are the fifteen *Mark* liked the best," Ann mimicked.

"This is only her first experience" Harold said with a twinkle in his eye.

"Stop it!" Ann scolded him, before saying, "She will get much better."

Harold concluded, "Thank you for showing it to me." They chorused, "May heaven have mercy."

Even before the lighthearted moment had passed, uneasiness clouded Ann's mind. Katie was, after all, the daughter of her close friend.

"I think that went fairly well," Mark said on the drive back to the Byler farm. When she didn't respond he touched her arm. "Katie?"

"Yes?"

"Where were you just now?"

"I guess I was daydreaming."

"A penny for your thoughts?" No response.

After a few moments she broke the silence. "Was that really your dad's idea? About Midnight, I mean, and the photo album?"

"He thinks it was, and that's all that's important."

Katie smiled and shook her head. "You know you can't enter my pictures at the fair, don't you? I can't take the money."

"If you want to see how good your pictures are, we could enter them and refuse the prize money."

"That's an idea," she said, as they entered the springhouse for the eggs. "I'm learning a lot from you, but I'm not sure it's all good."

"Why on earth would you say that?"

"It just feels *too* good. I feel jealousy and doubt creeping in."

"What are you jealous of?"

"Your family relationship. Your life. How easily you navigate it."

"What do you doubt?"

"Whether I belong there."

"So life is supposed to be hard? We're supposed to do without? It's bad if we're having fun?"

"Our worlds are so different. All of a sudden it scares me," Katie murmured.

"We're not either of our societies. We're two people who care for each other—just learning to care for each other, actually. All I want is that you give us a chance."

As Katie filled the egg bucket, Mark continued, "I'm not giving up on us." But he was growing alarmed. Her whole demeanor seemed to spiral downward. She was no longer the Bright Eyes he knew so well. A darkness lurked there that he did not recognize.

"I don't know what's come over me. Let me think this through," she said.

He held out his arms to her. She came into them, though Mark could feel her detachment and sense she wasn't giving mentally to the embrace. He tried whispering soft words to her and kissed her hair at the front of her cap. Nothing seemed to help.

"What if I'm never accepted in your world or feel comfortable there? I need to have time to sort this all out. It would be best if we didn't see each other until then so my judgment is not clouded by my emotions. I will contact you when I am at peace with it."

Mark returned home in a daze... no apologies, no lovelorn eyes, just a sharp and sudden put-off.

His mind reeled. Was it really his voice telling Katie he would respect her wishes and not contact her until she reached out to him?

Had he gone mad?

Chapter Nineteen

Mark's worst fear had become a reality, and it was painfully clear that he had a mountain to climb. Two, actually. It wasn't like he'd gone into this unaware, or even naïve. He had simply hoped it was an Appalachian mountain – maybe the Rockies, even. Just not an Andes or Himalayan, he'd asked God. He tried to console himself – Lord knew no one else could do it. If he didn't make the climb, he'd never be on top of the world.

Mark gave Katie the space she requested. He existed without her for more than three weeks. Throughout their separation, he hunkered down - withdrawing within himself. Harold and Ann saw the change, but there was nothing they could do. Ann would stop at the Bylers' for eggs, and Mary usually waited on her. Each assumed that a tiff had occurred between their children, and each had their own reason for avoiding the topic. Ann even bought eggs at the grocery store to avoid the awkward situation.

January's weather was typical - cold with snow - and it seemed like the whole world was hibernating. Peggy was working on her quilt and finally came to a point where she could use Katie's help. She could have sought out her mother's advice, but the knowledge she had gained in December while snooping through Mark's room drew her toward the Bylers'. Then she had a dream that demanded a response.

The sun was shining, and the temperature was above freezing for the first time in weeks. Peggy asked the school bus driver to let her off at the Amish farm at the end of Old Mill Road.

Mary greeted her cordially and invited her in. "Would you like some hot tea or hot chocolate, Peggy?"

"No, thank you. I was hoping to talk to Katie about my quilt."

"She's in her room. Let me see if it's all right for you to join her." Mary soon returned and informed Peggy that Katie had fallen asleep. "Wait a couple minutes then go on back. How are things going at Lane Farms?"

"I think everyone is just trying to survive the winter," Peggy replied.

"Amen to that," Mary said. She glanced toward the doorway as a sleepy-looking Katie shuffled into the kitchen. Katie brightened when Peggy greeted her.

"I need a hot tea," Katie announced. "How do you take yours, Peggy?"

Peggy smiled impishly and shrugged as she glanced toward Mary. "A little milk and a teaspoon of sugar."

When the tea was ready, Katie suggested that they go to her room where it was warm and comfortable.

"This is comfy," Peggy enthused as they entered.

"I've got my own stove, so I can keep it where I like it. Have a seat in the rocker," she offered, easing herself onto the edge of the bed.

"We've missed you," Peggy said. Katie raised an eyebrow as she processed the statement. "Our house isn't the same without you in it."

"I'm rarely in your house."

"You're in Mark's heart, so you're always there. But Mark hasn't been himself. I know it's cold, gray, and depressing, but there's another depression that fills our house. How long have you been away from my brother?"

"Twenty-two days," she answered with a sigh.

"For that same number, Mark has escaped inward, and you have battled the enemy alone. Have you imagined your world without him?"

"I have been without him," Katie stressed.

"And what has it been like?"

"A world without love."

"What was life like before the enemy infected our homes?"

"Filled with love and joy."

"Mark is doing what he believes he must. He is waiting. What were his final words to you the last time you spoke?"

"'I'm not giving up on us.'"

Katie sighed as she thought back over the last three weeks. She was alone. It had been a January of mental unrest. So many nights of despair while clutching Raggedy Andy and just trying to hold on. And her days had been filled with pain as her emotions pulled her further into the abyss. There were times she feared she might succumb, but some small event kept her going.

It had not been a total loss, she knew. Near the beginning, she had gone to Sampson's Drug Store and bought four rolls of film: one in black and white, and three in color. When the snow and cold came and the melancholy had overtaken her, Katie escaped out into the winter with her insulated camera case, her telephoto lens, and her film. She had poured her anguish into her pictures. She went everywhere... on a sunny day, a cloudy one, and in a snowstorm.

Katie had taken ninety-six pictures to help fulfill her promise to Harold Lane. She had pictures of the meadow with huge snowflakes falling. She had Lane's lower farm, her own family farm, and the Wagners' ponds with ducks sitting on the ice. With her telephoto lens, she had captured three deer standing at the edge of the woods.

Katie smiled inwardly as she thought of the picture of the cats by the shanty door and Midnight in his pen. She had a picture of those, too. While the winter weather and the battle in her mind had threatened her, Katie had used them to create. The four rolls of film now sat in a row on her table, undeveloped.

"This enemy you speak of. Do you know him?" Katie asked.

"We all fight the enemy in one form or another."

"I have prayed mightily and not heard an answer."

"Not until today. I awoke this morning with many things on my heart. I believe they're for you from God. Message number one: 'Tell her I have already answered her prayers in the hospital. If she didn't believe Me then, why would she believe Me now?'"

"Why did you break away from Mark?" Peggy inquired.

"I went to your house to show your parents the pictures, and a wave of doubt swept over me. I care for Mark very much, but I felt inadequate. I felt I would not be good enough for him. That I would not measure up to his world."

"Now it all makes sense," Peggy said. "Message number two: 'Tell her the enemy does not come once and admit defeat, but he comes again and again.

Tell her as long as she lives, she will have to be on guard. When she could not be defeated physically, the enemy came against her mentally.'"

Peggy sat beside Katie on the bed and took her hand. "When I awoke this morning, I knew I had to come to see you. I asked, 'Why me, God?' I think I know the answer. You are already doing His work in me."

"In you, Peggy? I don't understand."

"I was so inspired by your and Mark's experience in the hospital that I have decided to dedicate my life to nursing and helping others. God has had His say, and now I want to have mine. These feelings of yours that you aren't worldly enough, or smart enough, or good enough for Mark - I know my brother, and he's getting the better deal here."

The corners of Katie's mouth turned up. "Do you really think so?"

"I know so, and you'll find out eventually. I told you, we're friends for life, and I meant it. We girls have to stick together."

Katie felt the weight of winter's darkness lifting from her shoulders as she stood. She and Peggy locked in a firm embrace. "Our God has a sense of humor, Katie. I mean, look at Mark as a great example." They shared a look of understanding and chuckled.

"God had a third message for you, but you'll have to figure this one out for yourself. He said, 'Tell Katie her guardian angel is weeping constantly, and it's driving Me crazy.'" Katie burst into laughter, and Peggy joined her.

"Is there any chance of you coming to my house tomorrow afternoon to advise me on my quilt?" Peggy asked.

"I could come about two."

"That'll work. Thanks, Katie."

"Give Mark a message for me. Tell him to come for eggs at mid-morning, and that I'll be upstairs in the barn cleaning it out."

"What if we don't need eggs?"

"Tell him to get some anyway."

As Mark's car approached the Byler farm, he could see the big barn doors were slightly ajar at the top of the barnhill. He parked in the courtyard and walked up to the doors. The scent of hay filled his senses when he stepped inside. He stood there for a minute, allowing his eyes to become accustomed to the dim light.

Mark could hear her before he saw her. She was moving something in the back of the barn. He called to her, and she appeared, as if by magic, from a darkened doorway. She was silhouetted by the sunbeams streaming through the gaps between the boards behind her.

He moved toward her, and Katie broke into a run - a mixture of joy and desperation displayed on her face. She leapt high into his arms as he encircled her thighs and held her against him. While framing his face with her hands, Katie leaned down and kissed the top of his head. He held her there, never wanting to let her go. She wrapped her arms around his neck and pressed him to her, burying his face between her breasts while she hugged him in an embrace of pure joy.

Mark let her slide down along him until he could look into her eyes. "I'm never letting you go," he told her huskily.

"You'd better not, or I would be sad."

They broke into a laughter of relief and rapture, and Mark eased her to the floor. Katie held onto him for dear life, refusing to release him.

"I'm so sorry," she croaked.

He forced a space between them, and Katie's eyes begged for mercy. "Forgive me, Mark."

He wiped away a tear with each thumb. "I do forgive you. Now show me your bright eyes again."

She smiled, overwhelming his senses.

"How can I tell you how precious you are to me?" he asked.

"You can show me instead."

"Just tell me what to do."

"Let me jump into your arms again. That was fun."

Mark nudged her toward the back of the barn. Katie turned to face him when she reached the back wall. She undid her cap and let it fall to the floor. Her beautiful hair cascaded about her. She looked steadily into his eyes and broke into a run.

"Bright Eyes!" Mark called out as she neared him, and Katie leapt into his arms again - higher still than before.

"Hold me against you," she implored, sliding down over him once more, while golden waves of hair surrounded him. When her feet reached the floor, he buried his face into the crook of her neck, while she surrendered to him eagerly.

"I love your hair," Mark exuded, inhaling its aroma.

"I've been waiting all morning to drown you in it," she told him between shivers.

"Drown me with all of you," he begged, holding her tightly against him.

"Running and jumping feels so good! Let's do it again."

So they did, and then again. As she slid down over him, she looked into his eyes and asked, "Is this the kind of fun you meant?"

"We're getting there. Show me more."

"Sure," she said.

When Mark caught her this time, Katie wrapped her legs around his waist, locking her ankles behind his back. He held her there, and she pressed against him while her heart pounded against his chest.

"You're breathing hard," he said.

"Life can be hard and fun at the same time, you know. Even though this is getting harder."

"Are you ready to quit?"

"Not unless you are."

So they did it again and again, until both were exhausted. When Katie had her fill, she asked sweetly, "Did you need some eggs?"

"One dozen please," Mark answered, as Katie pinned and tucked her hair back under her cap. "Now where were we, before we were so rudely interrupted?"

"We were learning to care for each other, remember? And I believe you were about to kiss me," Katie informed him.

"No, I wasn't."

"You should have been."

Mark took her in his arms, and Katie raised her lips to meet his. They kissed softly and tentatively. When they parted, Katie said, "See, I told you so."

Mark lived up to his reputation of not knowing when to quit. "You seem to be better than me at knowing what I should do next, so what is it?"

"I think you should kiss me again. I'm not sure we got it right the first time."

After a sweet kiss, Mark asked, "How was it this time?"

"Better. I think we're beginning to get the hang of it." Katie stepped in close and laced her fingers behind his neck. "And what would you do if I was to hold you like this and wouldn't let you go? Would you be able to read my mind?"

She gazed into his eyes, and more words were unnecessary. When they finally parted a third time, she smiled. "Perhaps, your mind-reading powers are returning."

"You and Mark made up," Peggy said as she pulled Katie into Grandad's room and closed the door.

"How did you guess?" Katie asked innocently.

"You have an airport spotlight shining from your face."

Katie smiled. "We're all better now."

"Better than before?" Peggy questioned. At her reluctance to answer, Peggy made a face. "Awww, come on, Katie. We're friends!"

"Well... he kissed me."

"What was it like?" Peggy pried.

"Soft and gentle, romantic."

"Was that your first kiss?"

"Of course."

"Wow, Katie Byler got Mark to kiss her. I'll bet you had to ask him, didn't you?"

Katie blushed. "I'm not telling."

"I knew it! I knew you'd have to prod him 'cause he wouldn't have the nerve to do it himself. Did he kiss you only once, or were there more kisses?"

"I am not answering any more questions," Katie stated emphatically.

Peggy teased, "Mark's got a girlfriend." Katie couldn't keep the smile from her face.

They had Peggy's quilt problem straightened out in plenty of time for them to sit and talk. "I told Mark to make sure he's back by three, if that's all right with you?"

"Why did you tell him that?"

"So he could take you home. Plus, I want to see him squirm when he's around you. There's something I've been dying to tell you. I just don't know if this is the right time, with you and Mark patching it up."

"You've got my attention, for sure."

"I was snooping in his room last month, and I found a bunch of poems he's written. One was titled, *Bright Eyes*. I think Mark wrote it for you."

"Will you keep a secret?"

"You know I will."

"Bright Eyes is what Mark calls me in private."

"Has he given you the poem?"

"Not yet."

Peggy frowned. "I shouldn't be ruining your surprise.

"But that was nothing compared to what else I found: two large pictures Mark had drawn of you. They were done with colored pencils, but you'd swear they were photographs." The words had no sooner left Peggy's mouth when she gasped. "Oh, Katie! I never thought about your beliefs against pictures of people. You're not going to be mad at him, are you?"

"No, I won't be mad."

"It's just that they are soooo good-looking. You look beautiful in both of them."

"What's in the pictures?" Katie asked.

"The one is a picture of you standing behind the counter in the bake shop in your summer attire. You have a big smile on your face, and your eyes are glowing. Mark titled it, *I'm So Glad You Came*."

Katie's reaction confused Peggy. The happiness had left the older girl's eyes. "What is it, Katie? What did I say wrong?"

"It's not you, Peggy. It's me. It's a long story, but Mark never saw me looking like that in the bake shop. Don't mind me. What was the other picture?"

Peggy hesitated. "It's really not my place to tell. Not if you and Mark are only friends. I will say this, though, it opened my eyes to your true beauty. I didn't realize it until I saw the picture, but you're better looking than I am. I don't mean to offend you, but it's the Amish look that hides it."

Katie chose her words carefully. "Would you accept me as more than a friend to Mark?"

"Oh, yes! I like you, and you are good for my brother."

"Then tell me about this other picture."

"Mark has captured you so beautifully," Peggy began. "Not as a friend, but as a woman. I knew it was love the moment I saw it." Peggy described the picture in detail. "You looked so mature, so in love, and the drawing seemed so otherworldly, somehow. He titled it, 'I Await My Prince.'" Peggy sighed. "Mark has never seen you in a yellow sundress with your hair falling all about you, has he?"

"No," Katie answered. It was only half a lie.

Peggy heard a car door close. She glanced out the window to see Mark trudging up the driveway along the snow piles lining the edge of the yard. "It's Mark."

The kitchen door opened and closed. Peggy and Katie heard the footsteps slowly approach, and Mark poked his head inside their room. He saw four shining eyes returning his gaze.

"Why is the door closed?" he asked.

"For girl privacy. Don't you ever knock?" Peggy quipped.

"Yeah, I'll knock. Knock your block off," he said with a grin.

"Now children, behave," Katie scolded them.

Peggy sprang from the couch. "I'll let you visit while I go to the kitchen and fix a cup of tea. Can I get one for anyone else?"

"I'd like that," Katie replied.

"Sure, Sis. Make yourself useful."

After Peggy left and closed the door, Katie stood and went to Mark. "Don't be too hard on her. She admires you, you know."

"I suppose, but she can be so aggravating."

"And she learned it from….?" Katie said with a twinkle in her eye.

Mark put his arms around her and she leaned into his embrace. "I've been thinking about this morning," he said into her ear. "It was so fantastic!"

"What part?"

"All of it."

"Any special parts you liked better?" she persisted.

"If you made me choose the best part, it would be when you asked me to kiss you. However, my memory of that part is not clear like the rest. Would you help me remember it better? I've been wondering if you'll ever let me kiss you again."

Katie ran her hands up his back. "I guess if you don't try, you'll never know."

Mark released her and stepped away. She matched him look for look, only this time there was no darkened barn. Bright sunlight shone in the windows. He leaned down ever so slowly, taking it all in, absorbing this moment completely: her face as she tilted it upwards, the hair he adored, the freckles under the enchanting eyes which held his gaze, the lips - those beautiful red lips -the long, slender, pale neck in need of the summer sun, and the ample breasts gently rising and falling with each breath.

He leaned closer and touched his lips to hers. Softly and tenderly he caressed them – sending out tendrils of sweet longing. An eagerness rose within him, and he kissed her with more energy, more passion, as he parted his lips against hers. This was what he wanted – what he had always dreamt of.

Katie could wait no more. She threw her arms around him and pulled him to her, matching his parted lips with her own passion. She trembled in his arms and let herself be swept away. When they separated, she looked into his eyes and sighed, "Oh, Mark!" She laid her head on his shoulder and pressed herself into him.

Mark was not the only Lane who could plan. Peggy left the room and closed the door. She grabbed her coat as she passed through the mudroom then went quietly through the large dining room and into the hall which lead to the front door. She moved just as she had rehearsed it earlier. The door was already unlocked, as well as the storm door. She slipped out through them, careful not to make a sound. She stepped onto the porch that ran the full width of the house, then approached the big window and carefully peeked inside. She need not worry about disrupting the participants within, for they were completely absorbed in each other.

Peggy saw it all and marveled at the event. When it was over, the lovebirds sat on the couch talking and making 'goo-goo' eyes at one another. Peggy was cold and lightly tapped on the window. A startled couple looked her way, and she gave them an exuberant double thumbs-up. While Mark snapped the shade down, Peggy's last glimpse into the room was Katie laughing in the background.

Chapter Twenty

"You seem happy for the first time in weeks," Mary said to her daughter on Sunday evening as they shared time over tea.

"I feel good about a number of things, Mama. I'm excited I'll be seeing my pictures soon, and this rare, sunny weekend lifted my spirits. Peggy is becoming a good friend, and I enjoy the female companionship. I know you have been concerned about this since Lydia moved away."

"Have you considered attending the Sunday Sings?" her mother asked. "Deborah mentioned to me today that it has been a long time since you've been there. I told her I'd speak to you about it."

"Someday soon Mama, but you know why I haven't gone lately, and I'm still not ready."

Katie stared at her hands. How could she tell her mother that she didn't want to go to Sunday Sings? How could she tell her parents she wanted to spend her time with Mark Lane? They would be heartbroken and would never consent for her to see him, and there would be severe consequences.

"I haven't seen Ann in a couple of weeks," Mary said. "Did you see her yesterday when you helped Peggy with her quilt?"

"No, she and Brenda had gone shopping. It was just Peggy and me."

"I noticed that Mark brought you home." Katie maintained a cool exterior in spite of the churning she felt inside. She could never divulge the extent to which she and Mark had made amends.

"Yes, he said he had to go see Jim Fowler about skating on Wagner's pond next Saturday. He offered me a ride, since he was going right past."

"It's a shame you don't have Lydia's pond for skating. You really enjoyed that."

"It was the most fun I had all winter. Even sled riding at the Sings was second. Peggy will probably be going skating on Saturday, too. I suppose I could ask her if it would be all right for Jacob and me to join them. I just hate to invite myself."

"I know what you mean," Mary said. "You're always wanted at the Sings."

"I think I'll retire to my room and do some reading." Then Katie added, "I forgot to take my film when I went to help Peggy, so Mark will stop and get it on his way to school tomorrow."

In her room, Katie sat on her rocking chair and let her mind drift. She hated deceiving her mother, but if she didn't, she and Mark were over. She tilted the chair back, closed her eyes, and thought of being with Mark the day before. "I'm never going to let you go," he had said. She wondered if he really meant "never." She thought of their sweet kisses in the morning and then moved on to the afternoon. He had boldly kissed her, and the sharp need that arose in her surprised her. She relived the fire that passed through her and let it sweep her away once more.

Katie retrieved her journal and began to write. An hour and three pages later, she retired to bed feeling content.

The next evening, Katie was in her room day-dreaming about Mark again. He had entered the barn quietly as she milked the cows. She felt his hand on her back as he took the bucket from under the cow and set it aside. He raised her off her feet as high as his arms would reach. While she looked down at him in wonder, he said, "Good Morning. I wanted to see if you still looked as good up there." He smiled, and she turned to putty in his hands. He put her down and kissed her, right there between the cows, then nuzzled her neck.

"It tickles," she told him. Katie recalled her spontaneous shivers, and once again, felt the heat that had surged through her.

Mark left as quickly as he had come, taking her film, promising to be back on Thursday after school, and leaving her wanting more: more kisses, more cuddling, more shivers, and definitely more Mark.

Now with only her desires for company, Katie reached again for the two poems lying on the quilt beside her. She nearly had the second one memorized. *Winter Blues* she read at the top of one, and *Sunny Skies* was on the other.

Katie had finished her early morning chores, and came to the house for breakfast. She was washing up at the sink in her room and reached into her pocket to retrieve her hanky. She knew instantly what they were when her fingers touched them. She smiled as she unfolded the papers. Her heart soared now, as it had done this morning, when she read the second one.

I see her there within God's beauty.
While sunbeams dance she rushes to me.
She leaves her feet and floats on air,
And surrounds me with her golden hair.

Katie couldn't hold the tears back then, as she couldn't hold them back now. They flowed freely as the full measure of Mark's love radiated from the page.

On Thursday afternoon, Katie answered the door eagerly when Mark knocked carrying a bag. "You're in a good mood today," he said.

"I'm in a good mood because of what you have for me."

"What makes you think I have anything for you?"

Katie reached to take the bag from him, but Mark was too quick. "Oh, no! Trying to steal the kids' candy," he said. "Shame on you!"

He now had five sets of young eyes on him. He reached into the bag and pulled out a package of Tootsie Rolls and one of lollipops. "Who wants some?" he asked.

Mark passed two of each to everyone except three-year-old Ruthie, whom he gave one lollipop. Before Katie could get her situated, Mark said, "Let's give her a horsey ride."

"No, Mark," Katie shook her head. "Mama will be home any minute."

"Party pooper," Mark said, as he scooped Ruthie up and handed her to Jacob. As Mark got down on all fours, he instructed Jacob to balance her on his back.

Around the living room they went while Ruthie squealed in delight. Rebecca asked, "Can I do it too, Mark?" Mark looked to Katie with raised eyebrows.

"Oh, all right!" And she joined the fun.

Rebecca rode Mark, and Daniel rode Jacob. Around and around they went, bumping into one another and sprawling across the living room floor. Sarah sat on the couch, sucking her lollipop and clapping while Katie laughed. Ruthie ran and jumped on the pile. Everyone was having a great time, but the scene in the room was mayhem.

Mark looked up to see Mrs. Byler standing in the doorway, her mouth agape. Katie saw the surprise on Mark's face and followed his gaze to where her mother stood. Katie yanked Ruthie off the pile, as the other four struggled to their feet. They stood in a row, waiting for judgment to be handed down, or in Mark's case, handed up.

"Where did you get that sucker?" Mary asked Sarah. She pointed at Mark. Rebecca shouted, "Horsey, horsey!" pointing at Mark. Everyone laughed, and even Mary couldn't keep a straight face. She looked from Mark to Katie. "Don't you two have something better to do, such as pictures to sort?"

Mark handed her the two bags of candy. "Sorry, Mrs. Byler. These are for the kids."

"Thank you, Mark," she said as she took the bags. Gesturing toward Katie's hallway, she added, "Now git!"

Katie grabbed the bag with her pictures before she went.

She closed her bedroom door and looked at Mark. They burst into laughter, trying to keep it quiet, but looking at each other only made it worse. She fell into his arms and hooked her chin on his shoulder. Her pulse quickened and all she could think about was touching him.

"Dare I kiss you here?" he asked.

"Dare you not and see how that goes for you." He swallowed her words with his kiss.

"That's better, now let's look at the pictures," Katie said. She spread them across her bed from the earliest to the latest taken.

"Wow," Mark commented when the ninety-six pictures lay before him.

He held one up and studied it. "If you had a wide-angle lens, this one would have been a great shot. You could have been twice as close and still gotten everything in the picture. When's your birthday, Katie?"

"March fifth. When's yours?"

"I'm not telling. I never divulge my birthday."

Katie made a quick move with her eyes toward the door. As Mark nervously turned to see for himself, she slugged him on his arm just below the shoulder. "Owww! That hurt!"

"You deserved it," Katie said smugly.

"February fifth. Nine days from now, and counting."

"Why did you want to know my birthday?" She gave him a sweet, genuine smile and stepped in close, daring him to kiss her while trying to make him feel better.

"I'm going to buy you a wide-angle lens for your birthday," he replied.

"Why did you tell me that? You sure know how to ruin a surprise."

"Some things are better than being surprised. You'll have five weeks of anticipation. Each time you take a shot, you can visualize the same shot if you were much closer, and could still capture the entire scene."

"I just have one request. Will you please surprise me on my birthday next year?" Being of reasonably sound mind, Mark agreed that he would.

They analyzed the pictures, chose the ones for the Lanes' photo album, and separated the negatives to get reprints. "The quality of some of these shots is phenomenal," he said. "I love this one of the bankhouse with the huge snowflakes falling and the snow hanging off the roof. Weren't you cold?"

"Yes, and tired from walking through the deep snow, but now that I see the picture, it was worth it. Cold as I was, I couldn't help wishing that this was the storm we battled in the bankhouse."

"Especially, if it was just the two of us." Mark winked at her.

"And some nice warm blankets," Katie added with a smile and a caress on his arm.

"What's with the snow angel?" he asked.

"It's a picture for your poem."

"These black-and- white photos really make you feel the winter, and I want you to go ice skating with us on Saturday."

"Where did that come from?" Katie asked.

"I just remembered you told me you liked to skate on Lydia's pond. I should have thought of it sooner."

187

"I can't go at your invitation," she said. "My parents must never think we want to do anything together."

"I understand. I don't like it, but I understand."

Mark hugged her one last time, and she whispered into his ear, "Thank you for the surprise in my pocket on Monday. You really do understand surprises, don't you?"

"I understand you, or I'm willing to concede to you, Katie."

"Did I ever tell you how much I love the sound of my name coming off your lips?"

"That doesn't fall into the realm of pride, Katie dear?"

"No, that falls into the realm of love, Mark dearest."

The following afternoon, the Byler children were once again drawn to the front window when the screech of school bus brakes caught their ears. "It's Peggy!" Sarah said.

Mrs. Byler was waiting at the front door when Peggy ascended the porch steps. "More trouble with your quilt?" she asked as she invited her in.

"No, Katie got me straightened out last weekend. I came because of our ice skating dilemma tomorrow."

"Oh?" Mary asked, intrigued.

"We and the Fowlers usually get together a few Saturdays each winter to ice skate and play hockey on Wagner's pond. Betty Fowler came down with something last night and won't be able to come. That leaves us one short for playing hockey. Does Jacob know how to skate?" "Jacob is a good skater," Mary replied, "but he has never played hockey."

"We can teach him hockey, if he knows how to skate," Peggy said. "Mark will have him shipshape in no time."

"I don't doubt that he will. The skating might do Jacob some good. He's been winter-bound like the rest of us. The best skater in the family is Katie."

"I didn't know," Peggy remarked. "I'd love to have her come, also. How about the rest of the kids?"

"They don't have skates, I'm afraid. And it might be a little cold for them."

"I understand," Peggy said. "Anyone who wants to come on Saturday, right after lunch, would be more than welcome. Tell Jacob and Katie I'll see them tomorrow."

Mark was coming out of the barn when Peggy arrived back at Lane Farms. "How'd it go, Sis?"

"What a silly question," she said. "I talked with Mrs. Byler, and I'm sure Jacob and Katie will be there tomorrow."

Mark gave her an appreciative pat on the back. "Thanks for your help."

Peggy smiled and headed for the house. "Mark said he might be a little late for supper," she told her mom. Ann heard the tractor come to life across the road. She walked to the front window and watched Mark drive through the snow in the lane, all the way out of sight to the meadow.

When he returned, Ann was holding supper for him. "Everyone else has eaten. Get washed up, and I'll have yours on the table." Ann kept him company as he ate. "How'd it go on the Wagners' pond?"

"I cleared the usual spot and a little more. The snow was light, so it pushed easily. I'm going to call Mr. Wagner and get his okay to take the equipment and straw bales down through his lane tomorrow morning. I have to conserve my energy to beat Jim."

"Do you think Jim will let you?"

"Mom, are you trying to irritate me on purpose?" Mark asked with a grin.

Ann just smiled. "I better get the kitchen cleaned up."

Mark reached out and grabbed her forearm and looked up at her. "Thanks for holding supper."

She leaned down and kissed the top of his head. "You're welcome."

Peggy and Mark were sitting on the straw bales keeping warm by the fire when Katie and Jacob arrived.

"The gang is almost all here," Mark said as they approached.

"Is Jim still coming?" Katie asked nervously.

"Why, are you afraid you'll be drafted to take his place?" Mark returned.

"I was just wondering, is all."

189

"Don't let Mark fluster you," Peggy said. "If you don't want to play hockey, then you don't have to. Let's all lace up, so we can show you how to play."

Jacob was slinging pucks in the goal in no time, but Katie struggled. Peggy took her aside. "Just concentrate on the space between the legs of the sawhorse, and do what I do. Get the right mindset, then shoot swiftly and accurately." Peggy completed the maneuver with precision.

"What is this mindset you speak of?" Katie asked.

"Pretend it's Mark's head in that space." Their raucous laughter drew Mark's attention, but they paid him no mind. Soon Katie was making goals with regularity.

Mark was instructing Katie and Jacob on the fine art of passing when a voice called out from across the pond. "Afternoon there, cousins!" Jim Fowler waved as he trudged through the snow.

"Do you know Katie and Jacob Byler?" Mark asked.

"Just to wave in passing," Jim said, holding out his hand in greeting. When Jacob shook it, Jim commented, "Strong grip. I want him on my team." Jacob grinned and looked down.

"Why don't we let him choose?" Mark offered. "Whose team will it be Jacob, Jim's or mine?"

"I'll play with Mark, if that's okay."

Jim replied, "No offense taken. He's going to need all the help he can get anyway, especially with Peggy and me on the other team."

Mark and Jacob came close to winning one game, but Jim and Peggy won all of them.

Jim complimented Jacob on his play. "You did well for your first time. Keep practicing, and I'm sure you'll be beating Mark in no time."

"Did I hear you say he'd be beating you in no time?" Mark chimed in.

"Well, then at least someone could," Jim said with a smile.

Mark laughed, and Jim patted him on the back. "Your day will come. Better luck next time. It wouldn't be right if I just let you win? Same time next Saturday?" Jim asked.

Mark looked at Jacob. "Do you want to play again next Saturday?"

"Sure," Jacob responded eagerly.

"Betty will come next time," Jim said. "If Katie could play, we could have a three on three, which would be even more fun."

Everyone nodded their heads in agreement, except Katie, who just gave a weak smile.

"See you all next week," Jim called, as he headed for home, back across Byler's hollow and the fields to his parents' farm.

"Come and sit by the fire," Mark said to everyone.

"We didn't think to bring refreshments," Katie voiced sheepishly, as she watched Mark and Peggy set out brownies and hot chocolate.

"There's plenty for all," Mark assured her.

As they sat by the fire getting warm and enjoying their snack, Peggy blurted out, "Next Saturday is Mark's birthday. He's going to be King For A Day, and Mom will bake him his favorite cake."

"What kind is that?" Jacob asked.

"German chocolate, of course," Peggy replied. "You know Mark has a sweet tooth. It's that gooey, sweet stuff all over it and between the layers that he craves."

Mark grabbed a handful of snow and showered Peggy with it. "You talk too much. If Katie is going to play next week, we need to play some hockey to give her experience. Jacob! You and Peggy against Katie and me."

By the time they finished practicing, it was getting late, and Katie and Jacob still had the cows to milk. "I'll give you a ride home on the wagon," Mark told them.

"Just drop us off when you get to the road," Katie said, "We'll walk the rest of the way."

"And miss the opportunity to help you down off the wagon?" Mark asked when only she could hear.

On the ride to the Bylers', Peggy remarked, "I was thinking Sarah might like to learn how to skate. I have old skates I wore when I was ten or eleven. I'll bring them next Saturday in case your mom lets her come."

Mark stopped in front of the bake shop and hopped off the tractor. He went back to help Katie off the wagon. "See you next Saturday, Jacob."

"I'll talk to Papa about it. I'd sure like to come."

Mark stood beside the wagon just out of Katie's reach and held out his hand. She smiled and stepped forward, reaching out her hand for his while deftly overstepping the perimeter board. They locked hands, and Katie easily jumped to the ground.

"Thanks, Mark," she said. "I guess we won't need the bandages this time. And, thank you for a lovely day."

As Katie walked away, Mark called her name and went to her, out of Peggy's earshot. "Will you think of me while you milk the cows?" he asked.

"I always think of you now when I'm between the cows."

The following Saturday, everyone gathered again at Wagner's pond for another day of winter fun. Betty and Sarah attended, increasing the day's enjoyment.

They played three-on-three hockey with Mark's team winning the first game, but eventually losing the rubber match.

Jim and Betty left shortly thereafter, allowing the Bylers and Lanes time for leisurely skating. Mark turned his attention to Sarah.

"What can I help you with?" he asked her.

"My feet don't want to stay together. And when I hold them together, I fall over."

"Let's skate together, and I'll give you some suggestions." Mark held one hand out and Sarah clutched it gladly. After a little coaching and some failed attempts, Sarah could finally skate on her own, albeit unsteadily.

"All it takes is more practice," Mark encouraged her. "You'll be skating like a champ before we leave here today," he called after her to Sarah's delight. "Good job!" he shouted as she went by him the next time. "I'm watching you."

Katie glided over and came to a stop beside him. "Thank you for doing that. I'll take over now if you'd like to skate."

"No, I like standing here. It makes me feel important." She glanced sideways at him, and Mark knew she was waiting for the grin. But he was enjoying this and continued showing interest in Sarah's skating.

"She'll try harder if she knows someone is watching and truly cares about her progress," Mark said. "Sometimes all we need is for someone to believe in us."

Katie lost her balance and began to fall, but Mark caught her by the arm then steadied her for a moment. "I *believed* that if I was falling, you would catch me before I did," Katie attested with a twinkle in her eye.

Mark gave her a look of admiration. "You're good," he said. "Do you also grant birthday wishes?"

"Maybe. Depends on what it is."

"Give me a kiss for every year since I was born."

"And how many years is that?"

"Sixty-two," Mark replied emphatically. Katie muffled a laugh with her gloves, and the merriment shone from her eyes.

As the afternoon wound to a close, Mark started a snowball battle that soon escalated out of control with everyone pelting everyone else. Katie scored a direct hit on Mark's shoulder that showered him with snow. She laughed triumphantly, raised her arms in the air, and exclaimed, "Yay! I hit my mark."

Mark raised his hands above his head, "I surrender!"

Peggy skated slowly by him and said, "I hit my Mark! Are you going steady now?"

"Shut up, Piglet," Mark snapped. Even though the exchange was meant for only their ears, Katie overheard it.

When it was time to go, Sarah thanked Peggy for inviting her and allowing her to use the skates. Peggy gave Sarah a hug and told her she was glad they fit so she could learn to skate. Sitting on the wagon waiting to leave, Peggy placed the skates in Sarah's lap.

"I can't wear these anymore, and I want you to have them. I hope you enjoy them as much as I did."

Sarah rode all the way home smiling happily.

Before leaving the frozen playground, Katie gave Mark a brown paper bag. "Happy birthday. I made you some cookies."

"What kind?"

"Sugar cookies, of course. There is also a poem at the bottom of the bag. It isn't as good as yours, but I hope you enjoy it. You've written several for me, and I wanted to reciprocate. It's like a story, only written as a poem. It's all right to give me pointers on it later if you'd like. It's my first poem ever, so don't be too critical."

Mark squeezed her hand as he took the bag and thanked her all the while their eyes said what their lips could not. Alone in his room, Mark opened the sack and found a half-dozen crunchy sugar cookies. Katie had wrapped them in waxed paper, which puzzled him until he looked beneath them and found a hand-knitted, dark-blue scarf. He pulled it out and wrapped it around his neck. He thought of Katie's face pressed there and how warm that felt.

Katie's poem was folded and laying at the bottom of the bag.

Kisses, Hugs, and Stuff

When I close my eyes I can see your face,
As I still feel the power of the good Lord's grace.
I reached for your hand and found comfort there.
It filled me with peace where there once was despair.

I remember the poems you have given to me,
One about a spider and another about a bee.
I gaze at three pictures hanging here in my room.
Without you in my life there'd be silence and gloom.

For you are the voice ringing loud in my ear,
Bringing arms full of hugs, joy and good cheer.
Kisses and more kisses, let that be my fate.
Come give me your kisses if it's early or late.

He knew Katie would be pleased if he committed her poem to memory. It was truly a labor of love, which he accomplished by lights out.

Katie's sweet voice saying, "I hit my mark!" was his last memory before sleep overtook him.

Chapter Twenty-One

The following week brought milder weather, and it seemed like Mother Nature might at last be easing her grip. To Mark and Katie, the weather didn't matter. In fact, there was very little that could faze them anymore for they had a belief in each other. But in spite of that, they each had their mental insecurities to deal with.

Mark feared that Katie would reject his world in favor of her own. Hadn't she almost done so already? And he couldn't help but wonder if she was finally opening her eyes to a particular boy, or boys in general. Would she also open her eyes to the Amish boys around her? He took comfort in the fact that she had made no moves to reconnect with youth social gatherings since her hospital stay. He was well aware of Amish courting procedures, and Katie was almost eighteen. That fact was never far from his mind.

Katie wondered about the girls at Mark's school. Surely there were pretty girls whom he could give his attentions to: English girls with makeup, jewelry and fancy clothes. What did she have compared to them: dirty fingers from farm work, a milk bucket, and high-topped leather work shoes? Sometimes she felt inadequate and wondered why he'd even been interested in her in the first place.

When Mark stopped at the Byler farm on his way home from school, Katie was unusually quiet as she retrieved the eggs from the can in the water trough.

"Cat got your tongue?" Mark finally asked.

"No," she replied. "I'm just unsure how to ask you something."

Mark gently turned her toward him. "Don't be apprehensive about asking me anything. Not ever."

She ventured carefully, "I want to be with you, and I have been wishing we could live out your poem, *Snow Angel*."

"You mean make snow angels together?" he asked. She nodded. "When?"

"The moon will be out tonight, and the temperatures are warmer," she said. "We could meet at Wagner's pond."

Mark couldn't help smiling a little. "What a great idea."

Katie's demeanor brightened, and she gave him a big smile. "You're not upset at my asking?"

"Are you kidding? Why would you think I might be?"

"You might think me too forward. Peggy said the English girls approach you at school, and you pretty much ignore them."

"She did, did she? You can stop worrying about me ever ignoring you. I don't ignore the girls at school because they're forward. I don't chase after them because I have no interest in them."

"And you have an interest in me?" Katie pressed.

"I'm here getting eggs when we don't need eggs."

She would have reached for him, but they heard the barn door slide open just outside the springhouse.

She handed the egg bucket to Mark. "We'll talk more tonight. How about eleven o'clock?"

"I'll be there," he assured her.

Mark lit a small fire and set the straw bales near it. There were a few clouds in the sky but still lots of light from the half-moon. He watched Katie coming toward him across the Byler and Wagner fields. The night felt balmy compared to what it had been lately. Still, the fire took the chill out of the air and the light made it possible to fully appreciate Katie's beauty as she entered its golden glow. They embraced, and she sat beside him on a straw bale.

"Is there any chance you were seen leaving the house?" Mark asked.

"Very little. My parents' room is on the opposite end of the house and faces the road. This is my third nighttime walk in the last four, so my tracks won't mean anything either."

"You've had trouble sleeping lately?"

"Not really. I've been making tracks in the snow so tonight's tracks aren't the first."

Mark gazed upon this girl who had stolen his heart. For the first time, he was truly alone with her - even at the hospital they weren't alone. He wished she could see into the depths of him so she could see the love he felt for her that filled his inner chambers and raced through the hallways of his mind. Their road ahead was unclear, and the end was not assured. He knew the end as he saw it, but he didn't know how to inspire Katie to join him in his dream. She's my dream, he thought. How do I become hers? A voice on the inside said, "Show her who you are. Show her your heart."

Mark rose, turned to face Katie, and bowed. "Milady, are you ready for tonight's performance?" Her eyes flickered in the firelight as he began his recitation. *"When I close my eyes I can see your face..."* He continued without a flaw to the end of the poem.

Katie clapped her approval. "Do you like it?"

"It's as good as I could have done," he said honestly. He leaned down and kissed her tenderly. "It's a wonderful poem to match the wonderful girl who wrote it."

Katie looked into the fire then at Mark. She seemed content, but thoughtful. When she reached out her hand, he raised it to his lips and kissed her fingertips.

"Maybe we'll be too warm if we stay this close to the fire," he said seductively.

An amused smile played across her lips. "I'm certain it's not the fire that's making me warm all over."

Mark slipped off his coat while Katie let her hat and coat fall to the ground behind her. They straddled the bale facing each other. Mark ran his hands along her arms, caressing them, squeezing them, then moving on to her shoulders. He massaged her neck and rubbed her temples with his thumbs. She undid her cap and set it aside.

"There is something I must talk with you about," Katie said. She paused, then asked, "are you ashamed that I am Amish?"

He stared at her, trying to imagine where the question came from. He could see she was serious. "No," he replied, "a thousand times, no! Where on Earth did that question come from?"

"Last Saturday. And I have pondered it ever since."

"Please explain what you mean."

"After I hit you with that last snowball, I heard Peggy tease you, 'I hit *my* Mark. Are you going steady now?' You told her to shut up—as if you were ashamed of me."

"My dear, sweet Katie, I *am* your Mark. I was still angry from losing the hockey game, and I lashed out at Peggy for teasing me. It was the wrong thing to do, and I apologized to her when we got home. Ashamed of you being Amish? Never! I am respectful of it. We both know the line we're walking here."

"Well, stop being so respectful of it. I wish to be treated like an English girl."

Mark sprouted a crooked grin. "You want me to ignore you?" Katie gave him a sweet smile, and slugged him on the shoulder when he looked down. "You keep doing that," he whined.

"I thought your grandma had an expression about whiners."

"I never told you that."

"Yes, but Peggy did."

"I'll tell you what, Miss Blue Britches, I invite you to have lunch with me. I'll pick you up at eleven-thirty sharp tomorrow. We'll go to Isaly's and have hot roast beef sandwiches with mashed potatoes and gravy. We'll get chocolate milkshakes made with real ice cream. Wear your best Sunday dress, apron, and cap. Scrub your face until it glows rosy red. I'll make all the other guys green with envy, and we'll be the talk of the town. I'll kiss you in front of everyone while I play "Let It Be Me" on the tabletop jukebox."

Katie listened attentively until Mark had finished. "I'd like to do all those things, but you know I can't."

"It isn't you. I'm just frustrated that I can't display to the world that I'm proud to be with you."

"I understand, and I want to be with you, too." She massaged his shoulder. "I'm sorry I slugged you. Do you still want to hold me?"

"Only if you promise not to slug me again," Mark joked.

"I promise," Katie played along. "And I'll make it worth your while," she said with a gleam in her eye.

"Now you're talking," he replied.

Mark rearranged the straw bales so they sat on two while he leaned against the others. Katie sat in front, between his legs, and he folded his arms around her. Every now and then she'd turn and scoot onto his lap so he could kiss her, then she'd slide back in front of him to snuggle against his chest. She finally drifted off to sleep.

When at last they went their separate ways, the snow was beginning to fall and would soon cover all traces of their meeting. "Fresh snow for snow angels," Katie said. "I want you to bring your guitar and sing this song, Let It Be Me."

"When?" he asked.

"Tomorrow night. Eleven sharp. I'm not waiting and wondering when I'll see you again. In the meantime, we'll catch some sleep when and where we can."

They met as planned. They made their snow angels, and even the angels held hands in the freshly fallen snow. There were flurries in the air but next to the fire Mark had rigged a lean-to roof using the straw bales, a couple poles, and the tarp. Their world was private and secure.

"I've waited all day to hear your song," Katie said anxiously.

"First, I want to sing a song I wrote for you to set the mood."

Mark began to strum softly. Soon his mellow voice surrounded her. "Oh, the stars from the sky…"

"Where?" Katie asked, looking at the cloudy sky.

Mark stuck out his tongue. She giggled and said, "Sorry, please start again."

Mark cleared his throat and began to play. "Oh the stars from the sky twinkle in your eyes. You are my bright eyes, the girl my heart beats for. Say you'll stay near me. Say you'll be mine for evermore. My sweet bright eyes, I'm yours."

Katie dutifully clapped when he finished. "I eagerly await the main act."

Mark sang his best imitation of The Everly Brothers' song, "Let It Be Me." When he finished, Katie sat quietly, her eyes bright and shiny.

"Could you sing it one more time for me?" she asked. "I want to feel the song in my soul."

Mark closed his eyes and put his whole heart into a repeat performance. When he finished Katie was standing before him.

"I need you to hold me," she said unashamedly.

He set his guitar aside, and she came into his arms as he lay back on the straw bales.

"Sweet breath and sweet kisses – play them upon me like I play the guitar. I'm never going to let you go."

"I don't want you to," Katie replied, "so there."

One kiss led to another, and time was of no concern to them as Mark and Katie made sweet music together.

"Poor Mrs. Kimes," Katie lamented.

"What brought that up?" Mark asked.

"All she wants is to get out of her wheelchair and walk."

"I'm sure there is going to be a story behind this," Mark muttered.

"It started in December," Katie began. "Lydia had been writing to Mrs. Kimes ever since she moved back to Lancaster. She sent a Christmas present to me and asked that I deliver it to Mrs. Kimes. Lydia was worried about her and said that she sounded mighty depressed in her letters lately. I visited one day to deliver the present, and we got along very well. She told me she's been hoping for years to walk again. She subscribes to medical journals and reads everything she can about the spine. New techniques are being used today which have given her renewed hope for her situation. Even though she's been in a wheelchair for six years, she has continued to exercise and perform physical therapy, especially with Lydia's help. After Lydia left, she carried on alone."

"How old is she?" Mark asked.

"She's seventy. She went to see a leading expert on spinal surgery last fall. But they told her she was not a good candidate for the surgery."

"That's unfortunate. She's a nice lady, and I always admired her spirit. I know she's been through a lot in her lifetime, but it hasn't defeated her. Did you visit her often while you and I were apart?"

"Several times. It helped me get through it. She was so much worse off than I that it made it harder to wallow. We didn't talk about what I was going through, but I think she knew it was something major. She said to me, 'Whatever you want in life, you have to go for it.' The same day she said that, I bought four rolls of film."

"When will you see her again?"

"I may see her on Saturday."

"Make a point of it, if you can. Find out as much as possible about her injured back. Don't get her hopes up, but tell her you have a friend of a friend who will do some snooping."

"Oh, Mark! Do you?" Katie asked.

"She doesn't know it yet but, yes, I do."

"I will get you as much information as I can," she assured him. "This 'she' you speak of wouldn't be Dr. Ford by any chance?"

"My, how intuitive you are. I know she did a lot for us, but we did a lot for her, too. Let's see if she can help Mrs. Kimes."

The following week, Mark was well armed when he called on Dr. Janice Ford. Mrs. Kimes had supplied Katie with a detailed description of her injury, as well as pertinent information. Mark had called Dr. Ford's office the day before and secured fifteen minutes of her time before regular visiting hours began. He arrived early, and Dr. Ford greeted him as he came through the door.

"How did you manage to get out of school for this?" she inquired.

"I told them I had a doctor's appointment."

"So your mother knows about this meeting?"

"Not yet, Dr. Ford."

She raised her eyebrows but did not pursue the issue. "This is not about Katie, I hope."

"No, Doc, it's about a good friend of hers and a member of your own medical profession."

"How is Katie?" Dr. Ford asked.

"She's great, and she said to pass along a hearty hello."

"Tell her a hearty hello right back at her, and please give her a nice big hug from me."

Mark gave her a quick rundown on Greta Kimes's case.

"And, what do you feel I can do for her at this time?"

Katie and I were hoping either you know someone, or you know someone who knows someone in this field."

"You said she's been turned down by an expert group in Pittsburgh? If they've done a thorough analysis and determined her to be unsuitable, there is a good possibility that will be her answer wherever she goes."

Mark sat and waited. He looked into Dr. Ford's eyes and stayed pleasant and calm. Seconds ticked by. She shuffled the papers before her. Mark added, "She helped patch people back together for forty years, Dr. Ford. Now it's her turn."

"Am I correct to assume that regardless of my answer today, this doesn't end here?"

"I have no other sources, so if you'll help us, our chances of success greatly improve. We're not asking for a guarantee, simply a chance through your contacts. Katie's friend wants this to happen. She's been working toward a recovery since the day of her accident. We don't know where the leading experts for spinal treatment are in our country. Her son is onboard with this, and she's willing to be a guinea pig, in a manner of speaking."

"Mark, it's refreshing to see that you haven't changed a bit. Tell Katie I will try, but do not pass on hope to Greta Kimes."

Mark took a deep breath. "I told Katie we could count on you. Thank God you haven't changed, either."

Katie clapped happily when Mark gave her the news. "Let's pray for her success." After a moment of silent prayer, Katie elbowed him in the ribs. "Where's that big hug Dr. Ford told you to give me?" Mark didn't need to be asked twice. He wrapped his arms around her, lifting her off her feet in a warm embrace.

He sat her down and kissed the top of her forehead.

"Is that supposed to last me until I see you again?" she asked with an inviting look.

Mark grabbed her for a passionate kissing exchange. "You are going to drive me nuts," he uttered as he released her.

"I can only hope," she said, with a satisfied look. "I've been trying to remember the songs you sang to me, but I've forgotten many of the words. Would you write them down so I can learn them?"

"I assume no one can ever hear you singing English songs?"

"You assume correctly, wise sir."

"And you have a secret place where you safely keep all this material?" Mark asked.

"I keep all our correspondence in a locked box on a shelf at the back of my closet, along with my journal."

"You have a journal? You should let me read it sometime." Mark grinned as Katie flushed a little. "Someday we should write each other a letter and tell how we feel."

"When you tell Mrs. Kimes that Dr. Ford has agreed to contact those she knows, it would be best if you left my name out of it."

"Why?"

"There's only one person who has an inkling of what might be going on between us. It would be best if we kept it that way."

Chapter Twenty-Two

If the owner of the camera store in Granville thought it was unusual that a young Amish woman was patronizing his shop, he gave no indication of it. However, the same could not be said of the other patrons shopping there. If Katie was aware of the attention she drew, she pretended not to notice.

Only a few times in her life had she ventured beyond the familiar surroundings of Powder Mills, where her people were a normal fixture of everyday life. But here in Granville? Only a few miles apart but a world away, and yet, in a camera store of all places. It could certainly be considered one of life's contradictions. Katie's purchases were so... English. She bought a bottle of lens cleaner, five photo albums, an instructional book on photography, the monthly issue of *Photography* magazine, and, of course, a few rolls of film. Even ears were tuned in as the owner and woman in blue casually discussed the selection of film on display. Yes, tongues would wag today in Granville.

Returning home, Katie had time to let her mind wander about her interest in photography, about the coming year, and about Mark. She relived the two nights at Wagner's pond, feeling the stirrings rising up within her as they did every time she recalled their time together.

As Katie approached Deborah's house on Morefield Road, she resisted an impulse to stop. She didn't feel like idle chitchat about dresses and wedding plans today.

Katie hadn't told Deborah about the photography, knowing Deborah wouldn't understand. Only a few people who knew her could understand, and they were all English. She approached Hogback Road and guided her horse toward Mrs. Kimes's house. She wanted to share the good news.

Katie studied the now-familiar red-brick Cape Cod house out the buggy window. She liked the projecting center entryway with its steep-pitched roof and white wood-crown trim. The double garage attached to the right end on the level lot, and against its right wall was a large, open lean-to roof, perfect for protecting an extra car, or in this case, a horse and buggy.

"Come in, Katie!" Mrs. Kimes called out from the open door as Katie approached. "What a beautiful February day. I was just enjoying the sunshine at my front door when I saw you coming down the road."

Katie accepted her warm greeting and leaned down to give her a hug. "I came to visit you because I wanted to enjoy the beautiful sunshine *and* your sunny disposition."

"It is I who am always blessed by your visits. May I fix you a cup of tea?"

"That would be nice." Katie followed her into the kitchen.

"I'm not supposed to get your hopes up," Katie began, "but I can't keep it to myself any longer. Dr. Ford has agreed to use her contacts to try to find a doctor who will see you about your back."

Mrs. Kimes silently sipped her tea.

"That is what you still want isn't it?" Katie asked tentatively.

"Yes, it is. After I was refused in Pittsburgh, I simply didn't know where to turn. How do you feel about my chances with Dr. Ford?"

"She's a good and caring person, but even she doesn't know whether her contacts will pan out. Only time will tell."

"Well then, let's drink to time," Mrs. Kimes said raising her teacup. "Isn't this the doctor who treated you for pneumonia?"

"How did you know?"

"When you're in my condition, you have plenty of time to read. I see everything published in the *Granville Herald*. Was it a miracle, Katie?"

"I believe it was. I was just grateful to receive the gift."

"Then I'm in good company. I could use a miracle." A knowing look passed between them. "Tell me about yours."

Katie hesitated. Mrs. Kimes reached out and patted the back of her hand. "We are not so different, you and I. You've received a miracle, and I need one. Our relatives still live, perhaps even as neighbors, in the land of our origin. I want you to call me Greta, as I call you Katie."

"I would feel honored to count you as a friend," Katie said. "And friends address each other by their given names."

"Then Greta and Katie it is from now on," Mrs. Kimes stated. "As friends, my first statement to you is that you can trust me with whatever information you feel so inclined to share. Your secrets are our secrets, 'so long as we both shall live.'"

Katie smiled, and her heart felt at peace. "Do you want another cup of tea, Greta? You'd better fill your cup if you are going to listen to the story of my healing. I'll take another cup, too, but may I use your bathroom before I explode?"

Greta laughed understandably and pointed her in the right direction.

When Katie returned she launched into her story. "The gift I received involves a common acquaintance. His name is Mark Lane, and we are neighbors."

"I know his mother quite well," Greta remarked. "They're a good family."

Noticing the clock on the wall, Katie exclaimed, "Oh my! It's much later than I thought. I will have to come another day to go into detail because my mother is expecting me home shortly. I will explain enough today, hopefully, to satisfy your curiosity."

"Whatever you have time for is fine," Greta replied. "The good Lord knows I'm not going anywhere."

Katie made the short trip from the Kimeses' home to her own pondering the prayer Greta had made while holding her hand. It was Greta's closing statement that returned again and again to Katie's mind, "Thank you, Father, that Mark cared enough to seek medical help for Katie's illness, and that he obeyed your greatest command, 'to love one another.'"

Katie couldn't help but wonder if Mark truly loved her. Neither had spoken the words.

And did loving him have to mean that she should want to spend her life with him? She would have to give up everything to live in his world. Would she be able to make that sacrifice? There was still the matter of whether she could be happy there.

She had no answers, but she drifted off to sleep confident in Mark and all that he stood for, and confident that time was on her side.

Katie returned to Greta's house not long after her previous visit. She told the story of the healing powers. Greta was inspired by what she heard, and Katie skirted the issue of romantic involvement.

The iron grip of winter was lifting on Wilson County. February had yielded to March, and the sun came back to life as each day became longer. As Katie's birthday neared, Mother Nature unleashed her fury, as she so often does. The snowstorm started on Friday afternoon, and by bedtime, seven or eight inches had fallen. The weather report said to expect two or three more inches.

Mark slept like a baby. When his alarm went off, he gazed out the window to see that the snow had stopped. He knew what he'd be doing that morning and the thought brought a smile to his face. He liked pushing the snow with the pickup truck and snowblade. It was especially impressive when there were ten or eleven inches of snow. He was already running through the process in his mind and anticipating first light.

Ann was in the kitchen when Mark entered. "Where's Dad?"

"Hiding under the covers. He took one look out the window toward the barn and went back to bed."

Mark went through the kitchen door onto the closed-in porch. What his eyes beheld, he might never see again. "How deep is the snow?" he asked.

"Deeper than your father wants to think about. The radio said some places got as much as twenty-six inches, but I don't think we got that much here. Why don't you take the yardstick out and measure it?"

"Why don't I watch you do it?" Mark suggested, restraining a smile.

"Because, it's a man's job."

"Aw, shucks, Mom. You make me feel so grown up."

Where do you start pushing twenty-some inches of snow? Mark shoveled a path through the white fluff from the house to the driveway and he was pleasantly surprised by a shallower channel that ran all the way to the road.

From the depth of it, Mark guessed that his dad had run the plow up through the driveway once before he went to bed.

"I better get this cleared out next to the road before the plow goes through, or I'll spend the rest of the morning shoveling," Mark muttered. With the channel his dad had provided, he painstakingly cleared the forty-foot-wide driveway. He even cleared in front of the other buildings before the road plow buried them again. When Mark had all entryways cleared a second time, he turned his attention to the lower farm.

Mr. Wagner was struggling in deep snow with his tractor and high-lift. Mark stopped and offered his assistance which his neighbor gladly accepted. He had the Wagner driveway and barn area cleared in good time and went on his way.

Mark didn't think about the Bylers until he topped the knoll heading for the lower farm. They had no equipment, so they would be stuck hand-shoveling. As he approached the buildings, not a soul was in sight. There was a 'people trail' through the deep snow from the house to the barn. They must still be inside milking the cows and doing chores. He decided to make their lives a whole lot easier.

Mark cleared out the courtyard and then plowed up to all their buildings, pushing the snow away from the entrance of each one. He started to leave when he looked up toward the house. Multiple sets of eyes watched him through the glass.

Oh, what the heck. Why come this far and not finish it?

Up through the yard he went and off to the right—just missing their bottom porch step. Mary came out onto the porch as Mark came to a stop. She had a big smile on her face.

"You're a blessing, Mark. We can't thank you enough. You saved us hours and hours of work."

"Glad to help, Mrs. Byler," he yelled as he backed down to the road. Straightening the truck to go on his merry way, he spotted Moses, Katie, and Jacob coming toward him. He reached across and rolled down the passenger window.

"Merry Christmas!" he called out as they approached. Jacob grinned, but then, he grinned at everything Mark said.

Moses nodded appreciatively. "Morning, Mark. We're sure glad to see you on this fine morning."

"Glad to be here. I just couldn't see you working up a sweat for nothing. Happy Birthday, Katie."

"Thank you. Most people walk up to the front door when they come to visit," she added in a serious voice, but with eyes full of amusement.

211

"Hush, Katie!" Moses admonished her. "It's a good thing Mark has done. Now children, thank him proper."

"Thank you, Mark," Katie and Jacob said as one.

"I don't know, Mr. Byler," Mark drawled, "Katie is eighteen today. If you continue to call her a child, you're liable to get whacked on the head with an iron skillet."

Moses smiled and nodded. "Yes, I'd better keep my eye on her. Thank you for moving our snow. You saved us from a lot of back-breaking work."

"You're welcome. I gotta get down to the lower farm." A thought crossed Mark's mind. "Say, Katie, Midnight has his five-month birthday coming up in just a few days. I think it would be an impressive photo to have mother and son together standing in the snow or with the snow as a backdrop. I could get my dad to help. What do you think?"

"Black against white. That might be a great picture," she said with a smirk.

"Next weekend, then," Mark said.

Later that afternoon, the day had warmed with the sun bringing the temperature above freezing. Everyone in the Lane family was involved in their own activities when a knock on the door announced a visitor.

"Come in, Katie," Ann greeted. "What brings you out on this bright, sunny day?"

"I came to give Mark a blueberry crumb pie," Katie responded as she watched Mark enter the kitchen.

"But, it's your birthday. You should be getting presents today, not giving them," Ann said.

"This is a 'thank you' pie, not a gift. Mama told me we should do something nice for Mark, since he plowed out our whole place this morning, including right up to our front door."

"I wondered what took him so long at the lower farm," Harold remarked.

"I did Wagner's, too," Mark interjected. Katie handed him the pie, and he thanked her profusely.

Mark suggested they sing Katie '*Happy Birthday*.' Ann and Harold joined in as soon as he began, and Katie smiled broadly as they sang. When they finished, Mark continued with a new verse of his own. "May you bring me many more. May you bring me many more. May you bring me many more pies, many more pies for me!"

Mark reached into the cupboard and brought down a stack of plates. "I guess I could share just this once."

He promptly stuck a candle in the pie. "Make sure Katie gets this piece, Mom."

Katie ducked her head and said, "Don't give me any. It's your pie."

"Exactly. It's my pie, and now I'm giving you some, along with vanilla ice cream."

Mark held out the knife to his mom. "I'll let you do the honors. You are much more practiced at divvying up a pie for a group than I am."

Katie elbowed him in the ribs. "Do you really eat a whole pie by yourself?"

Harold snickered. "Let's just say if he ate this one alone, it wouldn't be his first."

Katie stared at Mark, her face a mask of disapproval.

"Hey. I buy 'em, I eat 'em," he said in his defense.

"The fact that you're sharing this one is a step in the right direction," Katie said.

Harold and Ann waited for his response that never came.

Harold handed Ann a pencil. "Write that on the calendar, Hon. March 5, 1966. 'Mark didn't get the last word.'"

"Yeah, and Mom put an asterisk after it and write, 'It took three people to accomplish it.'"

"That's my boy, all right," Harold responded, "doesn't know when to quit. I hope someday he meets the woman who finally gets him to admit defeat."

"Just like us, right, Hon?" Ann winked at her husband.

Mark let out a whistle. "Look who'd better be speechless now."

Ann's laughter filled the kitchen as she left to see if Brenda or Peggy wanted any pie while Mark was in a sharing mood.

Harold and Mark agreed on one thing: Katie's pie was one of the best ever eaten. Katie beamed. "We should make this a yearly tradition, huh Dad?"

Mark and Katie couldn't take their eyes off one another as Harold concentrated on finishing his pie. "I'd best be going," Katie said when Ann returned.

"I'll drive you home in the truck," Mark offered. "Just give me a minute to run up to my room."

Leaving the house, Mark was in the lead and warned Katie to be careful on the slippery cement. He held his arm out for her to hold onto for support.

Mark thought he heard his dad whistle back in the kitchen. I guess I didn't pull that one off very well, he said to himself.

"You know that was all for show, right?" Mark asked once they were in the truck. "I try not to act different when I'm with you and my parents, and that's pretty close to normal, but my mom and dad are hard to fool."

Katie nodded. "It's the same for me at home. Hiding this in plain sight is not easy."

Mark pulled a package out of his coat pocket and handed it to her. "Happy Birthday, Bright Eyes."

"Thank you. I've been anticipating it like you said and reading about its proper uses. I think I'm ready, but I have to tell you honestly, I believe using my wide-angle lens will be better than pretending. It's a lot like us. Being with you is better than pretending I am or remembering when I was."

"You got me there, Katie. I agree with you and hope you'll forgive my prior arrogance. Did you get lots of cards in the mail today?"

"And yesterday," she acknowledged. "We are big on cards."

"Did you get any that you liked a lot from someone special?"

"As a matter of fact I did, now that you've jogged my memory," Katie replied with a grin and a smile lurking behind it. "You took an awful chance, you know."

"I know I did, but I'm not ashamed of my feelings for you."

"Nor am I, for you. It's the timing that makes it difficult." Katie sighed. "If we were a couple years older, it might be simpler."

"If we were a couple years older, we probably wouldn't be a we. You'd be married to some guy with a beard."

"Don't say that, Mark. Don't ever put those thoughts in my head." Katie reached for his hand as he drove, and Mark gave it to her gladly.

Chapter Twenty-Three

"Dr. Ford is expecting you," Becky told Mark upon his arrival at the physician's office. "Go right in."

Mark knocked softly as he peered into the doctor's office. "Come in," she said and motioned to the chair beside her desk. "Have a seat. I'm sorry to interrupt another school day."

"No problem. It's only English Lit... *Shakespeare*," Mark said in a guttural voice.

Dr. Ford chuckled then continued. "We may have good news for Greta Kimes. A young doctor at RHB Hospital in Chicago has responded through a mutual acquaintance that he would consider accepting her as a patient. I'm sorry to take so long to get back to you. I took the liberty of making copies of the information you gave me and sent them to the doctor. He just called me at home this past weekend." She handed Mark a folder. "I'm returning your original papers, and there's a note inside with his information. He's making no promises until he meets with and thoroughly examines Katie's friend."

"So this is how it can really work." Mark shook his head in wonder. "I only hoped you could help Mrs. Kimes, and you've come through for her. You have no idea how much this means to all of us, but especially Mrs. Kimes. We want to pay you for your time and expense."

Dr. Ford smiled. "This one is on the house. I'll be pulling for your friend along with you and Katie. By the way, did you give Katie my greeting?"

"Yes, I did, and she enjoyed it very much."

"Then give her another."

Mark passed the folder on to Katie, who delivered it to Mrs. Kimes the very next day. Greta cried at the news, and Katie was there to embrace and comfort her. That weekend Mrs. Kimes and her son, Will, drove to Chicago. Will had taken a leave of absence from work, with the promise to return as soon as possible.

Katie told Greta that the Lanes were the contact family for reaching her. "Keep me posted on your development. The Lanes will bring me the messages."

"The Lanes, or Mark Lane?" Greta asked with a twinkle in her eye.

Mark became the usual courier, although Ann used it once as an excuse to visit and arrange to have the Bylers over for Mary's birthday celebration the following week.

Mrs. Kimes had gone through a busy week of tests at the hospital, and her doctor was still undecided. As promised, she called the Lanes almost daily, and Mark or Ann wrote down everything she said to relay to Katie.

Finally, on Saturday, the call came that she had been given the green light, if she was willing to go through with the surgery. Mrs. Kimes told Ann that when the doctor delivered the news personally, she told him, "Why, hell yes! How soon can we get on with it? I'm not gettin' any younger, you know."

The operation was scheduled for the following Tuesday morning.

"I want to surprise Mrs. Kimes on Monday evening," Mark told Katie. "Why don't I pick you up after supper and take you to our house? I'll place the call, and you can talk to her personally."

"I'd like that, and thank you for thinking of it. Tomorrow's not our church Sunday, and I'm going to be too excited to sleep tonight, thinking about Greta." She winked at him.

"All night or just part of the night?"

"I'd probably wake up a little before eleven from a bad dream, or an alarm clock ringing under my pillow. I probably won't go back to sleep."

"What will you do then?" Mark asked.

"Oh, go for a walk like usual. Maybe make my way to the meadow."

Mark gave her a playful grin. "Our meadow?"

"I believe it is your meadow. Have you missed me, Mark?" she asked suggestively.

"You know I have. I told you in blazing detail in my last letter. Oh wait! I never mailed it because it's too risky."

"It wouldn't be too risky to hand-deliver it," Katie said demurely.

"How is eleven at the bankhouse?" he asked. "I'll bring blankets, and we can sit on the big log by the fire pit. Bring your flashlight. There won't be much moonlight tonight."

"I know. There wasn't much last night."

Mark decided against building a fire. On a night this dark, the light would stick out like a sore thumb. Although there was no moonlight, a million stars shone above. He anxiously awaited Katie's arrival as he enjoyed the beauty of the sky while keeping an eye to the east. At last a light was visible across the fields, and Mark watched it come toward him. A light in the darkness was such a simple thing. It wavered with her every footstep. Katie sought the crossing, found it, then deftly crossed the stream on rocks placed for that purpose.

Mark went to meet her, and they embraced. He took full advantage of the night to scoop her up like a bag of feed and sling her over his shoulder.

"Stiffen your body and stick your arms out like you're flying," he said as they neared the bankhouse.

She did, and he twirled her around while she shrieked with laughter. Mark eased her down and they held on to one another.

She kissed him, then said, "Hold me above your head so I can pretend I'm flying."

When he brought her down, she swung her feet around him and locked them behind his back like she had that day in the barn. Katie clung to him like a bear cub clinging to a tree. "I should call you Smokey," he said as she nibbled on his neck.

"Or you could call me, 'Katie the Bear.'"

"You surprise me again. I didn't think you'd know Smokey the Bear."

"I read, remember?" She bit him playfully as she slid off of him.

Mark sat on the log by the fire pit and gently guided her down beside him. They wrapped the blanket around them to keep warm and explored the language of touch. And every touch was a promise. Her body softened as sweet, unpretentious Katie leaned into his caresses. And their kisses... oh, those kisses... brazen explosions of emotion that held nothing back.

And, yes, parting was such sweet sorrow. On his walk back to the house, Mark thought that he'd finally gotten something out of English Lit.

During Monday's wash-day duties, Katie let her mother know she'd be going to the Lanes' after supper to call Mrs. Kimes. "It is good that you have befriended this lonely widow. I am proud of you, Katie, but do not be drawn into the English ways. I, too, have been praying for a successful surgery for her. Am I correct to believe that helping Mrs. Kimes has helped heal the rift between you and Mark?"

"I feel it is helping to complete the work my pneumonia began in the relationship. We both know Mark can be an irksome individual."

"Yes, individual describes him," Mary agreed with a chuckle.

"But he did offer to come and get me after supper. He said it would only take him a few minutes, and he wanted to do it for Mrs. Kimes, so I accepted."

Her mother was silent. "And the Sunday Sings? You didn't go again last night."

"It was too far, Mama. Clear over at the Mast farm. Don't worry, one day I'll return. Deborah keeps me informed of all the goings-on. You know the main reason young people go to them is to find a match, and I'm not ready for that."

"In God's timing," Mary said. "But hopefully before you're an old maid."

"I'm only eighteen. You were twenty-two before you married Papa."

"I married outside my community, as you well know, and I was very fortunate to find a good husband."

"I still have years, Mama. Besides, you and Papa need me here on the farm."

"It has always been our way to get by. Regardless of when it's your time to leave, the rest of us will make do."

Mark's horn beeped from outside the bake shop, and Katie promptly came out of the house.

"Casual. Very wise," Katie commented when she entered the truck.

"Yeah, I thought my car might make it seem like it was a date."

"Where would you like to go on this 'date?'" she asked.

"We could go bowling, see a movie, play miniature golf, go to the drag races - which my parents forbid me to race my car in, even though I'd probably win - or we could just hang out, like you and I already do."

"So 'hanging out' is a date?"

"In a manner of speaking," Mark said.

"So, we have already been on dates, but I didn't even know it."

"Someday I'd like to take you on a real date."

"But I'm not allowed to date an Englishman."

"I believe I already knew that, but thanks for the update. And don't slug me."

"Hello, Mrs. Kimes, this is Katie."

"What a pleasant surprise. I'm so glad you called, but how did you manage it?"

"I'm at the Lanes' house, and I wanted you to know I've received your messages. We're all praying for you."

The two friends engaged in a pleasant conversation until Katie finally said, "I'd better let you rest up for your big day tomorrow."

"Before you go Katie, there is something I want to let you know. I told Will if I don't make it through the operation, I want you to have my books."

Katie closed her eyes, at a loss for words. Mark watched the color drain from her face as he sat nearby. They were alone in the dining room, and Mark instinctively reached out and stroked her arm.

She quickly composed herself. Mark could hear Mrs. Kimes speaking on the other end. "Katie? Katie, are you still there?"

"Yes, Greta, I'm here. You surprised me is all. But your son will not be turning over any of your possessions to me. You are the best friend I have, and I know that God is going to bless you greatly tomorrow. You have half of Powder Mills praying for you. That includes both English and Amish, not to mention the good folks in Lancaster, led by Lydia. You will come through the operation with great success."

"Thank you, Katie. You're right, of course. I look forward to seeing you when I get home, but you simply must bring Mark with you."

"You have my word on it," Katie replied. "Tell Will to keep us informed tomorrow."

"I love you, Katie."

"I love you, too, Greta." Katie hung up the phone and exhaled heavily.

Mark told Katie he hoped to have an answer from Will by suppertime, but the call did not come. He knew what she must be going through, but all he could do was wait.

Katie was becoming more and more anxious as the hours ticked by. She only picked at her supper. Now it was getting late, and still they waited.

It was almost eight when the call from Will Kimes finally came. The doctor said that things had not gone smoothly. The operation took almost two hours longer than expected, and they had to revive Mrs. Kimes once during the surgery.

Right before the operation Greta had told the surgeon, "Bring me out of this room with a chance. That's all I ask."

"I just couldn't picture this feisty old gal wheelchair bound forever," he said. "That image wouldn't let me quit."

Greta spent extra time in the recovery room, and the doctor wouldn't give his analysis until she was out of immediate danger, resting peacefully in the ICU. His current prognosis was a 50/50 chance of a successful recovery, including a chance to walk.

Mark's money was on Mrs. Kimes. He grabbed the keys and rushed out the door - running headlong into Katie. He wrapped both arms around her to keep her from falling.

"Why, Katie, how nice to see you. I was just hurrying to give you the news. Greta is all right!" She let out a huge sigh of relief. "I'll drive you home."

"I'm sorry I came to you," she said, "but I had nowhere else to go."

"I just now got off the phone with Will. I knew you'd be worried." As he drove, Mark ran through what he knew.

Her forehead creased in concern. "Will she be all right?"

"She's all right now. Let's see what the next few days bring."

She slid closer and laid her hand on his thigh.

Mark took the risk of stopping on the knoll. He cut the engine and the lights. It was a pitch-black night, so no one would see them. He pulled Katie to him and held her close. "I want to be there for you whenever I can, but we must protect the secrecy of our relationship at all cost."

"Of course," Katie said. "I have pictures, and I'd like to show them to you."

"I have a poem, and we need lots of eggs for making lots of ice cream to share with a certain girl I know and her family on Friday night."

"Why don't you stop on your way home from school tomorrow?"

"I'm already looking forward to it," Mark replied.

"Do you have a poem now?" she asked hopefully.

Mark chuckled. "It's in my room. I left the house in kind of a rush."

Katie stroked his cheek. "That's all right. You've already done quite a lot for me tonight. But there is one more thing I need you to do before you take me home." She slid her hand up behind his head and gently pulled him down to her waiting lips.

As promised, Mark stopped to get eggs the next day. Katie soon came out to meet him. "Fill-er-up please," he said as he held out the egg bucket. "I need all the eggs I can get. Homemade ice cream gobbles them up." He gobbled like a turkey and she laughed. "How long do I have before it's too long?" he inquired.

"As long as it takes," she assured him. "I told Mama I'd bring you in to look over the pictures. I already have them spread out on the table in my room. First, let's get your eggs. If you don't hold me in your arms in the next thirty seconds, I swear, I'm going to explode."

Katie took the pail from him and casually crossed the courtyard into the springhouse. As Mark stepped inside, she wrapped her arms around him and held on tight. "There, now I feel better. I've wanted to feel safe in your arms ever since last night."

Katie filled the bucket with eggs, then led him back to the house.

"Hello, Mrs. Byler. Katie has some pictures she wants to show me."

"I'll bet it's those pictures of Midnight. He and his mama sure know how to pose for the camera."

Mark looked over the pictures, voicing his admiration for the ones of Molly and Midnight in the snow. "How did you get these developed?"

"I bought a magazine on photography, and there were ads for film developing where you mail in your rolls of film. When I received my pictures, they included a couple postage-paid mailing envelopes. The developing charge was cheaper as well."

"How did you get these two of the snow sliding off the barn roof?"

Katie held up her index finger. "Fastest finger on Old Mill Road!"

"I've never seen it in a picture. This is the kind of shot that would win a prize in a photo contest."

"I was preparing to shoot the snow hanging from the roof when it let go. I was lucky," she admitted.

"You were lucky you weren't under it. May I have one of your envelopes for film development?"

"Sure." Katie handed him one.

"Thanks. I think I'll give it a try."

"The fine print warns you that any nude pictures will not be returned," she said softly.

"What?" he exclaimed.

"You heard me."

"Thanks for warning me. I was wondering about that."

Mark burst out laughing when she stared him down. "I was just kidding. Now give me a hug, and I have to leave."

She held onto him. "I won't let you go. Not until you give me something."

"Oh, you remembered."

Katie held out her hand, and he laid a folded paper in it.

"It's a poem," he explained, "and the words to the songs that you asked for."

"Better late than never," she remarked. "That was weeks and weeks ago."

"But I forgot, and you didn't remind me."

Katie smiled sweetly. "It's always the woman's fault. Even Adam said so."

"I never wrote a letter like I said, but I'd very much like to. If I could mail them, I would enjoy writing to you regularly."

"But we can't take the chance, Mark, as much as I'd like receiving them. What's the name of the poem?"

"*A Light in the Darkness.*"

"What inspired this one?"

"Waiting for you in the dark."

"So my flashlight is the light?"

"You'll have to read it to find out."

Chapter Twenty-Four

Mark sat in the cafeteria during lunch and overheard Kim Price ask another student if he was going in the direction of the Tastee Freeze after school. She deflated when the boy told her he had ridden the bus to school. Mark liked Kim and would occasionally joke around with her. The ice cream stand had recently reopened after its winter shutdown, and Kim had just started working there. A cherry milkshake sounded like a great idea.

"I'm going there after school," he said to her. "Would you like to ride along?"

Kim's face brightened. "Thank you, Mark. Should I meet you at your car right after school?"

"You got it!" he answered. All the kids knew his car was one of the first to leave school grounds after the final bell rang.

When Mark pulled into the Tastee Freeze parking lot, all the front-row spots were taken, so he parked off to the side next to the owner's red '65 Mustang convertible. "Better let me get your door, Kim. We wouldn't want to put a scratch on your boss's new car. Not if this job is important to you anyway," he said with a smile.

He joked with her as they walked toward the ice cream stand. She laughed and gave him a playful push on the shoulder, knocking him off balance. They laughed all the way up to the stand.

Because of her involvement with Mark and her concern for Mrs. Kimes, Katie had put off her trip to town to pick up her mother's birthday gift. She'd be busy tomorrow with the party, so she had told her mom she was going to see Deborah and would only be gone a couple of hours. That would be more than enough time to accomplish what she needed to do. Her travels took her past the ice cream stand just in time to clearly see it all.

Alone in bed that night, she used her pillow to muffle her sobs.

How could he do this to her? Just yesterday he held her in his arms and kissed her like she was the only one for him. And it was just last weekend that they had made out like crazy. Didn't that mean anything to him? It had meant everything to her. At last she cried herself to sleep.

Katie hoped for a miracle, but she was a realist. She accepted the world as she saw it, which is why she had fallen so hard for Mark. He had shown her love even though it was unspoken. She saw it in his eyes and felt it in his touch. And yet, did she not see plainly with her own eyes at the Tastee Freeze?

She had heard stories of treachery and had been warned to keep both eyes open at all times. Two years ago, her mother's sister visited from Ohio and gave her a talking-to about getting yoked to the wrong man. No one would know better than Aunt Martha. She was one of the few women in the Amish world who had been granted a divorce by the church. It was a case of severe physical abuse.

"Just because men make promises doesn't mean they keep them," her aunt had said.

Katie considered feigning illness to avoid Mark that Friday night, but her emotions drew her back into the presence of the one she no longer trusted. If Mark could pretend, then so could she.

Everyone seemed to have a good time at Mary's birthday celebration. All the Byler children enjoyed the homemade ice cream and toppings along with the marble sheet cake Ann had ordered from Robert's Bakery.

Ann and Mary were busy cleaning up the kitchen while Harold and Moses chatted at the large dining room table as the evening was winding down. The younger children were playing games on the living room floor.

"Would you like to see my finished quilt?" Peggy asked Katie and Mark.

"Very much," Katie answered.

"I'll get it from upstairs and meet you in Grandad's room where we can spread it out."

They waited in awkward silence as Katie brushed off Mark's attempts at communication. She hadn't made eye contact with him all evening. At first, he assumed she was playing it safe, but now he sensed that something was wrong.

Peggy arrived and Mark stood back as the two girls examined the quilt. "It is beautiful," he added, when he could get a word in.

Mark and Katie were alone again when Peggy returned the quilt to her room. Mark glanced toward the doorway and reached out to touch Katie's arm. She stepped back and leveled an icy gaze upon him.

Her coldness puzzled him. "What is it?" he asked. "Have I done something? I can tell you're hurting, and I want to help."

She didn't answer, but Mark could see the confusion in her eyes. Before he had an opportunity to delve deeper, Peggy returned.

"I wanted to show you a project I've been working on for school. Mark, you should find this interesting, since it's your family tree, too."

Peggy spread out a rolled paper on which was drawn a big tree without leaves. Family Tree was written at the top. "We've been studying genealogy, and this is our family tree." Peggy pointed out the two forks for father and mother. "Here are our grandparents and then great-grandparents, as well as their parents. We don't know further back than that," Peggy said somewhat sadly. "Do the Amish keep track of their ancestors, Katie?"

"We have family names written in our Bibles, but we are more about the living than the deceased."

Peggy rolled the paper up. "I can't help wondering what my great-great-grandmother was like. Was she nice? Did she like kids? She had nine of them so you'd hope she liked them." Peggy chuckled at her own joke, and then she was gone again – leaving a heavy room in her absence.

Mark searched his mind for anything to get the conversation flowing. "I'll bet you didn't know my grandparents both grew up Amish."

Katie's eyes seemed to bore through him. "Are you ever going to grow up?" she snapped. "I never know when you're making up one of your stories, but this one is definitely not funny!"

"If it means I've got to become a sour-puss like you're acting then I'm never going to grow up," he retorted.

"Maybe some people have reasons to become sour-pusses," she countered. She snatched her coat from the peg in the mudroom and stormed through the closed porch to the outside with Mark close behind. "Tell your parents I appreciate their hospitality this evening, and that I suddenly wasn't feeling well. Tell mine I'm walking home." She turned on her heels and started off through the yard.

Mark ran after her calling, "Katie, wait!" She stopped, and he slipped a folded paper into her pocket. "Talk to me Katie."

She pulled it out, waved it in his face, and asked, "What's this, more fairy tales?" She ripped the paper into pieces, dropped them on the ground, and disappeared into the dark night. This time, Mark let her go, wondering what in the world that was all about.

"What happened to you last night?" Mary asked, as they prepared the Saturday morning meal.

"I suddenly felt ill. I'm fine now. Maybe it was too much cake and ice cream." Katie shrugged. "Or too much Mark Lane," she said under her breath.

"I'm sure there is a story behind that," Mary said with a cringe.

"Physically, I'm fine, Mama, but I'm mentally uneasy."

"About what?"

"I shouldn't let it bother me, but Mark was telling his tall-tales again last night."

"Sometimes they are entertaining," Mary said, "but what was this one about?"

"He said that his grandparents grew up Amish. That would mean that they both had to leave the Order, and you know that rarely happens, especially in the old days." Mary was silent as she worked.

"We've met his grandma," Katie continued. "I even remember her name because it is the same as yours. And the last name is Miller. There are no Amish named Miller in Powder Mills."

As Mary's silence continued, Katie stared at her, waiting for a response. Finally, her mother met Katie's gaze. "You are correct," she answered, "but

230

Mary Miller and I both come from the same county in Ohio, and Miller is a common Amish name there."

Katie struggled to maintain her composure. She remembered when Mark had tried to explain last night. She had rejected him and torn up his paper. Dread filled her consciousness.

"Are you saying that Mark's grandparents did grow up Amish?" Katie asked.

"It's not my place to say. That would be spreading gossip. If it involves Mark's family, then it's only theirs to tell."

If Mark's words were true, were his actions also true? Had she misunderstood and assumed things that were not? His voice saying, 'Talk to me, Katie' rang loudly in her ears. But she hadn't talked to him, and she hadn't asked him to explain. She had cast him off in a fit of anger and now realized that she may have been wrong. There was nothing she could do. She had no reason to approach him.

When Katie looked at her mama, Mary was watching her. "I thought you and Mark were finally putting your differences aside and learning to get along," she said. "It seemed to be going well lately, and he has helped you with the photography."

In spite of her angst, Katie was still intuitive enough to recognize opportunity. "Why do you think Mark helped me, Mama? I'd wager it had a lot to do with wanting to get rid of me after my hospital stay. What English boy wants to play nursemaid to some Amish girl?"

Mary's mouth dropped open. Then indignation set in. "Katie Byler, it seems you've stepped in it once more. Life is a learning experience, but it takes maturity to get through it successfully. Perhaps it's best that you are not following the path of Deborah Yoder at this time. Did you treat Mark in an unchristian manner last night?"

"Yes, I suppose I did if he was telling the truth."

"This is not our way, Katie. If you can't get along with our neighbor, then how are you going to get along with a husband?"

Katie spent the next two days reliving the events of Thursday and Friday. By Monday morning, she desperately wished she could talk to Mark to straighten the whole thing out. He had been concerned for her. She knew that now as she played his words again and again in her mind, "I can tell you're hurting, and I want to help." Even in the face of her anger, he had been worried about her and not himself.

Mark didn't have a single clue for this strange turn of events. He certainly couldn't discuss it with anyone, either. Anyone, that is, except the one person who made it quite clear she wanted nothing to do with him.

He, too, spent the next two days remembering, and it left him anxious. For the first time, doubt crept into his mind. Or maybe it was righteous indignation. He waffled between pity-party and anger.

Mark went to school as usual on Monday. As he passed the Byler buildings, he tried not to look at the springhouse or the barn that held such vivid memories. He thought of Katie, who would probably be in the barn now doing the milking. He resisted the temptation to stop, as he had once before, to take her in his arms, and kiss her between the cows.

Today he must submit a report to Mrs. Weber and the English Lit class. He had spent hours yesterday reading and rereading the romantic parts of Romeo and Juliet. He almost felt jealous that they never had enough time together to have their first fight.

"Now, class, let's listen as Mark answers the question, 'What was the bond between Romeo and Juliet?'" Mrs. Weber said.

Mark stood and began. "I see no sense of making something complex that is simple. I read the section of the play several times that involved their relationship. Initially they liked the way the other looked. I believe they were subsequently drawn by the emotion that only humans can feel – passion. I believe Shakespeare was trying to get all of us to feel this same entity called passion. The end result was they simply loved one another completely and without reservation." Mark paused and looked at his classmates. "My assignment was to write three hundred words. What I just read was fifty-six words, so I wrote it six times, equaling three hundred and thirty-six words." Mark held up the pages for the class to see.

All eyes shifted from Mark to Mrs. Weber. No one breathed as they waited for their teacher's response.

"Since you read the story several times, how do you feel about the way Shakespeare chose to end it?" Mrs. Weber asked.

"The ending is sadistic, because no one wants it to end that way, and he surely did it for effect."

"To what purpose?"

"Who doesn't know the name of William Shakespeare or remember the story of Romeo and Juliet? I don't believe our lives should be a tale of woe. I believe they should have happy endings."

"Amen to that." Mrs. Weber replied.

Mark drove slowly past the Bylers' on his way home. He almost gave in to his desire to stop. When he entered the kitchen, his mom greeted him happily. "What's gotten into you today?" he asked.

"Mrs. Kimes called, and we had a lovely chat. She's recovering well, and they're beginning therapy to see if she'll walk. I wrote it all down if you'd like to take it to Katie."

"Mom, would you mind running it down to the Bylers? I have too many chores to do, plus an assignment for school. That is great news about Mrs. Kimes."

The next afternoon, Mark approached the Byler buildings when Katie stepped boldly into the road. He slowed to a stop and watched her from behind the windshield then rolled the window down as she approached. "You could get run over doing that, you know."

"You'd probably like to do that, wouldn't you?" she asked, with just the slightest hint of a smile.

"Not me. It would damage my car."

"How long are you going to ignore me?" Katie asked.

"I believe it was you who made it plain you wanted nothing to do with me."

"I did that, and I'm sorry. There's a whole explanation that I can't tell you standing in the middle of the road."

"Are you able to meet tonight?" he asked. He could see the deep lines across her forehead, the sag of her shoulders, and the sadness in her eyes.

Katie let out a sigh. "I will. Just tell me where and when."

"The bankhouse – between ten-thirty and eleven. Come whenever you feel it's safe to leave."

"I'll be there," she assured him. "It's wonderful news about Mrs. Kimes, isn't it, Mark?"

His demeanor brightened, and he smiled up at her. "I think she's going to be all right."

She gave his shoulder a squeeze. "We can pray together for her tonight. I believe in the power of combined prayer."

"Tonight, then," Mark confirmed.

Katie watched his car go up the road, and she knew he was holding back. Would she be able to explain in a way that he would understand?

She sensed that their relationship could continue or end depending on the outcome of tonight's meeting.

Chapter Twenty-Five

Mark arrived early in the meadow to prepare for their meeting. This was not a night for darkness. It was a night for shedding light on a problem. They would talk inside, and he had brought his Coleman lantern to hang from the ceiling.

After their two nights together by Wagner's pond, he had brought two straw bales over to the bankhouse. He placed them three feet apart so he and Katie could sit facing each other while they talked. The temperature would dip into the thirties on this late March night, so Mark had brought a blanket, a kerosene heater, and a thermos of hot chocolate. He was sure they would drink the hot chocolate, but he had no idea if they would use the blanket. "Is this love?" he asked himself. "Here today, gone tomorrow."

Passing by Wagner's pond, Katie remembered the two wonderful nights she and Mark had spent there. She remembered the feel of his arms around her, and she paused. She wished she could go back to before Thursday, when everything was fine and the only hurt created by love was a good hurt.

Katie looked across the long meadow and saw a glow in the night. Mark was waiting for her. She forced herself to continue on. She longed for him but felt a pang of fear as she approached the bankhouse. Drawing near, she could see him sitting on the big log where they had held each other less than a week ago.

Mark rose to face her, silhouetted by the light. Katie was glad she couldn't see his face in the dark when he softly said, "Hi, Katie."

She didn't want to see the troubled look that was sure to be there, radiating from those blue eyes. She returned his greeting and laid her flashlight on the log. Without hesitation, she reached out and wrapped her arms around him, holding him tightly in the cool night air.

Mark encircled her with his arms. "Just hold me," she whispered pressing her cheek against his shoulder. Once again, he was struck by the power of her embrace, and her need filled his consciousness.

"Thank you, I needed that," Katie said as she released him.

"You sure know how to get a meeting started," he said. "Does this mean you still like me?"

"I'll always like you, even when I don't like you much."

"Yeah. Let's go inside and talk about that."

Katie studied the interior with a thoughtful expression. "I don't remember exactly what it was like during the storm, but now it looks like a miniature house, windows and all." Observing the two straw bales, Katie said. "I especially like your choice of furniture. It gives the house a certain country atmosphere."

Mark smiled as she stood in the little house, and his heart melted again.

Katie sat down on a straw bale and faced him. The familiar lines on her forehead gave away her worry. "I'm sorry I got angry with you, and I'm sorry I was nasty to you," she quavered, her face drooping.

"Please explain to me what that was all about," Mark said.

"I saw you on Thursday with the girl at the Tastee Freeze. I just happened to be in town getting Mama's present and was passing by."

"That explains a lot," he acknowledged. "But why didn't you simply ask me about it?"

"I believed what I saw was quite clear. You held the door for her. You were laughing together and she playfully pushed you."

"It was nothing," he insisted.

"Do English girls always laugh and push you when it's nothing? I know when I laugh and push you, it's something. It's even something when I slug you."

Mark sighed. "I held the door so she wouldn't scratch the car beside mine. It belongs to her boss."

"Whose boss?"

"Kim's. The girl I gave a ride to the Tastee Freeze. She just started working there, and it was the owner's car. Kim is simply one of the girls at school. We aren't even friends, just acquaintances. She was looking for a ride to work, and I was going there anyway."

"It was nice of you to offer her a ride," Katie admitted, "but what did you say to her that was so funny and prompted her to push you?"

"I said, 'Try not to poison anyone today.'"

A thin smile played across Katie's lips. "Yes, that sounds like something you would say."

"That's just what we do. We joke and kid around. We laugh with and at one another. It doesn't mean anything."

"I misunderstood," she admitted, "but our societal differences had a lot to do with it. Maybe if our societies are going to cause this much trouble, we don't belong together."

"Do you really believe that?" Mark asked, watching her closely.

"No! I was just lamenting."

"Good. Because you'd only say that if you don't care about me as much as I care about you."

"I got angry because I care too much," she shot back.

"And I say if we don't care too much then we don't care enough," Mark countered.

Katie sighed. "Let me explain something. While courting, we don't do some of the things you and I have been doing together. I have let down my defenses and allowed you to get very close to me. You are the only man I have looked upon with interest. I didn't even like men when you came along, and that was partly your fault. Yet I have put myself out there on a limb with the possibility of you chopping it off. I mean, it was just the day before that we were all lovey-dovey. Can you understand?"

"I do now," Mark responded. "We've demonstrated our feelings for each other, but they've gone unspoken. You gave me your assurance that you have no interest in some other guy, but I didn't respond in kind. Maybe if I had, this wouldn't have happened."

"I saw you with the girl at the Tastee Freeze, and I was afraid you might like her more than you like me. I feared that you were just playing with my feelings. It was not a feeling I want to experience again, or inflict on someone else."

Mark leaned forward, took both of Katie's hands in his, and looked into her eyes. "I'm sorry you went through that. Let me put your mind at ease. I am not interested in any girl but you. As long as we both agree to pursue our feelings for each other, I will not have an interest in any other girl. We were doing a pretty good job of learning to care about one another. If neither of us wants to experience pain like this again, then we need to make some changes."

"What do you suggest?" Katie asked, biting her lower lip.

"We're at a disadvantage. We can't interact out in the open like normal couples. We're also not completely versed in each other's worlds, so there are bound to be misunderstandings. We have to trust and give each other the benefit of doubt. We need to be completely open and honest, and good communication is paramount."

Katie exhaled a long, slow breath. "I agree. And I *have* trusted you— except for this misunderstanding. We are good for each other, and you have been honest with me. I only wish there was some way we could communicate on a regular basis."

"Let's write letters," Mark replied. "It will help us get to know each other better. If we put our heads together, I'm sure we can think of a drop spot where we can leave them."

Katie squeezed Mark's hand. "There is another thing we need to communicate about tonight—your grandparents. I cut you off the other night because of my anger, and I thought you were making up stories. I'm truly sorry."

Mark wrapped the blanket snugly around her and rubbed her briskly with his hands. She gave him a weak smile while he poured her some hot chocolate.

"I don't know much myself," Mark said. "Someday we can get Mom to fill us in. The only reason I said it to you is Peggy showed you our family tree, and I assumed you had seen Mom's branch with all the names on it."

"Her hand covered the one side. I only saw your dad's family before Peggy rolled it up. What were the names on your mother's branch?"

"Miller, Mast, Yoder, and even Beiler and Hostetler way back."

Katie was quiet and he waited for her response. "Why were you afraid to tell me all this?" she finally asked.

"I wasn't afraid. I just hadn't gotten around to telling you yet."

"Complete honesty," she reminded him with a stern look.

"All right. I was saving it to bring it out if things weren't going so well… to get you to like me more," Mark admitted.

"So you had this all planned out?"

"Tell me you didn't connive," he retorted.

"Such a harsh, unladylike word," Katie objected.

"Would you like 'manipulate' better?" From the tight set of her mouth and the narrowed eyes, Mark knew she was about to slug him. "About *that*," he said, looking directly at her clenched right hand. "I was going to ask you if you would please not do that anymore. It was kind of cute the first time, but since then, it's no longer cute. You do understand there is a lot of wallop in your punch, right? I mean, it's not like you're a weakling."

Katie reached out and Mark flinched. She rubbed his arm just below the shoulder. "What are you doing now?" he asked guardedly.

"Pretending," she answered with a smile.

"Pretending feels a lot better," he said.

"Tell me what you know about your grandparents," Katie prompted again.

"Grandad Samuel was sweet on Mary Mast whose father happened to be the Bishop. He was an ornery old goat. Mary loved Samuel, too, only he didn't agree with certain things about their church's strict rules. Sam decided to become English, and he told Mary he understood if she wanted to stay. Grandma Mary didn't want to leave Sam, so she left the community with him."

"Bishop Mast never forgave Grandma, even though she hadn't joined the church. The Bishop was on his death bed when Grandma Mary got the call that he wanted to see her. Mrs. Mast had already passed a few years earlier and when Grandma attended the funeral, they continued to shun her. But Grandma went to see her dad anyway. He had asked that his grandchildren accompany my grandma, but only my mother went. My two uncles wanted nothing to do with him. They figured if he hadn't been interested in them their entire lives, why should anything change now? My mom did get to meet her grandfather, but he died less than a week later. Still, she does have that memory of him. Uncle John and Uncle Lucas have no memory. Who can say which is better?"

"Do your uncles live handy?"

"They both learned carpentry from their father. John stayed in the area, and he buys old houses to fix up and rent. Luke went to California to build houses, met a girl, and stayed. I've only seen him twice. He owns a construction company near San Francisco. The last time he was here, he told me if I ever needed a job, he'd give me one."

Katie tapped her foot on the floorboard. "How did your father take that?"

"Oh, he was none too happy, but he also knows I'm not running off to California."

"What do you intend to do?"

"I'll attend four years of agricultural college starting in September. Dad and I disagreed for the last couple years on whether college was necessary, but he finally relented. I think Mom had something to do with it. She knew I wasn't going to take no for an answer. It's hard to imagine that in just a few months, I'll be in college."

Katie's heart quickened. "And after that?"

"Right back here at Lane Farms. I'll be the seventh generation to work this land."

"Your dad must be happy about those plans."

"He doesn't say he is, but I suppose so. I mean, if I had a son, I'd be happy to see him continue on the farm."

Katie shook her head. "It will be over four years before you start your life's work. You English sure take your sweet old time, don't you?"

"I plan on living to one hundred, so that's only one minute out of twenty-five. When are you going to get on with your life's work?"

"I'm only eighteen. I'm going to let my life's work come to me. Besides, your Grandfather Samuel didn't live to one hundred," she stated.

"He might have, if he wasn't German," Mark said.

Katie looked puzzled. "Lots of Germans have great longevity. How was your grandfather different?"

"Actually, he was quite common for a German: stubborn, inflexible, and opinionated. But you can quite possibly thank God *and* my grandfather for you being alive."

"How is your grandfather involved?"

"He died of pneumonia. Sam was not one to go to the doctor. When he got sick on a Thursday, he refused to go in spite of Grandma's urgings. On Sunday, Grandma wanted him to go to the hospital, but he wouldn't. She called an ambulance Monday morning, but Grandad died before it arrived. That's why I acted when you became ill. When you get to Heaven, be sure to look him up and thank him."

"I surely owe him my gratitude," she said softly. "Now let's pray for Mrs. Kimes."

Mark took her hands in his and they bowed their heads. Katie waited, and finally he took the lead. She added a few words of her own before they both said "Amen."

She squeezed his hand when they were done, and he could see that her bright eyes had returned. "We can be grown up, can't we, Mark?"

"I never doubted it, but tell me what you mean."

"We can work out our problems and sit and talk with each other. Your English and my Amish don't need to get in the way."

"I didn't know when you came tonight whether we could continue seeing each other."

"Nor did I," Katie assured him.

"How do you feel now, Bright Eyes? I'm glad to see you have them back."

"I want to have bright eyes only for you."

"And I for you, oh dearest one," Mark said, raising her hands to his face and kissing each one. "There is something I wonder about that we have never discussed. You're obviously more religious than I. For me, it's not difficult, but how do you justify lying to the entire world about our relationship?"

"I may have a more personal relationship with God than you, but I question that I am more religious. Were you not chosen to save me? As to my lying, I do not lie to God. He knows my every thought, my every need, and my every desire. I hide nothing from Him.

"My lies are to man because of his rules. Even though I break no rules by being friends with you, many would frown upon it. However, having a romantic relationship with you would be unacceptable. My family would not be pleased, and there would be consequences."

"In my experience, rules are made to control people," Mark said. "If two people care about each other and are doing nothing wrong, then what right does anyone have to control them?"

"I agree with you in principle, but there is a limit to how far I can stretch the boundaries."

"Does that mean I can't take you dancing on Saturday night?" Mark asked.

"Yes, I believe it does."

"Pity. I've seen you with your hair falling down, and you would look really good in a dress out for an evening of fun or romance."

Katie took one of his big hands in hers and held it tightly. "To finish the subject on lying to be with you, we attend a lot of weddings, and one of my favorite lines is, 'Let no man put asunder what God has joined together.' If I must lie to be with you, then so be it. I have nothing to explain to Him."

"Your mother and father would say you are not honoring them." He knew he was pushing his luck, but he wanted to know how strongly Katie felt about this. Their future together depended on it.

"I honor them in my heart where God can see it. If it would seem to them that I do not do so, it is only because of man's rules."

A peace filled Mark's soul. "Is there anything else you feel we need to talk about before we go our separate ways?"

Katie swallowed hard and looked into his piercing blue eyes. "The paper you slipped into my pocket on Friday night. Do you still have it, and would you consider sharing it with me again?"

Mark stiffened and she apologized for shredding it. She added, "I also wouldn't blame you if you didn't share it with me."

"Would you prefer I tape it back together or make you a new copy?"

"I deserved that," Katie said. She looked away and after a long moment gazed upon him again. "I wish I could take it back. Do you forgive me?"

The tension built until he could stand it no longer. He pulled Katie toward him and sat her down on his lap while she wrapped her arms around him. "I forgive you, but promise me we won't fight like this again. Fighting may be beneficial to some couples, but I don't believe it's conducive with our personalities."

Katie smiled. "Are you trying to say, you don't think it's good for us?" Mark began to tickle her, but she jumped up. "Close your eyes," she told him.

Mark looked at her warily. "Why?"

"Just close them, please. And, no peeking."

"You sure can be bossy sometimes," he jokingly grumbled but closed them.

Katie nudged him to the back edge of the straw bale. She pulled her dress up to her waist and stepped onto the bale with one foot on either side of him. She eased herself down onto his lap, letting her dress fall around them.

Mark's eyes popped open to see Katie beaming at him. "See. Good things happen when you do what you're told." And she wiggled against him to get comfortable.

"I'm not going to accept responsibility for what your pretty little fanny is doing to me," Mark avowed. He nuzzled her neck and proceeded up to her ear.

"You sure got that right because I'm going to hog it all for myself," Katie murmured. She ran her hands over his back and her fingers through his hair.

He moaned. "You're playing with fire."

"No, I'm playing with our desire," she corrected him. "Just hold me, let yourself go, and let me worry about what happens next. I am here to please you."

Mark reached up and turned down the light. She softly touched her lips to his then deepened the kiss.

He let out a guttural moan and joined her completely in a deepening kiss that swept them away. "Kiss me like that again," he breathed in a near whisper.

But lips alone would not satisfy them and kisses yielded to long minutes of sensual embraces as they moved together while each pleased the other. Wave upon wave of desire flooded over them, though it was more than the physical contact, more than the sweet thrills that swept through them. As they blended into one, their souls were reaching... reaching together

243

through the corridors of time, down the pathways of tomorrow. All their tomorrows, actually.

Finally, Katie sighed and leaned back. "Now I can let you go home and take a cold bath."

Mark chuckled. "It's *shower*. 'Now I can let you go home and take a cold shower.' But I don't think that will be necessary. I'll just run naked to the house. That ought to do it."

They both laughed and held on to one another.

Chapter Twenty-Six

Mark set a record the following day in school. He fell asleep in three classes and slept until the bell rang to end study hall. School was a blur as he had visions of Katie when he was asleep and when he was awake. But even more than that, he could feel the exact form of her sitting on his lap and pressing against him everywhere she had touched him.

Her hands, those caressing hands. Where did she learn to touch him like that? She had no experience in such matters, which left only books and instinct. He was just thankful that he was the lucky recipient of the knowledge. And he was glad for the books he needed to carry in front of him.

Katie, meanwhile, claimed not to be feeling well, and her mother agreed that she didn't look good, either. However, she did seem better after a long nap. She set her alarm clock for 2:50 pm, knowing it gave her precisely twenty-three minutes to splash water on her face and to "just by chance" be walking to the barn in time for Mark's return from school. Katie was fairly certain that if she was sitting on the smokehouse steps, he couldn't pass her by without stopping. Not after last night, at least.

She was right.

"Hi Mark! What a pleasant surprise. What brings you by today?" He looked around in all directions while Katie laughed inside. He had a wary expression on his face as he stepped closer. "There's no one within ear shot," she said.

"It's a good thing you couldn't read my mind all day in school," he admitted sheepishly.

"Why? Were you angry again? I thought I should have taken care of that last night, dear one."

"Funny. Very funny. What's my excuse for stopping today?"

"To apologize," Katie informed him.

"Right… do you want to explain that?"

245

"Well, yesterday I flagged you down to apologize and discuss your grandparents, and you told me you didn't have time. You said you'd stop today to tell me when you'd have time, but you don't have time until tomorrow."

Now Mark was really confused. "Why don't I have time now?"

She gave him a cheeky grin. "I've already seen you now, and this way I get to see you for a longer time tomorrow while we hash out our poor relationship and you tell me about your grandparents. I'd say all that should take a good thirty minutes."

Mark shook his head and massaged his temples. "You need to get a telephone," he groaned.

"What on Earth for? You know they are not allowed."

"To keep me abreast of my schedule. It sounds rather complex."

Katie giggled. "Did you think about anything special today?" she asked, playfully batting her eyelashes.

"Yes," Mark said, not taking his eyes off her. "How about you?"

"It's a good thing your back is toward the house or my family might see your eyeballs ogling me," she said with a nod as if agreeing with him in conversation. "To answer your question, I did think about you. I'm looking forward to thinking about you tonight, too, and writing in my journal. Maybe you'll have a poem for me tomorrow, or even a letter. I can only hope... 'and then Mark said goodbye,'" Katie concluded.

"Damn, you're good. I think I might have met my match."

She waved as Mark drove off. Love you, too. That's how to make a relationship work. Now if she could just act like she was dragging along while she was actually floating on air. Katie went about the rest of her day wondering if Mark would be more inclined to categorize her actions as conniving or manipulating.

Bedtime couldn't come soon enough for Mark or Katie. Mark retired to his room early and began to write his first love letter. It began in bold letters at the top, "Dearest Katie."

He chose his words carefully, explaining how he had been drawn to her after her fall from the wagon. He admitted that the jolt of them hitting the

246

ground together awakened something within him. *I know it didn't do the same for you, and I certainly never received encouragement from you. It was like a force that was living within me had taken control. It came like the wind – uninvited – to change my world.* He smiled as he thought that Katie would probably say it was God.

Mark wrote of his admiration for her that went much deeper than her obvious external beauty. *I could see it in your eyes and in the way you carried yourself – in your deference to others. You have so many attractive qualities, and I was drawn to all of you. There was a yearning in my soul that even now, I do not fully comprehend. It is this force that drives me forward to know you. I want to know all of you, my dear, sweet Katie.*

Two pages of written emotion and truth, simply signed, *Mark.* He recopied the poem he had waited so long to give her - the poem she had torn to pieces. He included *Bright Eyes* with his letter. He folded the pages and slipped them into a small envelope.

Mark remembered how they had maneuvered through their difficulty last night. Their relationship had weathered the storm, and they had come out of it stronger than before. It gave him an easy feeling that their future was going to be bright. He thought about the coming summer and the potential it held. Thoughts of nighttime swims in the pond and meetings at the bankhouse lulled him to sleep.

A few hundred yards away, a similar scene played out in the bedroom addition on the back of the Byler farmhouse. Sitting at her small table, Katie recorded her thoughts, feelings, and desires for Mark in her journal. It was a private record meant only for her eyes, so she wrote frankly and boldly.

Katie thought of her friend in Lancaster as she wrote, "Oh Lydia, you were right. He warms every part of me."

After finishing her journal entry, Katie took a piece of paper from her drawer and began to write: *Dear Mark… How do I put into words what these last several months have meant to me? How much richer is my life than before? Let us continue getting to know each other.*

She stated in simple words how he made her feel and how much she enjoyed being with him. She concluded by thanking him for his patience and kindness during her recent emotional upheaval. She signed it, *Thinking of you, Katie.*

Katie remembered the girl she used to be and how nights had sometimes been a struggle. She thought of her moonlit walks in the cool night air and how different things were now. All she had to do was think of Mark, and she could drift off to peaceful sleep anytime she wished. He had said, "I am interested in no one but you." The words spread contentment through her soul. She replayed her boldness with him last night. Mark had matched her touch for touch, kiss for kiss. He might have a laid-back easy exterior, but there was nothing laid-back about the way he held her, kissed her, and moved with her.

Katie fell asleep surrounded by good feelings and dreamt that she and Mark were picnicking on a blanket beside the stream in the meadow. Her hair was falling all around her, as Mark lay with his head on her lap. She was mesmerized by his voice and his eyes as he sang to her – one love song after another.

The next day, Katie waited patiently on the smokehouse steps, gazing at the scenery. It would all look much different a few weeks from now when the greenery returned. A faint scent of spring was in the air on this warm, sunny late March day.

Mark pulled in right on time. "Howdy Neighbor!" he said as he ambled toward her.

Katie struggled to balance her inner excitement with her need to show exterior distress. When it was just her and Mama, she had pulled it off magnificently, but now in his presence, easy was nowhere to be found.

She felt the warmth of his boyish grin and understood why the girls at school would flirt with him.

Mark sat on Katie's left so she would not be visible from the house. He spent a moment running his eyes over her and laid his hand on the step between them. She caressed it as she said, "Nice to see you," giving him a smile that he had never seen on any girl, anywhere before.

"Are you ready for the performance?" he asked.

"I've been performing all day. Maybe you need to get warmed up?"

"Perhaps you should sit on my lap again. That warms me up." Mark pretended to look off in the distance. He winced and softly said, "Ouch," when Katie poked him in the ribs.

"I'm sorry. Did I hurt you?" she asked.

"Say you're sorry again, only with more emphasis. And lean outward and toward me so the house can see you."

Katie played along.

Mark stood and paced around a little with a serious look on his face. He leaned against his car and folded his arms across his chest while giving her a hard look. Katie gave him puppy eyes, and she patted the step to encourage him to sit down again. He slowly lowered himself onto the step. Leaning forward and placing his elbows on his thighs, he bent his head down and looked at the ground. "I thought about you last night."

"We're doing really well, so far," Katie said. "Pretend you're being forgiving."

"Can I hold your hand or pat your head while I forgive you?"

"I don't think that would be wise, but I thought about you, too. I even had a dream about us."

Mark turned slightly and looked at her. "Oh yeah? What about?"

"We were having a picnic in the meadow."

Mark nodded his head.

"Now would probably be a good time for you to explain about your grandparents," Katie said, "for about the next fifteen or twenty minutes, and I'll be very attentive – asking questions here and there."

Mark turned his body to face Katie, and gave her a wink. "When will you begin your spring picture-taking?"

"As soon as there are clear signs of spring, I guess. I'm chomping at the bit to get on with it. When will Lane Farms get up and running?"

"It won't be long now."

They spent the next twenty minutes lost in casual conversation until the creases appeared on Katie's forehead and the corners of her mouth drooped.

"What is it?" Mark asked.

"I believe our time is up, and I must let you go."

"Oh, that's a relief. The way you looked, I thought it was something serious."

She reached out to rub his arm but quickly stopped herself. "If you came to my room tonight, would you sit on the edge of my bed and hold my hand?"

"Both hands," he assured her.

"Would you lie beside me while you held my hands, like you did in the hospital?"

"I would."

"You'd better not. I know I could feel you this time and would not be satisfied with it ending there." And she gave him that *certain* look.

"I think about lying beside you in the hospital from time to time, though I probably shouldn't," Mark said.

Katie smiled knowingly. "I wrote you a letter and thought I'd hand-deliver it since I'm with you. Tomorrow I will look between our back field and your meadow for a good drop spot."

He slid his envelope across the space between them. "Why, Mark, I'm so glad we've cleared this up." She slipped the letter into her pocket and stood up.

Mark rose, and Katie held out her hand to him. Spotting Mary watching from the window, he shook it as one friend to another.

"I brought the egg bucket."

"I was so *hoping* you would," she said with a smile. "Race you to the springhouse!"

Mark laughed. "Yeah, like you're going to beat me in a dress."

"If I had pants, I could give you a run for your money."

"I seriously doubt that."

Mark could barely see in the low light when he stepped inside the springhouse. His gaze swung around the room looking for Katie. He found her to his left, sitting on the old rickety table.

She crooked a finger at him, motioning for him to come closer. When he did, Katie pulled her dress up to her knees and hooked her heels behind his legs. Raising her lips up toward him, she gently pulled his head down to her, and they kissed slowly and softly. "To be continued, I hope," Mark whispered.

Katie recited. "Kisses and more kisses, let that be my fate. Come give me your kisses, if it's early or late."

Mary was busy in the kitchen when Katie entered the house. "It's okay, Mama. Mark and I patched it up."

Mary looked at her approvingly. "I knew you could, if you put your mind to it."

"Now that I'm going to learn to get along with my neighbor, I believe I'm ready to rejoin my peers. I'll begin with church on Sunday followed by the Sunday Sing." Her mother was smiling broadly as Katie walked away.

Katie went to her room and sat on the edge of her bed. She looked at her name on the envelope. She felt its bulkiness and wondered about its contents. When should she open it? Not now. Not in the middle of the day. She should wait until after she retired tonight so she could be alone and uninterrupted in her thoughts of Mark.

Mark entered his room and went straight to his old roll-top desk, and he opened the paper Katie had given him. Her letter covered the front and half of the back on a normal sized sheet of paper. He read the letter all the way through and then read it again, this time trying to analyze the words for any hidden or implied messages.

"Katie, Katie, Katie," floated through his mind. Here it was in black and white. She clearly reciprocated his admiration. He had to make sure no one ever found out, or his goose was cooked. Make that "their goose" was cooked. He decided to get a tin box to hide his letters in the attic of the shanty. No one ever went up there.

The rest of the day, Katie could think of nothing but the envelope from Mark. Try as she might, Mark was never more than a few seconds from her mind.

At dinner, Mary announced to the family that Katie would begin to attend the Sunday Sings again and even host the event soon. Her father congratulated her on a proper decision.

When she was finally alone in her room, Katie retrieved the journal and letter from her usual hiding place. Sitting at her table, illuminated by the kerosene lantern, she opened the envelope. She removed its contents while she thought. Her first love letter from the one she...? Adored. She couldn't bring herself to speak the four-letter word because it had not been spoken to her... yet.

Katie unfolded the pages and counted them. Three pages. She smiled and began to read. *'Dearest Katie.'* Her heart soared as Mark described the birth of his feelings for her. They really weren't so different after all. It took an act of God for both of them to realize their feelings for the other. He thought she was beautiful. Katie almost said the words out loud. She had never seen herself as such, but she didn't spend time looking into a mirror, either. The important thing was that Mark saw her that way. He knew lots of good-looking girls, and he said she was beautiful.

Katie read his words, though some of it was beyond her ability to understand completely. She had never seen herself that way or in that light. There were words like precious, cherish, and revere. There were phrases like "amorous delight" and "ardent persuasions." And there were sentences that were both dazzling and mystifying. He plainly confessed that she, and she alone, inspired the passion that he felt in his soul. How could she believe that which she had never heard or seen?

This need Mark spoke of to know all of her... what if he didn't like what he saw and learned? Should she wish to learn all of him as well, and having learned, might suffer the same fate? Maybe it would be better to have not learned so much in the first place? Mark also spoke of the feelings he had for her—the appreciation and the overwhelming reverence. He admitted his yearning to have her at his side. He stated that he did not fabricate any of this, in fact, did not wish it upon himself. But here it was, staring him in the face. He said all he had to do to be overcome by these feelings was to think of her or look upon her person.

She realized they were her words, too. It was as if he reached into her soul and stole them from her. She wanted to go to him and hold him in her arms forevermore. Why did she hurt so much when she wasn't with him? She wondered if it would be so bad to lose themselves in one another.

Katie read Mark's letter again. Then a third time.

She finally turned to the poem Peggy had told her about.

Bright Eyes
If ever a love as sweet as yours
Were to pass my way through my doors,
I would drive it out with a shout or scream,
"Be gone! My word, you're only a dream."

And if in dreaming I would be
Forever bound to a world of fantasy,
What better place to pass my time
Than locked in a world of joy sublime?

But could the joy be passed on to
The one whose heart I wish I knew?
Are there forces in the universe
To open your heart to my lowly verse?

Pray tell, is this too much to ask?
That hearts could join and forever bask
In the union of two lives made new,
Where hope springs eternal for me and you?

I give it up, I abdicate
To the One who is love so great.
I humbly bow, I bend my knee,
And pray, "Lord guide sweet Katie and me."

There it was, written by his own hand. The word "love" staring boldly back at her on the very first line. Would Mark write it if he didn't feel it? How much longer than she had he felt this way? And having felt, how much stronger are the emotions raging through him than her feelings that threatened to overrun her. Like a bumble bee on a flowering rhododendron, Katie hovered over the words "the union of two lives made new." She drank in the sweet nectar and felt her heart reaching out. "Come and be my love," she whispered.

Katie fell asleep clutching Raggedy Andy.

Chapter Twenty-Seven

Mark answered the phone when it rang shortly after eight on Friday. "Is this Harold?" the voice inquired.

"No. This is Mark, Mrs. Kimes."

"Oh, I'm sorry to confuse you with your father. I have a hard time telling the two of you apart. I'm glad I got you. I'm sorry to call so late, but I've had an exhausting day, and I was hoping to get a message to Katie. Can you deliver it to her tomorrow?"

"One of us will be sure to deliver it." His mother was within earshot, so he chose his words carefully. "I'm ready to take your message."

"Tell Katie that the therapy is going fine. I get the feeling my physical therapist wishes it was progressing faster, but I'm doing as much as I can. I'm exercising and eating well, and I believe it's only a matter of time."

After the call ended, Ann asked, "Did you want me to run that note down to the Bylers in the morning?"

"I'll do it since I'm going right past. Was there anything else you'd like from there?" She was slow to answer so Mark suggested, "We haven't had one of their hams in a long time."

"Yes, a ham would be nice," Ann responded while watching him.

"What is it, Mom?"

"I don't know. You tell me. Is everything all right at school?"

"You know school. One good thing is we're finally finished with Romeo and Juliet. Now we don't have to be assaulted with all that drama day after day."

"You don't like Shakespeare?"

"Not especially, when the play we're studying has a lousy ending. I mean, look at you and Dad. You lived happily ever after, didn't you?"

"We're doing a good job of it so far, but you never know when life will throw you a curve. Romeo and Juliet got their curve kind of early."

"Kinda?" Mark exclaimed. "And I'd say their curve was a doozy."

"Sometimes life's curves are doozies," Ann continued, "but I must agree with you that the story is heart-wrenching."

Ann took his hand as she looked into his eyes. "You have to keep your eyes open and anticipate the curves. Every decision you make affects lots of people besides yourself, so make your decisions wisely." Mark nodded as he silently mulled his mother's words. "I'm glad we had this little talk. I miss what used to be our frequent conversations."

"I'm sorry, Mom. I've been rather preoccupied lately. I'll try to do better."

"I'd like that," Ann confirmed. "How about giving your mother a hug?"

As Mark wrapped his arms around her, he was ever so conscious of the difference between the love for a mother and his love for a girl. Mark squeezed her tightly. "I love you, Mom."

"I love you, too." Ann planted a kiss on his cheek. "I'll get the money for the ham."

On his way back from the lower farm, Mark pulled the truck into the Bylers' courtyard. Moses came out of the barn, and they exchanged greetings.

"Since you have a message for Katie anyway, I'll let her get you that ham," Moses said. "Jacob and I are busy in the barn with a cow having a calf, but I guess you know what that's all about."

"Speaking of which," Mark said, "Midnight will be six months old next weekend. Is Katie going to be able to take pictures for us?"

"I'm sure she'd be happy to. She said that she can't wait for spring to take lots of pictures."

Mark was crossing the road when Katie came out on the porch. He waited there and greeted her cordially.

"I had to wait to see if Father would take care of you," she explained.

He handed her a paper. "Mom wrote out her instructions because she knew I'd forget something."

Katie opened the note and began to read. "Please give my son four quick squeezes, three really big hugs, and eighteen kisses – one for each year I've enjoyed having him around – until you came along, that is." She quickly ducked into the smokehouse and Mark followed.

"How did you know I came for a ham?"

"I didn't. I needed a place to hide my embarrassment."

Katie couldn't get the knot loose on the ham. "Give me your penknife," she said, pointing to his pocket.

He held the object up for her to see. "It's not a knife. It's a sassafras root."

"Why do you carry that in your pocket?"

"Smell it," Mark said as he handed it to her.

"Mmm, this smells really good."

"I smell it once in a while," he admitted.

She took another long inhale of the aroma. "Did you bring one for me?"

"Keep that one. I have another at home."

"Yes, everyone knows you should always have an extra sassafras root."

She turned the root in her hand. "It's freshly cut. Where did you get it?"

"At the back edge of the meadow where the woods begins. There are oodles of them. I dug some for Mom to make tea. She says it's better than buying it at the store."

Katie cocked her head. "You say there are oodles?"

"Sure. If you want, I'll dig some for you."

"Maybe a burlap bag full? I could sell them in the shop."

Mark rubbed his jaw. "Do you think people would buy them?"

"I know lots of people who buy pies and bread when they could make their own. Just show me where they are, and I'll do the rest."

Mark scoffed. "I don't think so. You'd need help." He just let his comments lay there like a dead fish on the cutting table.

Katie bristled until the real meaning of his words occurred to her. "Maybe some strong, young man could help me?"

"Now you're thinking. Hold up on the ham and I'll untie it." While Mark worked on the knot he suggested, "Why don't we dig enough to fill half a bag until we see if it catches on?"

As they walked outside, Mark handed Katie the message from Mrs. Kimes. "She's coming along slowly, but she seems to be satisfied," he said. "Say, I cleared it with your dad that you'd take Midnight's six-month pictures next Saturday."

"I was hoping we could dig sassafras roots Saturday morning."

"I can't. I told Dad I'd go with him to an auction, and I'd like to take the pictures right after lunch, while the light is still good."

Katie agreed, but he could tell she was disappointed about the sassafras.

"I'm going to be off school on Thursday. Why don't we dig then?"

She gave Mark a dazzling smile of gratitude. "Why is your school closed Thursday?"

"It isn't. I have a dentist appointment Thursday morning, and I'm taking the rest of the day off."

"Why?"

"If you must know, I haven't been feeling good since early last fall."

Katie was now concerned. "What's the matter?"

"I'm allergic."

"Allergic to what?"

Mark shook his foot a little. "It started out slow at first, just a slight twitch, but then it intensified." He jerked his left arm and shook his hand. "It spread up into my neck." He rubbed it.

"Any other symptoms?" Katie asked, as she stepped back a little.

"Teary eyes sometimes. Throbbing head, especially my temples." He rubbed them. "And restless feet."

"Have you gone to Dr. Ford?"

"Sure."

"What did she say?"

"It wasn't good, I'm afraid." Katie waited, not even breathing now. "I have an acute case of boredom, and she advised that I stay away from the offending location. She even warned, if left untreated, it could lead to mental instability."

Katie took a deep breath. "Have you ever been hit up the side of your head with a ten- pound ham?" she asked stepping closer.

"Can't say I have," Mark answered, as he backed away. The scowl on her face left no doubt in his mind that she was considering it.

Suddenly, Katie's face broke out in a big smile, and she laughed. "I can't believe you got me with that. *You are just awful!*" They enjoyed the moment as they watched each other. She wanted to punch him and kiss him, all at the same time, but was unable to do either. "What time on Thursday?" she asked.

"Is twelve-thirty in the meadow acceptable?"

"That sounds fine."

"Bring a burlap bag and the camera. I'll bring the tools and the tractor. We can tie the bag of sassafras on the back. No sense carrying it to your house. Is your mother going to be all right with us doing this?"

"I'm sure she'd much prefer it was some available suitor, but I am eighteen. Besides, you and I don't get along very well, remember?" Katie gave him a wink and a grin. "I enjoyed your letter and your poem. I would thank you properly but it would be unwise standing here in our courtyard. By the way, I found a good hiding spot for our letters. Why don't I show it to you on Thursday?"

"I enjoyed your letter very much, also," Mark assured her. "Thank you for all the nice things you said."

"We could write another to exchange on Thursday," she cajoled.

"My day has gotten brighter because I've seen you smile," Mark said.

Katie awoke with a start. The clock on her nightstand indicated that soon her alarm would sound. She lay her head back on the pillow and tried to remember her dream. What had startled her so? Some of it was coming back. Mark was standing off in the distance and motioning for her to come toward him. As she approached, a large wall sprang up between them, and she could no longer see him. A great emptiness enveloped her, and her world spun out of control. Time sped past. Her surroundings were not the same, and she became afraid. She could hear Mark calling her name, though she could not see him.

That evening, Katie contemplated her second letter to the one she adored. Dare she tell him how much she missed him when they were apart, or that she played his antics over and over in her mind? Perhaps she could share snippets of her journal with him. Mark said to be honest and open, but shouldn't there be limits? Surely she could explain to a minor degree how much she appreciated all that he had done to enrich her life. She didn't feel comfortable sharing her recent dream about the wall but the one of them picnicking in the meadow was perfect, so she wrote a half-page about that.

Mark was busy making plans for Thursday afternoon with Katie. He had played in the meadow his whole life, and he knew all the tricks. There was jumping from bank to bank across the small stream and playing with the moldable, gray clay in the creek bottom. Tree-bending popped into his head, but that was too dangerous. They could climb the big beech tree growing among the blackberry bushes and carve their initials high up where no one would see them.

How would they have time to dig sassafras roots and have fun together? Mark allowed his mind to drift as he sat in church on Sunday. He could dig the sassafras before Thursday and put it in the bankhouse. No, he'd better dig a hole and bury it so there would still be fresh dirt on the roots. Also, Katie couldn't jump the stream in her dress.

Mark considered buying her jeans and a top, though he wasn't sure she'd agree to wear them. He decided to borrow old ones from Peggy since they were about the same size. He'd have to find some time between now and Wednesday to search Peggy's room. He could ask her for them, but it would be best that she not know.

That afternoon provided the opportunity he needed. Peggy and Brenda were watching a movie while his mom and dad were finishing up taxes.

Mark quietly entered Peggy's room and opened her closet door. He spied a stack of jeans on the top shelf, lifted them down, and removed the bottom pair. He found tops in a box on the floor and pulled out the one from the bottom. He liked the multiple shades of blue stripes.

Mark slipped back into his own room and stashed the clothes in a safe place. He sat at the roll top desk and began his second letter to Katie.

Oh Precious One,

I was sitting in church today - one of the family occupants of Lane Row. That would be the pew that all other church members know is reserved for the Lane Family. We actually paid for it when the church put in new padded pews last year. Some might ask, "Well how do you know you didn't pay for the pew behind it or the one across the aisle?"

That is a fair question, but it must have been this one because the Lanes have always sat on the right side, third pew from the front. I offered to sneak in some night and carve our name on the end of it, but my mother was not amused. I also said if we are going to buy a pew, why not the third from the back? That way, when I fell asleep during church, it wouldn't be so obvious.

The pastor was preaching on tithing so I had a lot of time to daydream. I mean, think. I came up with some things we can do on Thursday afternoon that you will already know about when you read this letter. If you're still reading it, that is. Pay attention, because there will be a quiz—those infamous teacher words. Somewhere between, "God wants you to..." and "You'd be better off..." I wrote you this short poem.

> *There once was a girl named Katie.*
> *A blueberry crumb pie she gave me.*
> *I don't like to swear, but I do declare,*
> *The thing was so hot that she made me.*

Well, I like to say that one good poem shouldn't be left lonely so here is another for my one and only.

> *I sit here alone, entombed in my room,*
> *Surrounded by four walls, darkness and gloom.*
> *Where is my Katie, that good looking lady?*
> *Ah, here she comes perched high on her broom.*

I want to tell you that thanks to you, today I received high praise when shaking the pastor's hand as we left church. "I am twice blessed," he said to me. "Why?" I asked innocently. "I couldn't help noticing you taking notes today, and you didn't fall asleep. It is good that our young people are interested in tithing," he replied.

261

I hope your day was as enjoyable as mine. The only thing that could have made it better would be having you in it.

Your humble servant,

Mark

Chapter Twenty-Eight

"Are you sure you shouldn't go back to school after your dentist appointment?" Ann asked Mark on Thursday morning.

"I'm not going to feel like going back," he answered.

"I'm going to Granville shopping, then I'll stop for groceries. I could get home as late as three-thirty or four, so you're on your own for lunch. How long will you and Katie be digging sassafras?"

"Oh, a couple of hours ought to do it. Plus, Katie was hoping to get some early spring photos of our farm. What time is Dad getting back?"

"Probably not until suppertime or after."

Mark went out the door whistling. "Dreaming, I must be dreaming," he sang softly. He'd have to write a song about this. Eli had taken the day off to help his father, which meant no one would be at Lane Farms all afternoon. His mother's words of caution to behave himself around Katie Byler had already become a distant memory. He wouldn't do anything Katie didn't want him to do.

Mark relaxed on the outer side of the sloping bank at the deep end of Wagner's pond and looked across the fields in the direction of the Bylers. This day was already shaping up to be a beauty – partly sunny skies, and the temperature in the mid-sixties.

His heart quickened as Katie came into view. He rehearsed all he hoped to accomplish in the next three hours. She looked in his direction and waved. His heart ached as he watched her close the last hundred yards between them.

"Do you have a hug for me today?" she asked, and he gladly obliged.

"Why are you here?" Katie inquired.

"Because you're here."

She smiled warmly. "I figured you'd be in the meadow."

"This was a good place to wait. It brings back fond memories of days gone by."

"And nights," she added, with a twinkle in her eyes.

"Actually, I thought I'd save us some time, and you could show me the hiding place now. I looked for a spot while I waited, but couldn't find a great one."

"Did you see the hollow log at the edge of the woods?" Katie said, pointing.

"It looks like a log all right, but it's not hollow."

"Not at this end, but did you check the other?" He shook his head, and Katie smiled. "Maybe you should have."

Mark maneuvered through the fence wire and examined the log. The open end faced away from the pasture and was half covered by vegetation already. It was deep enough to conceal a tin with their letters. "I see what you mean. In a couple of weeks you won't even notice it.

Good job, Katie. I missed it completely."

"And so would anyone else," she added.

As they entered the meadow together, Katie spied the tractor.

"You brought the big one!" she exclaimed with delight. "You remembered I wanted to ride it, didn't you?"

He shook his head. "This one was the easiest to get out of the shed."

She playfully pushed him. "I know you're lying. So where do we dig?"

"We don't. I already dug. If we spent all our time digging, we wouldn't have any time for fun."

"Fun?" Katie asked with a gleam in her eye. "You have plans for us, don't you?"

"More than you know. This would be a great picture of the green meadow with the barren woods surrounding it."

"Walk out a few steps so I can get you in a picture," she instructed.

"I thought you didn't believe in that," he said.

"You don't look Amish."

After she got the shot, Katie followed him to the hole he had dug for the sassafras roots. They transferred the roots to the burlap bag and shoveled the dirt back in the hole.

"Now what are we going to do?" she asked.

"First stop is my favorite climbing tree - over this way among the blackberry bushes."

Katie looked up through its branches. "I can see why you like it."

Mark asked her if she was good at climbing trees.

"I do all right, but this tree doesn't look like one I'd better climb in a dress." She looked at him then burst out laughing. "Is that your best sad face?"

"I was hoping we could carve our initials way up high where no one would see them."

"I'd love to, but…"

"Could you climb if you wore jeans and a top instead of a dress?" he asked sheepishly.

"I suppose I could, but where would I get those?"

"I took the liberty of pilfering some from Peggy's closet without her knowledge. They are old ones she doesn't wear anymore, and she won't miss them. They're in a bag in the bankhouse, but if you're not comfortable with doing this, then we shouldn't."

Katie asked him to give her a ride to the bankhouse while she thought about it. As they approached she instructed him to pull up along the west side, the way he did the day of the storm.

"I'd like to get a picture of the way it was that day," she said as she dismounted the tractor.

Katie took a couple pictures and then asked Mark to sit on the log, so that she could get a close up of him and the bankhouse. She adjusted the lens and snapped two pictures before putting the camera away. "I'll slip into Peggy's clothes, then we can climb that tree. I've always wondered what it would be like to wear English clothes. No peeking!" she said, as she closed the door behind her.

Nothing had prepared him for the emotional high that pounded in his brain when he saw her in Peggy's clothes. As if that wasn't enough, the top was too tight. There should be limits to what a guy has to endure. He studied the lovely face with the tentative smile, the blue striped top covering shoulders that were just right, the perfect breasts that were more than right, the slim waist that needed a belt, and the rounded hips giving way to her long, slender legs. Only her cap and black work shoes brought him back to reality.

"How do I look?" she asked, while turning around. He opened his mouth to speak but was too enthralled. "This top seems a little tight," Katie opined, as she flexed her shoulders forward and back.

"You're not going to hear me complain." Mark was wide-eyed with appreciation.

Katie blushed and looked down, but she had seen the admiration on his face. She looked up once again, holding her head high, as she unashamedly displayed her womanly attributes. She slowly did another turn and moved her arms and hands in a gesture that begged an answer to "What do you think?"

Mark whistled softly. "You look way better in those than my sister, and the top will stretch." Without thinking, he continued, "Are you titillating me on purpose?"

Katie blushed again, only she wasn't smiling. She turned as if to retreat to the bankhouse, but then changed direction and marched up to him. With lightning speed she swung her right hand up, headed for a collision course with Mark's cheek. But he saw it coming and easily blocked her attempted assault with his left forearm. He stepped in close and clamped his hands around her wrists.

"What are you doing?" he demanded, as he stood staring into her defiant face.

"I am a lady, and you can't speak to me like that."

"Like what?" he asked, meeting her glare for glare.

"Don't make vulgar comments about my breasts."

He released her and stepped back to a safe distance. "First of all, your breasts - no, your entire shape from head to toe - is absolutely gorgeous, and if any man can look at you and not admire it, then there is something wrong with him. But what did I say that was vulgar?"

"Something about my bosom," Katie retorted, standing her ground.

Mark's expression softened and he smiled kindly at this lovely creature planted before him. Katie took a step toward him, then another.

"I'm sorry, Mark!" she said before he could get started. "You're going to tell me I misunderstood again, aren't you?"

"I'm afraid so," he said slowly, "and no one knows better than I that you are a lady."

She stepped closer, biting her lip. "What was the word?"

"Titillating. T-i-t-i-l-l-a-t-i-n-g. You can look it up in the dictionary. It means, 'to excite in a pleasurable way.' I was asking you if you were trying to excite me in a pleasurable way on purpose."

"Yes," Katie answered. "I certainly was." Again she moved toward him and stood her ground, allowing his gaze to wash over her. As he closed the space between them, she raised her lips to meet his, and they clutched in a powerful embrace.

When they parted he said, "I'm glad we got that little misunderstanding out of the way." "Me, too. Want to try again?" she asked, giving him a sultry look.

Mark scooped her up in his arms and while she clung to his neck, he swung around in circles. When he was too dizzy to stand any longer, he laid her in the grass. She wouldn't let him go and pulled him down to her, seeking his mouth for more kisses.

"Now, where were we?" she finally asked.

"I believe you were about to explain how much of a lady you are."

"Do I still need to?"

"No, I'd say you've made a believer out of me."

"Are you sure?" She laughed and tickled him. They rolled over with Katie ending on top.

"Now that you're in charge, what are you going to do with it?" Mark asked.

She kissed him softly, her tongue gliding across his lips. "I'm going to tell you that I love it when you kiss me and hold me in your arms." After a long embrace Katie said, "Let's go have some more fun."

"If you give me that shirt, I'll stretch it for you," he said.

She smiled inwardly. "Nice try, but I think I'll keep it on."

"I brought a bigger one if you want to try it."

"Why didn't you say so?"

Mark shrugged. "I think someone got me a little sidetracked."

He retrieved the shirt from the tractor and tossed it to her. She held it up displaying the 4-H emblem. "It's one of my old shirts," he explained.

"I'll be right back." When Katie emerged from the bankhouse, he was looking out across the meadow.

"Oh, Mark," she called in a sweet voice.

He turned and there stood a beaming Katie in his over-sized 4-H shirt with her beautiful hair falling all about her. "It's just not right that you do this to me. You know that don't you?"

He chased after her as she squealed and ran away. Mark caught up to her at the stream's edge. "Jump!" he called to her. She stopped, but he easily soared over the small stream, landing on the other side.

"It's only six or seven feet from bank to bank. You can do it."

"I don't think so," she said.

Mark laid two sticks on the ground, the same distance apart as the two banks of the creek. "I've been jumping this creek since I was about ten. Even if you don't make it, it's not the end of the world. You're going to get a little dirty and wet, that's all."

"That's all?" she repeated. "These aren't even my clothes."

"Okay, I give them to you. Now they're your clothes, so let's practice."

Katie soon realized that she could jump farther than the distance between the sticks. "I think I'm ready," she conceded.

"How would you like to try something new first?" Mark asked. "It could be a lot of fun."

"What is it?"

"You run toward me then jump into the air as high and far as you can, like you're going to sail right past me, only I catch you."

"How will you catch me?"

"With my arms stretched out in front of me." He scooped her up and held her in front of him. "Put your feet straight out and lean back from the waist up."

Katie went quickly from short jumps right up to the entire seven feet and more. Mark caught her smoothly each time.

"This is fun! I want to jump the creek."

After a couple successful jumps, Mark suggested they try it together while holding hands. The synchronization was tricky, but they mastered that, too.

"Okay, I'm ready," Katie announced.

"Ready for what?"

"Ready to jump across the creek into your arms, of course."

"Katie, I never suggested that."

"You didn't have to. I knew where this was going, Mr. Daredevil. I know you're willing to risk my life and limb."

"Okay, but I want to watch you cross the creek alone a couple more times to be sure you're ready."

Mark watched as Katie ran, took flight, and soared through the air. He watched her lightly touch down - full of grace while at the same time strength and power with her golden hair trailing out behind her. He couldn't see that once and not want to see it again.

"One more time, Katie. I think you have it just about perfect, but I want to be sure." He was definitely smiling on the inside. As he watched a second time, Mark yearned to have a camera in his hand, but dare he ask?

"Okay, you're ready. Now remember, don't be afraid to bring your legs up. You must trust me to catch you. Only one thing can make this go wrong, and that is your fear."

Katie ran, leapt, and soared - and Mark caught her. "A perfect ten," he declared. He dropped her feet to the ground, buried his face in her hair, and held her close. "I want this in a picture," he rasped.

"Then take it, silly boy." She leaned fully outward, trusting him not to drop her on the ground. "But first, we must do that again." And Katie being Katie, insisted on another jump after that.

Then Mark got the shot of a lifetime: Katie midstream, walking on air, looking his way with "her smile" while her long, blond hair streamed out behind her. His 4-H t-shirt rippled in the wind, showing an oh-so-slight section of bare midriff. He would always call it "the greatest shot ever made."

And, of course, Katie took a couple of Mark alone in flight.

She was inserting a new roll of film when he said, "Since you're letting me take your picture, I want one of you sitting on the tractor."

She mounted it and slid onto the seat. Mark climbed the bank in front of the tractor and took shots from both left and right. She clutched the steering wheel and leaned forward, cocked her head slightly to the side, raised her chin, and smiled in a pose right out of a fashion magazine.

Katie had no reservations of the camera, and she reveled in it. She laughed and smiled while he emptied the roll of film. He took pictures of her sitting on the tractor fender with her knees against her chest, leaning against the old oak tree, poking her head and locks out the cabin window, and standing at the door. Mark took a picture of her sprawled on the bank, spread out like a snow angel in the grass, her arms and legs sticking out in all directions. He had spread her hair from arm to arm, in a huge fan shape above her head.

"Do you have any more film?" Mark asked when he took the last picture.

"One more roll is all. You're costing me a lot of money."

"No, I'm not, because *I'm* sending these in. You don't dare have them mailed to your house." Mark didn't dare have them mailed to his house, either. He would take them to the camera store in Granville and have them developed there.

"How much longer do we have?" she inquired.

Mark glanced at his watch. "Less than ninety minutes before we need to leave this meadow. We're running out of time."

"What else did you want to do?" Katie asked eagerly.

"Climb the beech tree and carve our initials." He tossed her one of the knives he'd brought.

"Who's going up this tree first?"

"It's your tree, so it should be you. Besides, I'm only looking out for your safety."

"What's that supposed to mean?"

"If I go first, I know what you'll be gawking at the whole way to the top. You could fall and get hurt."

High up into the tree they climbed and carved their initials – 'K.B. + M.L. 1966.'

As they returned to the bankhouse, Mark paced off one hundred steps across the meadow. He pushed an upright stick into the ground as he began and when he finished his paces.

"What's that for?" she asked.

"Maybe your statement, 'Race you to the springhouse' will help jog your memory," Mark said with a devious smile.

"From here to the springhouse?" she bantered.

"Wanna race?"

Katie looked from one stick to the other and then at Mark. "Is this where we start?"

"Uh huh," he nodded.

"Who's going to say, 'ready, set, go?'"

"Why don't you go first since you'll be finishing last."

"Oh," she replied with a flirtatious look. "Are you going to give me a head start?"

"Do you need one?"

"Not me." She glanced back toward the bankhouse with enlarged eyes.

How could he help but look? She had baited him perfectly. And she was gone in a flash.

He tore off after her – angry at himself for being duped. He caught up to her, but Katie could run and for a while she matched his speed. Finally, he began to pull ahead.

Just when it seemed the race was decided, Mark caught his toe on a tuft of grass and stumbled. He tried valiantly to regain his stride, but Katie had closed the gap between them. She dove and wrapped her arms around his thighs. He landed flat-out on the grass with Katie on top of him. She jumped up and ran across the finish line.

She turned and exclaimed, "I won!" while he was picking himself off the ground. Mark gritted his teeth and glared at her... then started toward her. She began to run again. He caught her and grabbed the back of her shirt to slow her down, but she struggled and fell with Mark straddling her.

Katie lay beneath him between his hands and knees that were firmly planted on the ground, but she was nowhere near corralled. She gazed into his eyes, and with a saucy smile, mimicked him. "Now that you're in charge, what are you going to do with it?"

"Tell you that you should be punished for cheating."

"Go ahead and punish me," she implored, giving him a look that could start a fire.

Mark groaned, and her open invitation continued. Her bright eyes crinkled merrily. She ran her tongue around her already opened lips, then stroked his arms.

"What are you doing up there? Come down here and punish me with kisses."

In a guttural voice, she pleaded this time, "Punish me." She reached up and pulled him down to her, and their lips clashed in a powerful attempt to consume. Mark pulled her tightly against him while she stroked his back. As the exchange concluded, her breathing came in gulps and her chest heaved as she clung to him.

Mark raised his weight off her. "Are you all right?" he asked, his voice filled with concern.

Katie laughed. "No, I'm not all right. You're driving me crazy." And she kissed him again... tenderly, yet clearly conveying her desire.

Their movements became a slow dance – gentle and methodical with each caressing the other. Their kisses transformed to sensual as they shared the raw emotions that joined them.

When their lips parted at last, their eyes would not. Mark leaned on his forearms as Katie lay beneath him with his hands for her pillow. For long moments they gazed into each other's soul.

Finally, she stroked his cheek. "I don't want to, but we must go."

There was one more endeavor Mark had saved for last. On the way to the bankhouse, he hoisted Katie above his head and she got to experience the thrill of soaring in the daylight.

Afterward, Katie ducked inside to change, and Mark waited patiently until she emerged. "All good things must come to an end," he muttered.

She handed him the bag of clothes. "Maybe I can use them again someday… or night."

"I'll hang onto them," he assured her.

"I'm looking forward to that tractor ride," she said.

"Since I won't get my proper thanks at the end, how about if I collect it now?" he suggested.

Katie smiled and moved in close. "You didn't think I was leaving this meadow without thanking you properly for the best afternoon of my life, did you?"

A little while later, Mark helped her onto the tractor and tossed her the camera case. Before he started the motor, she slid onto his lap and asked sweetly, "Want something to remember me by the next time you're driving this tractor?"

"Uh huh," was all Mark needed to say.

"Do you have a letter for me?" she asked as they drove through the lane.

He reached into the toolbox and retrieved it.

He smiled at her look of satisfaction. She put his letter in the camera case and withdrew one for him. He placed her letter in the toolbox, then put the camera case between his feet on the floor.

"Ready for some fun?" Mark asked above the clatter of the motor, as they turned onto Old Mill Road. "Let's go for a ride!"

Katie's face lit up when he didn't turn left toward her house but instead turned right. It was a half mile to the next farm, which the Lanes also owned. Mark ran through the gears and soon had the tractor at top speed. Katie was tentative at first, but before long she was beaming with delight. He watched her out of the corner of his eye and every once in a while stole a sideways glance. He turned the big tractor around in front of the barn and headed home.

Mark checked his watch and brought the tractor to top speed once more. His mom would be coming home soon. He glanced behind him, but no cars were in sight. He slowed as they neared his home buildings, and Katie squeezed his arm.

"Can we go up and back again?" she pleaded. "This is fun with the wind rushing by me." Her honest exuberance was too much to resist.

On the way up the road, she held one hand then both hands in the air, almost giving Mark heart failure. When he turned the tractor around, he stopped in front of the barn.

"Katie! You have to keep one hand on the handgrip," he cautioned.

"I'm sorry. It felt so liberating."

"All right," Mark said, "When I get up to top speed, stand beside me and I'll hold you. Then you can put your hands up." She nodded, and he started out again. As he slid his arm around her midriff, she pressed something between his legs. He glanced down to see her white cap.

There they were: flying down a rural road with his arm around her while she stood beside him. Her arms were raised to the heavens while she enjoyed every second, like a kid on a roller coaster.

When they passed his home, Mark slowed the tractor, and Katie sat down on the big fender. He handed her the cap, and she smiled and placed it on her head while Mark held firmly to her leg. He motioned to the hand grip, and she took hold of it once more.

What they were too busy to see was Mark's mother coming up behind them in the car. She never got closer than a couple hundred yards, though that was close enough for her to see what was going on.

Katie squeezed Mark's arm and with a contented look said, "That was a heavenly ride."

"I'll have to take you on the roller coasters someday," he told her.

He swung into the pull off in front of the bake shop. Katie hopped down and walked around the tractor to the side hidden from view. She leaned toward the tractor and patted its number plate. "Nice tractor," she cooed.

Chapter Twenty-Nine

Ann was waiting for Mark when he sauntered into the kitchen to return the empty thermos. He hoped her look wasn't meant for him.

"How'd the shopping go, Mom?" he asked nonchalantly.

"Great, until I was almost home." She pinned him with a glare.

He knew his hope was futile. "Then what happened?"

"Don't play dumb with me, Mark. You know very well why I'm angry."

"All I was doing was giving her a ride."

"Correction, young man! All you were doing was playing with fire." He bowed his head. "Why, Mark?"

"All I was doing was giving her a ride on the tractor."

"You had your arm around her! And she wasn't wearing her cap. Not even her Promised is permitted to see her that way."

"She liked the freedom of flying with no tethers. It was only a loose precaution."

"Everyone likes that feeling, but that doesn't make it all right. It appeared to me there were a lot of loose things happening."

"I was just making sure she didn't fall off the tractor."

"Why would you do it in the first place?"

"Because. We haven't been getting along lately. That's why I agreed to help dig the sassafras, and I promised her this ride last summer."

"Why did you promise her a ride?"

"It was the day of the storm. I took her back to the meadow on the tractor to find their blackberries. She remarked how impressive the 4020 was. I told her that she should ride it at top speed, and she asked if I'd take her someday. I didn't see any harm in telling her I would."

"The harm would be to our friendship with the Bylers if any Amish saw or heard of your little escapade. The harm would be to Katie's reputation as an available future wife. Her people wouldn't look kindly upon such an activity."

He sighed. "Nothing happened."

"I've got eyes, Mark. I can see that she's a good-looking girl. You have this under control, right?"

"There's nothing to control," he insisted.

Ann pointed her finger at him. "See to it that you keep it that way!" Her tone said the discussion was over, but Mark knew the subject would never be far from his mother's mind.

Katie's return to an unsuspecting Mary was much more pleasant. Her mom was impressed with the volume of roots dug but did question her daughter about the cleanliness of her clothes.

"Oh, Mark did all the digging. He only brought one shovel. I just loaded the bag, and I rolled up my sleeves for that. I took some pictures while he was digging."

"The roots smell good," Mary remarked. "Why don't you clean a few, and we'll boil them for our supper beverage."

Katie was ready for the one question that she knew would come. "You thanked Mark properly for his help?" Mary asked.

"Yes, Mama." Katie smiled as she returned to the porch. She intended to thank him again the next time they were together.

When Katie retired to her room for the evening, she opened her camera case and removed Mark's second letter. She laughed when she read it and then quickly asked God to forgive her. She laughed again at the poems, cutting it short at the end of the second one. She read his last sentence, "the only thing that could have made it better would be having you in it" and thought of how wonderful this day had been because he was in it.

Katie wrote Mark a short letter thanking him for a wonderful afternoon. Would he stop to see her after school tomorrow? She planned to carry the letter in her pocket in case she saw him.

The Lanes' phone rang that evening. "It's Mrs. Kimes," Peggy called. Mark was the first to reach it. When Ann came up from the cellar, he was writing notes, and she heard him say, "Katie will be so happy. I won't take this

276

information to her tonight because she wouldn't be able to sleep, but I promise first thing tomorrow we'll pass everything along. I have it all written down, Mrs. Kimes... you are very welcome... no, it's not necessary to feel indebted... if you were to invite me, then I would... we look forward to your homecoming, and I know Katie will be seeing you soon... please call as soon as you are ready for her to visit. It looks like you'll be home just in time for Easter."

Mark was helping himself to some ice cream when Ann entered the kitchen. He glanced sideways and found her looking at him. "It's wonderful news about Mrs. Kimes, and I'm sure you must be feeling very happy right now."

"I am, Mother, but the one who is going to be even happier is Katie. She deserves most of the credit for caring about Mrs. Kimes."

"She's a remarkable young lady who deserves to be congratulated, but remember our talk, Mark."

"I will, Mother."

"Do you want me to run the message down to Katie in the morning?"

"No, I think I'll do it on the way to school. But thanks anyway."

Mark retired to his room and began a letter to Katie.

My Dear, Sweet Katie,

I have thought long and hard since I first read your letter this afternoon. I am grateful for having you in my life.

Twice in your letter you used the word "debt." I do not want you to think that you are in my debt. In the beginning, I did everything out of friendship and because I cared about you. As our relationship developed, I've come to know the real you, and I could not be happier. But I want to know for sure that what you give of yourself is because you care for me and desire to be with me, and not because you are repaying a debt.

I believe we made another great step forward today in learning to care for one another. I hope you enjoyed our time together as much as I did.

Let's make a pact… no debt.

Am I dreaming,

Mark

P.S.   If this is a dream, please don't wake me!

Mark put the letter in an envelope and placed it with the message from Mrs. Kimes to deliver to Katie on his way to school. He reached for a sheet of paper and began to write again. He wasn't sure if it would be a poem or a song he could sing to Katie, but he wrote the title at the top of his page, "A Love That Never Ends." After a few failed attempts, Mark wrote on a clean sheet of paper:

Katie is a Verb

The word is out, or haven't you heard?
Katie's not a noun, it's a verb!
Katie's not a verb I know you'll say.
You'll change your mind by the end of day.

You just came, and it's still early.
There's plenty of time for you to get surly.
Hang around. She'll make you a believer.
Can't keep up? You may as well leave her.

The debate lives on. It never ends.
A word to the wise to all my friends.
Noun or verb, what does it matter?
If you see her coming, by all means scatter.

"Oh, Katie?" Mark called, as he entered the Byler barn the next morning. Katie stepped out from between two cows, milk pail in hand.

"Shhh," she held a finger up to her lips.

He gave her an apologetic look and whispered, "What's the matter?"

"I'm not sure where Father is."

"Gone, I suspect. His buggy isn't out there."

She relaxed and her face lit up to see him. "It's good to see you."

"You know I'm going to remember that look all day long, don't you?"

"That was my intent. You've heard about the armor of God, haven't you?"
Mark nodded.

She laid her hands on his chest. "That is your armor against all those flirtatious girls."

"You worry for nothing," Mark said.

With big, trusting eyes, Katie assured him, "I'm not worried."

"That's because you know how much I adore you."

"True," she admitted. "Do you have something for me?"

Mark took the papers from his pocket. She spied the envelope then reached out and slowly removed it from his fingers. "Is this another letter for me?"

"Uh huh."

"I'll trade you." She gave him her own, and slid his letter into her pocket. "Thank you. What else do you have for me?"

He stood quietly, looking at her with a twinkle in his eye and the paper in his hand. "It's Mrs. Kimes, isn't it?" Katie's eyes lit up. "Tell me what she said. Is it good?"

"It's really good. You can read all about it later, but the short version is she's beginning to walk and coming home tomorrow."

Katie threw her arms around him. "This deserves a celebration!"

"Yeah, we'll have to throw a party."

"I meant you and me."

"There will be lots of moonlight tonight," he began.

"Keep going," she encouraged.

"I could make a fire, and we could drink hot chocolate and toast marshmallows."

"I'll bring a couple of cookies," she offered.

"Let's say eleven," Mark said.

"We don't have to stay long," Katie added. "I was hoping to spend some time with you after the great time we had yesterday."

"Will you let your hair down?"

"I'd be glad to." Her look said even more. She gave him a quick kiss. "Thanks for your last letter, too."

"You're just so…" Mark began.

Katie knew it was coming, and she held up her index finger - moving it back and forth in front of him. "Don't say it. I know you want to, but please don't - for me."

He gazed upon her and capitulated. "You're just so very delicious."

Katie hugged him. "I knew you could do it. See you tonight."

When her work in the barn was done, Katie headed for the house to share the good news about Mrs. Kimes with her mother. Although she was anxious to read Mark's letter, Katie went about her morning routine and then helped her mother prepare the noon meal. She later feigned a headache and retired to her room. After reading Mark's letter, she composed her own short letter to give to him that night.

Dearest Mark,

Our times together are all like a dream and I sometimes wonder if I am dreaming too. I've actually had several dreams with you in them. Only one has left me puzzled, and I'm still waiting to see if it can be explained. I have heard that dreams have a connection to our lives.

I have never told you this, but thinking of you brings a peace to my spirit that allows me to sleep at night. It all started last summer in the aftermath of the spider incident. Your letter of apology and the drawings of the meadow were the beginning. Before that, it was not unusual for me to be awake for an hour or more in the middle of the night. Now, it is a rare occurrence - unless I am with you! If I added up all the hours of sleep I used to lose, they would tally more than if we met once a week.

You asked me once, how I stay awake in church. Saturday night, before our church Sunday, is not a good time for you and I to meet. To stay awake during Service, I need to get a full eight hours of sleep. When I had a restless night before church, it was very difficult to stay awake. I have been known to nod off a time or two.

Eyes Wide Open,
Katie

Mark listened to the weather forecast on his way home from school. An idea came to light when he heard the low temperature would be in the mid-fifties. "Tonight will be my first night at the bankhouse," he announced to his mother as soon as he arrived home. The plan justified all he would take with him and his absence from the house the entire night. God bless spring.

Ann tried to object. "You'll freeze. You don't have the bankhouse cleaned out."

"It's only going down to fifty-five," Mark informed her. "You know I've stayed there when it was colder than that. My sleeping bag will keep me plenty warm."

"You've got to get up early to go to the sale with your father."

"I'll take my alarm clock with me."

Ann finally relented. "Oh, all right, but take Bella with you to stand guard. And take your shotgun, too."

Mark hitched the wagon to the tractor and loaded it with gear. He hurried through his chores and finished them before supper so he'd reach the meadow while it was still light.

Though Katie's arrival was still several hours away, Mark started a fire in order to have a bed of coals and positioned the cooking rack above it. He felt quite satisfied as he sat on the log by the fire, strumming his guitar and playing a tune in his head. "I want a love that never ends. Give me a girl to be my friend." As the words came to mind, he wished he had brought a pencil and paper.

After throwing more wood on the fire, Mark entered the bankhouse and crawled into the sleeping bag, intending to close his eyes for just a few minutes.

281

Something woke him, then he recognized Katie's voice. She was renewing old acquaintances with Bella.

Mark emerged from the bankhouse and Katie said, "There's that sleepyhead."

He grinned while stretching. "Hi!"

"Hi, yourself. What's all this?" She made a sweeping, motion with her arm.

"I'm moving in for the summer."

"You do know, don't you, that spring just started?"

"Yes, but they have this new-fangled device called the radio, and it said the low tonight was only going down to fifty-five."

Katie remarked, "I would have gotten here a little sooner, but I had to walk tonight, since I can't see to ride my broom in the dark."

He looked at her sheepishly. "I hope my attempt at humor didn't put you off."

She pretended to scowl. "Come over here and sit on the log."

Like Bella, Mark did as he was told, though he pulled her onto his lap and kissed her playfully.

"Did you bring the jeans?" she asked.

"They're on the straw bales, along with both tops."

Katie stepped out of the bankhouse into the firelight with her hair more beautiful than Mark had ever seen it – waves abounded. She was wearing the blue striped top, which looked better by firelight than daylight, although Mark wondered if that was even possible. He watched as she came toward him and was physically affected immediately.

"Do you like my choice?" she asked.

She held her arms out to him while he sat on the log. "I can't stand up right now," he confessed.

Katie gave him a devilish smile. "Was it something I did?"

Mark looked into those tantalizing eyes and replayed the words her sweet lips had said. "Are you really that quick?"

"Not always," she said honestly. "We'd better let you calm down. There is always Wagner's pond, if necessary." A look of pity crossed her face.

"I sure wish I had my camera."

"Would you like to use your other camera?"

"Did you bring it?"

"Right here," and she reached behind the log to retrieve it.

"Sit on the log, and let me look at you." Mark walked to the far side of the fire, squatted down, and focused the lens for a close-up of all of her.

"Before I take these pictures, I want you to know that you are the most beautiful thing I've ever seen and not just the most beautiful person. Remember when you smile for the camera… 'Mark thinks I'm gorgeous.'" He took two pictures, then zoomed the lens in on her head and shoulders and took two more.

"I'm glad you put that top on, but I know it's not the most comfortable for you. If you want to change tops, feel free to do so."

"I would prefer the other one," she admitted.

When she reappeared from inside, he asked, "What did you do to your hair tonight? It looks different."

"I washed it after supper and put it into two braids instead of one before I laid down to catch some sleep."

"It has more waves and looks so good on you. Be my guest to do it anytime."

Katie smiled appreciatively. "I'd be glad to."

"I'm curious why you brought the camera tonight."

Katie began mixing up some hot cocoa in the pot hanging over the fire. "I brought it in case you wanted to take a picture. After yesterday, I realized how much it means to you to have pictures. If you're used to having them then you want them, I guess."

"So you did it for me?"

"Partly. For me, too," she said.

"But you're violating the rules."

"Our youth violate the rules all the time - maybe not this one, but some others. Why should my violation be any worse than theirs? A sin is a sin."

"So you view this as a sin?"

"No. This is man's rule. I don't believe God views it as a sin. Are the English going to hell because they have their picture taken? I don't believe in all our rules. Some are a yoke around our neck. There are principles on which I should stand, but I don't believe this is one of them."

"Tell me how you feel about becoming English," Mark ventured.

She studied his face. "You cut right to the heart of it, don't you, Mark?"

"You should talk. I was hoping to get the little things out of the way at the beginning." He waited and watched until her eyes danced and she cracked a smile. "I was hoping you'd smile at that."

Katie looked off into the night while she contemplated what he had said. "Are we at the beginning?"

"I hope so!" Mark exclaimed with conviction. "I don't want it to be anywhere else."

"To answer your question, if we decide that we should be together then I believe a woman's place is with her husband. We promised each other total honesty. I would be less than forthcoming if I didn't admit that there are worse places to be than at Lane Farms."

They sat side by side, sipping their cocoa and eating date-filled cookies that Katie had brought. They looked into the fire and into each other. It was only the beginning, but a bond was forming all the same. The most critical question was not how deep the bond would become, but how long they would have to strengthen it.

"About riding the broom," Mark said. "I hope my attempt at humor didn't put you off."

"That's the second time you've mentioned it," she acknowledged. "It didn't put me off. It made me laugh." She hooked her arm around his and laid her head on his shoulder. "Also, I couldn't help picturing us sitting there in church together." She leaned over and kissed him on the cheek.

"Well," he drawled, "this Sunday is Easter, and they always encourage us to bring visitors. This isn't your church Sunday, so why don't you tell your mom I invited you?" She rubbed his arm.

"I take it that's a 'no' then?" Mark asked.

Katie turned his face toward her. "Thanks for the offer. Now kiss me to make me feel better." He gave her a soft, tender kiss, and she sighed in approval.

"Why are you really staying all night in the bankhouse?"

"It's Mother, I'm afraid."

Apprehension seeped into Katie. "Why are you afraid?"

"She's beginning to suspect you and I may be more than just squabbling neighbors. She saw us cruising down Old Mill Road on the 4020. I think I successfully diverted her suspicions, but she'll be a lot harder to fool from now on. I knew sneaking out of the house tonight was not a good idea, but my staying here all night is not out of the ordinary." Katie's tension eased as they sat in silence holding hands. "It made me realize we'll need to write letters and use the drop spot if something ever happens to keep us from seeing each other for a while. I will not stop seeing you unless I hear from your own lips that it's what you want."

"If we commit to each other, you know I won't do that," Katie stated.

"I suspected it, but it's good to hear you say it."

Mark added wood to the fire then retrieved an old blanket from the bankhouse. He spread it between their straw bale and the fire, draping the outer edge over the bale.

He rubbed her bare arms. "Are you sure you're warm enough with only my shirt?"

"Near the fire, it's plenty warm enough, but a girl has other needs you know." She stepped closer, and slipped her hand into his. "What are your plans for the blanket?"

"Would you like to cuddle?"

"Does a newborn calf like milk?" She leaned in against him and looked longingly into his face. "I have a letter for you in my jeans pocket."

Mark nodded then suggested, "I could use the bale for a back rest, and you could lay against my chest like we did those two nights by the pond."

"It's a start," she replied. "Let's take our shoes off and get comfy."

Mark surrounded her with his embrace, and she leaned into him while stroking his arms. He collapsed his knees in upon her, and they moved against each other in a full body palpation.

She murmured her contentment between sighs and unintelligible sounds. "That's what I want… to feel you around me… to feel you touching me. Please don't stop… don't ever stop."

Katie sighed contentedly. "I really loved the ride yesterday."

"If you thought that was something, you should do it in my car with the top down. That would be three times faster than the tractor."

"I can't even imagine such a thing." Her voice was filled with wonder.

"I can only imagine it myself. It's rather difficult to drive and stand on the seat at the same time."

Katie snorted and quickly put her hand over her nose while she was turning red. Mark watched her saucer eyes and deadpanned, "Is that the new chortle?"

"Uh huh. Sorry."

Mark chuckled and squeezed her. "I can't believe my sweet Katie snorted."

She elbowed him and said, "Enough, Mark," and quickly changed the subject.

"When you were holding my waist and my hands were in the air, it was so liberating with the wind rushing by me."

"The wind wasn't rushing by you. We were travelling through the air, which was virtually still yesterday."

"Mark?"

"Yes, Katie?"

"Are you always going to be so literal?

"Why? Is that strike one? How many strikes do I get before I'm out?"

"If this is kickball, you get one more."

"You're a hard woman, Katie Byler. Can I do anything for extra credit?"

"Yes, be nice. No wait! You can kiss me again… and by the way, how did you get to be such a good kisser?"

"It certainly wasn't from smooching on other girls."

"Seriously. The first time we kissed up in the barn it was good, but you were tentative. You're not anymore."

"If you promise not to laugh or get mad at me, I'll tell you," he bargained.

"What you tell me might make me laugh or get mad at you. What do I do then?"

"You're not going to make this easy for me, are you?"

"Nope."

"Oh, all right. I stopped at the bookstore in Granville and bought a book called *The Art of Kissing*."

Katie stared at him. "They had a whole book on kissing?"

"Yes, all one hundred and sixteen pages."

"How many did you read?'

"About forty, I guess, but what does it matter?" Mark asked defensively.

A thoughtful look came over her. "So," she began, "if you were to read the rest of the book, you'd be three times better than you are now."

"How do I know? Would you like to read the book?"

"I believe I would," she responded, much to Mark's surprise.

"You never cease to amaze me."

"I've got something for us to try," she said, "but you must take me seriously. Let's stand facing each other. Now I want you to give me your very best, most passionate kiss."

"Really?" his eyebrows shot up.

"Do I look like I'm kidding?"

Moments passed before they finally parted. "Wow!" Mark uttered.

"Wow, yourself," she agreed. "Did it feel like I was repaying a debt?"

"Okay, you got me. Want to shake on our new pact?" he said, extending his hand.

She shook her head. "Give me another kiss to seal the deal, then I must go home."

Katie quickly changed clothes and they spoke briefly before she slipped away. "Don't forget we're taking pictures of Midnight tomorrow. Dad will pick you up in the truck about one o'clock. We need to throw my parents off the scent. I'm going to ask you to do something that will be difficult for me to do, as well. Let's act like there's nothing between us. That means no smiling eyes, no looks, or sideways glances. You are simply our friend and photographer. Is that okay?"

"You're right, Mark. It will not be easy, but I can do it."

Chapter Thirty

Harold and Mark rode quietly on the way home from the auction Saturday morning, each lost in thought. "Maybe I should have bought that tractor and high lift," Harold said breaking the silence, "but I couldn't justify paying so much for equipment that is half worn out. I thought I might get it for a reasonable price until Moore joined the bidding. I swear, he did it to spite me."

"What's he got against you?" Mark asked.

"Your mother," Harold replied with a cocky smile.

"Huh?"

"He was sweet on her when I came along."

"Mother obviously made the right choice. He's so unrefined and coarse. I can't imagine my mother liking him."

"Sometimes people develop into one thing or another. He wasn't always that way." Harold glanced at his son.

"Speaking of your mother, she's been a little concerned about you lately. She says things are changing and doesn't know exactly when it started. She's sure you've been different since Katie's pneumonia."

"Well, yeah," Mark said. "You go through that, and see if it doesn't change you. You know as well as I do that Mom gets these mistaken ideas sometimes. The hospital incident changed things between Katie and me, for sure, but we're only friends. She's grateful I've been helping her with the photography."

"You know," Harold said, "I've always wondered how you got Moses to agree to that."

"I think he wanted rid of my influence on Jacob and Katie more than he didn't want her taking pictures."

"You don't think you're being a little harsh?"

"No. It's real easy to see what other people's problems are, just watch and listen. Anyway, this is partially your fault, Dad."

"How did it get to be my fault?"

"You always said, 'You learn a lot more by listening than you do talking.' Actually, if you had only included the word 'watching' in that phrase, I could have blamed it all on you." Harold glanced sideways at Mark, saw him grinning, and just shook his head.

"If you could convince Mother to give it a rest, that would be nice," Mark added.

They grabbed a quick lunch before setting out for the lower farm. Mark took the tractor, pulling a wagon of feed for the cattle, while Harold drove the truck and stopped to get Katie.

Harold and Mark led Molly and Midnight into the alfalfa field. Katie used the hillside as a background and snapped most of a roll of film on the duo. She finished the roll on a few pictures of the herd and property.

Mark and Katie were alone for only a few minutes while Harold tended to Molly and Midnight in the barn. "Did you get my letter?" she asked, handing him the roll of film.

"It was right where you said you had it. I was worried about you when you headed home. We should have ended it sooner. How are you now?"

"I'm fine, but looking forward to an extra-long sleep tonight."

"Be sure and think about me."

"I always do," she said with a smile.

"I want you to tell me about that someday soon. I had a great time last night."

"So did I."

"I slept with your jeans in my sleeping bag."

"How come?" Katie asked.

"I could smell you on them all night long." She blushed and looked down. "I'm sorry to embarrass you, but total honesty, remember?" he said gently.

"It's all right, Mark. Honesty is good."

While Mark fiddled behind the tractor, Harold emerged from the barn. "Well, Katie, do you think we'll have some good pictures?"

"Many good ones, Mr. Lane," she said confidently. "The light was perfect, and Molly and Midnight were majestic."

"Here's the film, Dad," Mark said as he tossed it to him. "Geez, I just remembered, I left the pin in the wagon." Mark spun on his heels and ran to get it.

"How is the photo album progressing?" Harold asked.

"Quite well, but I must admit the day I went to the camera store in Granville, I caused quite a stir."

"Oh? In what way?"

"An Amish girl buying five photo albums, film, a magazine and an instructional book? All eyes were glued on the girl in blue."

Harold chuckled. "I guess if I had been there I would have been watching you, too. Don't forget I'm paying all your expenses. When I drop you off, why don't you run into the house and get your receipt? I'll reimburse you."

"Thank you, Mr. Lane. That's kind of you."

"If you need to return to the camera store in Granville, please let one of us drive you. It's an awfully long distance for you in the buggy."

They walked toward the truck, and Harold held the door for Katie as she stepped into the cab. He turned to Mark. "When a young lady leaves your presence, it's good manners to say goodbye."

"Huh? Oh, bye Katie," Mark said.

Later that evening, Ann and Harold were discussing Mark's behavior. Ann had shared her suspicions with him, and she was anxious to hear what he observed.

"It's a hunch," Harold said. "You have no proof. I agree it was foolish of them to be flying down an open road with his arm around her, but I believe he was doing it for the reasons he stated. There would be negative consequences if your hunch turned out to be true, but even if it were, what are we supposed to do about it? They're both eighteen and mature enough to be responsible for themselves. If you're asking me, I'd say there's nothing going on. Mark and I talked about this on the way home from the auction, and he explained it to my satisfaction. Besides, they hardly looked at each other today while Katie was taking pictures. When you and I were dating, we couldn't keep our eyes and hands off one another."

"Mark isn't stupid, and Katie Byler is quite aware of the consequences of having a relationship with an English boy. Maybe they were playing it cool."

"Ann, you only confronted Mark on Thursday night. How could they have collaborated on this already?"

"I'm not sure," Ann conceded. "I've been trying to figure it out. Mark dropped off Mrs. Kimes's message to Katie on his way to school yesterday morning. He could have told her then. Did they say anything to each other today?"

"Katie asked him if he knew what time Mrs. Kimes was expecting to get home. Other than that, they didn't say two words to each other. Here's the real kicker... when I was holding the door for Katie to get in the truck so I could take here home, Mark was rooting in the glove box of the tractor and wasn't even going to say goodbye. I had to give him a lesson on manners."

"How did Katie take it?"

"She just chuckled and said it was all right. What do you have to go on, really?"

"Woman's intuition," Ann insisted.

"Is that anything like voodoo?" Harold asked, the beginning of a smile tugging at his lips.

"Got me to marry you," she retorted.

"You've read too many spy novels, methinks. Conspiracy, conspiracy, conspiracy."

"I'll be getting home from school about an hour late tomorrow," Mark warned his mother Sunday evening. "I'm going to the music store in Granville to get new guitar strings. While I'm there, I may as well stop at the camera store and get Katie five or six rolls of film. They cost more at Sampson's, and Dad promised to pay all her expenses."

"He told me he just reimbursed her yesterday," his mother informed him.

"News to me," he shrugged.

"Your dad gave me the receipt from the camera store in Granville."

"How did she get there?"

"Your dad said she went in the buggy," Ann replied, as she studied him.

"All the way to the camera store in Granville?" Alarm flared briefly in his eyes. Ann brushed it aside as his entire demeanor changed.

"I wonder if her parents know she did that," Mark mused, then gave his mom a mischievous grin. "I'll bet she could get in trouble if they don't know but somehow found out." His eyes lit up like the Mark she knew so well.

"They'd better not find out, or you'll have to find yourself another photographer," Ann warned him.

"Maybe I was wrong about Mark and Katie," Ann confessed to Harold later that evening. She repeated her conversation with Mark. "He was genuinely surprised. If they had something going, I believe Katie would have told him about going to Granville, but it's more than that. His reaction to all this was vintage, old-time Mark. I know he would have bet me that Katie's parents don't know about that trip, and if they found out she'd be in big trouble."

"Is that it?" Harold asked.

"Not even the half of it. His eyes lit up at the prospect of getting her in trouble. I almost told him to make sure he keeps his mouth shut."

"What are you going to do?"

"I'll never tell them," Ann said.

"Do you think I should speak with him? I don't want to lose my photographer, and I like Katie. I can see where photography has helped her."

"My gut feeling is Mark won't do anything, and we shouldn't either," Ann replied.

Mark did indeed get new guitar strings in Granville after school on Monday. He also bought six rolls of film with his father's money and left three rolls at the camera store to be developed. And he stopped at the Goodwill store.

"Are you going to Bylers anytime soon?" Mark asked his mother when he passed through the kitchen.

"I'll probably stop on my way to town tomorrow," Ann said.

Mark dropped the bag of film onto the counter next to the door. "Would you take this film to Katie, please? And you may as well give her Mrs. Kimes's message from Saturday night."

"I'll take that, too. Thanks for the reminder."

As Mark left the room, Ann had an uneasy feeling. She hated to be wrong, and she was beginning to suspect she might be. That thought was still fresh on her mind when she knocked on Mary Byler's door the next morning.

"Hello, Ann," Katie heard her mama say when Mary opened the door. "Nice of you to stop by. Come on in."

"May I offer you a tea?" Mary asked. "We have lots of fresh sassafras brewed. I'm sure you heard where that came from."

"Yes, Mark told me all about it," Ann answered. She watched Katie out of the corner of her eye. If Katie heard or cared, she gave no indication of it.

"Hello Katie," Ann called to her and waved. "I've got a message for you." Katie paused from her cleaning and greeted Ann. "Will Kimes called Saturday evening to let us know they had made it home safely. He said his mother was pretty tired, and the ride home was very taxing to her back. He said she'd probably spend all day Sunday resting and recovering. It might be awhile before she can accept visitors."

"Thank you for the message. I'll get back to my cleaning and let you visit." Her eyes brightened when Ann handed her the bag of film. "Thank you, Ann."

The two women sat at the large dining table. "I was on my way to town, and stopped to see if you needed anything at the grocery store," Ann said, "and I wanted to ask you for a favor. I was hoping I could get you or Katie to make a blueberry crumb pie for my supper tomorrow night."

"What's the special occasion?" Mary asked.

"Mark's prom is only a month away, and he hasn't secured a date yet. I asked him if he knew anyone he could take, and he said he wasn't going. I think he's still feeling snake-bit by that girl from Granville. He hasn't gone on one date since then. Although I will say he's been spending a lot more time this winter playing his guitar. I can't help wondering if he thinks that instrument is going to win some girl's heart."

"Stranger things have happened," Mary said. "What's your plan? I know you, Ann, and you're not accepting defeat this easily."

"I'm going to give it one more try," she confessed. "I thought I'd fix Mark's favorite meal tomorrow for supper and top it off with a Byler pie and vanilla ice cream. I figure if that doesn't do it, nothing will."

Ann saw Katie smile. "What do you think, Katie?"

"We'll make the pie, and you can try to persuade him, but I was just thinking, 'Who knows what a man will do,' and they consider us fickle." Ann and Mary chuckled in agreement.

"That's my Katie," Mary added. "She's not too keen on men yet."

Katie scrunched her face and when she had left the room, Mary said in a low voice, "But I did have to put my foot down about the way she treated Mark."

"Oh," Ann said, "Mark didn't mention it."

"Except for that time in the hospital, you know they have never been too friendly with one another. Katie got mad at him the night of my birthday celebration, and I made her apologize. They sat right out there on the smokehouse steps for a good half hour talking. I saw them shake hands when it was over, and everything seems to be fine now. I'd say it's about time."

"Goodness," Ann remarked. "What could they have talked about for that long?"

"Besides the apologizing part, I'm sure a goodly amount of the talking was Mark explaining about your parents. He tried to tell Katie when we gathered at your house, but she thought he was just telling tall tales. I will say it didn't start out well. At one point Mark jumped up, paced about, and leaned against his car. I was afraid he might get in it and leave, but I could tell Katie coaxed him to sit down again. All's well that ends well, I guess."

"That's for sure," was all Ann could say, but she did a lot of serious thinking on the drive to Powder Mills.

The next evening Mark was pleasantly surprised to view the meal set out on the table: rib roast, mashed potatoes with homemade gravy, and his mother's special way of serving corn - heated with milk and sugar. "And it isn't even Sunday!" Mark complimented his mom.

"You should see dessert," Peggy piped up.

"What's for dessert?" Mark asked his mother.

"Blueberry crumb pie with vanilla ice cream," was her answer, but it was the way she said it that made him nervous.

"I love you too, Mother, but what's up?" Mark asked staring her down.

"I wanted to ask you if you'd given any more thought to attending the prom."

"Not really, but you most likely have my date all picked out for me."

"Cathy Parker," she informed him, "who lives at the other end of the road, doesn't have a prom date yet."

"Yes, I know who Cathy Parker is. She and I were just talking in the cafeteria yesterday. Wait a minute! Did you say something to her mother about the prom?"

"Actually, it was her mother who said something to me. I only agreed with her that you and Cathy would make a sharp prom couple."

"Since you seem so hep on helping me, Mother, there is something you can do. I want to go to Granville again on Friday, and I was hoping to get out of last period gym. We both know I don't need the exercise that class has to offer."

"What do you need in Granville? You were just there the other day,"

"I don't need anything. I want to pick up a couple of speakers for my backseat. Jim said he'd help me put them in Sunday afternoon if I had them. If I skip gym, I'd get home at the regular time, so I could get my chores done."

"You shouldn't skip school," Ann countered.

"I'm not skipping school. I'm skipping one gym class. I'll consider your suggestion about the prom if you write me an excuse to get out of gym."

Ann acquiesced. It might not have been the food that did it but at least her goal was partially achieved.

"We haven't heard from Mrs. Kimes yet," Mark said to his mother on Thursday. "I hope she's doing all right."

Ann thought for a moment. "I'll bake a casserole and take it down to them tomorrow. It would have been neighborly to have done it before this."

"Thanks, Mom. Let me know how she's doing. By the way, I'll be sleeping at the bankhouse tomorrow night."

"Do you have to? It's going to be colder."

"I've got a fire, a nice warm sleeping bag, and the radio to keep me company."

He called to Bella and headed for the meadow to make preparations.

Mark was ready for bed, though there was still one more job he wanted to do. Like his work at the bankhouse, this was a labor of love.

My Dearest Sweetest Katie, his letter began. Katie would read it the following night before closing her eyes, in spite of the hour.

How could Mark know the reaction a simple word could evoke in her entire being? That simple word was "My." She would read it again and again, dwelling on its implications. "Am I really yours, Mark?" she'd whisper aloud. Do I dare be so bold in my future correspondence? Will you one day soon declare your complete feelings for me and await my response? And what will be my reply?

The letter continued: *I have been searching for weeks to find a word that best describes you, one that I can call upon to bring instant memory and recognition of what and who you are to me. I could run through the scrapheap of words rejected, but the one I have chosen is "exotic." Being a man, I could have changed one letter and been quite happy with my selection, but it would not do you justice. While erotic is a strong part of your being, it pales in comparison to the totality of you. No, the choice must be exotic. The dictionary defines it as "strikingly unusual" or "having the charm of strangeness." In this case the word strange means "different," not odd or weird. I can see that look in your eye and on your face even though I am not with you, and it makes my heart do strange things. It makes me want to grab you and hold you. It makes me want to laugh out loud and revel in the wonder of you. Which reminds me; my second choice for you was "wondergirl," the explanation of that to be reserved for some point in the future.*

I am including the poem I wrote after our afternoon in the meadow. "Katie is a Verb" exemplifies the spirit of exotic.

Sweet dreams,
Mark

Chapter Thirty-One

Mark was a man on a mission as he added wood to the fire Friday night. Invigorated by two hours of sleep, he looked forward to Katie's imminent arrival. When Bella gave her first low woof while staring east, he was checking the pot of water over the fire. After school he had rummaged in the shanty and found a large cast-iron pot, a true relic belonging to his grandfather or great-grandfather Lane. Mark brought that pot to the meadow, filled it in the creek, and now the water was nice and warm.

Bella's continued woofs accompanied Katie's shimmering flashlight as she crossed the meadow. The Border Collie thumped her tail and looked at her master. Finally, Mark gave in with a laugh. "Go girl." Bella was off like a rocket, reaching Katie after she crossed the stream. The two girls trekked the last hundred yards together.

Mark patted Bella and told her she was a good girl. "I've been a good girl, too," Katie said with a hopeful look.

"I'm sure you have," Mark said. He reached out and took her into his arms. After a long embrace, he held her at arms' length. "Let me just look at you."

"Tell me what you see," Katie entreated.

"I see a very lovely lady who is standing before a very lucky man."

"Why are you so lucky?"

"Because you're about to go in the bankhouse and change your clothes."

Mark pointed her in the direction of the cabin and gave her a nudge to get started while gently slapping her on the bottom. Katie turned and glanced at him as she went. "Is that an old English custom?" she asked with a smirk.

"The bag of clothes is lying on the chair," he called after her.

"We have a chair now?" she remarked. "That's nice. I won't have to sit on a scratchy bale of straw to get my jeans on."

With her transformation complete, Katie emerged from the bankhouse in Peggy's jeans and a light-blue sweater. "Where did you get this nice sweater?" she asked approvingly.

"Every time you do that it blows my mind."

"Do what?"

"Stand there looking good enough to eat, but secondly, change from one girl to a completely different one in minutes."

"So you approve then?" Katie asked, slowly turning full circle and giving him an inviting look. "I had my hair up in two braids to give it more curl like you asked."

Mark scooped her up in his arms, kissing her soundly.

"I stopped at the Goodwill Store in Granville and got you some stuff."

"Including this sweater?"

"Yes, the lady said it was fifty dollars brand new, but I only paid four. I liked the feel of it. It's so soft and inviting, and the sleeves are really loose." Mark encircled her wrist and slid the sleeve up to her shoulder. "It's so loose it must feel like you almost don't have it on."

Katie couldn't look at him without turning color. "Sorry," he murmured, quickly sliding the sleeve back down.

"It's all right. It's just an uncontrollable weakness," she said.

"It may be uncontrollable, but it's not a weakness," Mark replied. "You look so..." Katie held up her finger in warning.

"...very cute every time you do that."

She patted him on the back. "Good boy," she cooed. "What else did you get us?"

"I didn't get me anything."

"Oh, I beg to differ." Katie straightened up and pulled her shoulders back. "Don't you think this sweater does a little something for you, too?"

The firelight flickered in Mark's wide eyes, and he nodded. "Umm, where was I? Oh yes, I got us a couple lighter-weight tops, a pair of slacks, and an old suitcase to keep everything in. It's in the trunk of my car."

Katie turned her attention to the large structure of straw bales near the fire. "What have you built, Mr. Carpenter Man?" she asked, circling it.

"It's a chaise lounge," he answered. "Crude and homemade, of course, but serves the same purpose."

"Very nice, but that straw is going to be itchy."

Mark entered the bankhouse and returned carrying a quilt and a blanket. "This is the quilt my grandmother gave me a couple years ago for my birthday. She said she was sure I could put it to good use. For now, I can't think of any better use for her quilt than you and I relaxing on it."

"This is going to be very comfortable with our heads angled up like this, but I can't put my shoes on the quilt," Katie said respectfully.

"Lay back and relax while I remove your shoes and socks."

Mark placed them at the side and retrieved the big pot from the fire. He checked the temperature of the water. "That's too hot unless we're going to be eating your little piggies."

Katie looked on as Mark poured some cold water slowly into the pot. She tested it gingerly, rolled up her pant legs, and submerged both feet above her ankles. She sighed contentedly.

"Let me wash them for you," he said, reaching for the soap. Mark gently washed her feet, one at a time. He held each foot above the water, rubbed it with soap, gave it a thorough massage and then rinsed it in the pot. Sitting on the edge of the bale, Katie murmured her pleasure.

"Didn't you already do that one?" she asked.

"Uh huh. Do you want me to stop?"

How could she tell him that she never wanted him to stop: that she wanted him to touch her in other places, including places that seemed to have a mind of their own? Dare she tell him how he was exciting her?

Mark's caresses felt so good. She imagined his hands gliding upward along her leg. Her desire threatened to overwhelm her. And how could Mark help but notice? He ran one hand over her jeans up to her knee and beyond, caressing and massaging her leg as he went.

Katie reached down, placed her hand on top of his, and squeezed firmly. Her lips parted and she uttered, "Mark, oh Mark."

The sound of her own voice rasping, "That feels so good," brought her back. His eyes caressed her and a delicious shudder shot through her.

For a long moment, they searched the heart and soul of the other with Mark finally capitulating, "You're in control, Katie."

"I'm not very much in control," she admitted. She looked down at their hands then back at Mark. "I'm not going to pretend I don't want your hand there, because that would be a lie. You cannot know how you excite me. It's a powerful force to control."

"Excitement is good," Mark said lovingly.

"Not when you're going off to college this fall."

He leaned forward and she met him halfway. They kissed, soft and tender. It was a kiss that said, "All is well." Mark dried her feet with a towel.

"Do you have another towel?" she asked when he had finished.

"I have one more."

"Good. Get it for me, please?"

When Mark returned, Katie instructed him to sit in her spot. He acquiesced and Katie slowly removed his shoes and socks, then placed his feet into the pot of still-warm water. "Enjoy it, as I did."

Mark leaned back on his hands with his elbows locked, not taking his eyes off this woman before him for whom he cared so much, for so long. He let the warmth of the water and the feel of her hands sooth him.

Katie finished, crawled onto the lounge, and snuggled into his arms.

Mark spread the blanket over them, shielding them from the cool night air.

"I hate to spoil our good mood, but I have information about Mrs. Kimes. Mother baked a dish and took it to her today. She seems to have hit a brick wall in her progress, and that's why we haven't heard from her."

"Tell me the rest," Katie said.

"She was beginning to walk in Chicago, although no more than she still can walk here. It's painful and takes a lot of effort. The doctor had warned her that progress was going to be slow. I think when she was in unfamiliar surroundings being handled by strangers, her resolve was greater than now when she is in her home near people who care about her. She says she isn't sure she can do it, or if it's worth it."

"But she can't give up!" Katie bemoaned.

"You tell her that," Mark countered.

"Maybe I will," she replied. "We may as well get all the bad news discussed together. Your mom would be a lot happier if you'd ask someone to the prom."

"She was at your house whining to your mother, wasn't she?"

Katie nodded.

"Do you want me to hold another girl in my arms, dance close to her, and feel her body pressing against mine? She'll expect me to kiss her." Mark saw the tears welling up in Katie's eyes.

"I don't want you to do any of those things, but if it would be better for you at home, then I would bear it."

"I will not put you through that kind of mental torment."

"Thank you, but I have a similar situation," she confessed. Mark waited silently, rubbing her arm as she lay with her head on his chest. The tears had been averted, but he could feel the tension all through her.

"It's okay, Katie. I know your heart, and I don't care what it is."

"Since you and I were in the hospital together, I have not participated in all our social functions. I have attended church and accompanied my parents on Sunday visits, but I have had very little contact with Amish youth. Deborah is the only true friend I have. Lydia and I were so close, I didn't develop other friends. The main youth social event is the Sunday Sing on Sunday evenings. My parents have been putting pressure on me to attend them again for months. I knew my time was limited on holding out and I did, in fact, attend the last one."

"What do you do at these gatherings?" Mark asked.

"It's simply a social time. We sing songs, but we also play games, have refreshments and sit around and talk. If a couple is courting, they come together and leave together. Sometimes people will leave with someone even though they came alone."

"Do these gatherings often lead to courting and marriage?"

"That is the intent of most youth who attend. It's all rather tame and innocent, really."

"Until it is not," Mark added. "Do you have boys who dote on you at these gatherings?"

"Casual acquaintances, mostly," she answered. "I spend my time with the girls. It used to be Lydia, before she moved away."

"To appease my parents, I really should attend these Sings. I enjoy them, as well. We get to interact with our own age group, free from parental supervision."

"I can understand your feelings on that," Mark admitted. "Our parents are a serious threat to you and I being together. They have a real potential to sink our ship."

Katie leaned on an elbow and looked down at him. "I don't intend to let them."

"And I believe you feel that way," Mark assured her, "but we have a saying in our world: 'the road to hell is paved with good intentions.' Parental interference may never come to pass, but it should be our main concern. You're saying you should attend these Sunday gatherings to ease your parents' mind and for your own enjoyment. I have no problem with either reason, but why were you nervous about explaining this to me?"

"He means nothing to me, but there is one boy. Well, I should say 'man' because he'll be twenty-one this year. He has asked for permission to court me in the past. I turned him down flat without even telling him I'd think about it. I didn't even like boys then, let alone want one courting me."

"When was this?"

"About a year ago. He could have a girlfriend now, for all I know, but I really don't care. He means nothing to me."

"What's his name?"

"Rudy Hostetler. Now can we get off this uncomfortable topic? Our time together is too precious to say another word about it. Look at me, Mark! I promise you that as long as we are pursuing the possibility that there may one day be an 'us,' I have no interest in any other man. Do you understand?"

"Aye, aye, Captain! This ship will stay afloat until we sink it," he quipped.

"That's better," Katie said.

She took his hand and led him into the bankhouse. She asked him to turn his lantern on low. When the small cabin was filled with dim light, she stretched out on his sleeping bag with her head on his pillow and raised her arms toward him.

304

"Before I must leave you, I need some 'power love,'" she said plainly. "I want to look into your eyes, as I feel all of you. It is what sustains me until I see you again. Overwhelm me with the physical presence of you, here where you sleep."

Eyes held unwavering as the minutes passed. There was a joining of their souls as each gave completely to the other. "Controlled power" would describe their desires as their bodies moved together. Their movements were slow and gentle and words were not spoken, for to do so would only diminish the event. Then came Katie's urgent words. "Crush me, Mark. If I can't have all of you, then give me everything else."

Each mouth sought the other, and this time they climbed a mountain in their minds together as a crescendo of emotions carried them to the grand finale.

When their passion abated, Mark asked huskily, "'Power love,' huh? Where did you come up with that one?"

Squeezing his upper arms, Katie looked up at him. "You're the muscle man. You figure it out."

He couldn't wipe the grin off his face. "You are fantastic," he said earnestly.

"No, you are fantastic. What do two fantastic people do if they don't want to get in trouble?" she asked mournfully, play acting.

"Jump in Wagner's pond," he ventured.

"You jump. I'll watch. I've already had pneumonia."

They laughed and Mark swept her up in his arms. "Next Friday, same time, same place?"

"I don't know if I can wait till then."

"I'll stop for eggs in midweek. You must get home to bed, so hurry and change your clothes."

Mark waited patiently for Katie to emerge from the bankhouse then entered to retrieve his book and letter. "If you find any good information after page forty, will you teach me?"

She smiled her classic smile. "I don't know if they'll accept that on deposit, but you can take it to the bank."

"There's a letter on page forty for you as well."

"But I didn't write one for you."

"It doesn't matter. You already wrote me four, and this is only my fourth tonight."

"But who's keeping score?" she opined with a smirk. Then her face drooped. "We didn't look at our pictures."

"We can open them together next Friday."

They embraced and kissed good night. As Katie turned to leave, she looked back at him. "Give me my starting momentum."

He was puzzled, but she continued, "You know, like when I was going into the bankhouse as our night began."

He understood and stepped closer. "Why don't I pretend it's an arm and just rub it instead?"

"Suit yourself, Lover Boy."

Mark gently rubbed her backside and gave her a nudge toward home.

Chapter Thirty-Two

Katie had turned her alarm clock back for fifteen more minutes of badly needed sleep. Still, when it went off, it was too soon. She quickly silenced the annoying device.

Her heart was heavy as she went about her chores in the barn. Mark's words about Mrs. Kimes giving up replayed in her mind. Katie didn't know what her next move should be, but she knew she had to do something.

As Moses said the lunchtime blessing, Katie knew what she must do.

"I believe the Holy Spirit is telling me to visit Mrs. Kimes this afternoon," she announced to everyone. "She has been home a week, and no one has heard from her. I fear that all is not well."

"I'll assign Sarah and Daniel some of your chores, and we'll get by," Mary responded.

Katie let her horse walk as she made the trip to Hogback Road. The slow journey gave her time to formulate a plan. Will Kimes came around the corner of the house from the back yard as soon as she pulled under the carport.

"How is you mother doing today?" she asked after dismounting from the buggy.

"I'm glad you came, Katie. Maybe your visit will brighten Mother's demeanor. I'm afraid she hasn't been well these last few days. She's in really low spirits."

"I know a Spirit that will cleanse that out of her," Katie said confidently.

A smile formed at the corner of Will's mouth. "Let's hope so. Mom is reading in the living room. Let me take you to her."

Will led Katie through the front door, but they stood together in an empty room. "Now, where did she go?" he mused. "She was reading here the last I knew."

"Greta! It's Katie. Where are you?" Greta appeared in the kitchen doorway in her wheelchair. Katie tried valiantly not to show alarm as she hugged Greta. Will quietly slipped out of the room. "What are you doing?" Katie inquired.

"Trying to get myself a drink while seated in this infernal contraption," Greta muttered.

"Let me help you. In fact, why don't I make us some tea? I brought a bag of sassafras roots."

"I've heard of it, but never had any," Greta said.

"I like it, and I'm sure if you add your usual cream and sugar, you'll like it, too. I swear sometimes you must be related to Mark Lane – you both have the same sweet tooth."

Katie and Greta sat on adjacent sides of the chrome-frame kitchen table with its colorful, blue Formica top and waited for the sassafras roots to boil. "Mark would like your table. Blue is his favorite color," Katie commented.

"That's the second time you've mentioned Mark," Greta pointed out. "Anything I should know about?"

"Greta! He's English. You know that's not allowed."

For the first time, Katie saw life in Greta's eyes. "You're getting mighty flustered over something that's not allowed," Greta opined.

"It was all worth it just to see you smile," Katie beamed proudly.

"Oh you devil, you!" Greta slapped her hand playfully. "I should have seen that coming. It's this back, you know. It has me seriously depressed. I'm sorry for not calling, but I wanted to show you my success, and I'm afraid I don't have much to show."

"You can start by eating a good meal," Katie admonished her. "Will told me you haven't been eating properly, even though he's been preparing full meals."

"Blabbermouth! That kid never could keep anything to himself."

Katie snorted out a laugh. "He must be forty years old!"

"Forty-one to be exact, but he'll always be a kid to me. Wait until you get your own children. You'll see what I mean."

"Try your tea, and while you're doing that, I'll fix you a late lunch. Let's see what's in your icebox to eat. Hmmm, I could make home fries with this leftover potato, and you have bacon and eggs. How do you feel about breakfast?"

"I'm not promising I'll eat it," Greta informed her.

"Do I need to go out to my buggy and get the whip?"

"Bossy young thing, aren't you?" Greta countered.

"So I've been told."

"Mark again?" she guessed. Katie busied herself with the task at hand and pretended not to hear.

"How's the tea?"

"Really good! It's fresh, isn't it? I could tell from the aroma of the roots."

"Yes, I just dug them last week."

"What, no Mark this time?" Greta asked innocently.

Katie continued preparing the meal and was thankful her back was to Greta. After placing the food in front of her, Katie was surprised and pleased to see Greta consume it all, right down to the last slice of toast with jam. When Greta finished, Katie took her hand. "Why haven't you been eating? Is your son that bad of a cook?"

Greta's face drooped. "No, I just haven't had the will. I had so hoped to be walking on my own by now."

"What's the reason you're not?"

"It's very painful, and I need help to do it. Will has to work, and by the time he gets home, I'm all tuckered out."

"If you had called, I would have helped you," Katie scolded.

"You have enough work to do. Besides, I'm losing confidence that I'll ever walk again."

"There is a whole passel of people at our house to do the work, and it's time for some of them to lighten my workload."

Greta's shoulders slumped as she stared down at the table.

"Tell me one of your favorite stories from your nursing days," Katie suggested.

Greta delved into a story. When she had finished, Katie requested another. She laid her hand on top of Greta's. "Both of your stories were amazing successes. Neither had even a so-so ending. They both had an element of miracle in them, as did my survival of pneumonia."

"My question is, 'Why you, Katie?' Why did God choose Mark, and why did He choose you? I hope that one day you know the answer."

"Perhaps you are the reason. Maybe this was all about you. God saved me through Mark so the two of us could team up with Dr. Ford, your son, and all the good medical staff in Chicago so you could walk again. You told me you had been praying for your healing for years, did you not?"

"Yes, I did."

"Your prayers have been answered, and God has done His part. Now you must do your part. You must fight to regain your ability to walk."

A sheen of tears formed in Greta's eyes. Katie took Greta's hands in her own, bowed her head, and began to pray. "Dear Heavenly Father, give Greta the will to walk again. Give her the strength to overcome her pain and the endurance to outlast it. We pray in Jesus' name that you bring long-lasting triumph over this injury. We rejoice in the success of her operation and ask You to lift her up, Father, so she may complete her recovery. Blessed is the Lamb, the Son of God, and the Father Almighty. Amen."

Katie squeezed Greta's hands then stood beside her wheelchair. "And Jesus said, 'Rise and walk!' The only difference is I am here to help you."

That first afternoon, Katie and Greta made only one trip from the kitchen to the front door. Greta gripped her walker while Katie shuffled along beside her. Katie helped move the walker forward and made sure Greta didn't fall. Near the front door, Greta sat and rested on the padded arm of a chair.

"You'd better get my wheelchair," Greta instructed her.

Katie shook her head. "We are going to walk back together."

And so they did, with Greta weeping as she returned to her wheelchair. Later Greta admitted that they were tears of pain and not the tears of joy Katie assumed. Her imagined success drove Katie to return the next day on her way home from church. The two women made that trip again, but not before Will intercepted Katie once more.

"Mother said you might return this afternoon. Thank you for coming. I don't know what you did to her, but it worked. She ate supper last night, and we had a hearty brunch late this morning. She looks better just since yesterday. Mother told me you received a miracle from God. Maybe you're her miracle."

"I am just a friend trying to help," Katie said.

"You're more than that. And Mother is blessed by your presence, so whatever you're doing, please keep doing it. She's not out of the woods yet, but at least she's not the negative, bitter person she was before you came."

"I am glad she is better today. It truly distressed me to see her so dejected yesterday," Katie confided.

"The timing of this couldn't be more perfect," Will continued. "My boss has been asking me when I can resume my business trips. I haven't been able to give him an answer. I know you were friends with Lydia. I paid her to stay all night and check on Mom during the day when I was gone. She slept in the spare bedroom down the hall from Mom's room. Would you be willing to take over that job? I'm sure we'll have no trouble agreeing on a wage if you consent."

Katie stammered. "I don't come to be paid. I come out of friendship."

"Please, don't be offended. I'm just trying to get the best care for my mother. You were her friend first, but I'm still going to pay someone to stay with her, and it may as well be you. You can still be Mom's friend. I'm the one who will be your employer."

"I will have to discuss it with Father and Mother."

"Understood," Will replied. "If you accept the position, my work will take me out of town next Sunday afternoon through Wednesday. If you can't do it, I'll have to hire a retired nurse I know. I'd much rather pay you, and so would Mother."

Katie paused, wondering what to make of all this. At last she said, "Your mother doesn't know it yet, but I intend to come back on Tuesday morning. I'll give my answer to her then."

"I can't ask for more than that. Thank you, Katie, and we sincerely hope you'll accept."

Katie found Greta in the living room. She was immediately struck by the difference that Will had described: the smile on her face, twinkle in her eyes, and the cadence of her voice. Katie was overjoyed and excited to begin their afternoon together.

They drank sassafras tea, exchanged ladies' gossip, and Greta shared another nursing story. Katie loved the stories about the expansive western

311

states. Greta and her husband, George, had lived in most of them due to his engineering job, and Greta had been a nurse everywhere they went. Katie shared her love of nature and photography with Greta and promised to bring pictures for her to view.

"If that isn't amazing, then nothing is," Greta exclaimed. "If an Amish lady can take pictures, then I can surely walk!"

They walked to the front door and back. "One day I will donate this wheelchair to someone who needs it, because I no longer will," Greta proclaimed when she sat down. She rested for five minutes and held her hand out to Katie. "Let's go again."

After another successful trip, Katie could tell that Greta was tired. "You've done a wonderful job today," Katie praised her, "but it's time for you to rest."

Greta eased into the chair and released a weary sigh. "This is very difficult, but it is getting better. I need to become more sure-footed so you don't have to hold onto my arm, and I wish my legs were stronger." She grew serious and touched Katie's arm. "When can you come again?"

Katie smiled. "Tuesday morning about ten, if that isn't too early."

"Goodness no," she responded. "I'm an early riser."

Katie leaned down to give her a goodbye hug.

"Please consider Will's offer," Greta whispered into her ear.

As Katie made the short trip home, she was elated over Greta's recent transformation. She thought about working for Will and getting paid. It would help greatly with her photography expenses, and she would even have money to help Mark add to her wardrobe. The Goodwill clothes were fine for now, but there were things she had seen the English girls wear that she was anxious to try herself: tennis shoes, fancy tops, colored pants, printed dresses and such.

That evening, Katie approached her parents as they relaxed in the large living room. She explained the progress Greta had made in two visits and asked them to excuse her from household duties on Tuesday morning. "I promised Mrs. Kimes I'd return to help her walk. I told her I couldn't do it tomorrow, since it's wash day."

"Poor Mrs. Kimes," Mary said sympathetically. "I'm sorry to see her struggling so."

"Oh, Mama, when I first saw her on Saturday afternoon, I feared that all was lost. Now it seems that she may yet have success."

"Praise the Lord," Mary stated. "We are proud of what you are doing."

"That is what I promised Will Kimes I would talk with both of you about." Katie explained Will's offer.

"The extra money would come in handy for everyone, including yourself," Moses admitted. "When would Mr. Kimes come for you on Sunday afternoon?"

"He said he was hoping for one o'clock, but it was flexible," Katie answered.

Moses looked thoughtful. "This means you would not attend the Sunday evening Sing, and I assume Mr. Kimes knows you don't do housework on Sunday."

"I suspect he already knows our Sunday beliefs since Lydia performed the same duties. He said many of his trips do not involve Sundays."

"Yes, but the Zooks were from Lancaster, and some of their ways are not our ways. If we give our consent to this job, it cannot repeatedly interrupt your social life. We are going to be visiting my brother Joseph's family next Sunday, and this means you will not accompany us."

"I am growing up, Papa," Katie asserted. "I would have requested to skip that outing anyway. I would rather spend the time here at home relaxing and reading. You know there are no girls my age at Uncle Joseph's."

Moses silently studied Katie. "You are growing up, I'm afraid. Where did the time go? I can clearly remember the day you were born. Wasn't it just yesterday?"

Katie gave Greta the good news soon after arriving on Tuesday morning. She was in high spirits, and her mood washed over Greta like a tidal wave. "Let's celebrate by skipping rope," Greta declared, and they both laughed. "Be sure to thank your parents for me."

Katie and Greta took time for a tea at the kitchen table. Greta was the one to break up the party. "I could sit here all day gabbing away, but I'm sure you have more important things to do than tend to an old woman."

"Hush, Greta," Katie admonished her. "I am fortunate to be in your company, but let's go learn you something." Katie leaned over and whispered, "Just don't tell Mrs. Walker I said that."

Greta patted her hand. "Don't worry. Your secret is safe with me." Katie knew that it was, but she couldn't know to what extent that simple statement would affect her future.

Greta's progress was slow and tedious, and Katie found patience that she didn't know she possessed. She was not patient by nature, but with Greta it was different. She simply pictured Greta as being Grammy, and she imagined what it might have been like to perform these same functions for her own dear grandmother.

"You must stay for lunch," Greta insisted. "I had Will pick up some lunchmeat to make sandwiches. I hope you like ham."

"I do," Katie assured her. "I like mine chipped the best."

"Then you are in luck, for that is what we have. I was going to have pickled beets, but Will said Thompson's was out of them."

"I could have brought a jar. We sell them in our bake shop."

"Really? Bring me a couple jars the next time you come, and I will pay you for them. No more buying them at the grocery store for me."

Katie washed the dishes while Greta peppered her with questions: How did she like school? What was it like to be Amish? Did she really like to bake?

"All done," Katie announced as she hung up the dish towel. "Is there anything else I can do for you?"

"Yes. Help me walk into the living room. I'd like to lie on the couch and stretch my back for a few minutes. I'll just close my eyes for a little bit, then I'd very much appreciate your help walking down the hall to my bedroom and library."

Greta was soon asleep. Katie slipped out of the room and walked down the hall to the study where Greta kept her extensive book collection. She glanced through some of the *National Geographic* magazines that filled an entire shelf. When she tired of pictures, Katie perused the books on the other shelves. She read one title, Catcher in the Rye, and chuckled. That's what Mark would do if we were running through a field of rye, she thought.

A book on the top shelf caught her eye. She reached up, pulled it out a few inches, and read the title, *Emotional and Physical Intimacy in Marriage*. She remembered Lydia telling her about this one. She even remembered some of the topics and information it contained. For a moment, Lydia flashed into her head once more, saying, "How I would love to have my hands full of him."

Katie was startled out of her thoughts. "Take it," Greta said from the doorway, while supporting herself on the walker.

"Greta! You're walking by yourself," she exclaimed.

"I am, aren't I?" Greta said.

Katie tried again to divert the conversation. "I didn't hear you coming."

"Obviously," Greta said with a chuckle. "I want you to take the book."

"I… I'm not married," she stammered.

"Yes, but are you sweet on a young man?"

"I don't have anyone courting me," Katie answered hesitantly.

"Why do I have a sneaking suspicion you're not telling me something?" Greta ventured. "No matter. Every woman should read that book once they get to your age. If you don't have a suitor now, I'm sure it won't be long until you do. And speaking of boyfriends you don't have, why don't you invite Mark to come for an early Sunday supper? Say about four o'clock. I'll throw a roast in the oven and have Will get a dessert at the bakery on Saturday. What kind does Mark like?"

"German Chocolate Cake," Katie answered, still flustered from their exchange.

"I thought you'd know the answer." Greta turned and started down the hall. "Don't forget the book! And I don't want it back. What's an old woman like me need with a book like that?"

Katie came slowly into the living room carrying the book. Greta looked kindly upon her. "Enjoy it, Katie. You've got your whole, wonderful life ahead of you. If you ever need to discuss anything, I'm here for you. I'm a nurse, remember?" She gave Katie a thin smile. "Please bring my wheelchair. I'm getting mighty tired," she admitted.

Katie helped her get seated. "Thank you for the book," she said. "You'll need to call Mrs. Lane and invite Mark for Sunday."

"Yes, I suppose I should. For appearances' sake," Greta said with a straight face. "It would hardly do for the invite to come from an available Amish girl. If you would prefer, I could have him come some day when you're not here."

"No," Katie responded, "I should be here to help you prepare the meal. Mark and I are friends, anyway, and he deserves your appreciation. Without his tenacity, none of this would have happened."

"I suspected as much, so let's get that boy here so I can thank him. Can you come again before Sunday?"

"I could come Thursday morning for a while," she offered, "but I can't stay for lunch. There is much to be done at home, especially now that I'll be gone for days in a row."

"I understand. I'll have Will help me with my walker in the meantime."

"Keep up the good work," she encouraged Greta, then gave her one last hug.

On the way home, Katie made a mental note to warn Mark to be very careful on Sunday around Mrs. Kimes.

As promised, Greta called Ann Lane to extend the dinner invitation to Mark. Greta explained how much she appreciated what Mark had done for her and that she wanted to express her gratitude in some way.

"What better way to thank a young man than to fill his stomach, right Ann?"

"Greta, it takes a lot to fill him up. I'd be more than happy to fix something and send it along with him. I don't want you to overextend yourself."

"I'll be fine. Katie Byler will be helping me. Will hired her to stay with me when he's out of town, and he's leaving on a business trip Sunday afternoon."

There was only silence from the other end of the line, and finally Greta asked, "Are you still there?"

"Yes, I'm here. If you change your mind and need me to make something for your dinner, be sure and call. It's no trouble, really."

After school on Wednesday, Mark stopped for eggs. Katie was already coming down the walk when he pulled into the courtyard.

"It's a little early for the top to be down, isn't it Mr. Lane?"

"Not when you're as hot-blooded as I am."

316

She grabbed the bucket and headed toward the springhouse. "Do you intend to stand here jawing about it or proving it?"

"Should I wait out here while you get the eggs?" he teased.

Her eyes narrowed. "If you want to wear them home, go ahead." He made a wise decision and trailed along behind her.

"I'm sorry," Mark said as he entered the springhouse and closed the door, "but I haven't had time to write you a let--" The ending was interrupted by Katie's lips over his, as she pinned him to the solid oak door.

Meeting passion with passion, Mark lifted her off the floor, turned them around, then pressed her between his hungry body and the wooden door. When their urgency subsided, she said, "Sorry, but I've wanted to do that for days."

"It's okay. So have I," Mark returned.

Their hunger flared anew. As he held her there, pinned to the door, Katie wrapped her arms around his neck while they melted into one. When they parted, she kissed his nose, eyes, and cheeks.

"You must have read past page forty," Mark commented.

"All one hundred sixteen pages. You should try it."

"Why don't you teach me instead?"

"I'd be happy to. How about Friday night?" she suggested.

Mark set her on the floor. "Why don't we just make Friday nights an automatic from now on?"

"Suits me fine," she agreed.

"There is a chance of rain in the forecast for Friday night. Maybe we should change it to Saturday. This isn't your church Sunday."

"And wait another day?" Katie asked with a yearning that was endearing.

"If there is lightning, I don't want you to come. It's too dangerous to walk across open fields. Besides, how could your parents believe you went for a walk on a stormy night?"

Katie changed the subject. "Are you going to Greta's on Sunday?"

"How did you know?"

"Because you'll have the honor of not one, but two ladies preparing your meal."

"You'll be there?"

"Uh huh," she said coquettishly, "to serve Master Lane since Greta needs assistance."

"Where does your area of expertise lie?" he asked with raised eyebrows.

"You'll just have to wait and find out."

"I'm not good at waiting."

"So I've discovered," Katie said, as she gave him her best smile. "Which is to my benefit," she added. She kissed him again. "Until Friday night."

Chapter Thirty-Three

On a cool evening in April, Mark sat alone in his room trying to decide where to begin.

My Dearest, "Oh My" Katie,

What do you say to describe that special someone in your life when she takes your breath away? When the things she does leave you speechless and hungry for more? Honey, Sugar, and Cutie Pie don't seem to cut it. When I think back to this afternoon and our time together, my mind goes numb, and all I can say to myself is "Oh my!" So for now, I shall think of you as my "Oh, my" girl while our passion plays continuously in my mind. Although we might control it, why would we want to?

Sometimes I ask myself, "Why are you not sitting on my lap right now? Why are my arms not around you? Why am I not gazing upon that lovely person named Katie E. Byler?" I know you don't have a middle name, but I have given you a middle initial. It's not fair that I have one and you do not. The E stands for Exotic, of course. We could put the initial at the beginning, like people who don't like their first name – E. Katie Byler. That actually makes more sense. "Hello, I am Miss Exotic Katie Byler." "Well yes, I can see you are," the gentleman replied.

Fifty-one hours and I will be with you. I'll try not to waste a second, for we have much to do. Why is there never enough time? Somehow, someway, I promise we will spend an entire day together. Time... if I could just figure out how to bottle it.

Let it be our time,
Mark

Meanwhile, in her private suite, Katie had just finished writing in her journal. If her parents ever read it she might have to appear on Mark's doorstep with her suitcase in hand. That thought was not totally disagreeable, and she spent a few minutes daydreaming along those lines before beginning a letter to the one she knew she loved.

Dearest Mark,

It has been a busy five days since our night together, but I have lost almost all thoughts of them, as a certain ten-minute span of time this afternoon has kidnapped all others and hidden them away somewhere in my mind. Maybe I should have addressed this letter to "Memory Snatcher."

I'm sorry for attacking you like that – well, not really – but you have been especially present in my mind and daily activities these past five days and nights. From reading your book, to the memories of our last meeting, to your last letter (which I've read more times than I can remember), you've popped up everywhere. Even my time spent with Greta was full of you. We must be careful not to give ourselves away when we are together at her house on Sunday. I am so much looking forward to spending the time together, even though we can't really act like we are together.

I'm becoming quite close to Greta, and I think she is to me as well. I believe she's someone we could trust if we had to. Helping her learn to walk is helping me, too. There is no sense writing it onto this page because I'll tell you about it Friday night.

What I will tell you is that I could not be happier than how you make me feel when we're together. We promised total honesty, so I'm going to admit that you are becoming a very important part of my life.

When I close my eyes tonight after my prayers, it is you I'll see in my mind and hope to meet in my dreams.

Sweet dreams of you,
Katie

Mark set his alarm for fifteen minutes earlier than usual in order to check for rain. Fortunately there was none, but he was still antsy and decided to head for the far side of Wagner's ponds to wait for Katie. She soon approached and he set out to greet her, flashing his light so as not to frighten her.

"What a pleasant surprise," Katie said as they embraced. "Did you miss me that much?"

"I was concerned about the weather. I don't trust it."

"I appreciate your concern. At least this way we'll die together."

"Don't say that," he scolded.

"You're in a good mood tonight, aren't you?" she said, her voice somewhat put off.

"It's my job to protect you, and your demise wouldn't exactly be a positive outcome." Mark reached out and tenderly held her. "I'm sorry for speaking sharply. Let's talk at the bankhouse; it feels like it might rain any minute."

A light mist was falling when they reached the cabin. As Mark swung the door open, Katie was greeted by a dim light from the Coleman lantern.

"I'll take your coat," he offered.

"It's warm in here," she said approvingly.

"I borrowed Dad's kerosene heater."

Katie glanced around. She noticed that he'd prepared a straw bale covered with a small blanket for their seat and two stacked bales for a table covered by his grandmother's quilt for a tablecloth.

"I like the two extra bales if we get company," she remarked, pointing to the additional straw bales in the back. "Are those our pictures laying on the old wooden chair?"

"Nah. Those are pictures of my other girlfriends."

Mark flinched as Katie quickly reached out then gently rubbed his upper arm. "Don't worry. I can't have this arm injured in any way," she said with a playful smile. "I'm looking forward to the back rub it's going to give me."

Mark held out his arms and gathered her against him. "Would you like to change your clothes?"

"A big, strong guy promised me a back rub, and it would be rather difficult in this dress."

"The clothes are in the bag, and I brought the slacks in case you wanted to try them. They have a stretch-band waist and should be more comfortable. The sweater you wore the last time would be great for getting a massage. I stopped at the five and dime after school today and bought you a pair of canvas summer shoes. I hope they fit."

"Then I guess I'll go into the bedroom and change."

"I take it that's my cue to leave."

"Uh huh," Katie answered, turning him around and pushing him toward the door. "Don't forget your umbrella."

Several minutes passed before the sweet sound of Katie's voice filled the night air. "I'm ready!" Mark turned and spied her standing in the doorway. She was dressed in the blue sweater and brown slacks and wearing her new shoes.

"How do you like the slacks?"

"They are very nice," she said stretching her leg out and back while holding onto the doorjamb. "They are less restrictive. Thank you for the shoes. Now come on, we've got pictures to view."

Katie opened the packages while Mark turned up the light. "Lay them out on the quilt while I close my eyes," she instructed.

"Why would you do that?"

"I've never seen myself in a picture. What if I don't look good?"

"I'll return them to the camera store and tell them to fix them."

She eyed him suspiciously. "You're teasing, aren't you?" He was busy spreading the pictures across the quilt and didn't feel the need to respond. When Mark finished, he started examining them and whistled.

Katie had been holding her hair in front of her face like a curtain. She parted it in front of one eye and peeked through the crack. "Are they good?"

"See for yourself." As he stepped behind her, Mark pulled back all of her silky, long hair. "Sit and enjoy them." She eased herself down onto the bale beside the makeshift table.

Katie looked from one to the next. "Do you think I look pretty?"

"No," Mark hedged, "you look gorgeous. I really like the ones on the tractor. You'd think you were a professional model. John Deere should pay me for these pictures to put in their ads. I'd write the slogan: 'Buy a John Deere and all the good-looking Amish girls will hang around.' They'll sell like hotcakes!"

Katie playfully pushed him off the bale. "I can't believe these pictures of us jumping over the stream," she remarked. "I'd like to take one home, but I shouldn't. However, I do want a couple of you. If I'm caught with them, all that would happen is I'd get in trouble for hanging out with an English boy. It's strange seeing myself in pictures."

Mark couldn't find the words to describe the beauty of the pictures by the fire, but his favorite was Katie hanging on the bankhouse door looking sexier than one girl should look in the presence of a normal male.

"You can take more pictures of me. I'm satisfied with these."

"You realize that's like the art world being satisfied with the Mona Lisa," Mark quipped.

"I don't know this Mona Lisa you speak of."

"And unfortunately, the art world will never know about you."

Katie picked three pictures of Mark and slipped them into her coat pocket. "How about that back rub?"

Mark handed Katie the quilt and blanket and began to line up the five bales through the center of the cabin. "Stand back and watch my house do a transformation. Sit your pretty little self down on that chair right there. Now stick your head out and shake it all about. Where's a pair of roller skates when you need them? I'm going to take you roller skating."

"Amish don't roller skate," Katie said.

"I know, it's not allowed. Have you ever heard of the Hokey Pokey?"

"No."

"I didn't think so. They have all-night skating parties sometimes at the Austintown Roller Rink. I'm going to find out when, and we're going. Help me spread the quilt."

"It sounds like fun, but what if I break something?"

"You'll just have to hang onto me all night."

"Now this is sounding like fun," she exclaimed while hamming it up. "But Mark, I have nothing to wear."

It took a couple seconds, but then it hit him. Mark collapsed onto the bales, laughing uncontrollably. Katie jumped on top of him laughing along with him. "Did I say something funny?" she asked, and they broke into laughter once more. Their laughter subsided, and they lay on their sides using an arm for a pillow simply gazing into the face of the other.

He leaned over and kissed her nose, then her cheeks. "Your loveliness is intoxicating."

She gave him a look that bared her soul, and Mark was no longer afraid. But he couldn't help wondering if this was the right time. Couldn't what he wanted to say wait? Why chance spoiling the magic of this night?

"Would you like to learn to Butterfly Kiss?" Katie asked.

Mark studied her. "Sure," he replied.

When school was finally out and a few other kisses were planted, Mark inquired, "What else have you learned that you can teach me?"

"Some of them we can't do because they're like my journal. They're private. However, I brought your book back, and I would suggest you finish it yourself if you wish to know."

Mark rose and reduced the light to a soft glow. He returned to the quilt and smiled down at Katie with her hair laying all about her. "I'll bet you didn't know it, but a Coleman lantern gives off a romantic glow." She laughed easily as he laid beside her and buried his face into her flowing locks.

"I washed my hair for you tonight using a lavender scented shampoo. Do you like the smell?"

"Very much. I like the smell of all of you, and I want you to do something for me before you leave tonight."

"What would that be?" she asked.

"I want you to get naked – when you're alone, of course, because I'll be outside – crawl into my sleeping bag and rub yourself around in it. Rub your hair all over my pillow. It will only take a few minutes and then I'll be able to smell you while I sleep."

Katie framed his face with her hands. "It's not fair that I leave my scent in your bed, and all I get is three pictures in return."

"What can I do to make it fair?"

"On Sunday, bring me your undershirt after you have worn it from now until then. I want it to be full of the scent of you."

"Does this mean you'll do as I've asked?"

"I will," she answered.

"There is only one thing better than you being naked in my sleeping bag."

"Don't go there, Mark Lane," Katie scolded him and gave him a loving push. "Now roll over, and I'll rub your back."

"Why don't I rub you first?"

"Because you'll never get yours if you do," she answered.

"I don't understand."

"You will at the end of the night." She smiled and pressed him down. "Did you bring any lotion?"

"Yes, dear. There's a bottle in the box." He raised his eyes to Katie who was watching him. "Did I say something wrong?"

"Quite the opposite. And it was the way you said it, as well - like it was as natural as breathing. You shouldn't do that unless you mean it."

"It caught me by surprise, too," he admitted. "But I do mean it."

Her eyes glistened as she said, "It would be better if you took your shirt off."

Katie sat beside him, leaned down, and kissed the three bold marks. "Your stitched spots have healed nicely, and one day they won't show much at all," she said softly. "I remember the morning in the hospital when you first showed them to me. You were taking such good care of me that I felt compelled to do something in return, so I kissed them then, too."

Mark turned and sat up beside her. "You don't think I forgot that, do you?"

"I don't know."

He took her in his arms. "I will never forget that. When I'm a hundred I will still remember. Quiz me if you'd like, but I can relive any moment I have been in your presence."

Katie kissed him briefly, then gently pushed him back onto the quilt. She folded the small blanket to serve as a pillow and slid it under his head.

She started at the waist and worked her way up, slowly and methodically while kneading the muscles with her strong fingers. He encouraged her on with his ooo's, and ah's. She couldn't help but notice what a fine specimen his upper body was from the waist all the way to his neck. She began again as she had initially and repeated the process. This time she straddled his thighs so she could get more leverage.

"Why are you so good at this?" Mark mumbled.

"It's because I want to do it, and because I read how to do it correctly."

"That was in the kissing book?"

"No, silly. It was in a book Greta gave me."

Mark twitched then asked if she knew about their relationship.

"No. She saw me looking at a book in her library and told me I could have it."

"What's the name of this book?" When Katie hesitated, he said, "Total honesty, remember?"

"It's private."

"How many times do you intend to play the private card?"

She wanted to say, "I'd play it much less often if you told me you loved me." She simply replied, "As many as it takes."

"Maybe I should have called you the Wonder Girl with Wonderful Hands," Mark said as she manipulated his muscles. He kissed her hands as she ran them down the front of his chest. When she finished, Katie gently rubbed his entire back, then caressed it with her fingertips.

"Please scratch it all over," he begged. "Harder... now faster," he coached, "Both hands, please. Okay, that's good."

Katie stretched out along the full length of him. She nibbled at his ear and gently ran her tongue around the perimeter.

"That tickles," he said.

"I didn't know," she countered. "I've never had someone kiss my ear."

"Neither have I, Smarty Pants."

"Do I get my back rub now?" she asked.

326

When Mark knelt beside her, he slid the bottom of her sweater up a few inches and slowly squeezed droplets of hand cream onto her bare skin. Katie kicked her feet on the quilt. "That's cold!"

"I'm sorry. Was that a problem for you?" he asked as he began spreading the moist cream across her skin.

"You know it was, mister! Please don't do it again."

He stifled his laughter. "How many other backrubs have you had?"

"Only the ones they gave me each night in the hospital. And I want to enjoy this one."

Mark's hand glided across her smooth skin all the way to her shoulders and back. "It was nice of you to get this stretchy sweater," she remarked.

"It works well, but I didn't know we'd be giving each other back rubs when I bought it. Uh, Katie? Where's your bra?"

"I took it off when you weren't looking."

Mark was quiet as he stroked her back.

"I trust you," she said. "Now give me a firm rub-down."

He massaged her lower back with gentle but firm strokes.

"Oh, yes, that feels wonderful."

"I could use both hands if you raised up and we slid this sweater up to your neck." Mark's suggestion was met with silence. "Since you trust me," he added.

She turned her head and their eyes met. "I do trust you, but when does prudence kick in?"

"Pretty soon, I'd wager," Mark replied as she eased her chest off the quilt. He slid the sweater up near her neck, exposing her entire back. "Your back is so beautiful," Mark remarked as he kneaded the muscles beneath the delicate pale skin. "It doesn't have one blemish."

"Because I had the good sense to stay away from bulls."

Mark concentrated on his endeavor. Beginning at Katie's slender waist, he manipulated her muscles with smooth, steady strokes: up to her shoulder blades and back down again. He used his large hands to maximum advantage as his fingers spread out over her feminine body. Her receptive flesh became putty in his hands, and Katie purred contentedly.

"I'd let you give me one of these every day," she said.

She sighed as he massaged the muscles of her upper back. "My neck and head, please," she requested.

"How I enjoy touching you like this," he whispered.

While he gently manipulated Katie's scalp, Mark studied all of her perfection and her imperfections, right down to the slight bump on the bridge of her nose and the ever-so-slight indent in the skin on the right side, just behind that bump.

She asked him to massage down along the sides of her ribs. He firmly ran his hands the length of her midsection.

Katie raised up on her elbows. "Do that again."

His fingers glided up along the perfect skin, and she shivered.

"Let me feel your hands massaging the rest of me."

Mark caressed her stomach and groaned softly as her muscles tightened. His hands against her bare skin sent longings through her. His fingers trailed down to her belly and one caught in her belly button. "Sorry," he muttered, and rubbed it out. He wanted to go lower. Katie's sensual murmurings said she wanted him to, though he forced himself higher instead and massaged each arm. Mark moved on to her legs – those long, slender, well-toned legs. His hands surrounded one leg at a time as he massaged clear to the ankles. Katie sighed as he manipulated her feet.

"See, manipulate can be good," he said.

"I'll let you manipulate me like this anytime you want."

When he finished, Katie took his hand and placed it on her bum. "Please massage my fanny that you love so much."

When she had enough, Katie turned onto her back and locked her eyes onto his with a sultry gaze. "Am I still in control?" she asked.

"For now, but you're making this awfully hard on me," he confessed.

Katie reached up and pulled Mark down to her. While they kissed, she moved her whole body against him and boldly showed him the desire within her as she trapped one of his legs between hers. "You make me want to love the living daylights right out of you," she croaked. They went to the edge of ultimate passion and pulled back. While caution could have been thrown to the wind, they took comfort in the knowledge that it had not.

Mark whispered, "I want to go, you and I. We'll ride the wind that takes us to the foreverland of magic and wonderment where we'll get lost in all our tomorrows – never to be seen or heard from again. Come soar with me, my dear sweet Katie."

At that moment, she'd have gone anywhere with him. "Let's hurry," she said. And she laughed, light and airy. Carefree.

They lay together on the quilt facing each other, while their eyes connected and their hands caressed. "I don't want to stop touching you," Mark confessed.

"Then don't."

"But you must go home to bed."

"I want to sleep here with you," she said honestly.

"I could walk you home at first light."

Katie sighed. "I'd like that."

"We could tell your parents we've become friends, at last, and we need more time together to get to know each other." Katie laughed as she snuggled close and requested that he hold her for just another minute. He kissed her on the forehead as was his habit.

And so, once more, they parted but not until Mark stepped outside to listen to the sound of faraway thunder while Katie undressed and crawled into his sleeping bag. When she emerged Amish once more, Mark said he would accompany her as far as they dared. "I'm not letting you walk through this unsettled night alone."

She didn't object, and they held hands as they went. Katie warned him to be careful on Sunday. "Greta already has her suspicions. We will need to be on our best behavior."

In the middle of a Byler field in the pitch black night Mark took Katie into his arms and kissed her tenderly. "You were right to give me my back rub first, and I look forward to more of your wisdom."

In the darkness, Mark could not see it, but Katie's face was beaming proudly, and she gave him one more, sweet kiss before they parted.

Chapter Thirty-Four

The windows were open in Greta's house on a pleasant Sunday afternoon in late April. A cool breeze wafted through the house as Greta and Katie prepared a late afternoon meal of roast beef, mashed potatoes, gravy, and a sweet-potato casserole with a streusel topping of brown sugar and pecans – their special guest's favorite.

Earlier that afternoon, Katie had pushed Greta in her wheelchair around the backyard to view Will's accomplishments and nature's rebirth. Katie's favorite was the large flower garden with its winding flagstone path, located just off the patio. The daffodils and hyacinths were in full bloom, releasing their intoxicating scent into the air. The tulips and irises were loaded with buds ready to explode and add their splendor to this floral display. A white wrought-iron loveseat sitting on the edge of the patio next to the garden enticed visitors to sit and contemplate the beauty around them. Accepting the invitation, the two ladies sat in silence looking out over the garden with expressions of peace and contentment on their countenances. Neither was anxious to return inside, so they lingered on the patio while the warm sun nourished their skin.

Katie helped Greta take hold of her walker, and they made a couple trips around the large cement patio. She helped Greta settle into a chair and went inside where a pan of sassafras tea warmed on the back of the stove. As she filled their cups, Katie closed her eyes and pictured Mark standing before her and opening his hand to reveal the sassafras root.

She touched her pocket where she always carried the root and smiled. She leaned down and inhaled the aroma rising from the cups. A short time from now, they would be together again. Could it possibly be only two nights since last they met? It felt so much longer. She wondered if he would notice that she had filled the house with the scent of sassafras.

"Tell me about our coming guest so I may be the gracious host," Greta entreated as Katie handed her the tea.

"Well," she began, drawing the word out into three syllables, "he is the youngest son of Harold and Ann Lane."

"Heavens to Betsy, Katie. I know all that. I want to be able to engage him in conversation. What are his likes and dislikes? How does he feel about school?"

Katie began again, "He likes working on the farm, especially driving their big tractor – which he drives fast most of the time, but he always slows down when he passes our buildings."

"Why does he pass your buildings?"

Katie explained about the Lane farm and the separated parcel on Morefield Road. That reminded her of Molly and Midnight, and she launched into the story about the calf's birth, its growth, and the Lanes' hope for the animal.

Katie described the meadow and the blackberries which led into the tale of last summer's violent storm. Greta heard about Mark's sweet tooth and his frequent trips to the bake shop. Katie mentioned that he didn't care much for high school but was looking forward to going to the state agricultural college in September.

"That's quite a start," Greta said. "I'm sure that will come in handy while Mark is here. I guess we'd better get crackin' if we're going to feed that young man when he arrives."

At two minutes to four, they heard the crunch of car tires on the stone driveway.

"We know Mark is punctual," Greta said.

Katie went to the window and watched him step out of his car. He was carrying a big brown bag. Surely Mark wouldn't hand her his worn shirt in front of Greta.

She heard her name being called and turned to see Greta standing with her walker, eyeing her intently. "Come on, Katie. Are you going to stand there gawking at him all day or let him in?"

Katie helped Greta into the living room. "I'll just stand here with this walker trying to look elegant while you let him in," Greta said.

332

The doorbell sounded as Katie reached for the knob. "Wow!" Mark exclaimed. "It's magic. The doorbell rang, and the door popped open. Close the door, and let's try it again. It's like a Jack-in-the-Box."

Katie's nerves fluttered while she eyed the bag in his hand. "Hello, Mark. It's good to see you. Come in and greet Greta."

"Don't mind if I do," he said in a strong voice.

He headed straight for Greta as soon as he stepped inside.

"I brought you a quart of Mom's best Red Haven peaches. Mom told me it was good manners to take something when you're invited out to dinner. I hope you like them." He withdrew the jar from the bag and displayed it for Greta to see. He handed the bag to Katie, and she peeked inside to see Mark's shirt folded on the bottom.

"I love canned peaches," Greta assured him. His host smiled up at him. "It's been a while. My, how you've grown."

"Yeah, I'm reminded every time I look in the mirror," he said with a grin.

"Katie, could you take my walker? I want to give Mark a friendly greeting." Greta held Mark's arm while Katie moved the walker aside.

They embraced in a warm and friendly hug as he squeezed her gently. "It's so good to see you again, Mrs. Kimes."

"Call me Greta, please. We're all friends here."

"I brought that book on photography you asked for," Mark said to Katie. "It's in the bag."

"I'll just put it in my room," she said quickly.

"Can you walk by holding my arm?" he asked Greta.

"I'm sure I can," she said, beaming up at him. "Is there any place special you'd like to go?"

"We could try a walk in the park," he suggested. "Then I'll take you on a rowboat ride. Would you like to retrieve your parasol before we go?"

Katie heard the laughter from her room, and she was amazed to find the two of them right where she had left them. They seemed to be having the time of their lives.

"You are such good fun," Greta said. "Ann has raised you well. I must compliment her the next time we speak."

"Speaking of Mother, she has sent her best regards and a message. She is overjoyed at what you and Katie are accomplishing together. She said she'll come to visit you later this week. She even mentioned taking you to lunch, but she'll call first." Mark leaned in close and whispered, "And she already gave you some peaches."

Greta laughed again while looking up at him. "All those beautiful, blond curls you used to have are gone."

"Now Greta, please don't embarrass me in front of the lady."

"Oh Mark," she said, slapping him lightly on the arm, "I'll bet you've never been embarrassed in your life."

"You're probably right," he said with a smile while looking at Katie above Greta's head. "How are you doing, really? And don't sugarcoat it for me."

"All right, I guess. It could be worse."

"Hold on to my arm, and let's sit on the couch," he suggested.

"I must sit in a straight chair. I can't get up from the couch yet, unless I roll off of it, and that wouldn't be very ladylike with company present."

"But I'm here to help you. Let's enjoy the nice, soft couch. The house sure smells good," he enthused, then inhaled deeply. "Let's see if I can name them - roast beef, onions, brown sugar, and there's another. Don't tell me... it's sassafras!" Mark's eyes twinkled as he looked at Katie. She smiled at his acknowledgement while looks of adoration passed between them.

"Did Katie tell you how much sassafras she dug?" he asked.

"She just told me she had dug some."

"She must have over half a burlap bag full. Saw 'em with my own eyes when I stopped to get eggs. Tell me, Greta, did she give them to you or make you pay for them?"

"Mark, hush! You're embarrassing Katie."

"So? Ain't nothing I haven't done before, and besides, she can't hit me because you're here." He grabbed onto her arm and feigned fear. "Protect me, Greta!'

She eyed Katie and asked, "Is he always like this?"

"Don't ask her. She'll only lie to you," Mark pleaded.

"You two must know each other fairly well," Greta remarked.

334

"Not really. I don't spend much time around her because she does all the talking, and I can't get a word in edgewise."

Greta peered at Katie sympathetically. "Would you care to take him out behind the woodshed?"

"Would I ever," Katie answered, squinching her eyes.

"Oh, boy. I know that look. My mother gives me that look. Okay, I'll be good." Mark swiped his hand down his face, like the curtain being lowered on a stage. When it dropped below his chin, he was a changed man; the friendly visitor was back.

"Has Katie told you about her interest in photography?" he asked. That topic yielded to a discussion about Greta's hospital stay in Chicago and her rough time at home. Mark patted Greta's hand as he hung on her every word.

A bell dinging in the kitchen interrupted their conversation.

"You can help me up, Mark. The meal will be ready before long." Greta held firmly to Mark's arm as he led her to the walker and then helped her into the kitchen. Sitting down in her wheelchair, she looked up at him. "Getting back into this chair reminds me how badly I want to be beyond it. I'm trying to progress with the walker so I can advance to forearm crutches, and then to a cane," she explained.

"You're on your way," Mark replied. "With Katie's help and your tenacity, I know you can do it." Mark spied a loaf of homemade bread on the counter. He closed his eyes and took a long whiff.

"Katie baked that for us," Greta informed him.

"Mmmm," Mark said. "It's a wonder to my nose... and my taste buds."

Greta chuckled. "I'll bet Katie makes lots of good things for the bake shop."

"Yes, but she doesn't like you touching, ogling, or smelling them."

Greta's stern voice broke in, "Mark! Don't get started again, or I'll take you out behind the woodshed myself."

He laid his hand on Greta's shoulder and squeezed it gently. "I'll be good."

"Thank you," Greta answered, rubbing his hand.

As Mark cut the bread, he watched the two ladies preparing the meal for the table. He admired the proficiency with which they worked together.

"Would today's honored guest care to say the blessing?" Greta asked.

"I will, but I'd like us to hold hands," Mark said. Katie smiled, catching his eye for just a second before bowing her head.

"Dear Heavenly Father," Mark prayed. "We thank you for the bounty that you have given us, and I thank you for the working hands of these two lovely ladies who have prepared it. We ask your blessing upon this food, and we ask you to bless Greta in her continuing recovery to walk again. In Jesus' name we pray, Amen."

As they ate, Greta asked Mark about school, Lane Farms and his plans beyond high school. He spoke with enthusiasm about going away to college. The worry in Katie's eyes did not slip past Mark's watchful gaze.

Mark asked questions about Greta's life in the U.S., her homeland, and the Great War. He mentioned Dr. Ford and explained the events leading up to the referral of the surgeon in Chicago.

"I would like to take this opportunity to toot Dr. Ford's horn," Mark said. "She still needs new patients, and I want to ask you and Will to consider trying her as your general MD. Our family goes to her, and so do the Bylers ever since Katie had pneumonia."

Greta remarked, "Katie told me about that. I could scarcely believe it, but I will admit her miracle gave me new hope that I might walk."

"Say, Katie. How do you like not having to milk the cows tonight?" Mark asked.

"It's a privilege I could get used to."

"Katie and I were just laughing about you the other day," Greta said. "I made that face I learned from you when you were about ten. You know, turn the lower lip down, stick your tongue out and up."

Mark grinned. "Did Katie tell you about the trick she pulled on me last summer by filling my blueberry pie with hot sauce?"

"I don't believe she mentioned it."

Mark launched into the story, embellishing the account, as Greta listened attentively.

"Aren't you going to tell her what you did to get even with me?" Katie asked.

Mark explained his retaliation, adding that he was unaware of Katie's fear and allergy to spider bites. He couldn't tell the story without regret creeping into his voice, and he concluded by saying, "I wouldn't have done it if I had only known."

"So you were the hero and the villain at the same time," Greta stated.

"That pretty well sums it up."

"Are your parents aware of all the shenanigans that go on between you?

Katie spoke up. "My mother knows some of it, but I'll bet his parents know very little."

"Why is that?" Greta wondered.

"Because he doesn't want them to know he's not perfect, would be my guess."

"Mark?" Greta prompted.

"This girl is way too smart for her own good," he admitted, giving Katie his best grin.

"This has all been very fascinating, but if you'll excuse me for a minute, I need to make a trip to the little girls' room. Can I trust you two to play nicely while I'm gone?"

"What are you doing?" Katie asked, when Greta was out of the room. "You are going to get us in trouble."

"Greta's a hoot. And she's not going to say anything to anyone."

"How can you be sure?"

Mark shrugged. "I just know. We could tell her every detail about us, and she would keep it to herself."

His comments earned a narrow-eyed gaze as Katie's forehead furrowed.

"You can trust me on this." He reached out and squeezed her arm. "Please enjoy the evening. I'm going to give you a very big kiss, if you don't relax."

The corners of her mouth curled. "Don't you dare," she said patting his hand.

They soon heard the sound of Greta's wheelchair coming from the living room. "My, it's quiet in here. Everything okay?"

"I was just telling Katie how much I'm going to enjoy watching her eat her favorite dessert in the whole world," Mark answered lightly.

"Oh? Don't you like German Chocolate cake, too?" Greta inquired.

"It's good, but blueberry pie is my favorite dessert. I get them at the Byler bake shop all the time."

"Katie!" Greta exclaimed.

"Once you get to know him, this will make a lot more sense to you," Katie informed her. "Now fess up, Mark!" And she kicked him under the table.

"Ouch," he grimaced. "Okay, I'll tell her. I like German Chocolate the best of all the cakes, but I like Katie's blueberry crumb pie better."

"Yes, but Greta said her son would get the dessert at Robert's Bakery, and they only have regular blueberry pie, which you aren't crazy about, so I recommended the German Chocolate cake."

"Okay, now I understand everything, children," Greta quickly interjected. "Let's have dessert. Katie, would you be kind enough to get the vanilla ice cream out of the freezer and cut the cake for everyone." Greta sat quietly with a look of astonishment.

"I'm sorry," Mark said. "Katie and I both love German Chocolate cake, and we are looking forward to tonight's dessert. I apologize for being a jokester. Sometimes I take my kidding a little too far. Please don't ever think poorly of Katie. She is somewhat of a handful, but then, I'm an awful lot to have to put up with myself. When the bake shop opens, I'll bring you one of her blueberry crumb pies. You and Will will enjoy it, I'm sure. They are heavenly."

As they enjoyed their dessert, Mark gushed, "Robert's Bakery makes the best cakes ever. Even my mother's can't compare."

"I won't tell Ann you said that," Greta replied with a smile.

"I know you won't. Mum's the word," he said. The look that passed between them spoke volumes. "You haven't told me how Katie got you walking again. Mom gave me a pretty bleak report last week."

"Katie has been a Godsend. She showed up here last Saturday and wouldn't take 'no' for an answer. I still say she's my guardian angel, although she insists everyone has their own." She gestured to Katie. "Cut a nice, big slice of that cake for Mark to take home."

Mark didn't object. "Thank you, Greta. It really is good cake, but don't cut too big a piece, Katie. Save most of it for you and Greta. I know how much you like it, too."

"Let's all go to the living room and sit a spell," Greta suggested.

Katie coaxed Greta into telling a couple nursing stories, and the time passed quickly. They all enjoyed a cup of tea, and Mark thanked her for inviting him. "The meal was one of my best ever and I'm pleased to see you are being so well cared for," he said, nodding toward Katie.

"Do you like milkshakes?" he asked Greta.

"Who doesn't like milkshakes?" she replied.

"Cherry is my favorite and chocolate is Katie's. What's yours?"

"Strawberry. Why do you ask?"

"Just wondered, is all." He rose and stretched.

"I don't want to overstay my welcome. It's getting late, so I'd best be going."

Greta smiled kindly. "Yes, you probably should go. Ann will be wondering what's keeping you. Help me stand so I can give you a goodbye hug."

Mark helped her off the couch and surrounded her with his arms. Greta laid her head on his chest. "You give the nicest hugs. My George used to give me great hugs all the time. How I miss them. Thank you for all you have done to help me. I am forever in your debt."

Leaning back, he held her at arms-length. "After a delightful evening such as this and the company of not one, but two lovely ladies, and the great food, I believe that debt is paid in full. Please consider what I said about Dr. Ford needing more patients."

"I'll talk to Will about it when he returns on Wednesday," she promised. "Hand me my walker. I need to make another trip down the hall to the necessary room. Katie can show you out." Greta started across the room and then paused. "Come back anytime. Our home is always open to you."

Katie was in Mark's arms before the bathroom door closed. "I'm sorry we picked at one another," she said.

"It's not your fault," Mark soothed. "I was the instigator, and I'm the one who should apologize. You know I only do it in fun, don't you?"

"Yes, I know. But we're two peas in a pod. Enough of that… I can't get Friday night out of my mind," she whispered.

"As great as it was, you know it's only going to get better, don't you?"

Katie agreed, but she chose to show him rather than tell him. Mark understood fully as he said goodbye.

"That was a pleasant evening," Greta remarked, as she returned to the living room. "After all that talking, I could use another cup of tea. How about you, Katie?"

"Sounds like a good idea. Why not come out to the kitchen and sit while I fix it?"

"I'm glad Mark came when you were here to help," Greta said.

They sat at the table sipping their tea when Greta flashed a tentative smile. "You love him, don't you?" It was more a statement than question. The color drained from Katie's face. Greta reached for her hand and squeezed it gently. "It's okay. I didn't mean to frighten you."

Katie inhaled deeply. "Was it that obvious?"

"Would you notice an elephant in a tea room? You must ignore each other if you are ever together when others are present. Powder Mills will know in hours. Have you told Mark yet?"

"Told him what?" Katie stammered.

"That you love him."

Her shoulders sagged. "We have not spoken those words to each other."

"Why not? It's obvious you both feel it."

"I have waited for Mark to say it first. He has not done so, and I don't know why. Sometimes I wonder if he is ashamed that I am Amish."

Greta smiled and shook her head. "That's the devil talking to you. Surely you know that's not the reason."

"I suppose, but I still don't understand it."

"Maybe he's afraid," Greta said.

"Afraid of what?"

Greta was silent a long time. When she finally spoke, she leaned forward and used a low voice, almost as if she were telling a great secret and feared that someone might hear. "Mark is a pureheart." It was a simple statement, yet said emphatically and with an air of reverence.

"What do you mean?"

340

"Nothing is hidden. All one has to do is spend a little time with him, and you see it all. He simply wants to love and be loved. Perhaps if I hadn't been married to George for almost forty years, I wouldn't have recognized it myself. I'll bet Mark is Ann's favorite, and she may not even understand the full reason why. You'll have to be very careful around her. Women have a sixth sense about these things, and I'm sure she already knows that her son's devotion is diminishing. It would be no surprise if she has already been on the hunt trying to track you down. 'You' meaning whoever is causing her son to withdraw from her, not 'you' personally."

"You were right the first time," Katie said. "She has already figured out that it's me, and she has tried to entrap me. Tell me more about this pureheart business."

"My husband George was a pureheart, although I didn't know it when I married him. I thought he was just different in a clingy way. You see, George had chosen me to be the love of his life, his soulmate. I was not always appreciative of what that meant."

"What did it mean, exactly?"

"How much time do you have, and how tired are you?"

"I'm wide awake and will be as long as you are. Mark and I are used to running on little sleep." Katie looked down, realizing what she had said.

"Oh, my dear, Katie. Even I am amazed at how well I hit this nail on the head. Could you be a union of two purehearts forming a great superheart? I have only met two in my lifetime, and their light brightened the world around them."

"Let me start at the beginning," Greta continued. "Most of us reach back thousands, or maybe tens of thousands of years in our mental constitution. I believe that purehearts, through some freak of nature or by God's plan, have reached back much further. In fact, all the way back to the Garden."

"The Garden of Eden?" Katie asked.

"Yes. Back to Adam and Eve before the Fall. Maybe God simply wants to get a glimpse of His grand design and what it could have been. Think of what it was like in the Garden before sin. There was no division between emotional and physical. All things were pure. Adam and Eve were of one flesh. As one

341

felt and thought, so the other thought and felt. Whether apart or together, they were always together in spirit, and they were in direct communication with God. Their world was perfect and uninhibited for there was no sin. They had no need to fear, and there were no distractions. Purehearts strive to recreate the Garden here on a sin-filled Earth."

"How is Mark different?" Katie inquired.

"To a worldly person like I was when I married George, Mark seems to be clinging, even a control freak. Think Adam and Eve. Their relationship would not be considered normal by today's standards. They were alone and so their entire social world was each other. 'And they were both naked, the man and his wife, and were not ashamed,' comes directly from Genesis in the Bible. I think your imagination and the book I gave you can paint a clear picture. As I have said, Mark wants only to love and be loved. He is willing to do anything and give anything to achieve his goal, just like Adam and Eve gave and shared totally with each other."

"So why hasn't he said he loves me?" Katie asked.

"It's a defense mechanism. The world affects purehearts more than other people, so they withdraw and put up walls. There is a good chance he hasn't professed his love for you because he's hiding behind that wall now."

"But why doesn't he just come out? Surely he knows how I feel about him," Katie implored.

"Have you and Mark ever had any true discord, particularly strife where trust was an issue?"

Katie looked down while Greta waited. She raised her head revealing sad eyes. "There have been two or three occasions that would qualify for what you have described."

"Who was the offender?"

"I was… each time."

"That definitely matters. Trust and assurance are very important to any pureheart. Mark will be cautious."

Now it was Greta who averted Katie's gaze. She was searching for what to say next, or how much to divulge. "Purehearts run the gamut of personality types, just like everyone else. Tell me about Mark."

Katie paused, then answered, "He is smart, particular, and organized. He plans everything out in advance, and I have rarely seen him caught off guard."

Greta gave a nod. "I call them 'super planners.' But give yourself credit, Katie. You are sharp yourself, and Mark is lucky to have you. Don't misjudge his awareness of that fact. The rest of the world would say he worships the ground you walk on, but he would say he knows the value you possess."

"And yet, he keeps his heart hidden behind walls."

"Yes, because of what he is. His personality raises the stakes. He is aware of the cost if he tries and fails. Fear keeps him hidden."

"How can I overcome his fear?"

"Always be there for him. Reach out to hold him both physically and emotionally."

"We surely do that a lot," Katie remarked.

Greta smiled with a faraway look in her eyes. "You remind me of George and me. Our life together became a lot easier once I learned that he had a simple need to be near me, touch me, hold me, and look into my eyes. Combine Mark's characteristics with your own and I can see the limitless potential. I know Mark can see it. It's obvious from the way he looks at you and the way he acts around you."

"He says he is my protector."

"Indeed he is," Greta affirmed. "Surely that makes you feel good."

"Yes," Katie said with an acknowledging smile.

"My George was the most loving and devoted man I have ever met. He was ultra-protective of me, and I know his thoughts were dominated by his feelings for me. I'm quite sure he never looked at another woman in the way he looked at me. He was loyal to a fault, and if I had died first, I believe he would never have remarried. I was the chosen one. It turned out he chose wisely because we lived a fulfilling life together. But how did he know that?" Greta shrugged.

"Mark will not settle for less than that which he has been inspired to achieve," she continued. "When he decides on his chosen one, he will not waver from the beginning to the finish line. For him, 'I love you' is a lifetime declaration, and he is well aware of what it means if he succeeds or fails.

"The purehearts know the Garden for it exists deep within them, but they recognize the world for what it is. Mark is Adam searching for his Eve. I tuned in to the Garden of Eden mentality, and George slowly drew me into his world. It is a beautiful place... being one both mentally and physically with another person. You are never alone."

"What do I do?" Katie asked.

"Mark is a purist, and he dwells in the Garden. When you think you can't love him more, find a way. Mark will reveal himself when he feels sure enough to drop the shield. Finally, I would recommend that you examine your intentions concerning this relationship very carefully. If your heart is not true, and you join as one with Mark, your union will tear your lives apart and destroy his."

Chapter Thirty-Five

The following day Greta made good progress. She was improving with the walker and even spoke of trying the forearm crutches. With the help of her medication, she could stand the pain in her lower back. Katie worked most of the day cleaning the house and doing laundry. This was the first time she had used a vacuum cleaner, and she was amazed at its usefulness. After Greta taught her how to run the washer and dryer, Katie washed four loads of clothes and towels, including her own clothes from the day before.

"How much simpler your wash day is," Katie said to Greta at supper. "And our home would be much less dusty if we had a vacuum gadget."

Katie and Greta never mentioned their talk from the night before. It was almost like it never took place. However, Katie remembered every detail, and her thoughts were never far from them.

"Have you ever taken a bubble bath?" Greta asked after dinner.

"No. What is it?"

"You fill the bathtub, clear up near the overflow, with water as hot as you can stand and dump in scented, foaming liquid. You lay in it for as long as you want, thinking of whatever you want. It's simply divine, and every woman should take one every now and then. I'm going to get washed up and retire early. I'll show you the overflow in the tub, give you the bottle, and you can help yourself. Don't bother setting your alarm. I'll wake you when I need you in the morning."

As Katie lay submerged except for her head and knees, she understood why Greta used the word "divine."

She lay her head back and closed her eyes, allowing her thoughts to drift. Katie came to the hospital scene with Mark. She had reached out to him in desperation, and he had saved her. He had always been there - all the way back to her fall from the wagon.

She thought of the wedding ceremonies she had so often attended and pondered words that were spoken. "A man shall leave his mother, and a woman leave her home." Could she leave her home? Without Mark, she couldn't imagine it, but if Mark truly loved her and they were meant to be together, then she would have to.

Katie tried to imagine living at Lane Farms with her Amish home just down the road, so close yet so far away. She would have to give up her family and all that she knew to be married to Mark.

Ah, there she had said it: *married*, that magical word. "Mrs. Mark Lane." She smiled at the idea. "Good day, Mrs. Lane. How are you, Mrs. Lane? Mrs. Lane, your order is ready." She loved her family, but she could think of nothing that would be more blessed than that.

Katie dwelled a long time on the events of Friday night. She thought of Mark crawling into his sleeping bag where she had lain naked. She could picture him breathing her aroma on his pillow and drifting off to sleep with her on his mind. Had she not done the same just last night with his shirt?

She pondered the long conversation she and Greta had had after Mark left on Sunday night. She still could not grasp the depth of it.

When her mind and body were satiated at last, Katie retreated to her own room. "I must thank Greta in the morning," she reminded herself.

Katie divided her hair into two braids, which was now her custom, and withdrew her journal from the bottom of her overnight bag. She sat at the small desk in her room and wrote until she was satisfied that everything had been documented. Then she prepared to write once more. Before she began, Katie removed the three pictures of Mark from her camera case and propped them in front of her.

Dearest Mark, she began. Katie told him about her day and Greta's continued improvement. She described her first bubble bath, making sure that he would be properly inspired by her descriptions: *the warm water soothing my skin reminded me of you. It was surrounding me as you surround me with your care.*

After a few paragraphs along that vein, Katie felt confident Mark would read her letter more than once. She smiled as she pictured him holding the paper and heatwaves rising from him like those off an asphalt roadway on a scorching summer afternoon. She thanked him for the closeness they had on

Friday night in spite of the weather. *I'm so glad we were able to be together. You give the best backrubs. Let's do it again this Friday. Remember to bring your hand cream, and I'll bring the cookies.*

I hope you enjoyed Sunday's dinner visit as much as I did. You really had me worried when you came in with that paper bag, but I should have known you'd pull it off. She drew a smiley face at the end of the sentence. *You take care of me all the time. It felt good to be taking care of you.*

Greta's words from the night before came to mind as Katie was about to write her closing statement, "When you think you can't love him more, find a way." Katie inscribed, *Forever yours, Katie.*

One more thought occurred to her and she added: *P.S. There is something I have wondered about for some time now. Every time we are together, you kiss my forehead, and I wonder why.*

That same evening, Mark sat at his roll-top desk formulating what he could write to Katie. He was going to give this letter to her at Greta's house tomorrow after school. Mark had a strong feeling about Greta. He didn't know why, exactly, but he believed that he and Katie could trust her. Lord knew they could use an ally.

My Dearest Darling,

I really like this salutation. I think I'll keep it if you don't mind, and no, I don't have any darlings other than you. You are my dearest and my only. My Dearest, Only Darling. There. Is that better?

Mark knew that would make Katie laugh since she laughed at most of his jokes. He often wondered if she really thought he was funny or if she was humoring him. Normally, he wouldn't care, but this time he did. He cared more about Katie than he had cared about anything in his life, even more than farming and Lane Farms. That admission made him cautious.

And there was the other thing—the dark thing that followed him always. That which the love of Gramps had rescued him from. Gramps and the meadow, that is. Forever lurking in the back of his mind was the thought that he had two mountains to climb—two chances to be denied.

Mark was familiar with the pull of Amish society on its youth, and Katie would be no exception. How much would she have to love him before it was enough? Would Katie walk away from all that she knew? Could he love himself enough to let her?

Mark wrote a flowing letter expressing his feelings of happiness, satisfaction, and hope concerning their Friday night, Sunday dinner, the moments in between, and the moments since. He finished it feeling satisfied that this precious soul he longed to call his own would want to be his, if he would only continue to show her his heart.

Tuesday afternoon was warm and sunny. Katie and Greta were at the mailbox when Mark approached in his car.

"Good afternoon ladies," he said with a smile.

"Mark! What a pleasant surprise," Greta replied.

Mark took her hand. "Come on, Greta, let's race."

Greta chuckled. "You are such a tease."

"I brought you something," he said.

"What is it?" she asked.

"I'm not telling yet, but it's in this here bucket." Mark brought it out of his car. "Let's go sit on your back patio." She agreed and Mark handed Katie the walker and scooped Greta up in his arms. "Follow us to the patio, my dear," he instructed Katie.

Greta was embarrassed so Mark lightened the moment.

"Now Greta, don't go getting mushy over me. I'm not in the habit of chasing after older women."

She relaxed and clung to his neck while Mark carried her around to the back of the house with Katie following close behind. He lowered Greta onto the patio and assisted her into one of the chairs.

Mark took the bucket from Katie and set it on the table. Removing the lid, he held the bucket out for both women to see. "We have a bucket filled with nothing but ice, as you can clearly see. Mark the Magician will now perform his feat of magic." Burying his hand into the ice, he brought out a milkshake. "Who in the audience likes chocolate?"

"Ooooo, me, me!" Katie chirped, playing along with his act.

Again Mark's hand plunged into the ice. "Who likes pink milkshakes with a C written on top? Oh wait, that would be me. That means last but not the least among us must be you, Greta. I hope there is something left in my bucket."

He reached into the bucket one last time, making a great show of flinging ice over the rim. "Oh dear! I hope my bucket is not empty," Mark feigned alarm.

"It better not be, Sonny Boy!" Greta quipped.

Mark guffawed, but quickly resumed his role. "Ah, wait. What is this I've found? A shake with an 'S' on top." He bowed, while handing Greta the milkshake. "Applause all around, please," he encouraged, clapping his hands enthusiastically. The audience gave him a rousing ovation.

Mark dropped into a chair and melodramatically wiped his brow with the back of his hand. "Being a magician is hard work."

"Do you have straws?" Greta asked.

"The straws! I almost forgot the straws." He stood and turned his back toward them, untucked his shirt, and three straws fell to the patio. Greta and Katie clapped again.

"Isn't your mother going to wonder where you are?" Katie asked, as the three friends chatted and drank their milkshakes.

"Nope. I told her I was going to the library in Granville to do research on a paper for chemistry class."

"Chemistry, huh?" Greta noted. "That would limit the conversation considerably."

"It did," he confirmed with a grin. "But I ought to get going." He looked at Greta. "I was never here."

"And I never saw you," Greta said with a nod.

"Is it all right if I stop tomorrow on my way home to see Katie? Say, for about as long as it takes to get a milkshake at the Tastee Freeze?"

"Park your car under the carport," Greta instructed. "It's less noticeable there. Use the door through the back wall in front of your car."

Mark leaned down and kissed Greta on the cheek. "Thank you, Greta," he said. She winked at him as he drew away.

"Come on, Katie. Show me that door." He grabbed the bucket and headed in that direction.

"Wait!" she called to him. "I've got a letter."

He stopped, turned, and looked at her with loving eyes. "I'll wait for a letter."

Katie hesitated, and Mark walked toward her. He wanted desperately to tell her to jump into his arms. "Well, go get it," he said instead, motioning with his free hand.

"You love her, don't you?" Greta asked when they were alone. Mark remained silent. "When will you tell her?"

"When I am sure," he said.

Greta didn't ask "When you are sure of what?" for she already knew.

On Friday, Mark stopped at the Bylers' on the way home from school, using the excuse of needing another envelope to mail film. Katie retrieved it from her room, and he mentioned he should get some eggs, too, and the pair headed out of the house.

Once inside the springhouse, she fell into his arms. "Why did you come?"

"We can't go to the bankhouse tonight," he said. "It's going to rain."

"I feared as much, but I was looking forward to being with you."

"Not as much as I wanted to be with you," Mark countered.

Katie stood back and eyed him suspiciously. "Do you think if you make me mad it will make it easier?"

He gave her a grin that was accompanied by a "you caught me" look, and she leapt into his arms. "Why do you do that to me?" she asked, hanging onto him.

"'Cause you are so... adorable."

"Kiss me, and we've got to get out of here," she prodded. Entering the courtyard, she asked, "Did you write me a letter?"

Mark shook his head. "Haven't had time. This is spring planting season, you know?"

"I hadn't noticed," Katie replied, holding up her dirty fingernails.

Mark smiled. "If I came to your room tonight, could I sit on the edge of your bed and hold your hand?"

"Both hands."

"Would you let me lie beside you while I held your hands?"

"No!" Katie answered. "I don't think Mama would appreciate having you there for breakfast."

The next four weeks were a blur as field after field fell to the Lane plows. Two tractors ran all day and sometimes long into the night.

Harold had rented a neighbor's fifty acres when it came available at the last minute, and he brought in extra help to get it planted. More than two hundred acres of corn were in the ground before the end of May.

Still, there was some time for play. Mark and Katie used the drop spot to exchange letters on the Saturday evening after the big rain. It was almost dark when he sat with Bella near the edge of Wagner's pond and watched the girl in blue come across the field.

As she retrieved his letter, he called to her and waved. She waved in return before carefully maneuvering through the fence.

"Hello there, Mark Lane," Katie said as she walked up to him. "Been sitting here like a bump on a log for long?"

"Long enough to do some learning," he answered.

"What have you been learning?"

"Learning to control my yearning."

"And what yearning would that be?" she asked seductively, rubbing his raised knee.

"Funny you should ask. Why don't I just show you?" He grabbed her arm and pulled her down to him.

She leaned into him, pressing her breasts against his chest. "You're in control," she said. Mark could hear the grin in her voice.

"Damn this rain," he muttered. She didn't scold him and her lips found his.

It was well past dark when they parted, but not before arms encircled, fingers caressed, and emotions ran high. And of course, before they said goodbye, Mark kissed Katie on her forehead once more.

Back in her room, Katie dressed for bed and snuggled down between the sheets to read Mark's long letter. The answer to her question came at the end: *You asked why I kiss you at the top of your forehead. Why do people everywhere celebrate birthdays? It's because that is the beginning of their existence here on earth. It's a joyous occasion and a celebration of life. No matter how old we grow, it's still celebrated. Technically, it's the actual moment of conception when life begins. That should be the moment of joy, the moment we celebrate. That slight mark on your forehead represents the actual moment of our conception. We didn't know it at the time, but it was revealed to us later, just as the child is revealed at birth. Each time I kiss your forehead, I am celebrating our conception.*

When Katie read his response, Greta's words came back to her. "Mark is a purist, and he dwells in the Garden."

"Oh, my dearest Mark," Katie murmured. "Can't you feel how my heart yearns for you?" She prayed, "Father, let him put down the shield and declare himself to me. I will dwell in the Garden with him, forever."

They met at the bankhouse six days later, on a beautiful mid-spring evening just past the full moon and perfect for campfires, toasted marshmallows, and stargazing. Backs had been rubbed under the stars beside the fire and lips had been kissed when Mark told Katie, "I bought you a present."

"It's not my birthday or Christmas," she replied.

"You're right," he said, slapping his forehead. "What was I thinking? Never mind, then."

"Come on," she urged.

"Come on, what?" he asked innocently.

"You can't tell me that and then do nothing."

"I did something. I agreed with you."

Katie waited.

"It's in the bankhouse," he confessed. "I'd rather give it to you there."

Mark sat on the old chair and Katie sat on his lap, unwrapping the small package in the light of the Coleman lantern. "It's a radio," she said.

"I want to share my world of music with you." He showed her how to use the earphone. "That way you can hear it, but no one else can. You'll be able to hear the weather forecast for Friday nights, too. Do you like it?"

"I'm not sure. I could get caught. I know some kids sneak them, but if they're discovered, their parents smash them."

"I brought mine too, and it's almost one o'clock. There's a song I requested to be played right after the news. Let's see if they play it."

Mark quickly had Katie's working, and he tuned into the same station. They sat listening to the news and weather, while he showed her how to adjust the volume.

The DJ came on after the news. "We have a request coming your way for a very special someone named Katie from a secret admirer. Hopefully, you can figure out who he is Katie, because it seems that he cares for you very much."

The music started followed by Tab Hunter's voice singing the words of Young Love. Katie listened, hanging on every word, scarcely bothering to breathe. She leaned her head against Mark as the song played on. When it had finished, she was silent for a long time while he held her.

"That was just beautiful," she said. "Are you my secret admirer?"

"I am if you want me to be," he murmured.

"I want that very much," Katie whispered. "Now what do you want to do?"

"Slow dance."

"But I don't know how."

"I'll teach you when the next slow song comes on."

They had no sooner stood and moved to the center of the room when a slow, soothing melody began to play. "Step with me. Simply listen to the rhythm of the music and move your body with it. You'll be doing fine in no time," Mark assured her.

A few slow songs later, Katie was laying her head on Mark's shoulder and dancing like she had been doing it for years. They had both arms wrapped around each other, taking baby steps. Every now and then, she raised her head to gaze into his eyes and he placed soft kisses on her neck. "I should let you go home," he said.

"One more song, then I'll go," she pleaded.

When the next song began Katie sighed, "Oh, Mark, I know this one. You sang it for me that night at the pond."

They melted into one another emotionally and physically as Let It Be Me set the mood. When it ended, Mark shut off both radios. He pulled her back into his arms, and they danced one more time while he hummed the same music.

"I have a surprise I've been waiting all night to tell you," Katie said. "Will Kimes is going on another business trip early Sunday and not returning until Saturday afternoon. Greta said you were welcome to come for Sunday supper."

Mark frowned and breathed out heavily.

"What's the matter?" she asked.

"I guess that means we won't be meeting at the bankhouse Friday night."

"I'm sorry, Mark, but it's my job, and I can't let Greta down. She's usually asleep by nine or nine-thirty. I could tell her you're coming over. I'm sure she wouldn't mind."

"That'll work," he replied, "but I'm curious to know how your parents took this Sunday to Saturday gig."

"I'm eighteen, after all, and I promised I'd walk home early Monday morning to help Mama do the wash. Greta said it was okay. They're sending Will clear across the country and there was nothing he could do."

"Change your clothes. Then I'll walk you as far as your fields."

"You don't need to."

"Yes, but I want to."

He hadn't asked her to crawl into his sleeping bag, but when Mark returned, he found it smelling very much of Katie.

When Mark pulled into the Kimes's driveway on Sunday evening, the garage door suddenly opened, and there stood Katie with a smile on her face and motioning for him to enter. He had no sooner cut the engine when the door closed behind him. She came up along his side of the car and ran her hand across his shoulder then around his neck.

"You're getting really good with the timing thing," he said with a grin. "I sure am glad I have the top down." She leaned down and he pulled her to his eager lips. "I've been waiting all day for that," he uttered.

Mark climbed out of the car and leaned against it. He held out one hand, and she took it lightly. He slowly turned her around.

"Is that a new dress and cap?"

"Why, Mark! I didn't think men noticed such things," she said in a flirtatious voice.

"You wore them just for me, didn't you?"

"No," she said flatly. "I wore them to impress Greta."

He laughed.

"I love to hear your laughter, but when are you going to give me a proper greeting?"

"Good evening, Miss Byler," he said, lifting her hand to his lips and kissing it softly. He looked into her sparkling eyes, and she returned his gaze. Mark touched his nose to her hair and inhaled. Down her cheek with soft kisses he traveled.

Warmth filled her being, and Mark could tell she was teetering. He responded with a kiss on her sweet lips that started out gentle but became a hungry fire out of control. Katie threw her arms around him and met him halfway, passion matching passion. Mark lifted her off her feet and sat her on the top of his car door while their desires kept raging. When they broke apart, he said, "I've been thinking about you."

"A penny for your thoughts," she offered.

"You'd better only give me half a penny because I can only tell you half my thoughts." His hands traced the contours of her body, caressing and stroking as he went.

"We'd better go in," Katie whispered. "But kiss me once more to have something to remember as I look across the table at your eyes that speak."

"Hello Greta," Mark greeted her as he entered the kitchen. His eyes showed his surprise as Greta stood at the kitchen counter while her forearm crutches leaned against a chair. Her walker stood nearby, but her wheelchair was nowhere in sight. "No wheelchair?"

"It's put away in storage till we find it a good home."

"I wonder if you'd like to take a leisurely stroll through your flower garden, if you have time," Mark joked.

Greta gave him a brief glance, trying to read his intent. "No. I think it would be best if I stayed inside for the remainder of the evening. Katie and I raced around the house earlier, and I'm a little tired," she said with a thin smile and a twinkle in her eyes. "Katie, why don't you be Mark's tour guide?"

Katie turned to look at him, but he was no longer giving either female his attention. His nose was in the air as he sniffed deeply. He walked along one wall of cupboards, stopped suddenly and leaned toward the crack between the doors. He inhaled again, then turned toward Katie and smiled. The endearing look she gave him melted his heart. In three steps he was beside her and grasped her waist and hoisted her into the air.

"Katie, my Katie," he said. He swung her around then lightly placed her back on the floor. "Will you never quit surprising me?" Katie gave Greta a thumbs-up, as Mark led her out the back door.

They walked along the path through the garden. She pointed out each new flower and perennial, explaining what she could remember that Greta had told her.

Mark listened as he watched her speak. He asked questions so he might listen to the sweet sound of her voice once more.

When they had completed the perimeter of the yard, they sat on the loveseat at the edge of the patio. Mark took her hand and threaded their fingers together. "Thank you for baking a blueberry crumb pie," he said.

She could tell that he wanted to say something, and she was pretty sure she knew what that something was. How could she draw it out of him? How could she give him the confidence he needed to say it? How could she make him understand that she wanted him to say it?

Katie squeezed his hand and then reached up and tenderly laid hers upon his cheek. "Please enjoy the little things I can do, Mark."

He tenderly kissed her on the top of her forehead. "The sweet sound of your voice takes my breath away," he confessed. "What you consider 'little things' are not little things to me." His voice caught. "Nothing you do with me or for me is little."

Katie sensed that this was not the right time and she forced a smile. "We can talk more about this later, if you wish. I must go and help Greta with the meal."

"Yes, I'm sure Greta could use some help. Why don't we go in together?"

Katie rose, not letting go of his hand. "We'll find something for you to do, too."

Mark declared it was the best blueberry crumb pie he had ever eaten. Greta agreed, although admitting it was the only one she had ever eaten.

He bid farewell to Greta, once again taking her in his arms for a goodbye hug. "Keep advancing," he told her. "Next time you invite me to dinner, I want to race you around the house."

"You keep praying about that," Greta chuckled. "Now that would be a miracle."

Katie accompanied Mark to his car, and they took a little extra time to say goodbye. Before Katie opened the overhead door, she handed Mark a large envelope.

"I didn't have time to write," he began.

"Hush, neither did I. It's something else. Don't bend it, and when you open it you'll understand why."

When Mark was alone in his room, he slipped the contents out of the envelope, discovering two 5x7 enlargements. The first was a wide-angle photo of Katie's room, including her bed with the farm scene puzzle hanging above it. It also included the wall with the three pictures he had drawn of the meadow and her bookshelves with Raggedy Andy sitting on the top shelf.

The second photo took his breath away. It was a close up of Katie's bed and the farm picture hanging above the headboard. Sitting on the edge of the bed near the pillow was none other than Katie Byler in her Sunday best with a beautiful smile lighting her face. Her eyes sparkled their most brilliant hazel, and sitting on her lap was Raggedy Andy. On the back she had written, "I'm so glad you came."

Greta waited patiently for Katie's return. "Let's have a cup of tea to celebrate what almost happened," she announced when Katie entered the kitchen.

"Greta! Nothing is private around you, is it?" She pretended offense.

They sat at the kitchen table sipping their hot tea. "You and Mark spend a fair amount of time alone together, don't you?"

"How did you know?"

"Woman's intuition," Greta said. "How's that working out?"

"It's been controlled up until now, but I must confess, it is getting harder for us to keep our hands to ourselves."

"I'll bet it is," Greta acknowledged, "but it won't get any easier. Where do you think all this is going?"

"Pretty much wherever Mark wants it to go."

Greta laughed merrily. "Oh Katie, I don't think so. Are you really unaware of the control you have over him?"

"Did you use much persuasion on George?"

"Sometimes, but George was an easy-going soul. We agreed on most things - the important ones at least. There would be times when, like all men, he just didn't get it."

"What did you do then?"

"He liked back rubs and kisses."

"Mark likes both of those."

"See, you are not so naïve," Greta complimented her.

"The chapter on massage in your book has helped already," Katie said. "But Mark has repeatedly ventured into new experiences that I would not have thought of or been bold enough to initiate, if I had."

"Tell me about these experiences since it's obvious they are not sexual," Greta cajoled.

When Katie concluded some time later, Greta exclaimed, "Oh my goodness; you've had a lot of fun together, haven't you?"

"Yes, we have," Katie admitted, "and we've gotten to know each other along the way."

That night, as Katie slept soundly with Mark's shirt pressed firmly to her chest and all the aromas of him soothing her mind, she dreamed. They were in the meadow playing hide and seek. She called out to him, but he did not answer. She caught a glimpse of him through the blackberry bushes and snuck up behind him to scare him. He was on his side on a pile of branches, as if asleep. Katie rolled him over and bolted upright in her bed, now wide awake.

What had she seen that frightened her? Try as she may, the ending was blank. "It's only a dream," she told herself. "Go back to sleep."

Chapter Thirty-Six

On his way home from school Monday afternoon, Mark was listening to his favorite Youngstown radio station when a song ended. He reached for the button to switch channels as a commercial began. *"Austintown Roller Rink announces their all-night, Anti-Prom Blast this weekend from 10:00 PM Friday to 6:00 AM Saturday. Eight big hours of fun you won't find in any high school gym."*

Mark turned the radio off and rode in silence. While he slowed the car to a moderate speed, his mind raced. The expression "divine providence" came to mind.

He was already making plans as he drove. He just needed to get alone with Greta. As he approached Hogback Road, Katie caught his eye. Her back was facing him and she was walking toward Greta's house. He cut the wheel, and the car slid through the turn.

Katie heard the sliding tires and jerked her head around. Her eyes lit up – first in fright, then in recognition. And then they darkened. She looked down sheepishly when Mark stopped beside her. "Anyone need a lift?" he asked through the open window.

She gave him a thin smile but was unusually reserved. "Are you going to get in or stand there looking at me?" He could see she was undecided and softened his demeanor considerably. "I'm sorry I spoke to you like that. Please, tell me what's wrong."

"I don't smell good. I've been working hard all day at home, and I can even smell myself. I planned to get cleaned up at Greta's house."

"Come on, Katie," Mark said, holding out his hand. "Come into the car. I don't care what you smell like."

"I know I can't look good, either," she added.

"Now that's plain crazy talk," he assured her. "You always look good. You may be a little stinky, but you definitely look good. Anyway, aren't I the one who requested the smell of you all over my sleeping bag?"

Katie smiled at last and got into the car. "I would prefer you not see me like this, is all."

"If I had to choose between not seeing you and seeing you like this, it's a no-brainer," Mark said reassuringly, as he started down the road. "Anyway, I've got all my windows down, and it's a short drive, so how bad could it be?"

Katie rubbed his arm and gave him a forgiving look. "Hello, Mark. What brings you by today?"

"I came to ask my girlfriend out on a date."

"Oh? Where were you thinking of taking Greta? Will you need a chaperone?" He pulled into Greta's driveway, letting her questions go unanswered.

"Let's get you cleaned up, so you don't need to feel self-conscious."

"Thanks for the offer, but I can do it myself," Katie said over her shoulder, as she hurried on ahead of him.

"You are a smarty pants," he mumbled under his breath.

Greta was sitting in a chair in the living room when Mark let himself in. "It's a beautiful day for relaxing on the patio," he suggested.

"I didn't want to take a chance on falling with no one here to help me," she admitted.

"Wise decision. Have you been walking around the house much today?"

"Can't you see the path I've worn across the living room and down the hall?" Greta remarked.

"I heard through the grapevine that Dr. Ford has a new patient," Mark said.

"Yes, she said to tell you hello, and she hopes you're staying out of trouble."

"Me?" Mark feigned innocence. "I'm always good. How does she think your back is doing?"

"I went to her for regulating my medications - especially my pain pills. She put me through my paces concerning my back though, and she gave me some helpful hints."

"I'll help you out onto the patio, if you'd like," he offered.

"Why thank you. Since Katie is getting cleaned up, that would be nice."

When they were seated outside Mark asked, "How did you manage all day without Katie?"

"I can take care of myself all right. Will is the one who thinks she should be here, especially at the beginning. Once I can walk better and am driving, Katie won't be as necessary. I am growing quite fond of her, so who knows when her assistance will no longer be needed."

Mark gave her a steady look. "I have a proposal to make and I may as well just say it."

"I'm listening."

He told Greta about the all-night skating party and his promise to take Katie roller skating.

"Is there a chance you'd be all right alone, and would you be willing to allow us?"

"How would you explain this to your parents?"

"I go skating once in a while, and I would simply tell them I was going. I'd just neglect to mention that Katie was going, too."

"You know your mother isn't going to be happy about this. She told me about your refusal to ask a girl to the prom."

"What was I supposed to do? I couldn't tell her why I wouldn't go to the prom. My relationship with Katie *must* remain hidden."

"What if it comes out in the open?" Greta asked.

Mark clenched his jaw, and his eyes turned cold as ice. "Nothing will stop my quest for Katie and I to be together. Only she has the power to do so."

Greta mulled it over. "If you pick Katie up at nine and have her home by five, I will go along with it. Listen to my words, Mark. If you ever do anything to hurt that dear, sweet girl, you will have God to answer to, but here on Earth you will know my wrath."

"Thanks for the warning, but you know me. I don't know how, but I suspect you know me better than I know myself. I would never do anything to hurt Katie."

"Did I hear someone mention my name?" Katie asked, as she came through the backdoor looking fresh as a daisy.

"Mark was just telling me about a proposal he has for Friday night. Help me inside, Mark, and then you can tell her all about it."

Mark and Katie sat side by side, holding hands while he explained and answered all of her questions.

"I can't give you an answer until I've talked with Greta," she said. "It sounds like fun, and I would love to go if we had no responsibilities. What about your work on the farm on Saturday?"

"My mother was gung ho for me to attend the prom. It would have been seven before I got home. I'll respect your decision, but I need the answer by tomorrow at the latest because I have to buy you a blouse, shoes, and socks. You can wear the brown slacks since they're dressy. Roller rinks have dress codes."

Greta watched from the bathroom window as the teenagers leaned against each other, holding hands in silence. She was puzzled at this subdued reaction. It had to be coming from Katie's side because she was well aware of Mark's enthusiasm.

The two women talked in the kitchen after Mark had gone. Greta took Katie's hand. "What did you tell Mark?"

"I would have to think about it and talk to you. What about my responsibility to care for you, and what if you need me?"

"Did he tell you I had already given my permission?"

Katie looked up with big eyes. "No. Why do you suppose he left that out?"

Greta, too, was speechless as she considered what had taken place. "I am here to help you, but I am not here to provide you with all the answers," Greta said. "Open your heart and become one in thought with Mark. Why would he not tell you? Go back to the purity of the Garden."

Katie thought for a while then replied, "He didn't want to sway me. He heard my concern for leaving you alone and had enough respect for it to let me decide on my own."

"What you're saying is Mark loved you enough to let you decide what was right for you to the detriment of his own desires. I will be fine for eight hours. Thank you for your concern for my safety and for being a responsible person. It isn't necessary to sacrifice a lovely time out to stay home with me. Before you go to bed tonight, I have one more task for you."

"Anything, Greta. "

"Take another bubble bath while you think about Mark and his feelings for you."

Mark stopped at Greta's house the following afternoon promptly on time. The garage door opened, he drove inside, and the garage door closed - all like magic. But the most magical of all was his passenger door opened, Katie slid onto the seat and closed the door behind her. She slid over to his side without taking her eyes off him. "I would love to go skating with you, and Greta said that it's all right. But then, you already knew that." Turning his head to face her, she concluded, "It's your move."

Looking out through the car windows, Mark replied, "You know a garage lightbulb gives off a romantic glow."

Katie's smile was swallowed by a hungry kiss that led to another.

"I'll go to Goodwill after school tomorrow then come here to make sure everything fits," Mark said. She still held him pressed against her. "You do know that if you loosened your grip, I wouldn't run away, right?"

"I'm holding you because I like you right where you are," she whispered. "That's the way I always want to be with you. I want you to be able to tell exactly how I feel." Katie's pulse raced. She took Mark's hand, placed it on her heart, and held it there. "Can you feel it?" she asked. "That's what you do to me. It's a force I cannot control that comes from deep within my soul."

Mark had just turned onto Hogback Road the following afternoon when he passed Deborah Yoder going the opposite direction.

"Did Deborah Yoder just leave here?" Mark asked when Katie greeted him.

"Yes," she said with a grimace. "I was so afraid you would come while she was still here."

"I would have said I came to see Greta. No big deal."

"I'm not so sure. It wouldn't have been a good thing."

"Well, if it ever happens again, I'll keep driving on down the road."

"That would be best. The suitcase in your hand might have raised her interest. Are you moving in?"

"Funny. Where's Greta?"

"Out on the patio reading a book." Katie took his hand and led him down the hall to her room. "What did you get me?" Her voice revealed her excitement.

"They had several blouses in your size, but I thought this one would look best." He held up a golden blouse.

"It's beautiful!" she exclaimed. She held the blouse in front of her and viewed herself in the dresser mirror. "I can picture it with my hair flowing all around it. Go stand in the hall while I try it on."

The blouse fit perfectly, and Katie called Mark back into the room so she could try on the shoes.

"Allow me." Mark picked up a brown loafer and reached behind her heel. "I feel like Prince Charming placing the glass slipper on Cinderella's foot."

"Who is Cinderella, and why would anyone have glass shoes? Sounds pretty impractical to me," she stated matter-of-factly.

"So much for fairy tales and chivalry," he mumbled.

"They fit, too. Looks like I'm all set," Katie said beaming happily. "Now if it were only Friday night. Did you tell your parents?"

"Yes, but they weren't happy about me going alone. I bought a few other things that you may like. You can look at them and decide for yourself."

Katie handed him ten dollars. "I want to help pay for the clothes. They are my clothes, after all, and Greta is paying me."

Mark studied her and decided her mind was already made up. He accepted the money. "You know you didn't have to do that."

"But I wanted to. Someday I want you to take me to a store that stays open late, so I can do some real shopping."

He held out his arms, and she came into them. "I want to hold you for a minute before I go." He whispered into her ear, "I miss you like crazy when we're not together."

"I miss you just as much. Now give me one of your long, sweet kisses to hold me over until Friday."

Mark greeted Greta on the patio before he left. She smiled kindly, asked if the clothes fit, and he told her that they did.

"Wonderful," Greta replied. "I'm already looking forward to helping her prepare for her big night out."

"I knew you would." He squeezed Greta's shoulder and kissed her cheek. "What are you reading?"

"It's a love story."

"Let me know how it ends," he requested. "I only read books with happy endings."

Katie and Greta were enjoying casual conversation over dinner on Friday evening when the subject turned to Mark - like it usually did if they talked for long.

"You know Mark will be punctual," Greta said.

"It's one of his traits that I admire," Katie replied.

"Rather than opening the garage door when he arrives, why don't you open it ten minutes earlier? I want his first glimpse of you to be as you enter the living room from the hall. He and I will be visiting while you are getting ready in your room."

Katie looked puzzled. "But I have plenty of time to get ready before he arrives."

"I know you do, my dear, but a lady always takes a few extra minutes to make sure everything is perfect while the man sits and anticipates her grand entrance."

Greta waited while Katie thought.

"Anticipation, grand entrance, the man gazes upon you lovingly..." Greta hinted.

Katie smiled, but then her face became serious. "Isn't that being devious?"

"No. That's being smart."

Later, the two ladies were in Katie's room putting the finishing touches on her appearance. Greta had pulled Katie's long hair up into two pigtails so it would be off her neck while she skated.

"That's such a lovely blouse Mark bought you," Greta said. "That young man has taste in colors, I'll give him that."

"I wish you could see the drawings of the meadow that he gave me last summer," Katie said. "They're enchanting." She looked at Greta in the mirror.

"The pictures opened my eyes to him, and it was afterward that we truly began. The letter of apology that accompanied them was a nice touch, too."

"I'll bet Mark has a lot of nice touches," Greta said suggestively.

Katie met her eyes in the mirror. "Your wisdom is showing again."

They were chatting in the living room when they heard the garage door closing. "Go Katie!" She motioned her down the hall. "Remember what I taught you. I'll call for you when it's time." The doorbell soon rang. "Now that young man has manners," Greta mused.

"She's surely ready by now," Greta told Mark, as they sat talking on the couch. "She's so excited about your date that she's probably making sure she looks perfect for you. Katie! Mark is here," Greta called.

"I'll be right there," Katie called back. She entered the living room and Mark rose to greet her. His eyes admired her from head to toe.

Katie paused and waited for him to say something… anything. "Do I look all right?" she asked.

Mark finally got his tongue to work. "Way better than all right," he gushed.

Katie revolved slowly then bestowed her very best smile upon him. "I'm glad you approve. How do you like the pigtails?" She tossed her head from side to side, making them bounce and sway. His eyes revealed his admiration, and Katie met his gaze with her own.

"You do scrub up nice," Mark finally said, harkening back to his comment in the bake shop all those months ago.

Katie smiled in remembrance, raised her arms out to him, and met him in the middle of the living room for a loving embrace.

"Greta, would you be able to stand long enough to take a picture of us?" Mark asked.

"I'm sure I can manage it. Where's your camera?"

"In the car. I'll run and get it."

When they were alone, Greta said, "See what I mean? You performed wonderfully, and this is a time he will not soon forget. In fact, he'll have it in pictures."

They stood before the fireplace with Mark's arm around her, and he told Katie how beautiful she looked. Greta snapped the picture as Katie looked lovingly up at him.

Greta handed Katie a shawl. "Put this on if you get chilly. Make sure you're home by five at the latest. Mark, it's Friday night. You need to be a defensive driver. Don't get into any trouble, and both of you return safely, or it's my goose that gets cooked."

Mark beamed with pride as he drove down the road. He glanced sideways at Katie. She returned his look and smiled.

"We're going on a real date," she said.

"Yes. So let me tell you the rules," he began. "First, and foremost, is front-seat etiquette. How close you sit to the guy shows how much you like him." Katie slid over some.

"If you like him a lot, it is even customary to sit next to him." She slid over a little more. "Of course," he continued, "next to him means different things to different people. To me it means I can feel your thigh touching mine."

Katie slid up against him. "You mean like this?" she asked, leaning against him.

"You're getting the hang of it already."

"What else do I do? This seems so simple."

"You could use your imagination," he suggested.

"I could put this arm around your shoulders and lean over and kiss your ear, but then I'd be afraid of distracting the driver."

"Fear not!" he proclaimed, as her tongue began to tickle.

Katie laughed and gave him a hug then laid her head on his shoulder. The night was a dream come true, and their happiness filled the air.

They rode in silence for a while. Mark thought about how far Katie had come, what lay ahead, and ultimately, how badly he wanted it. He wanted to tell her everything he was feeling - completely spill his guts and take his chances. His thoughts were interrupted by the neon sign announcing their arrival at the roller rink.

Mark explained the do's and don'ts of skating as he helped lace up Katie's skates. "Do hang onto me until you can be on your own. Don't fall on your tailbone. Don't allow one skate to come in contact with the other. Anyone who is a good ice skater will quickly pick up roller skating. By the end of the night, you'll be giving me a run for my money."

Bolstered by his confidence, Katie attacked the task with enthusiasm. Until she stood up, that is. Mark caught her before she fell. She was wide-eyed as they walked together toward the skate floor, clinging to his arm.

"These things go forward and backward!" she exclaimed to no one in particular.

It wasn't a snap, but before long, they were holding hands and circling the rink without needing to stop and help her off the floor. The announcer came on the loud speaker to announce the Fast Skate. The music flew into high gear and the skaters did, too. Luckily, they exited the skate floor just in time to escape the charging horde.

"Now we have an inkling of how the Chinese felt when Genghis Khan showed up," Mark commented when they had taken their seats. While the music played on, he explained to Katie about the Mongol Horde and the history of the Asian land.

"You have so much more knowledge than I," she remarked. "There are times when I feel inferior."

"Please don't," Mark said. "You can learn if you want to. How much you know about book-learned subjects certainly doesn't reflect your intelligence. In some ways you're better off, and you can learn whatever interests you. Photography is a perfect example."

"How about kissing?" Katie asked with a smile. "It's a good example for both of us."

"Let's go skate, you silly nymph. I need to get my mind off this subject. There's no kissing allowed in this building. I'm not even allowed to put my arm around you unless we are enjoying a Couple Skate."

"First, tell me what a nymph is," she demanded.

"A beautiful, graceful young woman."

She stood up carefully and held her hand out toward him. "Hold my hand, and let's go work on the graceful part."

Mark and Katie remained on the skate floor when the next Couple Skate was announced. They put their arms around each other and held hands as they slowly circled the skating rink to the rhythm of the organ music. They stole a glance at one another from time to time.

Katie wished Mark would just tell her how he felt. Greta had said, he would reveal himself when he was sure. Katie realized she should have asked, "When he was sure of what?" She had assumed that Greta meant, "When Mark was sure that he loves you," but did she really mean that? There could be other explanations, and the most likely reason was when he was sure that she loved him enough to be his Eve.

The Couple Skate ended and an All Skate began. Katie asked Mark if they could sit for a while. They had just finished a soda when "The Hokey Pokey" was announced. "Come on," he said, pulling her up by the hand. "You've got to learn 'The Hokey Pokey.'"

The participants formed two rows facing each other from one end of the skating floor to the other. The song began, and Katie followed Mark's lead. He admired the way her pigtails bounced when they came to the verse, "You put your head in, you take your head out."

Of course with the rink full of teenagers they couldn't omit the verse, "You put your backside in." Katie and Mark had their own private joke and laughed out loud, as they watched each other "shake it all about."

During the Advanced Skate, Katie enjoyed watching a few expert skaters put on a show.

"I need to use the restroom, how about you?" Mark asked.

"No, I'm fine. I'll stay here till you return."

Mark hesitated. He wasn't sure he should leave her sitting here alone, but nature was calling. "Okay, don't go anywhere. I'll only be a couple minutes."

The Advanced Skate ended, and an All Skate began before Mark returned. When he came out of the men's room, the seating area had cleared out. He glanced in Katie's direction then tensed. Katie was sitting in the same spot, but standing in front of her was a boy about his age engaging her in conversation. She shook her head. Mark approached them just as the boy grabbed her arm and pulled on it.

"Come on," the boy said. "All I'm asking for is one little skate."

She tried to pull away, but the boy wouldn't let go. Mark came up behind him, jammed his index finger into the offender's ribs, and muttered into his ear, "Get your fingers off my girlfriend's arm." Startled, the boy released her and glared at Mark before finally skating away.

Katie was visibly flustered as Mark sat down. "It's okay," he said. "He won't bother you again."

"He asked me to skate, and I told him no. Why did he grab me?"

"Because he's no gentleman, and he's probably gotten away with it before. We'll just sit here until the next Couple Skate, if that's all right with you."

"I'd like that," Katie replied. "You do a good job of supporting me during the Couple Skate."

"You're actually getting quite good for your first time," Mark complimented her, "but I'm not surprised. I'll bet you'd do well on a bicycle, too."

"Where could we ride one of those?" she asked.

"I could bring mine to the meadow on a full moon night.

"It would be nice to be somewhere more private than here," Mark said, stroking her arm. He looked at his watch. "We've already been here more than four hours. Are you getting tired yet?"

"Do you know somewhere more private?"

"Inside my car in Greta's garage is a lot more private," he assured her with a gleam in his eye.

She returned his look. "Why don't we skate one more Couple Skate, then go?" Katie slid her arm through his and leaned up against him.

When the Couple Skate began, Katie looped her arm around him while he held her close, and they enjoyed a leisurely skate. Mark would lean over every once in a while, near the far end of the rink away from the seating and gently kiss her hair. She in turn would look up at him with starry eyes. "I'm glad you brought me," she said. "This has been more fun than I imagined. Can we do it again sometime?"

"We will do it again, I promise," Mark told her. She smiled and leaned her head against his shoulder.

The stars blazed as Mark drove across the interstate with Katie snuggled up close to his side. His arm was around her, and her head rested against his shoulder. In spite of the late hour, he was wide awake, and music played softly on the radio.

"I've been listening to the radio a little each night in my room," Katie said.

"Hear any good songs?"

"Some of them are good and some not so good. A lot of times the songs are sad."

"We call those tear jerkers."

Mark spied the lighted sign of a truck stop and took the exit. "Where are we going?" Katie asked.

"Did all that skating make you hungry?"

When they were seated in a booth at the all-night truck stop, Mark plunked some change into the tabletop jukebox and chose two selections.

"I've never eaten in a restaurant," Katie stated.

"I figured as much. Why don't you let me order for both of us?"

Young Love was almost over when the waitress came to take their order. "One hot roast beef sandwich with mashed potatoes and gravy and two chocolate milkshakes, please."

The waitress looked at Katie then at Mark. "You must be lovebirds," she remarked. "Only lovebirds sit on the same side in a booth. Ya always gotta be touching one another."

Mark's jaw dropped, and Katie held back a chuckle. The waitress looked at Mark and raised her eyebrows. "So all you're having is a chocolate shake?"

"I was planning on eating half of the meal," he explained.

"Can't you see that young lady sitting beside you needs her own? She's practically skin and bones. Don't you earn enough to feed her right?"

"Make that two meals," Mark capitulated.

After the waitress left, Katie elbowed him. "She got the better of you. She had you roped and tongue tied," she said with a playful smile.

"You don't mess with the cook," Mark muttered.

"She's the server and the cook?" Katie asked.

"She could be at this hour. It's probably just as well. You look like someone who doesn't share her food very well."

"Now Mark, if you had to choose between me sharing food poorly or sharing kisses poorly, which would you take?" And Katie shot him that *'Come and get me'* look.

"Is this a trick question?" he asked and began tickling her.

She wrapped both arms around his neck and pulled him to her waiting lips. That was all the egging Mark needed. He grabbed her and got rather frisky with his hands and passionate kisses.

"Mark! We're in public," Katie said nervously.

"I don't see anyone around. Besides, you started it by looking at me like you did."

Katie smiled sweetly. "There's that 'woman's fault' thing again. Please show some self-control… until we get to Greta's garage, that is." She puckered his lips with her fingertips and kissed him with a loud pop.

Mark threw his head back and laughed out loud. Katie soon joined him while blushing profusely.

When they finally stopped laughing, Mark couldn't tear his eyes away from her, and a silly grin filled his face. Katie couldn't help but grin back at him. He ran his hand up her arm. "I can't believe you started that."

Katie gave him an impish shrug. "So, at least I was honest."

"This was really good," Katie admitted while finishing her meal. "I think I could eat another."

"Go ahead. Eat me out of house and home," Mark said. "We can always join the old woman who lived in a shoe."

"Why did she live in a shoe?"

"Because she had so many children she didn't know what to do. But what I'd really like to know is how a woman that old had kids in the first place," he mused.

"All this is a mystery to me," Katie replied.

"You don't read fairy tales or nursery rhymes?"

She shook her head.

"So you don't know 'Mary Had a Little Lamb' or 'Humpty Dumpty' or 'Jack and Jill'?"

"None of those."

"Would you like to learn them?"

"Will it make me a better girlfriend?"

Mark laughed and laughed. Suddenly Katie said, "The clock is ticking. Remember Greta's garage."

"We'll have an hour," Mark said.

"Let's hurry. An hour is not enough."

It wasn't enough. First they tried the backseat of Mark's car, but it wasn't comfortable. Then they tried the couch. It was too narrow, although each enjoyed the top and the bottom of their time there.

Later that morning, Greta found them fast asleep on the carpeted floor, wrapped in Mark's quilt and using the couch pillows for their heads. Mark was behind Katie as they lay on their sides. His arm was around her while she held it firmly between her breasts with his hand against her neck. The look of sheer contentment on their faces was too much for Greta to disturb.

Six became seven. Seven became eight, and still, Greta let them sleep. The clock was approaching nine when Greta's noise while preparing tea caused Katie to stir. She turned and kissed Mark. His eyelids opened. Then he smiled and kissed her back.

"I want you to know it's morning, and I still respect you," he said with a mischievous grin.

"That's because we didn't do anything, silly boy. You fell asleep as soon as we crawled into your grandma's quilt."

"I am in so much trouble," he sighed. "I wonder what time it is?"

"I wonder where Greta is?" Katie added.

"Not really. Eight fifty-two. And I'm right here," Greta said.

They both sat up and saw her looking at them. "Greta!" Katie exclaimed. "You should have awakened us."

"You were sleeping so peacefully, I hated to disturb you. Besides, I had a lot of time to think. Mark, you probably should be going. I remember you told me last night you might stop for a bite at the new truck stop on the way home. Tell your parents you closed your eyes to rest for just a minute in your car and the next thing you knew, it was eight-thirty. They might not be happy, but they'll understand. Be sure to go out to the other end of Hogback, so you're returning home from the right direction. You'll have to stop by one day on your way home from school to get your suitcase. I take it your night out was enjoyable?"

"It really was," Katie said. "I'll tell you all about it after Mark leaves."

"I'm sure you'll leave out some of the good parts," Greta jested with a wink.

Katie blushed. "Come on, Mark. I'll get the door for you." She took his hand and headed for the garage.

Mark had to tell his parents he awoke at eight-fifty.

Chapter Thirty-Seven

Katie's clothes were washed, dried, and folded neatly back into the suitcase. She had cleaned the house one last time for Will's arrival, then showered and dressed for her return home. She wished it was Mark who was coming for her and thought about how different that would feel.

Katie had told Greta in detail about her date and the fun they had roller skating. She even told her about the persistent boy who wouldn't let go of her arm. "What bothered me the most was a stranger touching me." Katie asked if she could discuss something she didn't fully understand, but was hesitant to ask.

"What is it?" Greta inquired. "It's obviously troubling you."

"It's the most important thing of all," Katie answered solemnly. "It's the question of whether or not Mark loves me. You told me, 'Mark will reveal himself when he feels sure enough to drop the shield.' I thought I knew what you meant, but I'm no longer sure. It occurred to me that your response could have multiple meanings, and I don't know which applies."

Greta studied her, weighing her own words carefully. "You have obviously drawn some conclusions, so tell me what you've discovered."

Katie explained her recent revelations and Greta asked, "If I had told you what the problem was and what you should do about it, would you have accepted it as your own and acted upon it as faithfully?"

"I suppose I would not have."

"Have you done as I instructed? Have you thought long and hard about whether or not you wish to become Mark's Eve?"

Tears came to Katie's eyes. "I could have answered you the moment you instructed me, but I didn't out of respect. I have known for a long time that I wanted no man in my life except Mark, but in recent days I have realized just how much he means to me."

"You would forsake all others to be with him?" Greta continued.

"Yes! Can't you see how much I love him?"

"You would abandon the ways of your upbringing to live with Mark as

English?" Greta persisted. Now Katie's tears were freely falling and even though Greta shared her pain, she waited.

"'If it means I can't be with Mark, I don't want to be Amish. If Mark would only tell me he loves me, there would be no hesitation. Help me open his heart so he will know my love is true." Katie fell to her knees on the living room floor and beseeched her, "Show me the way." With head bowed, her tears kept falling.

Exhausted, Greta slumped onto the couch. She waited for Katie's tears to subside then held out her arms. "Come to me."

Katie rose and fell into Greta's arms. Greta held her as she would a small child, rocking her gently. "Forgive me for making you go through that, but I had to be sure that you loved him with all your heart. Mark loves you - spoken to me by his own lips - and you love Mark. Only time keeps you apart."

Katie surrendered completely to Greta's embrace. All the yearnings and unknowns came together as one as she waited on Greta.

"Return to your home. Go about your daily life and let your thoughts dwell on the one you love. Believe in your heart that his thoughts dwell on you. Express your thoughts and feelings in love letters. When you are together, allow love to flow from you. Mark will feel it, know it, and draw closer day by day until he knows beyond any doubt that you love him just as Eve loved Adam. Give him the kind of devotion that you reserve for the Father. Then love will rule on high, and fear will run and hide."

Once more the floodgates opened and tears fell like rain as Katie released her emotional turmoil. These were tears of joy, and Katie gave them up without shame. She clung to Greta long after the tears had subsided. "I love you, you know," Katie said.

Greta smiled and laid her hand gently on Katie's cheek. As the two women embraced, Katie knew their spirits, too, were forever joined.

Katie returned on Tuesday to help Greta walk with the forearm crutches. When the two women met this time, they embraced with a knowing look. The baton had been passed. Greta had given her the key to life's door, and without hesitation, Katie accepted all that went with it: maturity, responsibility, dedication, and love were now driving her existence.

"Will is taking a half day off work tomorrow," Greta beamed happily.

"Oh, and what good tidings do you have to share today?"

"He's taking me shopping in Granville."

"What is the occasion? No, let me guess, you need a new pair of driving gloves?"

Greta smiled and shook her head.

"Work boots?"

"Canes," Greta declared. "I told him I wanted to get ready for my next phase of living."

"Bless you, Greta. You're always prepared. And do you have a time line for this cane?"

"As soon as possible, so let's walk some more. The garden awaits us."

Katie smiled wistfully. "Ah, the garden. Maybe we will find Mark there."

"Tell me how your letter writing is coming along."

"It's doing fine," Katie replied, "but I was hoping you could help me with a poem I've been working on for Mark. He is forever writing me poems, and I have only written him one. This one is proving to be more challenging with many stanzas and shorter lines."

"Sounds like writing a song."

"Mark writes those, too. He sang one for me once, while he played his guitar."

"Did you ask him to play you any more songs?"

"No, but I guess I should have, huh?"

"Depends. Do you like music, and is Mark any good with that guitar? Does his singing resemble a cat getting its tail stepped on?"

Katie laughed. "I like music, he plays the guitar well, and his singing is very good."

"It's your life, I guess, but you might consider asking him to play another song or two. I used to write songs when I worked in a cabaret back in the old country, before I became a nurse."

"Is that why you have a piano?" Katie asked.

"Yes it is. I still enjoy banging on the keys every now and then, and singing my own songs." She gave Katie's arm a pinch.

"If I can write songs, I ought to be able to help you write a poem. What's the name of this poem?"

"Sweetheart."

"Sounds like a poem I'd like to read," Greta remarked. "Bring it with you next time."

"As luck would have it, I have it in my pocket today."

Greta helped tweak the poem, and Katie wrote out a finished copy to give Mark, along with the letter she had spent Sunday and Monday nights composing. The previous Saturday morning before they parted at Greta's, they had agreed to meet at the east end of Wagner's pond shortly after dark on Tuesday night. If either couldn't make it, they were to leave a letter in the drop spot by sunrise on Wednesday.

When Katie had waited five minutes beyond their agreed-upon fifteen minute wait period, she rose to leave and looked one last time toward the meadow. She saw Mark's light, and her spirits soared. Watching him come toward her, she remembered his poem *A Light in the Darkness*. She recalled the last two lines: I realized tonight as I watched you draw near/ You're my light in the darkness for all my years.

She couldn't wait for the days to come so she could show him how much she truly loved him.

At last Mark was with her, scooping her into his arms and holding her up high until he let her down slowly. He collapsed onto the grass of the pond bank and Katie flopped on top of him.

With only the moonlight to see by, they gazed upon each other while allowing their bodies to do the speaking. "Get closer," Katie implored.

Mark stroked her back and then up the incline to squeeze her fanny ever so gently. "Harder," Katie rasped as she pressed down firmly against him. "You have got to be the closest thing there is to Heaven," she said with a steamy voice.

"Did you change your name to Heaven?" Mark asked.

"Kiss me," she said demurely. "No more talking without some loving."

Katie yielded her sweet lips for the taking but directed the action with soft kisses. "Caress my lips tenderly with yours. Take me to your foreverland," she murmured. "Take me to that secret place in your mind."

Their union became magical as they blended together in a world of tender ecstasy. And for just a little while, they got lost in the wonderment.

When they finally came up for air, Mark said, "I'm sorry I was late. I just finished disking a field, and I'm dirty and smelly, too."

"I know where there's a pond to wash off in," Katie teased.

"You first," Mark said. "I really dislike cold water." Then he added suggestively, "But in another month or so it won't be cold."

"Oh, Mark! If you keep talking, *I'm* going to need to jump in that pond." Her desires were already raging, and she feared the thought of them skinny dipping would send her over the edge. "I have a letter for you," she injected to change the subject.

"And I have one for you."

"I've got to get back in case I'm missed."

"Friday night at the bankhouse?" he asked.

"Yes, but there's something I want to warn you about."

"Is something wrong?"

"It's a woman thing," Katie said shyly.

"Ahhhh. There are three women in our house, so I know all about periods. It's okay. We'll adjust. But if you'd rather stay in your bed, I'll understand."

Katie was quick to nix that idea. "I want to be with you, even if it's just to lay in your arms."

"We can talk more," Mark said. "I still have many things I'd like to know about you."

"And I you," she concurred.

"Make a list," he suggested. "We'll make sure we hit them all."

Before they parted, she told him she would be in the mood for music on Friday night. "I'll bring my radio in case I'm feeling well enough to dance. Can you bring your guitar? I want to hear you play and sing me some songs." She could tell he was pleased at her request and she silently thanked Greta.

Returning home, Katie was practically walking on air. Mark had said, "We'll get them all." It was good if he had no more unanswered questions.

"Oh, Sweetheart!" Katie called as she neared the campfire. Mark rose from his chair next to the fire and took her in his arms.

"Am I your sweetheart?" he asked.

"You are. And did you like my poem?"

"Immensely!" Mark said with a flair. "How are you feeling?"

"As usual. It didn't come until this morning, so I still have a lot of cramping." She looked at the two pots hanging over the fire. "What's for dinner, dear?"

"The one is sassafras tea, and the other is simply hot water."

Katie frowned and shook her head. "I'm sorry, but I'm not going to be able to hunker down to wash feet."

"It's not for our feet," he said kindly. "It's for your hot water bottle."

"I didn't bring one."

"I did. I brought you some aspirin, too."

"Where are we going to congregate?" Katie asked.

"In the bankhouse. It's a little cool this evening. I set up the straw bales to form the lounge chair."

"Do you mind if I keep my dress on tonight? My tummy feels better without the pressure." She removed her cap and undid the braids, letting her hair fall over her shoulders. Katie observed Mark's face as he watched her shake it out with her fingers. "I will never tire of seeing that expression on your face," she said.

Soon they were sipping tea by the fire and discussing events of recent days. "Where'd you get this neat old canvas rocker?" Katie asked as she rocked forwards and back.

"I found it in our junk room. I thought you might like it."

"Did you bring your guitar?"

"Yes. I have a couple songs I'd like to sing for you."

"Only two?" Katie turned her lower lip down.

Mark laughed. "I have a duet we can do if you'll sing the female part." He reached into his pocket and handed her a paper. She unfolded it to see the male/female lines written out.

He handed her another paper. She unfolded this one and read the title at the top, "God Bless America." He taught her the melody and sang along with her the first time. Then Mark was the one being entertained while he listened to the beautiful sounds coming from her lips. "Let's go inside where my guitar sound won't carry as well."

Katie relaxed on the lounge with the water bottle while Mark sang and played song after song. She clapped enthusiastically after he finished each one then asked him to play another. They ended by singing the duet. After Katie learned her part, Mark joined in and the song became complete. They were each gazing lovingly at the other when they finished.

"Either part is incomplete, but put the two parts together, and there is a burst of life and love," Mark said.

Katie could not be sure. Was it the song he was speaking of or their relationship? But still, he had said, "love."

Mark reached for a cardboard tube behind him. "I brought something to show you. I want to thank you for the pictures of your room, especially the one with you in it. The writing on the back described the look on your face completely."

Katie waited nervously for what came next. The phrase on the back had been written spontaneously and once written could not be removed; "I'm so glad you came." She knew it had come from Mark's own drawing of her in the bake shop that Peggy had described.

"At first I thought nothing of it, but then I realized it must be more than mere coincidence. Figuring it out was easy, but getting Peggy to admit it was more difficult. She did finally come clean. She insisted you were merely a listener to her gossip."

Fear gripped Katie. She wanted to tell him it was love that made her listen and love that made her write it on her picture.

"Since Peggy told you about the picture, I figured I may as well bring it and show you. I wanted to show it to you, anyway. I was always afraid that you'd be angry with me for making them."

Katie blinked. He was afraid that *she* would be angry?

"Please don't feel that way," she said. She slid to the edge of the chaise and placed her feet on the floor. "I can't bear that you be afraid." Katie stared down at the floor slats, not knowing what to say. "I'm sorry for invading your privacy, and I understand if you are angry."

"That's just it," Mark said. "I don't want my drawings to be private any more than I want my songs to be private."

"So you're not upset with me?"

"I'm glad this has come out into the open," he said.

"Do you want to show me your picture, or is it pictures?" she asked.

"Two, actually. Peggy said she told you about both of them. I want no secrets."

Katie laid her hand on his arm and looked into Mark's eyes. "That is what I want, too."

As Katie looked upon the bake shop picture, she could feel the love he had drawn into it. Mark said, "This picture has become a self-fulfilling prophecy."

"What do you mean?" she inquired.

Mark held the photograph of Katie sitting on her bed beside his drawing. She could hardly believe her eyes. The two faces were identical. "Peggy described the picture and told you about the words I had written at the top. You became the girl in the bake shop. The photograph is the proof of it in blazing color. If this can happen, it makes me wonder…"

"Go on," Katie urged.

"Can I become everything you want? Can you become everything I want? It has happened in this case. You have become every part of her: not just the smile and pretty face but the spirit behind the face. I'm drawing ever closer to that spirit, and it scares me because the closer we get, the more is at stake." He paused.

"I have one more picture to show you," Mark said.

Katie's mind reeled as she looked upon the girl in the yellow sundress. She could feel the stirrings deep in her soul. "Is that how you see me?" she asked. "Is my spirit that beautiful to you?"

"Look at her, Katie. That is you."

"No! You have added something spiritual… and you have added love beyond measure." Understanding bubbled up within her and Katie knew that she gazed upon the very soul of Eve; a soul that was one with God and one with Adam. She looked into Mark's eyes and asked, "Can you truly see back that far?" Katie stared at the picture, mesmerized by its aura.

"What are you thinking?" Mark asked.

"Will this picture, too, become a self-fulfilling prophecy?" Katie asked. She watched him and knew he was struggling.

He hesitated long enough to draw a deep breath and let it out. "That depends on you, I guess."

Katie responded without hesitation. "No! That depends entirely on you." She stared at him as if expecting him to say something.

Mark couldn't translate her body language, even though it was his turn to act on the information before him - to fully grasp the situation, to come out from behind the wall. In spite of all he knew and his yearning to be truly one with Katie, it was a leap too far.

A small voice from the enemy whispered into his ear, "What if she doesn't love you enough? She's left you before. She'll break your heart, you know."

The opportunity to unite forever had been lost. While Mark floundered, Katie withdrew.

Chapter Thirty-Eight

Adam and Eve were expelled from the Garden, and Satan ruled the Earth.

Mark wallowed in fear, and Katie was overcome by disappointment. Emotions, once their ally, drove them apart. "What God has brought together, let no man put asunder" was under attack.

There was no dancing in the bankhouse that night. With all the dignity she possessed, and soon after their discussion of the pictures, Katie claimed severe cramping and left in a flurry. Mark tried to accompany her as far as the Byler fields, but she told him curtly that his assistance wasn't needed. Then he was alone with his confusion.

Mark had never heard such a tone in Katie's voice before. He had heard her angry, but this was deeper. This was emotional hurt, and Mark knew that he had caused it.

"It was the woman's fault," Adam told God.

What did she expect from him? Wasn't this the second time she had rejected him... or was it the third? He had done everything to show her how he felt. Mark crawled into his sleeping bag, knowing that he had disappointed Katie and truly let her down. "She'll never forgive you," the enemy whispered in his ear.

Adam saw that he was naked, and he hid.

Mark turned inward and tried to find the answers there. He had no experience with this degree of turmoil, and he struggled with the upheaval. Unable to untangle the knots in his brain, he slept fitfully that night. And the next.

He finally found solace in work. Rain was forecast for Sunday night into Monday, and Lane Farms had many fields in various stages before planting. The Amish help was off on Sunday, but Harold fell back on an old reliable friend to fill in. Harold, Tom, and Mark worked all three tractors from sunup until long into the night. The rain held off until they planted the last field. The long, physically demanding day was just what Mark needed. Their accomplishments restored his mental balance and his confidence. He loved farming. Would it be so bad if this was the love of his life?

Returning to her room after leaving Mark in a flurry, Katie heard the voices in the night: you don't belong together; he'll never trust you enough; you were naïve to think it would work out. Swamped by discouragement, she clung to Raggedy Andy beneath her covers. Like Mark, she could barely think straight. Katie knew she was brooding, and even though it wasn't her way, she couldn't help herself. She did have a tinge of guilt but thought after all they'd shared that his reasoning was faulty.

While the enemy filled Mark's head with lies, Katie did forgive him. She was the first to come out of her misery because she had been down this road before. She worked through her angst on Sunday afternoon surrounded by all the love Mark had given her. She read his letters and poems, remembering that she had cried out to him once before, and he had heard her. "Hear me, now," she cried out again.

Katie arrived at the Sunday Sing at Deborah Yoder's house in a good frame of mind. Lots of people she knew were there, and she enjoyed the social gathering. It was a warm May evening, and there was an excitement in the air.

"Rudy is here by himself," Deborah said. "Maybe you should talk to him. He's been stealing glances in your direction. I think he still likes you."

Katie recalled the time Rudy Hostetler had revealed his interest in her. It was an awkward conversation. Katie had always liked Rudy, but she had had no romantic feelings for him. In fact, she had had no romantic feelings for any boy, and she wondered at the time if there might be something wrong with her.

To Katie, the situation was simple, as were most things to her. No interest meant no interest, and she told him they could be friends, but she wasn't interested in a serious relationship. That was a year ago, and she suspected the word got around. Since then, no boy had asked to accompany her home.

While she was getting refreshments, Rudy came up beside her and touched her arm. "Hi Katie," he said in a friendly voice. She greeted him pleasantly.

"I've been watching you all evening," Rudy said.

"So I've heard."

"You look lovely as ever this evening." Katie blushed and looked down. Encouraged by her reaction, he continued. "Would you sit with me while we eat?"

She accepted his invitation and they talked amicably while they enjoyed their food. Rudy was a good conversationalist, and she had always enjoyed his company. "Have you thought any more about what I asked you?" he ventured.

His question caught her by surprise, and a vision of Mark flashed through her head. Suddenly, Katie felt like she was being disloyal and mentally searched for a way out. "Why Rudy, that must have been almost a year ago. I didn't realize there was no expiration date."

Rudy fidgeted. "I know what you said then, but this is now, and I was hoping your feelings might be different."

"I am one year older," she remarked, "but I still am only eighteen. I realize that one day boys will have to grow on me, but not today." She could see the disappointment in his eyes, and she almost felt sorry for him. "What happened to Marian and Lena?" Katie asked. "I heard they were receptive to your attention."

He smiled. "I took a page out of your book on life. I told them that we could be friends."

"That's unfortunate for them," she said.

"You did say we could be friends," Rudy repeated. He brightened and asked, "Can friends give one another a ride home at the end of the evening?"

She looked at the black night sky with clouds hiding the stars. She remembered the forecast for rain she had heard last night on her radio. Would Mark view a ride home as a betrayal? Katie looked at Rudy who still waited hopefully. "As long as it's a ride with no strings attached. It looks and feels like rain, so a ride would be kind of you."

"It's still not that late," Rudy commented later when he dropped Katie off. "We could sit on the front porch and talk for a while."

"That could be misunderstood as encouraging you," she pointed out. "Before long, everyone would be talking about us."

"I'd never tell," he assured her.

"Even if you wouldn't, there is a whole group of people in the house who would. Thank you for the ride. I appreciate your kindness."

After prayers, Katie lay in bed with the lights out. She thought about everything that had happened since she awoke this morning. She had not written in her journal about Rudy because she was in love, and he was not the one. She went to sleep thinking about Mark and the feeling of his arms around her. If she could only be with him, everything would be all right again.

Throughout school on Monday, Mark thought of Katie and remembered their parting on Friday night. His inner voice asked how he could love her completely. Where's the foundation of trust? He thought about waiting her out but finally decided he should just tell her how he felt. If she was going to forgive him, then she would. If she wouldn't, then nothing mattered anyway, and he still had farming to love.

After school, Mark was on his way through town when he spied Katie's horse and buggy tied in the alley beside Thompson's grocery store. He parked and entered the store, alert for her presence. The aisles were empty until he came to the last one. Halfway down the aisle, Katie was studying the bottles on the top shelf.

Mark approached as she reached for a bottle of maple syrup. "Katie," he whispered, startling her. The bottle fell from her hand. He reached out and snared it but not well enough, and it began to slip from his grasp. As Katie turned toward him, he brought his left hand around and trapped the bottle between the back of his hand and her chest. They stood eye to eye, one set full of surprise and the other desperation. "Grab it," Mark implored, "before it drops."

She looked down at the bottle and his hand. "You've got two hands. They've worked pretty well, so far." She mimicked his grin.

Mark pulled his left hand away and caught the bottle under the bottom as it fell. "I didn't mean to scare you. I should have thought before I did that."

"You do that a lot, don't you?" Katie asked.

"Do what?"

"Act without thinking. You seem to be good at it, like you've had a lot of practice."

Mark tried to read her intent. "That was close," he countered. "We almost got ourselves in a sticky situation."

"We? I'd say it was you, and you're pretty well in the thick of it already."

Mark was about to fall on her mercy when she smiled. "I'm teasing you. You're so good at it, I'm just giving some back."

He looked intently into her eyes. "Do you forgive me?"

"For having your hand against my chest?"

"For Friday night!" he replied anxiously.

"That depends on you."

"I don't know what to do," Mark said.

"Surprise me," she answered. She knew her love was beyond reason and surprised him, in turn, by caressing his cheek and giving him a kiss on the lips. He nervously looked up and down the aisle. "I don't care," she said. "I don't care who knows about us."

Mark took her in his arms, and they kissed passionately between the rows of food.

When they separated, she told him, "Rudy took me home from the Sing last night."

"Why did you let him do that?"

"Because it looked like rain, and I didn't want to get wet. I wanted to tell you because we promised honesty and no secrets."

"It's okay, then," Mark replied. "I trust you. Are you planning on having a blueberry crumb pie for me tomorrow?"

"Is that any way to ask?"

"Will you have a blueberry crumb pie for me tomorrow?"

"That's better. Still needs improvement."

"Please make me one of your fantastic blueberry crumb pies."

Katie gave him her best smile and said, "Goodbye, Mark." As she walked away, Katie thought, "He loves me. I know he loves me. We are going to talk about it. And soon."

Tuesday after school, Mark stopped to get his pie. He had even brought the egg bucket just in case Katie wasn't busy. Mary Byler greeted him warmly as he entered the shop. "I'll bet I know what you came for. Oh, and I see you'd like some eggs." She reached out through the open wall and rang the new bell mounted on the outside. "Sarah will be right here to get your eggs."

Mark engaged Mary in idle talk as he paid for his purchases then casually asked, "What's Katie up to today?"

"She's weeding and doing some planting in the garden."

Sarah peered in the open wall. "Yes, Mama?"

"Mark would like two dozen eggs," Mary told her.

Walking toward the springhouse, Sarah told Mark about her new duties of helping with the baking and fetching the eggs. "Someday, I'll be taking Katie's place," she said proudly. "If she ever starts liking boys, that is."

Mark looked for Katie in the garden as he started up the road. She had been watching for him to leave and gave a quick wave of her hand. The letter Mark had written to her was still in his pocket. He wanted to hand deliver it because its message was precious to him - as precious as the girl whose name was written at the top - and its contents were time-sensitive. Mark remembered the events in the grocery store, and Katie's statement to surprise her rang in his mind.

"What can I do to surprise her?" he asked himself.

On Wednesday, Katie's alarm went off like every morning, announcing the start of another day. She stretched and walked across the room to retrieve her clothing. Out of the corner of her eye she saw a strange shape as she approached her table. She gasped and jumped back.

"What in the world!" Katie said aloud. Through the window behind the table, she made out a large shape in the semi-darkness. She peered through the glass for a closer look, and realized it was a quart jar full of wildflowers. She brought it into her room and set it on the table. Katie examined the flowers and discovered a paper wedged between the stems. "SURPRISE!" she read. She turned it over to see if anything was written on the other side. "Are you surprised?" The question was accompanied by a smiley face.

392

Katie smelled each of the varieties and then placed the note in the box with Mark's letters. She removed his t-shirt from under her pillow and locked it in the box, also.

Mary saw the flowers later that day and asked where they came from.

"There was no name with the flowers," Katie honestly replied.

Mary told Moses about them, as soon as she saw him.

"Your mother says you have a secret admirer, Katie," Moses said at supper. "Or maybe he's not a secret, except to us." He looked at Katie with raised eyebrows.

"Papa, I don't know who left me those flowers. Maybe you did. Mama, are you missing a quart jar?"

"I hear you didn't throw them away," he prodded. "If you ever figure it out, I'd sure like to know who it is."

Katie gave her mother a beseeching look.

"Oh, Moses," Mary said with a smile, "we should let it go for now."

By Thursday, Mark decided to enlist Peggy's help in delivering his letter. She asked their mom if they could have a loaf of homemade bread from Byler's for supper.

"I haven't spoken with Katie in weeks," she said. "It'll give me an excuse to visit." Ann acquiesced, and Peggy took off down the road on her bike.

She found Katie in the garden and gave her a hug.

"What brings you by today?" Katie asked.

"Mark wanted to come, but after due consideration of the ramifications, he decided against it."

Katie's eyes sparkled at the verbiage. "Mark tell you to say that?"

"No, but it's something he would have said."

"Amen to that," Katie agreed.

Peggy discreetly handed her the sealed envelope. "It must be important for him to solicit my help in delivering it." Katie quickly slipped it into her pocket.

"Mark doesn't talk about you and him, ever," Peggy said, with the accent on ever.

Katie was silent, not knowing what to say.

"It can only mean one of two things. I've kept my nose out of it, but I will tell you, it hasn't been easy for me to do."

"What do you mean?" Katie asked.

"Mark is my brother. He and I are friends, and I have no knowledge of what may be the most important event of his life. Either you two have nothing going on, or there's so much going on that Mark dare not speak of you. I vote for the latter."

"Please be patient," Katie implored. "We will fill you in when the time is right, but now is not the time. There is too much at stake."

Peggy gave Katie an understanding look. "May God help you. You are going to need it." She hugged Katie and said, "Be good to my brother. He has a pure heart, you know." Katie returned to her weeding to hide her tears. When Peggy was gone, she made a beeline to her room and cried again when she read Mark's letter.

My Dearest Katie,

I have been spiritually troubled since you left me Friday night. I have tried talking it out with God, but the message I keep getting is "talk to Katie."

I have always known that you are closer in spirit to our Heavenly Father than I am, and I have admired you for it.

I have wanted to have a serious conversation about something very important for weeks, but I have not had the courage to do so. I am looking forward to talking it out with you on Friday night.

Missing you like crazy,

Mark

P.S. How could I live without the feel of your sweet lips on mine or the embrace of your arms around me?

Katie cried for what hadn't been said. She cried for what would be said, and she cried out of longing for this man who had done so much to fill her heart.

She drifted off to sleep that night believing in her soul that love was everything. She slept soundly until just before the alarm.

Was it a vision or simply a dream? She could clearly see herself then hear her voice calling out to Mark. As before, they were in the meadow, only it was no hide and seek game being played. This time, fear permeated the air. It thrummed in her ears while she cried out his name as she ran. Then she saw him and screamed in terror as he reached out a blood soaked hand to her, rasping, "Help me, Katie."

She awoke in a cold sweat as her previous concern had turned to dread. She lay there in the dark knowing she had to warn him, but how? She would have to wait until tonight.

Chapter Thirty-Nine

The storm clouds rolled in by noon, and all afternoon Katie fretted. She had listened to the radio and knew they were calling for heavy rain. She was waiting on a customer when Mark's car pulled up to the bake shop. Her heart pounded with the anticipation of telling him now. The customer was slow while Mark waited. Before that one left, two more had entered the small shop.

Mark recommended the bags of sassafras tea to the other customers as he paid Katie for the one he was holding. The rain was already beginning to come down.

"Here comes that rain they've been predicting," he said loudly enough for everyone to hear. "It's supposed to be a real gully-washer. We'd best stay safe and dry in our houses tonight." The other customers agreed while Katie nodded in understanding and thanked him for his purchase. Then Mark was gone, and Katie could do nothing except watch him leave.

The bake shop had a slow first week, but it usually did until word got out that the Bylers were open for business once again. On Friday morning, Katie had talked with her mother about closing the shop on Saturday.

"That would give me the opportunity to catch up on my spring photography at Lane Farms," she pointed out. Mary agreed and posted a notice on the bake shop door.

Katie sat at her writing table Friday evening planning her next day's itinerary for picture taking. She'd follow her normal route each time she went to the meadow and stop at Wagner's ponds in case some wildlife appeared.

After writing in her journal, she wrote a short letter to Mark which she would leave in the drop spot. Katie told him she would come to the pond just after dark every night until he was there to meet her. She said she hoped to see him soon.

Katie sat at her writing table and thought about how loving Mark had changed everything. And she wondered how their love would change tomorrow.

She was surprised the next morning to find a similar letter already in the metal box from Mark. He had also written the last two stanzas of her favorite poem, Bright Eyes.

Pray tell, is this too much to ask?
That hearts could join and forever bask
In the union of two lives made new,
Where hope springs eternal for me and you?

I give it up, I abdicate
To the One who is love so great.
I humbly bow, I bend my knee,
And pray "Lord, guide sweet Katie and me."

Katie rejoiced as she headed for the meadow - the place where their love had flourished.

At Lane Farms, the day dawned bright and clear. There was peace and contentment in the air. The push was over. They had planted the last field of corn. The previous night's rain had cast a lull over most immediate field activities, except for one.

The electric fence box warned that there was a grounded fence somewhere on the north side of the road. Harold disconnected the wire to the meadow, and the remaining fences were clear of trouble.

"Take the crosscut saw," he advised Mark. "You may have to walk the entire perimeter of the meadow. It will most likely be a downed tree limb or simply a weed shorting out the wire. I'm going to reconnect it now, so you'll know when you find the problem that it's the only one."

Mark gave him his patented grin. "Aw shucks, Dad. You're going to come with me so you can test it, right?"

Harold smiled in return and gave him a friendly slap on the back. "This is your chance to be a man."

Mark followed the fence along the lane that led to the meadow. Once there, he began to search its perimeter. He passed Wagner's ponds at the east end, then headed west where the back edge of the meadow bordered deep woods. Halfway across the fence line and not far from the best blackberry picking, Mark found the problem. A single weed had grown high enough that last night's storm blew it onto the fence. It was diverting the electricity into the ground and weakening the jolt in the wire.

Mark took a minute to look around. He was just north of the grove of young trees that were perfect for tree bending. It had been three years since he had engaged in that activity. His parents would forbid such foolishness, so he did it in secret.

Mark ambled in that direction, and before long he was smack in the middle of his favorite place in the meadow. The young trees were bordered by blackberry and a few blueberry bushes: good eating and high adventure all in the same spot.

Mark looked up into the trees, remembering past days spent carefree in free fall. He picked a good tree and began to climb. The higher he climbed, the more precariously the young tree swayed. Eventually he came to that point where he could climb no higher. When the tree swayed one way then started the other, he threw his weight in that direction. He lunged outward into midair while holding onto the small trunk of the treetop.

For a moment, he was weightless as a battle waged between thrust and gravity. As always, gravity won. The tree arched, and Mark headed toward the ground with only the young tree's trunk standing between him and disaster. He felt the tension building in the trunk through his hands. When he knew that to hold on any longer would be to his peril, he let go and dropped to the ground.

It was a safe landing, even though he had dropped more than his height. There had been times in the past when some trees would allow him to get closer to the ground, and the landing was easy. Sometimes he had to let go much higher, and the landing could be quite challenging.

When starting up a tree, Mark always tried to pick his landing spot. He looked for level ground with no tree roots, rocks, or bushes - especially thorn bushes. His biggest adversary was two types of trunk failure. The easy one was when the trunk gave way but simply bent because the wood fibers failed and shredded under his weight. That was a slow ride down and a minor control problem.

The second type was the partial break. Mark had only experienced it once and that was three years ago. It had everything to do with why he had stayed out of the trees since then. As he lunged that time, his arc had just begun when he heard and felt it almost as one. The trunk tension was gone, and then came a loud crack as the trunk did a vertical split. The section Mark held in his hands split off, yet acted as if hinged, and pulled Mark backward toward the tree trunk. He crashed down through the lower limbs of the tree, catching one between his legs. A few more bruised his ribs, and one cut a big scratch down his side.

Mark untangled himself from the mass of branches and limped down to the creek to clean his wounds. In spite of the scrapes, bruises, and ribs that would take weeks to heal, he knew that he had been lucky. He sat at the edge of the small stream and looked back toward the stand of trees. He asked himself if the fun was worth the cost. That was three years ago, and time has a way of taking the edge off an acute memory.

Katie was enjoying her reprieve immensely. The sunshine was a welcome change to the stormy night. She entered the meadow and thought of last year's blackberry crop. She decided to check on the blossoms in hope they would be bountiful again.

Deep in the blackberry section, Katie was startled by a loud noise in the thicket just ahead of her. It sounded like something heavy had fallen to Earth. Curious, she moved forward in the direction of the noise.

Suddenly, Katie saw him. He was climbing a young tree not far ahead of her. She ducked behind a nearby bush, afraid that he might see her. She watched him climb higher and higher into the very top of the young tree. She was so intrigued that she didn't realize it was Mark until he turned his face in her direction as the treetop swayed. Her heart pounded in her chest.

One more step upwards, and all at once, he lunged into midair. As Katie watched, he held onto what little was left of the trunk. The treetop arched and headed earthward. Man and tree struck, then brushed past other tree branches.

It ended as suddenly as it had begun. Mark let go and dropped to the ground.

Katie gasped as she watched the spectacle conclude. She clapped a hand over her mouth, but it was too late. The sound had already escaped her lips. She thought surely he had heard her, but she remained crouched behind the bush.

When Katie looked in Mark's direction again, he was gazing upward - studying the other trees around him. She let out a long, slow breath. Apparently, Mark was too involved to have heard her gasp.

However, Mark had heard it: a moment after his feet hit the ground... off to his right not far away, a noise that only a human voice could make. He glanced over and saw nothing. Then out of the corner of his eye, he caught sight of a white cap. It had to be Katie.

Mark chose another sapling and began to climb in a manner that allowed him clear vision toward the bush she hid behind. He pretended not to see her.

What young man could resist the temptation to show off for the woman he loved? She watched intently as his feet touched down for a well-controlled landing.

Mark decided to climb one more tree before talking to Katie. When he reached the top, he lunged outward. Maybe he hadn't pulled himself close enough to the top. Maybe the tree was just a little too brittle. Or maybe the extra twenty-five pounds he carried since last he did this was just too much. For whatever reason, the tree snapped in a complete break, and he fell out of control.

Mark held fast to the treetop. It rolled along the branches of a larger tree, and those branches sagged under the weight. He thought about letting go, but the treetop was slowing his descent. He was hoping to come around, just another quarter turn to land on his feet.

Instead he crashed down into the entanglement of branches, back first, looking skyward. A sharp pain stabbed through him a split second before impact. A short, dead branch had been snapped off the big tree by the one he clung to as he fell. One end had stuck in the soft earth with the other pointing up like a spear. It pierced Mark's back, just below the rib cage and a few inches in from his right side.

Tree branches separated him from the ground, but the force of his fall drove the dead branch into the ground and all the way through him. He was dazed but conscious as he lay impaled. He tried to get up, but something was holding him. Puzzled, he looked to his midsection and saw his shirt held away from his body as if there was something propped under it. Mark reached down and pulled up his shirt to see the stick protruding from him. He tried harder to rise up and was met by searing pain. He grasped the stick and tried to roll sideways and experienced the same outcome. He was staked to the ground. Then he remembered Katie and called her name. She was beside him a moment later, eyes wild with fear, her lips desperately called his name.

"I need you to be strong," Mark gasped. "I must get to the hospital, but first I need help getting up. This stake must stay in me, and it's buried in the ground. I'll hold it with my left hand while you pull with all your might on my right arm. Be prepared for me to scream, but don't shrink from your task."

On the second pull, the stake came free from the earth. Mark struggled to the base of the big tree, picked up the crosscut saw and handed it to Katie. He gave her his knife, and she cut his shirt off the stick behind him. She gripped the stake with her fist against his back and used the saw to cut it off. Katie helped Mark out of his t-shirt and tore it in strips. She tied them together to make a long bandage. She wrapped one end around the stake at Mark's front, tied it snugly and then circled to the back, repeating the procedure.

"Your apron, Katie. Rip it lengthwise, so we can wrap it around me above and below the stake ends to hold everything in place."

She followed his instructions and tied it snugly.

"I'll start for the crossing. Get your camera case."

"I don't care about the camera. Let me help you."

With blood running down his leg, Mark stood his ground.

"You are so stubborn," she said.

"I don't have all day to stand here waiting. My head is starting to spin already." That said, Mark headed for the creek with Katie catching up just before he arrived.

Mark stumbled and fell when he came out the far side. He cried out in pain and then struggled to his feet with Katie's help. "Lean on me, and we'll walk together," she commanded.

They had made it into the lane when Mark told her he needed to rest. Maybe you should run on up to the house and get Dad." But he was slurring his words, and she had noticed that his steps were getting shorter. She dropped the camera case by a fence post and tried to help him. He motioned with his hand, "Go on. I'll wait here."

"I'm not leaving you here to die alone."

"Silly girl, I'm not dying." But Katie could tell from all the outward signs that he was in dire danger and that life was leaving him. She had heard more than one story in her community about blood loss leading to shock and then death.

"I'm not leaving you," she said firmly. She put her arm around him and helped him up. "Lean on me. We must keep going." While they plodded along, Katie talked to him, encouraging his forward progress. "Only another hundred yards, then we'll rest. You can do it."

At one point, Mark suddenly stopped. "Don't tell my parents what I was doing when I got hurt. Just say I fell out of a tree."

Katie latched onto an idea and threatened, "If you don't keep moving, I'll tell them exactly how you got hurt!" For a while he sped up, making good progress. But he tired and sat down to rest.

A minute was all Katie would give him. They could see the buildings now, and they were too close to give up. She helped him up and noticed that his lips were blue. Mark mumbled, "I think I'm dying."

Her gut knotted at his admission. "You're not going to die because I won't let you. Fight, Mark!" She forced him to move forward. "Don't you dare leave me in a world without you. I will *never* forgive you."

That got his attention, and for a while, he tried mightily. Then his steps became mechanical, while he floated in and out of consciousness. "Let me rest," Mark mumbled. "Just for a little bit."

"No, Mark! No rest! We'll continue on if I have to carry you."

He brightened once more. "That's a laugh. You can't carry a bag of feed."

"Only a few hundred yards. Keep walking. You've got to keep walking." Then Katie saw him. Harold was at the front end of the pasture changing the feed wagons for the cattle. She tried to speed up but could go no faster. "Your father is in the pasture. We must get his attention."

Mark looked toward the buildings and for a short distance found new energy.

Harold had unhooked the full wagon and was backing up to hitch onto the empty. Katie waved with one arm and held onto Mark with the other as the field drew closer with each strenuous step. One single strand of wire separated the lane from the pasture. When they reached it, she scooted under then turned to help Mark, who was on all fours. The stick protruding from his back caught on the wire and stopped his progress.

Katie grabbed the wire and braced for the jolts that she knew would come. Lifting it high enough for the stick to clear, she commanded, "Keep coming, Mark!" While the electricity pulsed through her, Mark struggled through to the other side.

Katie looked toward Mark's father. She jumped and waved her arms. With eyes fastened on Harold, she waved and pleaded, "Look at me!" She watched him rise from the tractor seat and knew he would dismount.

Did he hesitate? Was he looking in their direction? It was too far to be sure. She closed her eyes and kept waving.

Katie looked again toward Mr. Lane, but she couldn't see him. Then he reappeared and leapt onto the tractor. She waved wildly, keeping her eyes glued on him this time. He turned toward her and waved.

"He has seen me. Thank God, he has seen me!" She rushed to Mark's side. "Your dad has seen us, Mark! He's coming."

Mark did not answer, and he did not stir. He looked like he was sleeping. It was almost surreal, but then the alarm bells clanged in her head. "No, Mark!"

404

she cried. Katie shook him and commanded, "You cannot sleep. Wake up!" she shouted.

Katie pulled at his arm and forced her knees under him, trying to rouse him into consciousness. She held his limp form in her arms and cried out to God to save him. In anger and desperation, she slapped him hard on the cheek. She could clearly see her finger marks there as she screamed, "Wake up! You're not leaving me!"

Mark's eyes opened, and he frowned. "Did you hit me?"

"Yes! And I'll hit you again. Now keep those eyes open."

"Why did you hit me?" he mumbled.

"Because I love you!"

Mark smiled and his eyelids fluttered—then closed.

As Harold Lane and the "big, green machine" bore down on them, she cradled Mark's head and shoulder in her lap.

Katie went boldly to the throne while Mark's blood oozed into the fertile soil.

Chapter Forty

After the wagon ride from the field, Harold and Katie struggled to get Mark onto the seat of the truck.

"His head will rest on my lap," Harold said. "Ann and the girls are shopping so I need you to ride to the hospital with us. Crouch on the floor in front of him. Steady him and hold the stake away from the seatback. You'll have to lean over him. I apologize, but this is not the time to be modest."

The pick-up truck sped along Old Mill Road.

"Talk to him, Katie," Harold said. "Keep him awake. Pinch his cheek. Pull his hair and if that doesn't do it, then pray. Pray like you've never prayed before!"

Katie sat alone in the waiting room, her eyes clamped shut as she prayed. A hand on her arm caused her to open her eyes. She looked into the compassionate face of Dr. Ford.

"I overheard them say 'Lane,' and I'm here to help," she said solemnly. "First, we'll pray together, then I'll tell you all that I know."

Katie wiped the tears from her cheeks and nodded. "Thank you," she whispered as they bowed their heads.

Dr. Ford clasped Katie's hands tightly in her own and led them in prayer. Then she filled Katie in. "He's in the operating room now. Dr. Stewart is young, but he's a good surgeon. He'll do everything he can to pull Mark through. Mark has lost a lot of blood, and his father is giving blood at this very moment. I am also going to donate. Would you want to be tested as a compatible donor and give as well?"

"Yes, of course. I want to help," Katie replied.

"Let's get you tested then, but first we'll stop at the bathroom and get some of that blood washed off of you."

Harold's friend, Tom, and his wife, Alice, arrived at the hospital and donated blood, too. They took Katie home and stopped at the Lanes' house to see if Ann and the girls had returned from shopping. Tom had promised Harold that he'd leave a note on the door if no one was home.

Katie left the hospital while Mark was still on the operating table, not knowing if he would live or die. But she had no excuse to stay.

"Let me know as soon as you can," were her last words to Harold.

It was almost dark when Harold knocked on the Bylers' door. He gave the news to the family gathered in the living room.

"We believe that Mark's going to make it," he said hopefully. "Dr. Stewart said he's not out of the woods yet, but he's doing as well as could be expected under the circumstances. They've repaired his insides as best they could, and the rest is up to Mark. He is currently under sedation, and the doctor said the next twenty-four hours are critical. Ann is staying all night, and I have the girls with me in the truck, so I better get them home."

"We'll keep praying for his recovery," Mary said. "Tell Ann we'll prepare your meals on Monday and not to worry about cooking."

Harold nodded. "Thank you, and your prayers are appreciated. Thank God Katie chose today to take her pictures."

Harold eyed Katie steadily as her red eyes filled with tears again.

"Ann and I will be forever grateful to you for saving our son. We thank God for you, Katie."

Katie had just opened the bake shop on Tuesday morning when Ann pulled up.

Ann surprised Katie by giving her a firm hug. "Thank you for saving our son," she spoke into Katie's ear.

When she stepped back, Ann eyed her intently. "Mark has been asking for you."

Katie looked down, not knowing how to respond. Finally she asked, "How is he?"

"I think he's going to be all right. Each day he seems to be getting a little better. As bad as he is right now, I'm more worried about an organ the stake didn't pierce."

Ann paused as she let Katie think about that for a moment. "That would be his heart."

"Did the fall damage it in some way?" Katie asked.

Ann shook her head and graced Katie with a warm smile.

"There's a funny thing about this whole ordeal. Mark gave the doctor and nurses all a chuckle before they operated on him. It seems he came to and was babbling about a blue angel. Claimed she carried him out of the meadow and that she loved him. He said she told him so herself. Said she held him in her arms on the way to the hospital. The doctor told me not to worry; that it was normal for a person in Mark's condition to hallucinate."

A smile tugged at the corner of Ann's mouth. "Do you promise to tell me about it one day?"

Katie looked upon her with wide eyes.

"About the accident, I mean," Ann clarified.

"Yes. Yes, of course."

"But in the meantime, I have to take you to the hospital to see Mark. We had a long talk last night, and he wouldn't let me leave without promising I would bring you to see him today. A promise is a promise. I'll watch this shop myself if I have to, and Harold can drive you there. But first, I'll go talk to Mary and see if she can take your place."

"Wait in the hall while I go in and say hello," Ann told Katie as they neared Mark's room.

"Hi, Mom. I thought maybe you forgot about me today," Mark said.

She hugged him and gave him a kiss. "No, I was just delayed while getting you a present."

"I don't see it."

"It's out in the hall." She gave him another kiss and left the room, while Mark's eyes followed her out the door.

In the hospital corridor, Ann paused in front of Katie. "Go on in and see him. I'm going to the restaurant on the corner to have lunch… a long lunch. And I brought a book along to read. It's a love story."

Katie's heart rejoiced as she watched Ann walk down the hall. She turned and entered Mark's room with one thought on her mind.

"Where do we go from here?"

Today in the Meadow

Today in the meadow I saw a bee.
I got too close, so it was chasing me.
I ran so fast across the grass
Until I thought I had lost him at last.

I was so glad I began to sing.
It was then I felt that mighty sting.
I jumped back and looked in his eye.
"Why'd you do that?" in pain I cried.

"I had let you off the hook," he replied.
"You began to sing and my ears were fried.
I had to act fast. I had no choice.
I had to silence that squawking voice."

So now the bee is a friend to me
If I'm in the meadow and him I see,
I control my singing very well
'Cause I don't want my body to swell.

Snow Angel

I met with her on a full-moon night.
We frolicked in the snow just out of sight.
As angels were made upon the snow,
We asked our guardian angels to show.

To our dismay they never came.
We had a good time just the same.
Some night we'll have to go again
To play and frolic just as friends.

As we part and say goodbye
Fresh snow is falling from the sky.
Creations we made soon will be gone
But my Earth angel still lives on.

The Girl and the Spider

Have you heard the story of the spider
And the little girl who sat beside her?
The little girl didn't like spiders much.
She didn't like spiders, snakes and such.

As the big black spider was sitting there
The happy little girl was unaware.
Suddenly the spider said, "Hey that's mine!"
When the girl squashed a bug right at suppertime.

She's now the flattest spider you ever did see,
And the little girl no longer has company.
Here's how the moral of the story goes,
"Better keep quiet or stay on your toes."

The Spider and the Bee

Everyone knows the reality.
There are no friendships
Between a spider and a bee.

A spider builds its deadly web.
A bee's sting can kill,
But not from its head.

If a bee gets caught in the trap,
The spider will approach
While the bee's wings flap.

The job at hand is very serious.
If the spider gets stung,
He will soon be delirious.

The spider knows that he's the winner
As he whistles a tune
And he wraps up dinner.

Winter Blues

Here I sit sad and weary
While outside it's dark and dreary.
I am lost within my woe.
Where is Katie? Where did she go?

But time drives on, further still.
Cruel beast, he watches from the hill.
I shout to him, "Just leave me be!
Let me wallow in my misery."

I look to see that yonder hill.
I know beyond she lies there still.
My heart is heavy as I wonder
These same things does she ponder?

If I must wait then wait I will.
I pray to God my hours fill.
No new drug will pull us through
For we have got the winter blues.

Sunny Skies

I woke today, the sun was shining.
Is this God's plan? Is this His timing?
I feel a singing in my spirit.
Is this the end, or am I near it?

Over that hill today I go,
But it's for joy and not for woe.
Katie has asked that I come calling.
Will this be the end of my tears falling?

I see her there within God's beauty.
While sunbeams dance she rushes to me.
She leaves her feet and floats on air,
And surrounds me with her golden hair.

We lock and cling in loving embrace
With bright eyes shining from her face.
She presses my chest with her fingertips.
I lean and kiss her tender lips.

Kisses, Hugs, and Stuff

When I close my eyes I can see your face,
As I still feel the power of the good Lord's grace.
I reached for your hand and found comfort there.
It filled me with peace where there once was despair.

I remember the poems you have given to me,
One about a spider and another about a bee.
I gaze at three pictures hanging here in my room.
Without you in my life there'd be silence and gloom.

For you are the voice ringing loud in my ear.
Bringing arms full of hugs, joy, and good cheer.
Kisses and more kisses, let that be my fate.
Come give me your kisses if it's early or late.

A Light in the Darkness

A light in the darkness whose owner I cannot see.
A light in the darkness whose owner can't see me.
I marvel at my heartbeat and how much it quickens.
As its owner draws near, the plot greatly thickens.

The light is approaching. I can tell from my seat.
It's getting bigger and brighter. We two shall soon meet.
Should I be on guard? Do they mean me harm?
Or do they come to beguile me with charms?

As I sit and linger in this hour so late,
It will not be long till I know my fate.
My heart's in my ears. I hear it pounding.
I now see the form, as the last bend she's rounding.

It is my true love. She is my dear.
How silly of me. I had no need to fear.
Soon she'll arrive, and I'll give her a hug.
She now stands before me, but gives me a slug.

What is it my darling? What is it sweet one?
If I did offend you, I did it in fun.
I realized tonight as I watched you draw near
You're my light in the darkness for all my years.

Bright Eyes

If ever a love as sweet as yours
Were to pass my way through my doors,
I would drive it out with a shout or scream,
"Be gone! My word, you're only a dream."

And if in dreaming I would be
Forever bound to a world of fantasy,
What better place to pass my time
Than locked in a world of joy sublime?

But could the joy be passed on to
The one whose heart I wish I knew?
Are there forces in the universe
To open your heart to my lowly verse?

Pray tell, is this too much to ask?
That hearts could join and forever bask
In the union of two lives made new,
Where hope springs eternal for me and you?

I give it up, I abdicate
To the One, who is love so great.
I humbly bow, I bend my knee,
And pray, "Lord, guide sweet Katie and me."

Katie is a Verb

The word is out, or haven't you heard?
Katie's not a noun, it's a verb!
Katie's not a verb, I know you'll say.
You'll change your mind by the end of day.

You just came, and it's still early.
There's plenty of time for you to get surly.
Hang around. She'll make you a believer.
Can't keep up? You may as well leave her.

The debate lives on. It never ends.
A word to the wise to all my friends.
Noun or verb, what does it matter?
If you see her coming, by all means scatter.

Sweetheart

Today I awoke in your embrace
Then turned to see your sleeping face.
Your arm around me held me near.
I felt your warm breath on my ear.

While your breath my skin caressed,
Against each other our bodies pressed
While light came creeping upon the air,
Your nose was nestled in my hair.

I lie here thinking that life's getting better,
How happy I am since we've been together.
You are the joy that brightens my day.
I now can declare, "Come what may!"

But now what comes is wretched light.
I closed my eyes and wished for night.
For you'll soon wake and then be gone,
And I'll be left to face the dawn.

I think of last night and the fun we shared.
I dwell on the ways you showed you cared.
Sweet time together has swelled my heart.
How fitting the name, my dear 'Sweetheart.'

"Strive for perfection. You'll achieve some form of excellence, and that will have to be good enough."

G.R. Minner

Most admired person—Nadia Comaneci

🦩 🦩 🦩 🦩 🦩 🦩 🦩 🦩 🦩 🦩 🦩 🦩 🦩 🦩 🦩 🦩

G.R. Minner encourages reader feedback!

Visit his website at www.grminner.com

Learn more about G.R.Minner on Facebook.

Follow his page at G.R.Minner, Author.

Made in the USA
Middletown, DE
04 March 2018